D0327240

THIS GULF
OF TIME
AND STARS

*The Finest in DAW Science Fiction and Fantasy
by JULIE E. CZERNEDA:*

THE CLAN CHRONICLES:

Stratification:
REAP THE WILD WIND (#1)
RIDERS OF THE STORM (#2)
RIFT IN THE SKY (#3)

The Trade Pact:
A THOUSAND WORDS FOR STRANGER (#1)
TIES OF POWER (#2)
TO TRADE THE STARS (#3)

Reunification:
THIS GULF OF TIME AND STARS (#1)
THE GATE TO FUTURES PAST (#2)*

* * *

NIGHT'S EDGE:
A TURN OF LIGHT (#1)
A PLAY OF SHADOW (#2)

* * *

SPECIES IMPERATIVE:
SURVIVAL (#1)
MIGRATION (#2)
REGENERATION (#3)

* * *

WEB SHIFTERS:
BEHOLDER'S EYE (#1)
CHANGING VISION (#2)
HIDDEN IN SIGHT (#3)

* * *

IN THE COMPANY OF OTHERS

*Coming soon from DAW Books

THIS GULF OF TIME AND STARS

Reunification #1

Julie E. Czerneda

DAW BOOKS, INC.
DONALD A. WOLLHEIM, FOUNDER
375 Hudson Street, New York, NY 10014

ELIZABETH R. WOLLHEIM
SHEILA E. GILBERT
PUBLISHERS
www.dawbooks.com

Copyright © 2015 by Julie E. Czerneda.

All Rights Reserved.

Jacket art by Matt Stawicki.

Jacket designed by G-Force Design.

Jacket photograph by Roger Czerneda.

DAW Book Collectors No. 1671.

Published by DAW Books, Inc.
375 Hudson Street, New York, NY 10014.

All characters and events in this book are fictitious.
Any resemblance to persons living or dead is strictly coincidental.

The scanning, uploading, and distribution of this book via the Internet or via any other means without the permission of the publisher is illegal, and punishable by law. Please purchase only authorized electronic editions, and do not participate in or encourage the electronic piracy of copyrighted materials. Your support of the author's rights is appreciated.

First Printing, November 2015
1 2 3 4 5 6 7 8 9

DAW TRADEMARK REGISTERED
U.S. PAT. AND TM. OFF. AND FOREIGN COUNTRIES
—MARCA REGISTRADA
HECHO EN U.S.A.

PRINTED IN THE U.S.A.

To Dr. R. J. F. (Jan) Smith, who left us too soon.

Dr. Smith was my grad studies supervisor, a dear man with a neat dark beard and twinkly eyes. He introduced me to fish pheromones, as well as -40C winters, gumbo (the mud), and gliding over the prairies, and it was in Jan's basement lab at the University of Saskatchewan that the question of the Clan came to me.

I was examining the cost of growing features of use solely for reproductive success. Deer annually regrow antlers to fight for and attract mates, consuming nutrients and energy. Similarly, my study subjects, male fathead minnows, grow mucous disks on their heads to prepare nests and change their behavior in ways that make them more vulnerable to predators. Evolution drives such adaptations, but not beyond those costs. Selection pressure swings back to sensible.

When wouldn't it? I wondered, late one night.

What if an intelligent species realized a trait—of use originally for reproductive success—offered future generations a different advantage? What cost would they be willing to endure as a society, as individuals, to enhance that trait?

And when they went too far, when selection pressure swung back as it inevitably would—what then?

I remember staring at my busy minnows, thinking surely we'd know better.

There began the story of the Clan and Sira di Sarc.

Thank you, Jan, for this and so very much more.

Acknowledgments

I will always be grateful Sheila Gilbert of DAW, my editor-dear, believed in my first novel, *A Thousand Words for Stranger*. Even more, I'm grateful for her continued belief in me. What you hold in your hands is the result of her support, trust, and enthusiasm for my work, not to mention her vast skill as an editor to make that work worthy of you. Sheila's been nominated twice for the Hugo for good reason and I sincerely hope, by the time this is published, she'll have won.

DAW Books is more than my insanely talented (and adorable) editor, of course. Please, every one, take a very well-earned bow. Betsy Wollheim (Hugo-winning editor!), Peter Stampfel, Joshua Starr, Katie Hoffman, Briar Herrera-Ludewig, Marsha Jones, Paula Greenberg, Sarah Guan, and George! My thanks also to Jessica Cooney of Penguin Canada. An author couldn't ask for a better publisher-family, or friends.

My previous science fiction titles from DAW, including my first novel, have covers by the famed Luis Royo. How could we possibly match that? Well, we did. Thank you, Matt Stawicki, for the stunning, passionate, and accurate cover you created for this book. It not only stands proudly with the rest of the series, but you've captured Sira as she is now perfectly. (The Hair!)

Speaking of series. *Gulf* is book seven, after all, and I'd taken a long break from writing in this universe. (There were toads.) Coming back, I knew I needed help. I ran a competition to find betareaders for the series. A wonderful number entered, studying the books with glee. Thank you very much!

The following individuals read my first draft manuscript with an eye to any errors of content: my official Betareaders Carla Mamone and Lyndsay Stuart. They provided me with thorough (blush) lists of my mistakes and I thank you both from the bottom of my heart. Any goofs left in the book are my fault. (Thank you Timothy (Sir Tim) Bowie who stayed at the ready.)

Thank you, Jennifer, my first reader, for your always valuable thoughts on the book. (And for the photos of reading it in exotic Bali. Wow!) I couldn't let it out the door without you. My good friend Janet E. Chase jumped in to read when I had a shaky moment. Thanks, BF! Whew.

You'll find some familiar names in these pages, characters won at charity auctions over the past few years. Thank you all for your support of such excellent causes and for letting me do my worst to your namesakes. In alphabetical order: Andrea Knight (*Andi sud Prendolat*), Carla Mamone (*Arla di Licor*), Dennis Csurgai (*Deni* and *Cha sud Annk*), Destiny Nelson (*Destin di Anel),* Holly Hina (*Holl di Licor*), Jacqueline Lam (*Jacqui di Mendolar*), Jana Paniccia (*Janac di Paniccia*), Karina Sumner-Smyth (*Kari Bowman*), Kim Nakano (*Janina Michi*), Lawren Louli (*Magpie Louli, Witness*), Lee Sessoms (*Leesems di Licor*), Lyndsay Stuart (*Asdny di Licor*), Ruth Stuart (*Ruti di Bowart*), Timothy Bowie (*Ruti di Bowart* and *Hom M'Tisri,* the *Vilix*), and Victoria (*Nik di Prendolat*).

The past year was full of memorable events. I'd like to thank all of my gracious hosts and friends: Chattacon 40 (Chattanooga TN), Perfect Books and Can-Con (site of the Aurora-Anticipation Party) (Ottawa ON), Bakka-Phoenix Books, INSPIRE!, and Ad Astra (Toronto ON), #RRSciFiMonth, the fabulous Mindy and Mark Maddrey (Washington/World Fantasy), Manticore Books (Orillia ON), and Oasis 27 (Orlando FL). It was wonderful to finally meet my online friends, Susie and Lee, Cyn and Gabie, in person. Thanks for coming the distance! You made us smile then and still do! My thanks to Boko Bakery for inventing the perfect

Nyim Cookies. I gratefully acknowledge the hard work and enthusiasm of Catherine McLaughlin, Kristy Maddock, and Sandra Kennedy, (and friends), who made my events at their Chapters extraordinary. My thanks to Dr. Rick Wilber and his students for inviting me into their classroom. Thank you, 2nd Avenue, for Sparklers, Signs, and Celebrations!

To Scott Czerneda and Erin Stirling. May your road be ever filled with light.

My dear readers. Here you go. Reunification.

Buckle up!

Trade Pact Space

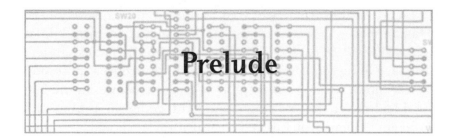

Prelude

FINGERS, four and a thumb, tapped the metal edge of the vent. The fingers were dark blue from tip to second joint, as if dipped in paint.

Or pox blood.

The fingers gripped and pulled. The covering grate came free without sound or resistance, revealing an opening twice the span of those fingers spread wide.

Wide enough.

The right hand led the way, scrabbling into the pipe. Body parts, riding on tough fleshy limbs and careful of clothing, followed in turn. The head produced eyes to survey the shadowed rooftop, but didn't tarry. It ducked through the opening, canting forward so its well-secured hat went first.

The left hand did what it could to pull the grate into place behind it, breaking a nail. Regardless, it subvocalized a chuckle.

At last, their time had come.

Barrels waited on their racks, the more costly brews festooned with cobwebs and dust. A pair of aged portlights hovered near the rafters, their fitful glow doing little to dispel the gloom. The cellar's chill suited only one of those gathered around a table made from two empty barrels and a sheet of real wood, and only one felt sufficiently at ease to sit on a stool.

Board Member Theo Schrivens Cartnell, representative for the Human species in the conglomeration of mutual interests known as the Trade Pact, trusted he appeared at ease and not exhausted. To reach Stonerim III unremarked, he'd traveled in a succession of starships, each more decrepit than the one before. In the last, he'd had the choice of being crammed together in a cabin with itinerant Lemmicks or Turrned Missionaries. He should have gone with the missionaries. After vomiting most of his insides at the stench, the rest of the journey had passed in a haze. He'd staggered into the first portcity hotel for a bath and change of clothing.

And the last of his stims.

What mattered was this gathering; typically, an important member wasn't here. Late, he hoped, or waiting to make an entrance.

Risky, with such as these. Cartnell lifted his glass in a gloved hand and pretended to admire the bubbles rising through the tawny liquid as his stomach roiled in protest. "Rare, this," he said. "Sure you won't join me?"

The other Humans in the room, a slim woman with her face hazed behind a vis-shield and an even slimmer man, his face pocked and scarred, didn't move. "Time's wasting," she said, her voice distorted. "You called us. Get to the point."

"I accept and gladly." A callused palm engulfed a glass, ivory-tipped fingers clicking together like castanets. The contents were drained in a single swallow. As Brill went, the male was almost dainty, no bulkier than a very large Human. Still, he'd opened his coat with an exclamation of relief. Warmth was a trial, given those layers of blubber and thick leathery skin, and the land above the cellar was in the midst of a tropical summer.

It couldn't be helped. This was their first—the only—chance to meet. They couldn't do so for long.

Not with the aliens known as Clan on all their worlds.

Not with what the Clan could do.

Cartnell put down his glass and stood. No more codenames.

"Cartnell, Board Member." He pulled a datadisk from his pocket and set it on the table.

"We know who you are." The other Human male touched finger to forehead and smiled without humor. "Sansom Fry, Deneb Blues." Fry put a second disk by the first. "My contribution."

The woman passed her hand in front of her vis-shield, shutting it off. Tiny black spiders spilled across her forehead and along her right cheek to her chin, tattoos that shifted and seemed to crawl with each movement of her lips. "Ambridge Gayle. Grays." Without hesitation, she tossed her disk on the table; it tumbled to meet the rest.

"I never thought to see Deneb's syndicate heads in the flesh, let alone in the same room. If you can do this, friend Cartnell, I am confident of wonders!" The Brill smacked his thick lips, then struck his chest with a curled fist. "Manouya!"

Fry's eyes narrowed dangerously. "Who?"

"You know him as the Facilitator." Gayle raised a brow, spiders scurrying in accent. "Whom I never thought to meet. Greetings." A gracious nod, during which her eyes didn't leave the others.

"You?" With deliberate disbelief. "Behind every major smuggling ring within Human space?"

"Why not me?" The Brill hit his chest again. "We're smarter than any of you. Who do you think got you here, safe and secret? Who'll get you back?"

"Is that a threat?" Gayle said, her voice like the flow of silk over steel.

He'd be lucky if they didn't kill one another first. Cartnell coughed. "If we could move along, please?"

Manouya chuckled. "Here's my share." A fourth disk landed on the table.

He'd planned for five. There should be—

So be it. Cartnell pushed aside the tray with its offerings and replaced it with a reader, outwardly typical of its kind. "This will copy across, once each disk is activated. As agreed, what we've brought will be shared with all."

"And better be worth this nonsense," Fry said, gesturing to their surroundings. He smiled unpleasantly. "Or someone dies."

If not "worth this," nothing was. Cartnell loaded the disks into the reader, their stubby ends protruding. "Then I'll go first. As you know, the Clan's advantage is that they can pass as Human."

"And there are more of you than anything else," grumbled Manouya. "There are," he stated as the others glared at him. "You're everywhere."

"It's not coincidence." Cartnell licked a finger, touching its damp tip to the disk end. An image glowed above the table, brighter than the portlights. It was a chart of the richest, oldest Human-settled span of the Trade Pact, the so-called Inner Systems.

What drew those viewing it an involuntary step closer, staring, was the red staining most of those worlds. "I give you the Clan."

The Brill rumbled in dismay.

Fry's fist rose, then fell to his side.

"Caraat claimed his kind were everywhere. Inescapable. That foul—" Gayle cursed, tattooed spiders writhing along her lips. "I shouldn't have come here," she finished harshly, but made no move to leave.

" 'Caraat'?" A Clan name. Cartnell frowned, withdrawing his hand from the map. "Our arrangement's full disclosure. Who is he?"

"Yihtor di Caraat," Fry said heavily. Gayle shot him a dire look; he spread empty hands. "You didn't think the *crasnig* was exclusive, did you? He dealt with anyone who could afford him."

An unfamiliar name, itself a shock, but what twisted inside Cartnell's gut like fire was the realization of who this Yihtor must be. Had to be.

The destroyer.

Three Human scientists had succumbed before anyone made the connection. They'd been in different systems; their projects, classified at the highest levels, in different fields. None knew the other, yet all three had been found curled in a fetal position, their once-brilliant minds ripped apart and barely functional.

One of them, Sarran Coffler. His Sarran.

They'd studied together as young men, Sarran's intellect like radiance itself. Fallen in love as fiercely as only first love could and might have been lifemates—should have been, Cartnell thought with that old and ugly pain—but for work they loved more. Oh, they'd kept in touch over the years. Always, they'd kept in touch. By vid, lately, being busy. Lazy. He should have visited. Made the time.

Too late. Seeing the name in the newsfeed, he'd cleared his schedule in frantic haste, tracked Sarran not to a hospital, but a hospice. There'd been a window. Flowers. Air rank with piss. He'd stood, looking down. At a body still fit and cared for. At a face, slack and drooling. Into brown eyes, terrible, empty brown eyes . . .

Cartnell swallowed bile.

He'd walked away, each step burning aside grief to leave one goal: to find who'd destroyed Sarran and how. Locking himself in his office, he'd sat at his desk and, for the first time in his career, used his executive codes to override protocol and privilege. Anything about Sarran's case—cases—came to him. Nothing led back. No one would be allowed to stop him.

Reports flooded in, of no use. Cartnell'd widened his search and there it was: a neglected, overlooked message from a lowly Port Authority constable, suggesting a link: all three scientists had been sensitives—their minds not telepathic but receptive, making them vulnerable to those with full abilities. The usual precaution, keeping away Human telepaths, hadn't been enough, the message went on to claim, because the culprit might have been Clan.

Who?

Cartnell'd followed any and every rumor, building a startling profile of an alien race living among Humans, as Humans. A race defined by wealth and power—being telepaths of unknown ability—without a single official document to confirm their existence, nor a single complaint registered against them, anywhere, ever, until this one Port Jelly sent her message.

Impossible.

His searches had an echo. The Port Jelly was slipping through channels, way outside her pay grade or clearance, hunting news of the Clan. Cartnell made a decision. Working from the dark, he arranged for the curious constable to be offered a post as a Trade Pact Enforcer, entitled to work offworld, then made sure she was assigned Sarran's case and any like it. Any request she made was granted, including the implantation of experimental mind-shields in her and those working with her.

Soon he had a report on his desk detailing rumors of a Clan renegade—or group—who'd flouted the laws of their kind and sold their Power. Nothing proven.

Nothing ever was, but whatever else had been suspicion about the Clan became fact, insofar as he was concerned. They existed. He had them under scrutiny. As for Sarran's destroyer? He'd taken comfort there'd been no more minds lost.

Freed from a meaningless career digging through musty cargo holds, the former Port Jelly—with Cartnell's now-public endorsement—advanced to Sector Chief, with a ship of her own and a reputation for results.

A shame he hadn't realized what else she was. "Are you still in contact with him?" Cartnell asked quietly. "Yihtor di Caraat?"

Gayle stiffened. "No. And I don't plan to be."

"Caraat's dropped from sight." Fry stared at the map. "He wouldn't like this. He wouldn't like this at all."

"I don't." Manouya's wide shoulders hunched. "So many Clan. Too many!"

"Too few," corrected Cartnell. He fought a wave of familiar dizziness. It would pass. He'd time. "Don't let this fool you. The Clan are scattered. Each of these—" he pointed at a red world "—has but one. At most, a small family."

"Fool us? I think you've been fooled, Cartnell." Gayle nodded at the map. "Caraat paid for ships to deliver luxury items, nothing but the best. Furnishings. Food. You name it. For more than a family, believe me. Where's his world on your map, Cartnell? What about Acranam?"

The name of the Clan's remote and solitary colony, a colony for which they'd offered no explanation. So much becoming clear at once—calm, he told himself. Calm and control. "Acranam's different, yes. There are twenty-nine families living there." He paused for effect. "Less than two hundred Clan."

She stared at him. "That's—that's not possible."

"Might be." Fry stuck his thumb in his mouth, then pressed it to his disk. A vid appeared, showing a wide street ending in dense jungle. The image moved from side to side, picking out buildings with windows but no doors. The viewpoint soared up, and foliage met over rooftops, hiding them; beyond, foliage stretched unbroken to the horizon. "Scans are useless—traded top of the line blockers to him myself—so I had my people drop a 'bot—what?" at Gayle's shake of her head. "Caraat disappeared mid-contract. For all I knew, the whole place had been wiped out. Besides, I wanted some leverage. In case it wasn't."

"It's always tech with you." Gayle spat tidily, catching the moisture midair with a finger's tip, touching that to her disk. "Now this is leverage." Numbers stacked themselves in tidy rows, then clustered. Lines drew between certain groups, names appearing in color along them. "While you took pretty pictures, my people uncovered those managing Caraat's offworld finances, as well as those of other known Clan. More than a few remain—how shall I put it?—free agents. Accessible." Spiders danced to her smile. "I've left them be, for now."

"I'd say that beats you, Blue." Manouya chuckled at Fry's dour look, then wiped sweat from his cheek, dripping the result on his disk. Green ripples appeared in Cartnell's chart, seemingly random until they converged around three points. "The Clan can't be tracked," the Brill said, "but lately they've drawn attention." An ivory nail went to the first point. "Plexis? Fair enough. Who doesn't shop there?" It moved to the next. "Ret 7. Some nasty business there, I'm told, but all's been quiet since." The final point. "Camos, however, remains active. Why?"

"Their ruling Council met there," Cartnell supplied. "Probably still does."

Predators in the wild gained that intent focus.

When Cartnell didn't elaborate, Manouya shrugged. "The Clan might be tricky to spot; not so a heavy cruiser. I found it fascinating, Board Member, how often Sector Chief Lydis Bowman, one of your Trade Pact Enforcers, has taken her ship to a world with a confirmed Clan presence."

Fascinating wasn't the word he'd use. Cartnell held his tongue.
Fry's eyes sharpened. "I know that name."

"Who doesn't? Someone rises that far and fast, people like us
better notice." Gayle gestured magnanimously. "In the interests
of 'full disclosure.' I was made aware that certain Human telepaths were abducted by the Clan. Bowman's constables recovered
what was left."

"As if she knew where to look. Yes, ours, too," Fry added at
Gayle's raised eyebrow. "Why'd a Sector Chief get involved in the
first place?" He hesitated, then went on grimly. "What are we
saying here—Bowman's one of them? Clan?"

"She's Human." Whatever that heritage meant to her. Cartnell
chose his words with care. "There is something between them.
Bowman's not controlled—" as he'd first suspected, "—but the
Clan have tolerated her snooping around them for years." Bowman's own reports spoke of how the Clan defended their privacy
by selectively erasing memories, a process so subtle it escaped
notice.

Unlike what had been done to Sarran's wonderful mind. Cartnell pushed that aside. "I believe they can't touch her. I don't
know why. Not yet."

"That could be of use." Fry's eyes narrowed. "On our side,
then? Is it possible?"

He'd thought so. Hoped so, until— "She's on theirs," flat and
sure. "Lydis Bowman made the arrangements to formally invite
the Clan into the Trade Pact."

The ensuing silence was more stunned than predatory.

"I was there for the signing." Hadn't that been the greatest
challenge of his long career, to smile and seem proud? "They
came. The Clan. Every single one."

Gayle spoke first. "You're saying you knew them for what they
were."

"There was no doubt." Cartnell repressed a shudder, remembering. Humans didn't appear out of thin air, to stand voiceless
and stare . . .

. . . stare at him. They still did, when he could sleep. Nightmares shaped like people, staring . . .

Cartnell collected himself. Why shouldn't Clan pass a visual inspection? They lived on Human-dominant planets for a reason. He'd been overjoyed to finally obtain internal data on them, until he'd seen for himself what they could do.

Of what use was a physiological scan on beings who never passed through shipcities or customs ports?

Who simply *wished* themselves where they wanted to be, like something out of a story.

Cartnell tapped a finger on the table, feeling their attention. Now, he thought. "Nine hundred and thirty-three."

"Which is?"

"The number of Clan in Trade Pact space, including children. The sum of their species. Nine hundred and thirty-three."

The three exchanged incredulous looks. "Less than—" Fry stopped and swallowed, hard. "My son's last music recital had more in the audience."

Gayle shook her head. "This treaty you say they signed—we would have heard."

He'd anticipated disbelief. "Board exec-level only, immediate staff excluded." Sensible, there being more species in the Trade Pact—each with its Board member—than there were Clan. Pragmatic, most of those species disinterested in Human-centric problems.

He'd known he was alone from the start.

"As it stands, few know the Clan exist, even less their—situation. The Board wants it kept that way. They think signing the treaty means the last of Clan meddling. Like that—" Cartnell snapped his fingers "—they've become model citizens."

"'Meddling'?" Fry echoed, eyes narrowed. "Ripping minds apart for their secrets? Rewriting memories so anyone you trust becomes your worst enemy? You can't be—"

Gayle silenced her colleague with a lift of her hand. "We're here for the same reason," she said almost gently. With a sharp look at Cartnell. "What 'situation,' Board Member? Why would the Clan reveal themselves?"

The right question. "They've run out of time." Cartnell clenched his hand within the stars, the fist spotted with red. "The

Clan are desperate. There's some reproductive issue. If it can't be resolved?" The fist opened and withdrew. "They go extinct."

The Board's reaction? Powerful, secret telepaths asking for help, each able to move between worlds without technology or trace? Like spilling syrup near a sippek nest.

The greater fools among his colleagues expected gratitude: Clan to serve in their offices, perhaps, or assist in negotiations.

Run errands. Fetch.

Steal. Assassinate.

Destroy the precarious balance between species who scarcely tolerated one another enough to trade, let alone sit in debate.

This was about more than his lost love. This was chaos. Inter-system war. He saw it so clearly.

While Cartnell had been frozen with horror, the rest of the executives had almost wet themselves, or whatever their species did, in their eagerness to come to the Clan's aid.

"The Trade Pact has offered every resource," he finished, pleased to sound normal.

"Have they . . ." murmured Gayle, a perilous smile elongating the legs tattooed beneath her lips.

These three understood; had hidden themselves almost as successfully as the Clan, acting from the shadows with an effective reach the Board should envy. Everything he had had gone into this toss: to find them, to reach out to arrange this meeting. He'd have their help.

After that? He'd have justice.

"Their desperation's our chance." Cartnell gestured to the map. "We know where they are—who they are. We can move against them—"

" 'We'?" Fry slammed his hands flat on the table and drove his face through the display, red dots careening into pockmarks and scars. "You mean us, Board Member, that's who you plan to do your dirty work. Take all the risk and blame. For what?"

"To put an end to the Clan." Spiders collided as Gayle scowled at her counterpart. "I didn't think you a coward."

Straightening, Fry yanked down his collar and turned, pointing to the gleam of dull metal where his skull met his neck, flesh ridged in callus along the edge. "We've all had these damned things installed just to keep our thoughts to ourselves. Knowing who the Clan are isn't enough. How can we know whose minds they control?" He took a ragged breath. "I want them gone, but nothing's worth the risk. If they're going extinct, I say let them!"

"Agreed." The Brill's voice rattled the glasses on the tray. "Grasis-sucking amount of gall, Cartnell, thinking to take on the Clan. Why can't we wait?"

He'd prepared for resistance, to bargain, but even as Cartnell readied his arguments, the leader of the Deneb Grays spoke.

"Because they're an imminent threat." Gayle faced the Brill and her counterpart. "Don't you see? The Clan tolerated us while we had use. Well, now they've the Trade Pact. Authority! They'll want to be seen as law-abiding. How better than to turn on us? How can we know," her voice lowered, "they haven't?"

Cartnell held his breath.

"Less than a thousand," Fry said after a fraught moment, staring past her into the map. "If we could get them in one place again . . ."

"That won't happen," replied Cartnell. The Clan had been summoned by their own leadership; they hadn't enjoyed being together. He'd seen it on their faces, in how they'd moved uneasily to keep apart.

"Then it's impossible." Fry rubbed a hand over his face, then shook his head. "They're spread across what, two hundred plus worlds? We don't have the numbers to hit them simultaneously and that's the only way, quick and clean."

The Brill grunted thoughtfully. "If we did—"

"Even if, forget it. Having Sector Chief Bowman on their side? The instant we struck she'd know exactly who made it possible. Our friend here might consider himself expendable. I don't."

"Leave Bowman and the Enforcers to me," Cartnell said firmly. "It's the Clan we must be rid of—only then will we be free and safe." He sat, fighting another gentle wave of dizziness. Expendable, was he? Fry wasn't wrong. The syndicate leaders were among the lucky ones. Mind-shield implants were risky by nature, being alien tech wired to Human flesh. When that flesh objected—

He'd time.

Just not much.

"Gayle. Say they give us up. We go low. Wait it out." Fry spat over one shoulder. "But if the Clan see us coming, we'll be done, forever. All of us. I say protect what we have. Look to our own."

She looked halfway convinced.

What was that? Cartnell went still, waited.

"They won't see us."

The Brill's great head spun around to aim at the form stepping from the shadows. Outlawed weapons appeared in every hand but Cartnell's, coming alive with snaps and whines.

"Our final guest," the Board Member announced, dizzy now with fierce hope.

Seams stitched themselves as the Assembler walked forward, the clothing a match in style and size, if not in color. It—she wore a hat set at a jaunty angle, and appeared weaponless.

Not that anyone with sense trusted what they saw, when it came to beings composed of sentient parts who didn't always agree. Weapons had lowered, not vanished.

"My name-for-one-minds is Magpie Louli," the Assembler told them, her voice strengthening as her upper torso began to inflate and deflate. "I bring information to destroy the Clan."

While Cartnell cleared the reader displays, readying the device for a new disk, Louli sat, more or less erect, on the facing stool. Her left fingers drummed on her hat as her right dug into a deep bag at her waist. With a sweeping gesture, she drew forth an object and laid it proudly beside the reader.

Not a disk. A mummified hand. The withered fingers curled as though they'd died cupping something while around the wrist glowed a band inset with symbols and controls.

"If this is some joke—"

Louli stared up at Fry, her eyes cold beneath long lashes. "The Clan robbed us first. We don't forget. We want what's rightly ours." She transferred her gaze to Cartnell. "It's true? You have their faces?"

He nodded. "More. I've personal idents and locations. If you have what you promised . . ." The final piece. The key . . .

Bowman.

Her shoulders began to quiver, as if dancing. A foot joined in; the other stepped firmly on its toes. "I do." Louli gestured at the withered hand. "I have their past."

No one moved or spoke.

"Their past," the Assembler insisted, her voice rising with an odd echo behind it. "Meet the Witness." She shook her right arm vigorously. The seam parted and what had been her wrist and hand dropped on the table, scurrying to their counterparts. Plump living fingers wrapped around the desiccated thumb, tugging it to where Louli could reach it with her left. She did something to the band on the wrist and deftly brought the wrist to meet the end of her arm.

Her face contorted as the two joined with a meaty click. The withered fingers trembled and moved, ever-so-slightly. "Nasty," she muttered, adding a string of syllables that needed no translation.

Fry snapped, "Well?"

Her eyes rolled back in their sockets, then dropped to stare at them. The pupils, once Human-norm, now had milky depths. When she spoke, her voice had changed, its Comspeak accented and so rapid it seemed she didn't stop to breathe. "The Clan arrived in Trade Pact space here. Not here, this room. This world, Stonerim III, in Norval, when it was, in what was our place, a fine place, *Doc's Dive*—"

Sarran, do you hear? I was right, Cartnell thought, flushed with triumph. I was right! He'd gambled on this world, guessed its significance based not on any facts—where would he find those— but on Bowman herself. Born here. A constable, here. Curious about the Clan, here.

"—Clan walked in, dressed like beggars, begging for help. Took a blood sample, always did, kept the data, want it? Would have tossed them but for the cases. Packed with artifacts— priceless, perfect, prime! No idea of their value till that fool told them—"

"What kind of artifacts?" Manouya interrupted.

"The kind worth coming back to life for, solo-brain." Fingers and thumb clawed at the tabletop, dead skin cracking at the knuckles. Bone glinted. "Hoveny!"

Manouya hummed a hasty prayer, the low sound resonating through Cartnell's bones and teeth. No one knew why the Hoveny Concentrix, that greatest of known civilizations, had fallen. Brill had been among the founding species of the next, the First, come together out of a shared curiosity. Or had it been dread?

To those not of the First, the word "Hoveny" meant one thing: treasure.

"Gods!" Fry grabbed one of the glasses of beer, the scars on his face whitened by a feral grin. "My grandmother'd talk my ear off about the Hoveny, how she'd send an acquisition team at the mere sniff of a find. Those were the days." He took a quick swallow, giving the drink a surprised look before taking a second, longer one.

"With that kind of credit lining our pockets," Gayle mused, "what couldn't we do?"

Fry lifted the glass at her. "Exactly."

"There've been no new Hoveny offering for years," Manouya pointed out. "The Clan must have sold any artifacts they possessed long ago."

He mustn't allow distraction. "Wait." Cartnell lifted his hand. "There's more." There had to be. "Witness?"

The Assembler's nose melted into her face, a second gasping mouth taking its place as words rattled from the first. "Sold them? Kept some, maybe. Hidden if they did. Worth the look. Not important. Not what matters! Aggsht—" as it gagged, then spat a stream of yellow goo over the table.

"What does, then?" Fry snapped. "Get to the point."

"I'm dead. Why should I?" Perhaps judging the mood in the cellar, the Assembler didn't wait for an answer. "Yes, more. Much more. Don't waste time. Cases had Triad seals. Authentication! Understand? Came from a Triad site, must have. But no world on record with finds like these. None. Ever."

"An unknown Hoveny world?"

"Where!?"

"Secrets. Secrets. Never knew, but someone does." A sly wink.

"Someone with the Clan before. Someone on their world. That world. Someone helps them steal Hoveny artifacts and wipe the source. Triad someone. Who? Who?" Both mouths snapped shut.

One smiled.

"Helped—or was *influenced*," Gayle ventured, breaking the hush.

Fry's gaze didn't leave the Assembler. "Wasn't there a new Hoveny find? Thirty years or so back."

"Fakes." Manouya sounded certain. "The First spend more to discredit forgers than fund new digs. They let the site at Aeande XII be covered by a glacier, for Grasis' sake; the finest Hoveny building ever found, not that anything inside worked or made sense." He rolled his head from side to side, a crackle of extra joints accompanying the movement. "An accessible Hoveny site, unrecorded? Hard to credit."

"This REAL!" Spittle flew from both mouths.

"What if it is?" Fry flung his drink against the barrel rack, shattered glass and beer spraying into the darkness. "That, for treasure we can't find."

"Not find for you! US! Belongs to us! Belongs to—"

Cartnell grabbed the withered hand and snapped it free at the band, grimacing as it collapsed into dust.

The rest of the Assembler fragmented, parts scampering in every direction. The Brill stomped at what had been a knee joint but wasn't fast enough. Gayle gracefully dodged the feet.

Fry spoke. "Board Member." Quiet threat.

Cartnell spread his arms. "It's Bowman." He'd had the pieces all along, just not how they fit. "Her great-grandfather was a Triad analyst. Here, on Stonerim III."

"Ah!" Excitement puffed the Brill's cheeks.

"Coincidence," cautioned Gayle.

"Certainty," Cartnell replied, ticking points on fingers that wanted to shake. "The timing. Marcus Bowman died or disappeared offworld while working in a Triad. The First seized any and all property owned by his family without explanation. We can guess why."

He paused to settle himself. No showing weakness, not here,

not to these. For Sarran's sake. For every innocent's. "Marcus Bowman was involved in how the Clan arrived—and succeeded—in Trade Pact space. That's why the Clan won't touch his great-granddaughter now."

"You imply gratitude, from the Clan?" Gayle's lips twisted, spiders pulled this way and that. "She's never taken a bribe. I've inquired."

"Maybe she's a pet." Manouya grinned. "Maybe the Clan's been raising Bowmans. A hobby. It could happen," as Gayle gave him a disgusted look. "There's a market. Your species is adorable while nonverbal."

Ignoring the interchange, Fry leaned forward, eyes glittering with renewed interest. "We're all thinking it. Not gratitude. Extortion. What if Bowman has something to use against them?"

"Something Marcus left his family for protection." Manouya's grin widened improbably, splitting his face. "Grasis' Glory! What if he left them the coordinates for the Hoveny world?!"

"No new artifacts means no one's been back—bah!" Fry smacked his fist on the table. "We're blowing smoke here."

"Unless what Marcus left was hidden from his family, too," Gayle said. They all looked at her; she nodded at Fry. "If I wanted to keep something safe from mindcrawlers, I'd go tech, not people."

"Yes." He narrowed his eyes. "Simple. Meant to last. Sentimental value, to keep it passing down; no more, or it might be sold. But how would it activate?"

Cartnell rose to his feet. "Get rid of the Clan and I'll give you Bowman. Ask her yourself."

Gayle laughed. "Really, Board Member. That's all you've got to offer? A chance for a hidden clue to a world that might not exist, for treasure we might never find—"

"Treasure exists! Wealth beyond measure! Share and we are prepared to cooperate despite your nasty manners." The Assembler adjusted her hat as she came forward, pointedly flexing the fingers of her own right hand once it climbed up her leg to reattach. "Clan can't see us. Think we're you." A nod. "Clan bleed like you." A sly smile. "Clan won't know we are many and more, till too late and dead! Give us good weapons. Take us all places!"

"Not adorable, ever." Manouya made a rude noise. "And you sneak on ships like pox."

"Saves fare," the Assembler said smugly.

"Grasis' Seventieth Hell." The Brill shook himself, sweat drops flying. "Could we actually pull this off?"

"The Clan aren't alone," countered Gayle. "What of their puppets?"

"Kill them," Louli said cheerfully. "Traitors!"

"Not by choice!" Cartnell objected, so sharply the Assembler scrambled away.

"Mind-wiped carrion," a disagreeable mutter from the shadows. "Almost dead now."

"About that." Fry licked his lips. "We do this, be a shame to see those Clan creds go to taxes. You said you found some who'd listen to reason." He looked at Gayle, then Manouya, as if asking a question.

Gayle's nod was almost imperceptible. "We'd need room to work. What about the rest of the enforcers?"

"Leave them to me," Cartnell replied, cold and sure. He'd been forced to sign a treaty absolving the Clan of past crimes against Humans. Well, he'd have his justice. Sarran's justice.

The Board Member representing Humans within the Trade Pact retrieved his disk from the reader and tucked it in a pocket. "Are we agreed?"

Gayle took hers. "We'll need to go over arrangements with our eager new—allies."

Cartnell assumed the malicious giggle from the dark was Louli's reply.

"The Deneb Blues agree," Sansom Fry said dryly. "And won't kill you, Board Member Cartnell." He smiled. "Today."

Vis-shield restored, Ambridge Gayle nodded. "The Grays agree."

"Manouya?"

Sweat beaded the Brill's broad forehead, trickling down his cheek. He collected his disk, the now-emptied reader crumbling into itself, then looked up, eyes somber. "Yes, yes. I agree."

"Hearing a 'but' in that," Fry observed. A needler appeared in his hand, business end aimed at the floor. "Are you with us or not?"

"We need you, Facilitator," added Gayle.

"Yes, you do." The Brill sighed and nodded. "I have questions. The Clan arrived. They settled in Trade Pact space. Why? Who are they? We don't know."

Sarran's sort of questions. For a fleeting instant, Cartnell felt the stir of doubt.

Fry took another beer. "Very soon, my friend, no one will care."

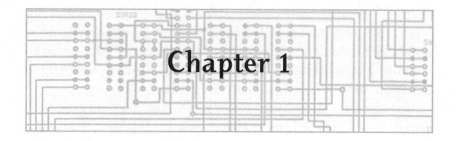

Chapter 1

"BALLOONS." I eyed the round objects orbiting Morgan's head and kept my distance. "Why?"

"It's an occasion, Sira. There should be balloons." At the lift of his hand, the objects clustered in a brightly colored mass, except for one—pink with an array of purple dots—that dropped to hover in front of his nose. He batted it away.

The balloon came right back, the purple dots sliding over the shiny pink to create a florid script. I read aloud, " 'Happy 150th Anniversary.' "

"I got them from the Lemmick on Level 3, spinward ¼." As if that explained everything. Morgan batted the balloon again. It spun back to offer alternative greetings, in rapid succession and not all in Comspeak; of those comprehensible—to me, at least— none were the occasion about to be celebrated and a few were anatomically unlikely for humanoids.

I couldn't help laughing.

My Human grinned. His was a pleasant, forgettable face, one he'd learned to control with precision long before we'd met to the chagrin of those who thought to best him in trade. Except with me. The grin lit the remarkable blue of his eyes, warming me to my core.

Morgan slapped his palms together, popping the balloon. It

released a receipt he ignored and a whiff of foul odor neither of us could. Lemmick indeed. "Who needs words," he said cheerfully. "We know why we're here."

"Here" being a chilly service corridor curving into station distance, the pair of us huddled by a burping waste compactor to avoid machine traffic. Servos who didn't expect flesh tended to run into it. There was, I thought wistfully, more to Plexis Supermarket than its unfortunately familiar underbelly.

We weren't hiding, exactly. Certainly not from anyone with access to the vid feeds omnipresent on Plexis. We'd taken our assigned parking spot and obtained the living air tags "fortheairweshared" and were, in fact, legal this trip. I even had a plas ident with my name and rank in my pocket: Sira Morgan, co-owner and hindmost crew on the *Silver Fox*. Yet my Chosen, the usually pragmatic and practical Captain Jason Morgan, insisted we wait here—complete with balloons—until all was ready inside.

"We didn't hide last time," I pointed out.

"Because the reopening of the *Claws & Jaws* wasn't a surprise."

True. Plexis had promoted the event to every system in range, saying their willingness to rebuild the restaurant after "that incident" proved the station was a fine place to do business. Those onstation were fully aware "that incident" had been caused by Plexis' heavy-handed security and that funds to rebuild had to be dragged from them screaming and kicking, but any publicity was good publicity.

The station had moved since, leaving the Fringe for the Inner Systems. I wasn't sure how I felt being so close to where I'd been born. In the Clan way, I'd been taken from my mother as a child, to be fostered offworld. If I *reached,* I'd feel the passage our attenuated link had etched into the M'hir before breaking.

Family life among my kind wasn't like that among Humans. This plan of Morgan's? I tried again to warn him. "Ruti and Barac might not react as you expect." That was putting it mildly. "I don't want you to be disappointed."

Morgan grinned, his head surrounded by balloons. "Who doesn't like a baby shower?"

Those who weren't to have children, I thought sadly.

For generations, Clan pregnancies had been planned by Council; their goal: to increase our ability to move through the M'hir. Only the most powerful were allowed to breed. It had seemed a good idea, till I'd been born.

A crossing of sud Sarc and di Bowart lines hadn't been on any list I'd studied. Barac hadn't the Power. Ruti's parents had been listed as dead, lost with dozens of other Clan in a starship explosion.

A tragedy faked so those involved could escape Council dictates, for the rebels had settled on Acranam and built a secret thriving community. However much I empathized with their motives, they'd been led by Yihtor di Caraat and his mother. The di Caraats had used their Power against Humans and other Clan, allying themselves with criminals.

And my father, who'd thought to force me to Join with Yihtor.

Yihtor was dead; my father exiled. I was blissfully Joined to my one love. Acranam had been forgiven.

Nothing, I knew, had been forgotten. Though she didn't deserve it, Ruti carried that taint and wasn't welcomed by most Clan. As for my cousin Barac? I still wasn't quite sure how he'd survived their Joining, though I was delighted for them both.

As Speaker and leader of the new Clan Council? I couldn't approve the result. Council still dictated Clan reproduction, we had to, but no longer to increase individual Power. Now it was for our survival as a species. Trade Pact researchers were working as quickly as possible to offer us a plan, a way out of the trap we'd created for ourselves. I'd promised them time. I'd begged it from my kind.

Presumably some were listening.

Admittedly, Barac and Ruti would have waited had they known, but we weren't like Humans, whose fertility could be managed. Clan Chosen were ripe from the onset, like flowers ready to be pollinated.

Pollinating, I thought with honest frustration, it seemed we couldn't stop.

"It's an occasion, Witchling," Morgan insisted. "Aren't you happy for them?"

He was. So happy, joy *sizzled* across our inner bond, pushing aside common sense and remorse. Deciding to be happy too, I leaned close, careful not to inhale any remaining Lemmick-breath, and kissed my beloved. My hair lifted to caress his cheek and Morgan responded with enthusiasm.

Time should have stopped right there.

Later, I would wish it had.

"Hom Morgan? Fem Morgan?"

We stepped apart, fingers last to untwine. A familiar oval face peered around the canister, gold faceted eyes catching the light. The upward tilt to the cilia framing Hom M'Tisri's thin lips was, according to Morgan, the Vilix version of a friendly humanoid smile. I took him at his word, having never seen the affable host of the *Claws & Jaws* anything but smiling. Of course, I'd never seen him anywhere other than by his podium at the restaurant entrance and suspected he slept inside it—one of those inter-species' questions impossible to ask politely—yet here he was, immaculate in a purple-and-red floral print, standing in the ser-vice corridor. "If you'd follow me, please," he announced calmly, "your table is ready."

I half expected him to hand us menus.

"Excellent." Morgan put his hand on the other's upper shoul-der, a signal sending half the balloons to hover around the Vilix. " 'Ri, they don't know we're here, do they?"

"I have informed no one, Hom Morgan." Leaving open any number of possibilities.

My Human didn't appear worried. "Good! Lead the way. Watch out!"

We ducked in time for the delivery servo to whiz by safely. The balloons, having scattered, reformed their unnervingly brilliant cluster over Morgan's head.

I could have sworn Hom M'Tisri looked relieved.

The *Claws & Jaws: Complete Interspecies Cuisine* was packed to the gills—or whatever breathing apparatus applied—with patrons, this being the supper hour for an abundance of those on Plexis and the menu famed for its surprises. Since the restoration, reservations were required station-months in advance.

Unless you knew the owner, Huido Maarmatoo'kk.

Morgan and I were in our best spacer coveralls, the ones without obvious patches and less faded blue. It wasn't as though there was a dress code; most of those on Plexis at any given moment were spacers or tourists, and restaurants used recyclable covers on their seating.

I expected to be taken to one of those seats. Instead, Hom M'Tisri led us, balloons soaring like our personal rainbow, through the antechamber into the organized chaos that was the kitchen. Steam clouded the air, filled with a confusion of delicious smells to make my stomach growl and some that made me queasy. Everyone was shouting to be heard over the sizzle of busy cooktops. We went between the main counters, careful of elbows and tentacles. For their part, the sous-chefs and assistants of varied species missed neither beat nor chop, acknowledging our intrusion by squeezing to let us by. We might have passed without causing the slightest disturbance.

A balloon full of Lemmick-breath met a hanging cleaver.

Pop.

Noses twitching, the current master chef—a Zingy—stared mournfully into the pot she/he was stirring. I kept walking, hoping she/he wasn't the sort to jump to conclusions—

She/he was. "Ruined!!" The pot sailed across the countertops, its creamy contents erupting outward in globules, strings, and thick bits. The others avoided being struck with a fine economy of motion, obviously well practiced. "My TRUFFLES—!" The word rose to a shriek. Hom M'Tisri slowed, his instinct as host to soothe matters. The chef brandished a gooey spoon in his direction and shrieked again, eyes popping.

The Vilix wisely picked up the pace. "This way, please!" he shouted.

I followed, watching where I stepped. Why did it have to be truffles? The credits now burning on stovetops or splatted on the floor could have provisioned the *Silver Fox* for a standard year—longer, if we were careful. We'd be heading back to Pocular at this rate.

It might not have been our balloon. Not that I wanted Huido to fire another chef, but better that than we spent another season digging fungi in the jungle. And that's what would happen, I thought gloomily. We were traders, good ones, but the lucrative truffle market was saturated with company ships. Could we still rely on our contacts among the locals and—

Words formed in my mind. *Don't worry about what hasn't happened yet, chit. We'll deal.* Under the words, a hint of amusement.

If my captain chose to ignore the ramifications of balloons and truffles on our meager budget, I decided with relief, so could I.

Swinging doors led into the main restaurant; traffic in both directions was brisk and argumentative. The *Claws & Jaws* prided itself on living servers and kitchen staff. I'd thought this was to cater to the idiosyncrasies of the wealthy, but Morgan admitted Huido had broken all of his servos within a week of opening, almost going out of business as a result.

"Through here, please." Hom M'Tisri opened the rightmost of a pair of less obvious doors and ushered us—and the balloons—into another, wider hallway. "With your kind indulgence," at a significant rise in volume from the kitchen, "I'll rejoin you momentarily."

"We know the way," Morgan assured him, balloons orbiting his head again.

I eyed my Chosen as we walked along the thick carpeting of the living quarters portion of the *Claws & Jaws*. The private dining room had a perfectly good entrance from the restaurant. If we were using Huido's own access?

It meant the Carasian was part of a conspiracy to surprise Barac and Ruti, something patently crucial to the success of the "baby-rainshower-occasion."

I abandoned any notion of warning the pair what to expect. I'd no idea anyway, except my Human was happy.

Much as I loved them, I thought with growing amusement, did the aliens in my life have to be so—alien?

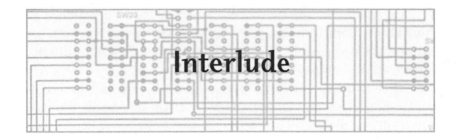

Interlude

DEALING WITH ALIENS, you never saw it coming, Morgan thought ruefully. That unforeseen consequence.

Who knew Lemmicks exhaled into their balloons? Now someone would miss a ridiculously overpriced supper, for which they should rightly thank him. More importantly, Lemmick-breath had Sira worrying about truffles and provisioning the ship, of all things.

Like any spacer worth the air.

Which she was, he thought proudly, and more. Born Sira di Sarc, she was the most powerful individual of her kind, the secretive humanoid Clan. Before he'd come into her life—rather, when she'd arrived at his air lock—Sira had been in self-imposed exile, for no unChosen male had the strength to survive the instinctive Power-of-Choice within her. She'd spent decades locked in the physiological adolescence of a Chooser, studying her personal curse and that of the Clan.

Her solution had been—him.

A lock of red-gold rose from the mass tumbling down Sira's back, curling toward him like a languid finger. Warm and sensual, that hair, strangely willful, and the mark of a fully mature Clanswoman. She'd become that by being near him. By being attracted.

By falling—that unforeseen consequence—in love with an alien.

As had he. For he wasn't, Morgan thought, the simple trader he seemed either.

When he'd met Sira he'd been a telepath of respectable skill, for a Human, with enough potential to make him uncomfortable around the noisy minds of others and wary of the Clan, who disapproved of such power in others. Since?

Suffice to say, he no longer noticed crowds. Sira had honed his abilities, trained and tested them to Clan standards, wanting above all else to protect him from herself. For Clan thoughts and bodies moved outside the known universe, through a dimensionless space they called the M'hir. It was real. He'd almost died there, when she'd lost the fight with her own instinct.

Almost. Instead, he and Sira had managed the formerly inconceivable. Not only had her body matured into its natural—and glorious—adult state before Choice could take place, but their minds and hearts had forged the permanent Clan pair-bond called a Joining.

While he remained wary of the rest of her kind, even the most xenophobic of Clan couldn't argue with that.

Not that he cared. What mattered? He was no longer alone, no longer empty and courseless. The clear brilliant sanity of Sira's thoughts, her passion and goodness, filled him. Each shipday he woke to the joy of discovering the universe with her. And when they made love—

Her head half turned, hair lifting to reveal the sweet curve of her jaw, the blue of the air tag adhered to her skin, and, yes, a coy dimple. *We could leave, you know.*

He came close to tripping over his own feet. *Witchling.*

You started it. With distracting *warmth.*

The Human tightened the mental shields she'd taught him, restoring privacy, and found his voice. "First things—"

He paused, the hall echoing with the bang and clank of carapace and claws in violent motion. A massive black Carasian scampered around the corner—itself worthy of silent contemplation, if not immediate flight—to come to a crashing stop by the dining room door.

In a blur of motion, the being arranged himself into a tidy, a little too obviously bored demeanor, his great handling claws tipped to the floor, lesser claws folded. Surely, that posture said, he'd been here the entire time instead of standing longingly at the door to someone else's pool.

A door unlikely to be breached by longing—or high explosive. Since the "incident" in the restaurant—during which plumbing and beams underneath had mysteriously been damaged, improvements had been made. Between the door security codes Morgan had upgraded and some additional, illicit, construction, the station itself could crack open and the chamber housing Huido's wives be unaffected. The wives could, of course, open the door from inside, making immediate flight by other species advisable. Their needs well satisfied, the prospect was unlikely.

The Carasian longing to introduce himself was Huido's so-called nephew, Tayno Boormataa'kk, a would-be rival Huido tolerated because no one in authority on Plexis could tell the two apart, a confusion as useful as it was entertaining. Tayno happened to be working off a significant portion of the construction costs, not that he'd admit it.

"Greetings, Tayno," Morgan said.

The Carasian pretended to see him for the first time. "Welcome, Captain Morgan!" he boomed. Within the pulsing disks of his head carapace, a row of gleaming black eyes suddenly tangled in their effort to stare at the balloons. "Who's this?"

Morgan sighed inwardly. New to life offworld, the young male tended to panic at the unexpected and there was a great deal of him to panic. "It's all right, Tayno," he said soothingly, "these are—"

"More guests?!" Claws rose, snapping in agitation. "I wasn't prepared for more guests, esteemed Captain Morgan. I wasn't notified. There aren't more settings. There aren't more portions!" An eye swiveled. "Hom M'Tisri! About time you arrived. This is your responsibility. You're fired!"

"You can't fire me." The Vilix's mouth cilia bent in a rare display of temper. The host had, Morgan conceded, been sorely tried in the past few minutes. "Only Hom Huido can."

Eyes untangled. Glared. "I am Huido!"

"No, you're not."

Sira covered her mouth with her hand, eyes shining. *Oh, dear.*

Tayno let out a bell-like sound of distress. "How did you know? How could you? I've molted! I've grown!"

"So," the Vilix observed, cilia rising, "has your uncle."

Tayno collapsed in defeat, his body clattering like pots dropped in a sink. "He'll fire me," he said in a woe-filled whisper.

"He won't. These aren't more guests, Tayno," Morgan assured him. "They're balloons. A type of decoration." He waved one lower. Eyes followed it warily. "See?" He batted the balloon away.

"A Human custom," Sira explained, batting it back.

"Fem Morgan." The giant alien visibly settled as his eyes rested on the Clanswoman. Sira—or more truthfully her *grist*, as they called it—elicited outright devotion from Carasians.

Those they'd met, Morgan reminded himself, careful of assumptions.

"If you say so, of course," Tayno continued, growing cheerful. "My apologies for the misunderstanding. Would you care to be seated? May I?"

"Hom Huido will attend to his honored guests. You watch the door—" Hom M'Tisri pointed. "—this door—as ordered."

Caught, the Carasian gave a rattling sigh. "Very well."

The Vilix saw them into the room and then took his leave, closing the door behind him. Morgan looked around with interest and some concern, for the elegant dining area, newly refurbished with rare wood and costly light fixtures, had been transformed again. A glittering web covered the ceiling and draped the walls, more hanging from the lights. At every delicate junction hung a cluster of small purple globes, dusted with silver. Pretty.

If you didn't look too closely.

"Are those . . ." Sira's voice trailed away.

"I don't think we should ask." Little doubt they were Retian eggs; hopefully empty of young Retians, but there was no telling. "If he offers any, just say no." Morgan waved the balloons to hover over the long and ornately set table. The low rest Huido preferred was at the head, for he'd host this gathering. The old romantic had insisted.

The remaining seats were chairs suited to humanoid anatomy. A slender crystal tank of water, lit from beneath and filled with, yes, more purple eggs, acted as a centerpiece.

Trust Huido to take the concept of a baby shower literally.

"Look." Sira went to the second table, set against a wall. Boxes of various sizes covered its surface, all but one wrapped in rich black material and topped with a neat bow, also black, of issa-silk. "This is—this is too extravagant." Her nose wrinkled. "Unless . . . they won't be more . . . you know . . . ?" With a gesture to the eggs.

"I'm sure they're not edible," Morgan reassured her, hoping he was right. The Carasian should know better, but he wasn't beyond a joke at Barac's expense. Never at Ruti's, though. His confidence restored, the Human nodded at the lone red box. Words chased each other over its surface: "Happy 150th Anniversary!" "Condolences." and "Congratulations!" The Lemmick party-favor dealer had been busy.

"Oh, my." She grinned. "From Tayno?"

"That'd be my guess." Morgan chuckled. He shrugged off his pack and set it under the table. "I didn't think to wrap ours."

Her hand rested on his arm. "You thought of this, Jason. It'll be a wonderful surprise, this baby rainshower."

"No rain. Just shower." Through her touch, he sensed the faintest trace of *worry* and realized it wasn't just the truffles. "It's what families do," he said gently.

The corners of her lips deepened adorably. "We're a family?"

It had come to him one morning, waiting for her to wake and see him, his heart overflowing. That this joy of theirs, wasn't only theirs.

"Yes. A family. You. Me. Huido. Tayno, but don't tell him," he suggested. "Our Clan heart-kin." Beginning with her sister Rael and Barac.

Add the few he'd trusted with her life and his: Thel Masim, who managed Auord's shipcity; Rees, tending bar at Big Bob's; maybe—he stopped there, then finished with, "Copelup."

Her hair drifted up in surprise, then settled over her shoulders. "Who isn't coming," she guessed with a *flicker* of disappointment. "Or we wouldn't be in this room." Drapsk traveled in such numbers they'd have filled the entire restaurant.

Not to mention they caused an administrative flurry every time they docked their massive and powerful ship at Plexis; word would have spread. "Copelup apologized for the better part of an hour," Morgan confirmed. "He said there was 'something in the air.' Repeatedly." Given the Drapsk were an olfaction-dependent species, the phrase could mean anything from something in the station air to an odorous message from home.

"I hope he wasn't too upset." She paused delicately. "Could you tell?"

Drapsk, they'd discovered, reacted to adverse stimulation in dramatic fashion, from rolling into balls to chemically exchanging occupations. "No *gripsta*," Morgan told her, then grinned. "He promised to send gifts."

"As if we could stop him." Sira looked pleased. "They'll be perfect, too."

The expression: "Drapsk know what you want before you do," being apt. The little aliens prided themselves on their knowledge of customer needs and preferences; best not to ask how they obtained it.

"Human, Clan, Carasians, and Drapsk," she mused aloud. "At a baby shower."

Morgan grimaced.

"What?"

"It sounds like the start of a joke," he admitted.

Denial! Sharp enough to make him wince. "It sounds, my dear Chosen, like more family than I'd ever thought to have in my life." Her gray eyes glistened. "Thank you."

Morgan took her hand and pressed the palm to his lips, letting her feel his smile. Her mouth twitched, then smiled back. "Our family," she whispered as if tasting the words.

"My brother!" With a clatter like a malfunctioning servo, Huido Maarmatoo'kk edged sideways through the door.

Post-molt, he was not only resplendent but changed, his

gleaming shell free of the dents and battle scrapes Morgan remembered all too well. The fasteners shed with the old shell had
been refitted into the new with, the Human noted with misgiving,
substantial additions. The Carasian's notion of useful armament
tended to weaponry on the shadowy side of legal, or so far beyond it wasn't worth mentioning, but there were those watching.
Unwise to provoke their attention—

—impossible to avoid his. Adapted as they were for the slick
rock of tidal pools, Huido's sponge-feet and thick legs worked
admirably on station flooring. "My brother!"

Morgan braced himself.

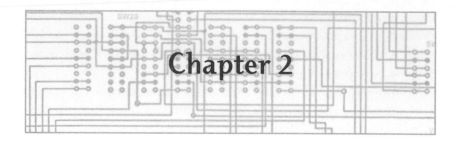

Chapter 2

AN IMMENSE CLAW seized Morgan around the waist and hoisted him to the ceiling, my Human pounding on what shell he could reach in protest. It wouldn't work. Huido's bruising gesture of affection was as inescapable as it was touching. Thankfully, I wasn't entitled to it, despite Morgan's inclusive notion of "family."

Eyes parted to allow twin needle-like jaws to protrude. I froze with Morgan as the tips of those jaws touched his cheeks with exquisite care.

Ritual complete, Huido dropped him with a hearty, "Ah! The lovely Sira Morgan! You've left the pool so soon? What a shame! Morgan, you disappoint us both."

The "pool" being where the Carasian's many wives awaited his attention—impatiently, by all accounts—I blushed. Huido boomed with pleased laughter and all was right in the universe. Even the balloons remained where they'd been sent.

So far.

Hom M'Tisri had followed Huido with a beverage cart. Having placed that to his satisfaction, he turned to his employer. "If there's nothing else, Hom, I'll return to my post."

A claw waved in agreement. "Yes, yes. Let us know when our

special guests arrive. I'll want them brought here at once. Wait." That same claw closed slowly. "A pretense. I have it! My nephew's stuck in a compactor or some such. Feel free to arrange it."

"Leave it to me, Hom Huido," the Vilix replied with ominous enthusiasm.

Once the door closed, the Carasian lowered his voice to an aggrieved mutter. "My nephew's been full of himself since the molt. Should have cracked him while he was soft. Too kind-hearted for my own good, that's me."

Not to mention too soft himself. I smiled to myself. Phero-mones encouraged simultaneous molts, Morgan had assured me, making it less likely one Carasian would have the advantage at that vulnerable time. The restaurant had closed for several days to accommodate this biological necessity. I wouldn't have been surprised if Huido had locked his nephew in a storeroom for the duration, rather than take any chances with their timing.

Timing being a factor today. "How are you managing to get Barac and Ruti here?" A point of keen curiosity Morgan had re-fused to satisfy.

"My invention: *Yipping Prawlies*," Huido announced proudly. "Fresh from the grills. Ruti's favorite! She has excellent taste, you know."

What I knew was a menu item wouldn't counter my cousin's suspicious nature. "And prawlies help how?"

"They're served the same day each station cycle." A grand wave. "Barac and Ruti share a plate every time. Trust me, Sira. They'll be here."

To share an appetizer? It made as little sense as a baby shower for Clan, unless—

They couldn't afford a full meal.

All at once, I understood. If there was a common factor among my individualistic kind, it was personal wealth. Mine as a di Sarc was gone, spent to redress at least some of the harm done to Humans by the Clan. I was happier without it, but I had the *Silver Fox* and a livelihood.

Others weren't so fortunate. When I'd tied our future to the

Trade Pact, it had spelled the end of Clan "First Scouts," those charged with dealing with Humans and eliminating any problems. They'd protected our secret lives.

Now they were a secret, to bury as deeply as possible. My people had always feared the mass of Humanity around them, well aware what would happen should the scouts' actions be made public, and no promise by the Board executive could reassure them.

I should have seen it coming. Scouts worked alone, in isolation. They were selected from the unChosen who lacked prospects for Choice: the expendable. It didn't take long for them to be cast aside, their families—willingly or not—severing access to funds and refusing contact.

As Speaker for the Clan, my authority—unless I took personal and direct action—was largely symbolic. There'd been nothing I could do other than be relieved none of the former scouts had been mind-wiped.

Barac sud Sarc had resigned his position as First Scout when he'd Joined with Ruti, well before the "new" Clan morality had taken hold. His family hadn't rejected him, in any sense.

That wasn't protection from others.

If Barac and Ruti needed help, they'd be too proud to ask. I looked at Morgan, unsurprised to find his face set in the so-innocent expression I knew better than to believe. "This happy 'occasion' we're having—" I began.

Heart-kin. With the warm greeting, figures formed, three of them. My younger sister, Rael di Sarc, smiled at both of us with equal delight. Barac's parents, Enora sud Sarc and her Chosen, Agem, stood with her, neither having the strength to 'port to Plexis on their own.

As 'di,' Rael had enough for all. I gestured the greeting between equals as our three Powers touched in gentle reacquaintance, surface thoughts mingling in the M'hir, for these were, in truth, heart-kin and trusted.

Formalities over, I stepped forward to offer my hands, first to Enora, then Agem. "Welcome! This is our host, Huido Maarmatoo'kk, and you know my Chosen, Jason Morgan."

Enora's dark eyes sparkled with unshed tears. She was taller than I, dignified and graceful. Lines left by laughter and smiles framed her eyes and mouth, for she'd aged when I had not, and she was utterly beautiful. *Thank you,* she sent, then took Morgan's hands in hers. He smiled warmly, touched by her gesture.

Agem was short for a Clansman, with a round, cheerful face. His Talents were minimal, but he'd a sensitive nature well suited to Enora's innate empathy. He'd grown distractible with age and didn't travel alone. He was no less kind.

Theirs was a good Joining, I thought. Enora sud Friesnen had fostered with me as a little girl and I couldn't have loved her more had she been my own. Once Enora's sons had been fostered, she'd returned to live with me, managing my affairs with skill and gentle tact until I'd left with my Human.

To this day, Enora didn't know I'd selected Agem sud Sarc for her Choice. The then-Council hadn't cared about the Joinings of mere suds. I had. To Council's surprise, her union with Agem produced a son powerful enough to be named di Sarc, Kurr. They'd wasted no time authorizing a second only to be disappointed. Barac hadn't the same Power.

He'd the same noble heart, I thought, proud of my cousin.

Agem's eyes widened when I introduced him to Huido. "My first Carasian." He began to sketch the gesture of recognition between equals only to wave his hands vigorously. "Hello!" His hands dropped. "Greetings. Fair skies, no, seas. Oh, my. I looked up what I should say, I swear. I made notes."

Enora brushed her fingers over his wrist and he calmed. "My Chosen," she explained, "is concerned he might give unknowing offense to you, Hom Huido."

Huido snapped a small claw. "In the presence of such exquisite grist, offense is impossible! Welcome, Hom Agem. Fem Enora. Welcome, Rael, sister of my blood brother's mate. In your honor, my home is yours! I vow tonight's meal will be a triumph. If it is not, I'll serve the chef!"

"Hardly ever happens," Morgan said cheerfully.

Agem looked relieved.

"Rael?" Enora indicated the table of boxes. "Our contribution, if you please."

My sister nodded and went to the table. Any Chosen Clans-woman was attractive—our Power and physical nature ensured it—but Rael was breathtaking. Black hair framed her expressive face and cloaked her shoulders, moving restlessly. A swath of deep blue fabric enveloped her from neck to toe. With each step, it parted over her long pale limbs, revealing the spiral of intricate tattooing from thigh to toe. She knew the Deneb fash-ion suited her.

No, this swagger was more than that. I lowered my shields, sensing profound *satisfaction*.

She'd been to her Chosen.

If Rael wasn't pregnant, she soon would be.

Something wrong?

No. Nothing would make me argue with Rael, who'd risked so much for my happiness, especially if she'd found some of her own. Besides, Morgan said I wasn't to worry about what hadn't happened yet.

He'd meant truffles.

I simply added a population crash and the potential extinction of my species, then put it all aside. After all, this was an occasion.

Complete with gifts. A wide plas crate winked into existence beside the table, its white sides covered in yellow-and-red dots. Rael rested her hand on the lid. "All we need are Barac and Ruti."

"Not quite." Morgan stood beside the dining table, his hands on the backs of two chairs, the look on his face that said there was something I didn't know. "We're waiting for Quel di Bowart and her Chosen."

"You invited Ruti's parents?" Enora glanced at me, concern warring with anxiety. "Here?"

I hadn't. That said, I could appreciate my Human's reasoning: parents of one, only fair to invite the parents of the other. It wasn't the Clan way, but I did my best to smile. "It's a Human custom."

"They aren't coming," Rael informed us. "I contacted Quel to ask about a gift for Ruti. She was disagreeable." Her ever-expressive face filled with disgust, her hair writhing over her shoulders. "She said seeing a Human once was enough for a lifetime."

An opinion my sister would have agreed with, before coming to know Jason Morgan. Rael was proof my xenophobic kind could change.

Quel di Bowart was proof it would take time. A great deal of it.

Huido rumbled, then roared: "Unacceptable!" Picking up the superfluous chairs, one per great claw, he flung them violently into a corner. They bounced instead of splintering, implying someone had thought ahead. He rattled his outrage.

"Just as well they didn't come, then," Morgan said with a deliberate smile. "Our happy couple will be here soon. Wine, anyone?"

"Yes! Whatever you would like. It's here, or I'll send for it." The Carasian hurried to loom over the beverage cart, eyes expectant. "Anything for my friends! First, a treat!"

I wasn't fooled by Huido's lightning change of mood. Insult Morgan? The di Bowarts had better be on their very best—and apologetic—behavior if they came to the *Claws & Jaws*. Or bring someone with them to taste their supper.

Their tableware had vanished. I wouldn't have put it past my Human to 'port the cutlery into the M'hir. Or to the *Fox*.

Blame your sister, he sent, amused. "Try this," he said aloud, handing me a fluted glass filled with blue froth. He'd one of his own.

As, I noticed, did the others. I took the glass and gave the liquid a cautious sniff. "What is it?"

Huido gave his booming chuckle. "Babyful punch! Harmless and nourishing."

As I went to take a sip, another Carasian appeared in the doorway. "Your pardon—"

Spotting one another, the pair turned to living statues, mirror images save for the metal rings and clips fastened to Huido's carapace. Tayno, I was relieved to notice, hadn't any. He was menace enough unarmed.

Morgan went to Huido and rapped on his shell. "Still bigger."

With matching rattles and clanks, the pair resumed their normal postures as if nothing had happened. "I thought you'd be in a waste compactor by now, Nephew."

"Indeed, my magnificent uncle," Tayno replied, sounding not the least contrite. His eyes wandered to take in the new arrivals.

"So?"

Eyes snapped back. "Unfortunately, I cannot put myself inside one and Hom M'Tisri has been preoccupied with an influx of Skenkrans. He said you'd understand. Something about perches."

"Have our guests arrived?"

"Yes and been seated. I can—"

"Oh, no, you can't. Remain at the door." Huido bent an eye toward Morgan. "I'll escort them myself. I am a master of subtlety. They will guess nothing!"

Morgan nodded, somehow straight-faced. "We'll be ready."

Agem's brows knotted. "Barac will sense our presence. His mother's, certainly." Enora grew suddenly interested in the egg-filled centerpiece; I could see the curve of her smile.

Not all Clan traveled offworld. Not all, I reminded myself, played games of Power with one another. "Our people keep tight shields on Plexis," I said before Huido could react to any doubt of his ability. "Trust me, Barac won't be scanning."

Trust me, our cousin won't be fooled for an instant by this big lummox, Rael sent, vastly amused. *Better hope Barac plays along.*

In answer, I lifted my babyful punch.

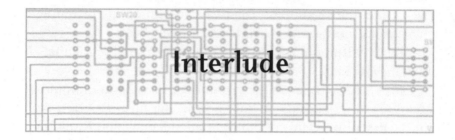

Interlude

RUTI DI BOWART SQUIRMED in her seat, her luxurious hair catching glints from candlelight as it twitched in sympathy. "I should be in the kitchen, not out here."

Feigning horror, Barac regarded his Chosen. "Don't let him know, or you will be." Him being the massive alien heading their way between the tables, one great handling claw balancing a loaded tray, the other clenched with incongruous delicacy around a single flower.

"I promise." Dimples appeared on her soft round cheeks.

Dimples he loved, among all else. The joy of it still amazed him. To have his emptiness not only filled by another, for any Joining would do that, but filled with—

Those kissable cheeks took on a hint of rose as Ruti shared his thought. Her eyes sparkled.

—love, like any besotted pair of the Humans he'd once thought fools. Not a Clan expectation. Not a Clan priority or need. Having discovered this feeling, having Ruti . . .

Who were the fools? Barac thought.

His cousin Sira's doing, this ridiculous contentment. And Jason Morgan. Not to mention Huido.

"Stop! It's not on the menu!" Huido lifted his claw to save the flower from the beak of a Chincomih. "Stupid grasseater. Go graze somewhere else!" This while his tray-laden claw swung wide for balance, just missing the heads of a pair of Threems at the neighboring table. "GO!" The bellow sent the Chincomih and its five companions galloping for the exit with bleats of outrage, their napkins fluttering from their concave chests.

"Oh, my." Ruti put a hand over her mouth to hide a smile. *He really shouldn't.*

You try to tell him that, Barac responded. The Carasian wouldn't admit to being sentimental, and few, seeing his servo-sized bulk for the first time would credit it, but since Barac's and Ruti's Joining, he'd insisted on bringing a fresh rose, a very expensive fresh rose, to their table.

The special attention might be because he'd introduced them to one another, but Barac suspected it had more to do with their grist—for Huido's species could sense something of the Clan in the M'hir. Theirs was, they'd been told repeatedly, exceptional.

Midstride, Huido stopped. "Do you smell that?" he asked in an anguished whisper most of the restaurant could hear.

Ruti wrinkled her nose. "What?"

Eyestalks bent to aim at the tray. "This isn't right. This isn't right at all!"

Barac's stomach growled to say yes, the food almost in reach was not only the right food but theirs and could they have it?

Ignoring the sound, Huido spun in his tracks. "Come with me! Both of you. We will accost my misery of a chef about her/his mistake together. We will demand satisfaction!"

"That's not—" The "necessary" died on Barac's tongue, for his Chosen had leaped to her feet, eyes flashing with indignation, and then there was nothing for it but to grab up their bags and follow the incensed Carasian wherever he was leading them.

Most of the other customers did their utmost to ignore their passage, rightly fearing to put their suppers at risk.

One turned her head to follow, smiling.

She wore a hat.

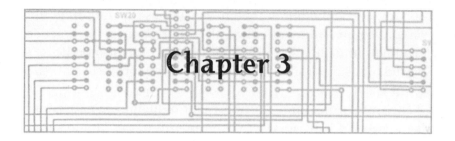

Chapter 3

"PARTY HATS," Morgan whispered.

I peered at my Chosen, seeing little more than the glint of his eyes. "What?"

A sigh. "I forgot them."

Given the five of us were crouched on either side of the door to the restaurant, ready to ambush poor Barac and Ruti, I couldn't see how hats would help, but I made a sympathetic noise.

"What are party hats?" Rael whispered from behind me.

"Human custom," I replied automatically. How many more my fellow Clan would accept before protesting, I'd no idea, but they'd followed along in good spirits so far.

Remember playing 'port and seek?

My own childhood was decades past and dimmer than the lights, but Rael's wistful tone made me smile. *I remember you and Pella refused to stop for lessons.*

A bright and happy memory.

I'd others. Of hiding in the dark, running, waiting. My heart thudded in my chest. I remembered waiting, alone, to die.

Not alone, Sira. Never alone. A hand found mine, gripped tight; he'd found me then, too.

Together, I agreed. *Always.*

Wordless *warmth* dispelled the cold of the past. Then, *Someone's coming.*

I passed the warning to the others, felt their *anticipation.* Morgan, ever the optimist, had instructed us to jump up in unison and shout "surprise!" when the door opened. In practice, Rael had shouted before jumping, startling Agem so badly he'd 'ported to the other side of the table. Hoping for the best, I readied myself.

The surprise was ours. The door that suddenly opened, admitting a flood of light, wasn't to the restaurant, but Huido's own, and though the silhouette filling in that doorway was unmistakably Carasian and two following behind humanoid?

They wore uniforms.

The room lights came up. I straightened with the rest, the flicker of alarm crossing Morgan's face proof he hadn't invited Trade Pact Enforcers to our family occasion.

Though these he could have, I thought, starting to smile. The short, stocky woman with bright intelligent eyes was Sector Chief Lydis Bowman, while at her side—as usual—loomed Constable Russell Terk. Gray battle armor showed at the collar of Terk's uniform but instead of any obvious weapons, he carried a pink box under one arm, tied with sparkly green ribbon.

Bowman, after a swift glance that took in balloons, egg-festooned webbing, and the table, spoke first. "My apologies, Captain Morgan. Guests. We hadn't planned to interrupt—"

The other door opened. In rushed another Carasian, with another two humanoid figures, this time Clan. As the door shut behind them, there was a momentary pause. Our three groups eyed one another, the Carasians having the advantage of being able to eye everyone at once.

Barac's "What—?" overlapped Ruti's "Who—?" They closed their mouths and stared.

"Surprise!" Agem shouted.

"What is the meaning of this intrusion?" Huido bellowed, snapping a claw at his nephew. "You were guarding the door!"

Tayno, clearly feeling himself on some moral high ground, dared bellow back. "I found Ruti's parents!"

"Idiot." Terk was built as close to a Carasian as a Human male could be, his uniform straining at the shoulders. He scowled, an expression well suited to a face made of planes and harsh lines. "Don't you recognize us?"

The Carasian hesitated an instant too long.

"My nephew truly is an idiot, friend Terk," Huido admitted. "Tayno. Pay attention. These fine beings have no grist. They are Humans. Important ones! This is Sector Chief Lydis Bowman and Constable Russell Terk." More sternly. "You insult them with your ignorance!"

Tayno collapsed on the floor, claws splayed out to the sides. "Crush me, Uncle! I am unworthy!"

Before Huido could be tempted, Morgan rapped a knuckle on his shell. "We'll need two more settings."

"Are those?" Bowman looked at the eggs, then shook her head. "Won't ask."

"You will join us, won't you?" I asked Bowman.

"Join us in what?" Barac asked, perplexed. During the bellow-ing, he'd taken Ruti to greet his parents and Rael. "Sira?"

Oh, this wasn't my doing. I turned to Morgan and waited.

His lips twitched. "This is a family occasion," my Human said smoothly. "Barac, Ruti. We've come together to celebrate—"

" 'Family'?" Ruti's face went ashen. "My parents—why would Tayno think my parents were coming?" Hair lashed her shoul-ders. "What occasion is this? Barac, they can't be coming here. They can't have her. You promised—"

Taking her hand, my cousin looked at me.

Something was terribly wrong. One day, maybe, we'd look back at this first Clan-Human baby shower and laugh, but right now, all I could see was Ruti. I went to her, took her hands in mine, and *reached*.

Emotion battered me. *FEAR! Protectiveness. Betrayal/grief.* Out-wardly she appeared upset, but inside, where it counted, Ruti was close to irrational. The M'hir roiled with her distress and I could see Barac wince as he tried to protect himself.

I extended shields around her mind, lowering those between us. *Tell me,* I sent.

Her eyes were wide open, pupils dilated, but Ruti was strong. Somehow she calmed herself, managed to form words. *They want my baby, Sira. They'll take her from me as soon as they can. Keep her on Acranam. Hide her away. I'LL LOSE HER!*

My fury at the former rebels wouldn't help, so I kept it to myself. *You won't.* I let her feel a brush of my Power, my will. *I won't allow it. Trust me.*

She swallowed hard and nodded, hair subsiding.

We do. Barac. He put his arm around his Chosen's shoulders, his eyes fierce, and if Ruti's parents discounted his ability to protect his own, I thought, they'd learn otherwise.

It wouldn't come to that. "This is a baby shower," I told them, aware of Morgan at my side. "A Human custom where family and friends welcome a new life."

"Even you?" Barac hadn't lost his fierce look.

Oh, and didn't I feel Rael's attention then?

I refused to flinch. "I've asked our people for"—there was no easier word—"restraint, but that's to ensure a future for all. Including your daughter."

"For whom we've gathered," Morgan put in.

"Our feast awaits!" Ever the vigilant host, Huido seized his cue with gusto. He leaped into noisy action, herding us to the table and summoning servers from the kitchen. Tayno, having not been crushed, roused to fetch the chairs from the corner for Bowman and Terk.

In honor of the "occasion," Huido, at the head of the table, set Barac to his right, Ruti to his left. Wordlessly, Terk moved his chair to the end, sitting where he could watch everyone. We were friends, of a sort; we certainly had history. It wasn't that he didn't trust us, I thought. It simply wasn't in the constable's nature to lower his guard.

Ousted from his spot at the table, Tayno settled without argument by the beverage cart, perhaps just as happy to be farther from his uncle. Or closer to the beer: he wasted no time pouring a glass into his handling claw, eyes parting to allow that appendage to tip its contents into the hidden cavity Carasians used for a mouth.

Enora, joy lighting her face, sat between Barac and Rael. Across from her, Agem was so frankly delighted to be next to Ruti that the young Clanswoman soon warmed to his attention. I'd thought to sit across from Rael, but Bowman arrived there first, leaving Morgan and me the seats to either side of Terk.

Once everyone settled, Morgan rose to offer a toast, giving Ruti a tender smile. "To family, friends, and the future."

"To success in the pool!" Huido bellowed, shaking the water in the tabletop tank. "But eat first!" he advised coyly. "You'll need your strength."

Barac blushed, Ruti laughed, and suddenly, it was an occasion after all.

Whatever was being served in the *Claws & Jaws* that station evening was nothing compared to what was on our table. Course after course arrived, each offering as irresistible as it was exquisitely portioned and timed. Bowman, known for her love of fine food, saluted Huido with a finger to her forehead and if not for his recent molt, I was sure Huido would have swollen from her praise and ours.

There was conversation, light-hearted and aloud. By our custom, it was rude for Clan to converse mind-to-mind in front of others; I was gratified to see my heart-kin extend that courtesy to the aliens. Only Terk didn't join in, but he paid attention, of that I was sure, and wasn't drinking.

Morgan leaned over the table, blue eyes sparkling. "Where are you putting it all?" he whispered.

"There's nothing wrong with enjoying an excellent meal," I informed him, loud enough that Huido broke out in a laugh. Much as I loved my new life, the *Fox's* galley supplied sustenance, not this level of satisfaction.

My Chosen chuckled, understanding completely, and turned back to catch what Ruti was saying at the other end of the table.

I loosened my belt in anticipation of dessert.

Bowman leaned close. "I'd like a moment of your time, Speaker," she said in a low voice. "In private. We need to talk."

I lost my appetite. So much for being legal, I thought with an inner sigh. Next time, we'd sneak aboard. "How did you know about—?" I waved my fork.

Terk looked up. "There's a Lemmick," he volunteered around a mouthful. "Level 3."

"Spinward ¼," I finished. So much for secrecy.

The top authority in the sector leaned back comfortably. "Glad to help celebrate. They—" a nod to the head of the table, "—deserve to be happy."

Morgan glanced our way. "Agreed."

"Been a while since my last baby shower." Bowman took a sip of her wine and cocked an eyebrow. "Could use some party hats."

My Human feigned chagrin, the other Humans chuckled, and none of it was real. Oh, I believed Bowman thought kindly of Barac and Ruti.

But she'd come for me.

The rich food sat uneasily in my stomach as I wondered why.

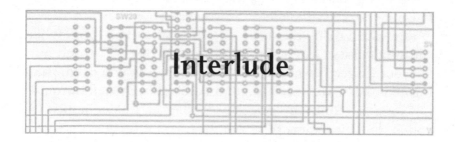

Interlude

WE COULD GO.

Barac met Ruti's somber gaze, the distress she hid from the others coursing like tiny needles beneath his skin. Being the center of attention unsettled her at the best of times. Being the cause? Worse. *Aren't you curious?* he sent, keeping it light. A First Scout's training concerned Humans and, while unfamiliar with the baby shower custom, he understood the significance of ornately wrapped boxes. *They've brought gifts.*

Her eyes flicked to the table. *For us?* As if it were unimaginable others cared about them. The new life within her made them both more protective. He hadn't guessed it would start Ruti building this shell of distrust around them, but that had been her response to her parents' outrageous demand.

Give them their baby?

He'd give them his force blade first.

After that, the bland-faced uncle who'd cut off his funds—

A touch on his knee. Barac turned to meet Enora's knowing gaze. *So much anger.*

Forgive me. He strengthened his shields. She couldn't help but feel the emotions of those close to her, and no one could care more.

If anyone could comfort his Chosen—he stopped himself. A mother wasn't someone Ruti was willing to have.

For now.

We're always here for you. Enora gave the tiniest of nods.

"Ruti, you haven't told us the name of your Birth Watcher." Rael tilted her head, smiling. "Anyone we know?"

Ruti gave a tight little shrug, the ends of her hair fitful. When she didn't answer, Barac spoke for her. "We don't have one."

Silence spread from Clan to Clan. Even Huido noticed, pausing mid-pour. His eyes clustered to stare at Ruti. "What's wrong?"

"Nothing." Ruti's lips pressed together and Barac hoped his cousin would leave it at that.

As well hope to be rich again while he was at it, for Rael frowned and snapped, "'Nothing'? This is ridiculous. You must have a Birth Watcher. To protect the baby. To help her be born."

"Don't you think we know?" Taking a breath, Barac gestured apology for his tone. His cousin didn't deserve it. "Thank you for your concern, Rael. We're working on it."

She gave a gracious nod, though she let him feel her *worry* and wasn't done, not Rael, but she'd wait. His father turned to Ruti and asked her a harmless question—

—Barac didn't hear, his mind abruptly tugged by another's vastly greater Power into the M'hir.

Explain this.

In the M'hir, Sira was brilliance and heat, as if a sun had found its way into the darkness, her mind voice like the clean scent of rain before a storm. And a storm brewed; he could sense its terrifying *edge.*

Barac kept his eyes on Ruti, dwelling on the face he loved. *They're trying to force her home. Her family's forbidden their Birth Watcher to leave Acranam. Anyone else we've approached has either turned us down or demanded more than we can afford. You know why.*

Regret rang through the M'hir, distant and soft. Then *RESOLVE* filled it.

What was Sira in this place brightened until he gasped without sound and would have covered what weren't eyes if he could.

The instant passed and they were no longer alone. Ruti was with him. And—

—another presence, like a pool of still calm water. *Ruti di*

Bowart, my name is Quessa di Teerac. I offer my service as Birth Watcher to your daughter-to-be, if that's acceptable to you and your Chosen. I can be on Plexis tomorrow, unless you need me immediately.

*But—you're—*Ruti's mind voice firmed. *Tomorrow would be fine, Quessa. Thank you.*

The presence vanished.

Their Birth Watcher would be the Chosen of the Clan's foremost Healer, Cenebar di Teerac, her own skills in such demand Barac couldn't remember the last time Quessa had left Camos.

My gift, Sira sent, and the M'hir released him.

Barac blinked, finding himself still staring at Ruti. In the span of three heartbeats, their lives had changed for the better, their greatest problem solved. His Chosen gazed back, her generous mouth starting to curve up at the corners, her eyes moist. *Sometimes, I forget who she is.*

Family, he insisted, for his beloved cousin was that. Above all, Sira was that.

And the Speaker of the Clan.

Chapter 4

BEING ABLE TO HELP BARAC and Ruti made me happy.
The need for it did not. It meant a visit to Acranam in my near future and I'd no friends among its Clan. I'd Chosen a Human over their leader, after all, not to mention rudely shoved their little kingdom back under Council authority. At least there were no di Caraats to poison the mix. Yihtor's House had been exiled by Council; the few remaining, including his vile mother, had vanished from sight. Doubtless they cursed me in their spite, but that was all. Exile had consequences, foremost being banned from traveling the M'hir.

The Watchers saw to that.

The strange disembodied things had their uses, I thought with distaste. Clan scholars—I'd been one—remained divided on what the Watchers were: some unconscious projection from living Clan; the dead whose minds had dissolved in that other space; the M'hir itself, expressing opinion. What mattered to most was that the Watchers protected the M'hir from unwanted intrusion and, somehow, *listened* to Council dictates.

They left Morgan alone. When I'd the choice, I left them alone, too. It was better for all concerned. Acranam, though—

"You going to eat that?"

I looked up, realizing I'd been transfixed by my egg-shaped pastry. "No."

"Allow me." Bowman held out her hand. I passed her my plate only to watch her give it to Terk. "Enjoy that," she ordered brusquely. "Take your time."

Terk's dour look expressed his opinion; that didn't slow his fork.

She rose to her feet. "That moment, if you will."

The Human had picked her "moment" with care. Barac and Ruti, having shared the news of their new Birth Watcher, were in the midst of an animated discussion with his parents and my sister—no doubt about babies—while Morgan, followed by the balloons, had joined Huido at the gift table to sort the order of presentation.

Having no choice, I stood as well. "Whatever this is about, we didn't do it," I said firmly, there having been certain instances otherwise in the past.

"Good to know." Her smile didn't touch her eyes. "I need a drink."

I accompanied Bowman to the beverage cart where she ordered a cup of sombay and scalded cream from Tayno. Given the jaunty tilt to his carapace and random motion of his eyes, this was brave or foolish.

She was never foolish. Brave, yes, I thought, studying her. As well as devious, complicated, and brilliant. The metallic tang to my inner sense near her—and Terk—warned against mental touch. They'd artificial shields implanted in their scalps, making their minds invisible to Clan. Brave, indeed, both to have the implants . . .

And to be so very interested in my kind they were necessary. Not for the first time, I wondered how Bowman had survived that interest.

I'd expected her to go into the hallway where we'd have some privacy. Instead, the sector chief took a few steps beyond the cart, as if to wait for her drink, then pulled out a thumbnail-sized disk, affixing that to her collar.

Silence. I could see lips moving, Tayno drop a spoon, but heard not a sound.

"Excuse the precaution," Bowman said evenly. "What we've to say shouldn't be overheard. I'm sure you agree."

I'm listening.

I smiled at that. Bowman's eyes narrowed. "Morgan, I take it?"

No need to confirm what she knew full well; my Chosen and I were partners in all things. "Why the secrecy?" Not that we weren't obvious. I sensed *interest, concern* from my kin. I sent a quick *reassurance,* feeling none myself. Rael stared back, unconvinced. "What's this about?"

Her disarmingly amiable features grew still. "You don't know?"

She'd a way of making you examine your past for misdeeds. It wasn't that we'd done anything wrong, I reminded myself, and Bowman knew it. Morgan and I had simply kept a prudent distance since our adventure on the Rugheran homeworld, White. The Rugherans were, presumably, happy with the result. The Drapsk definitely were, having experienced a procreative frenzy.

Ren Symon had died in Morgan's arms, having helped him do the unthinkable.

For Jason Morgan had *pushed* his starship through the M'hir to bypass normal space and reach me in time.

Something I couldn't do.

Something no Clan had ever done.

And something to never do again, lest Morgan become the target of every species in the Pact.

If that was why Bowman was here, let her try—I buried the cold dark thought deep inside, where my Chosen wouldn't feel it, schooling my expression. We'd scraped together repairs for the *Fox* and gone back to work. There'd been no sign anyone had paid attention; no reason to suspect Bowman even knew.

Until now. "That would be why I'm asking," I said as calmly as I could.

"I gave you time. Waited for you to get in touch. When I heard you were on Plexis, I was done—" Bowman broke off with a humorless laugh. "You really don't know. Here I'd half-convinced myself you'd decided against our arrangement and was prepping for the consequences. Should've trusted my instincts about you."

Arrangement? Consequences?

So this wasn't about what had happened, I thought with sickening relief, but I shared Morgan's puzzlement. "Is this about the treaty?" I hazarded. "I thought everything was going well." Or as well as could be expected with a bureaucracy the size of the Trade Pact. I'd honestly lost count of the Board Members who'd approached the Clan Council "off the record" with an offer of help; none had been worth the price.

"Treaty's solid." Her brows met, then lifted. "You haven't spoken to your father."

"Jarad di Sarc's been exiled." I could no more keep the chill from my voice than make sense of this. "He's no longer part of the Clan."

"Damn." Bowman unfastened her collar with a twist of her thumb and tugged it open. She didn't dislodge the device keeping us in a bubble of silence. "That's inconvenient."

What's Jarad know that we don't? Morgan asked.

Nothing that matters.

Nothing I cared to hear was more the truth. "If you've something to say to me, Chief Bowman," I told her, "please say it. Otherwise, I'd like to rejoin my family. It's time for the gifts."

Bowman's gaze went to the boxes, paused thoughtfully at the silly balloons, then returned to me. I couldn't read her expression at first. Curiosity, I decided.

Or was it wonder?

"All this," she said slowly. "Your doing, Sira di Sarc. Huh," a soft grunt. "What have I to say? You're the best of your kind. Oh, not because of your Power. How you use it. I'll admit, till you came along, I was ready to give up on the Clan, but you—Clan like you? You're why I'm here. Why I'm staying."

Bowman, complimentary? "Someone's not about to die, are they?" I glowered at her. "Or blow up? Because if that's what this is, you're wasting time."

A chuckle. "I imagine I am. This'll be interesting, me briefing the new Speaker. You'll have to take a lot on—" She stopped, eyes momentarily unfocused. In Clan, that sudden distraction signified communication mind-to-mind.

In Bowman, it meant one of her many implants was delivering a message.

Her eyes closed for an instant. When they opened, what I saw in them made me hold my breath and any questions.

For what looked out was deadly.

"We'll do this later, Sira. Got to go." Bowman yanked the device from her collar and dropped it in a pocket, alerting Terk with a nod, then paused, her expression easing. "Don't worry. You and me, we've something new. Trust. Hold on to it."

She didn't wait for me to answer, raising her voice. "My sincere apologies, Fems, Homs, but duty calls. Barac and Ruti, congratulations. Huido? Decent meal. I'll be back."

Sector Chief Lydis Bowman spun on her heel, her eyes raking me one last time as if a look alone could convey meaning, then was out the door, Terk pounding behind.

The dining hall felt smaller.

"But it's ready," Tayno announced plaintively, a steaming cup in one claw.

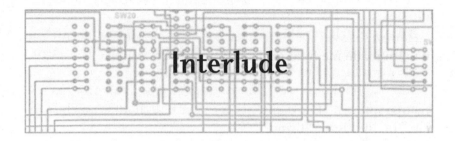

Interlude

WITH BOWMAN'S ABRUPT DEPARTURE, the room fell silent. If the Clan *sent* to one another, Morgan wasn't included, but they didn't hide their consternation. He shared it. Bowman in a hurry was never a good sign. Enforcers dealt with trouble at the species-species interface. With thousands in the Trade Pact, that trouble ranged from misunderstanding to major threat. The Sector Chief wasn't called for misunderstandings.

Sira walked back, red-gold hair twitching at the ends. She shrugged as if to say "Humans," and smiled. "Is it time for the gifts?" she asked, detouring to relieve Tayno of the cup.

Huido snapped his claw. "It is! Bring our guests."

Tensions eased as Ruti and Barac were herded, the pair adorably embarrassed, to the gift table and Morgan dared a quick sending of his own. *What's your read on this?*

That we'll be seeing Bowman again and soon. Her gray eyes crinkled at the corners. *Are family occasions always complicated?*

He had to laugh.

Chairs were brought for Ruti and Barac, the others standing to watch. The Clan appeared mystified, even Sira. Morgan paused, the first gift in his hands, wondering why. "Is this so different from how you give gifts?"

Rael lifted a shapely brow. "We don't."

"Not like this," Enora corrected, smiling. "For us, gift-giving is private, arising from impulse more than occasion."

"It's not as if we can't buy what we want," Rael stated. It was no idle boast.

Barac's flinch was almost imperceptible, but Sira noticed, too. She must have *sent* to her sister, for Rael looked at her. Her beginning frown turned to something appalled.

She hadn't known. "A baby shower's special," Morgan explained quickly. "These gifts are for your daughter as much as for you," he told Ruti. "Tayno?"

He was amused to see Tayno stay out of his uncle's reach as he came forward, though he knew full well the youngster was in no danger. Huido was blissfully content. The younger Carasian approached Ruti, his package pinched between both claws, stopping before risking her feet to lower the box into her hands with commendable care. "Happy Shower Anniversary," he boomed, the wrapping adding a cheerful "Have a Great Trip!" "You open it," he said helpfully, claws at the ready, every eye on the box.

"Thank you." Ruti waited.

Huido snapped a claw and Tayno scrambled backward.

Ruti undid the paper, which promptly refreshed its offerings to a repeated: "On Sale Now, Best Ever Party Favors, Level 3, Spinward ¼," and opened the lid of the box inside. Her face worked for an instant, settling into a bright smile. "How—useful. Thank you, Tayno."

She passed the box to Barac, who reached in and pulled out a tangled mass of string and, yes, spoons of various sizes.

"You hang it in a breeze," Tayno said eagerly. "It sounds like home. I made it myself."

Barac gave the contraption a dutiful shake, producing a clinking susurration that might, Morgan thought charitably, sound like waves on rock to a homesick Carasian.

"A treasure," Ruti said firmly.

Tayno stood a bit taller, self-esteem restored.

"Ours is next," Agem indicated the dotted crate with a proud smile.

"It's not new," Enora forewarned. She gave a small sniff, her smile tremulous.

With a curious look at his mother and father, Barac unlatched the lid. He gasped. "This was my cradle. And Kurr's."

"That's—" Ruti ran straight into Enora's arms, sobbing.

No one spoke. By their stricken faces, the Clan felt as he did. Morgan hoped so. This glorious ache, this belonging. How long had it been? Best not, he decided wryly, count the years.

A small hand slipped into his. *Good custom, this baby-rainshower. Good family.*

"There's something else in there." Rael's voice was less than steady. "From me. Well, not in there, but there's a card—"

The card, it turned out, was promise of delivery for an anti-grav stroller, a Denebian model so new and eagerly anticipated the waiting list, Rael explained, could fill a city. She'd obtained the prototype for them, an extravagant gift.

One she now regretted. "If there's anything you need more, cousin," she began.

Barac gestured his gratitude, echoed by Ruti. "This is perfect. We won't need it for a while."

"I'll 'port it to you when you do," she promised, her smile like sunshine.

Huido's pile of presents took the pair over an hour to open and exclaim over. None, to Morgan's relief, contained Retian eggs, preserved or otherwise, but rather what appeared a complete wardrobe, in several sizes, as well as bedding and other necessities.

Every item was practical and well-made. He'd bet Hom M'Tisri had done the shopping.

Though likely not the bibs adorned with tiny smiling crustaceans.

Bowman's gift sat alone on the table. Sira brought it to Barac, who opened it as though afraid it might explode. Inside was a new rattle, shaped like a starship. And—"Morgan?" He held out a small cylinder.

The Human took it, letting out a low whistle. "This is a voucher stick." A Trade Pact Enforcer Travel Voucher, to be precise, with an authentication chip on the base. The indicator read full. By treaty, such a voucher must be accepted, regardless of species.

So he wasn't the only one to suspect Barac and Ruti were homeless. His guess? The former First Scout was identifying vacant hotel rooms, taking that first look they'd need for a locate. Simple, then, to 'port in and out. "It entitles the bearer to accommodation and food, no questions, no record."

Barac took the stick back, turning it over in his hands. He looked at Morgan, eyes full of doubt.

"It's for the baby," the Human told him and risked sending, *No strings attached.* Ruthless as Bowman could be, this gift he trusted.

Whatever Barac read in his face reassured him. He nodded. "For the baby."

"Your turn," Sira said, smiling.

Huido'd talked him into going last. Morgan retrieved his pack from under the table. His fingers fumbled at the fastenings. A little late for self-doubt, he told himself, taking a deep breath. The second attempt succeeded and he pulled out the roll.

"I didn't wrap it—" he began, offering it to Ruti, who spread the canvas over her lap and stared.

Morgan surveyed the painting, critical of his own work. If he'd had time, he'd have gone back and done more sketches, tested color against light, refined a line—

Ruti's fingertips brushed glowing white petals, stroked a deep green leaf, followed the curl of a vine. She breathed out a word. "Nightsfire."

He hadn't known the name. Apt. The flowers unfurled after sunset, trapping hapless flying things. He'd—

"I thought I was willing. To pay the price. Leave it all behind. My home, its beaut—" Ruti choked and Barac moved behind her chair, resting his hands on her shoulders. Her hair coiled up his arms, the image of misery.

He'd never meant to—Morgan sank to a knee in front of her. "Ruti, forgive me—"

She frowned. "For what, Captain? You've given me what I needed." She took his hand, lowered shields to share with him a fierce *determination.* "I let fear guide me. Rob me. No more, I say!"

She twisted to look up at Barac. "We answer to Sira and the Clan Council, not my parents. Acranam is my home as much as theirs. I will claim it for our daughter."

Barac gave a grim smile and nodded. Morgan squeezed her hand. He rose to his feet and bowed. "I've no doubt you will."

Not alone. He wasn't the only one to *hear* Sira's promise.

"After she's born," Ruti added practically.

"Time for more babyful punch," Huido exclaimed, rattling his carapace. "Who'll be first?"

There was punch for those who wished it, sombay for the rest, and by the time Rael 'ported away with Enora and Agem, after fond farewells and vows for more visits, Ruti was half-nodding in her chair. Barac regarded her fondly, then turned to Morgan, shaking his head. "You might have warned us."

Tayno hiccupped, which in a Carasian produced a prolonged metal chain-through-ring sound. "Surprise was ess—seeential!" Another hiccup.

Morgan wasn't sure if it was the punch or the fact that the eggs on the walls had mysteriously vanished during the gift-giving.

"Have to agree, cousin." Sira sat cross-legged on the table— elbows on her knees, chin in her palms—and grinned. Her hair shimmered in contented waves down her back. "Human custom."

Barac gestured profound gratitude. "Thank you. Thank all of you." He hesitated, looking at the gifts.

Before he could confess—to not having a home, or anywhere to store them—Huido put down his beer glass. "Leave your gifts here for now. I insist. And," more slowly, as if thoughts took their time moving through that immense head, "the balloons. Tayno will put everything away with the greatest care."

The nephew hiccupped again, eyestalks drooping. Morgan raised a meaningful eyebrow.

Huido shrugged, tipping his carapace from shoulder to shoulder. "Tomorrow. He'll put everything away tomorrow." He swept a great handling claw through the air as though removing any possibility of worry. "Tomorrow, *Yipping Prawlies* shall once more grace the menu, and you and Ruti will return. I insist." Eyes milled furiously, then settled all at once on Ruti. "Tomorrow," very quietly, "everything will be as it should be."

What does he mean? Sira asked.

Morgan let her *feel* his smile. *The old softie. He's going to take in our homeless parents-to-be. They just don't know it yet.*

Her gray eyes surveyed him. *And Bowman?*

His smile faded. *The less we cross paths, the better.* Something was up, something more than some new relationship between the Enforcer and the Clan. The last thing they needed was to be drawn into one of the sector chief's convoluted investigations.

The best way to avoid that?

"Party's over. Time we lifted fins, chit," Captain Morgan announced cheerfully.

The sooner the *Silver Fox* hit open space, the safer they'd be.

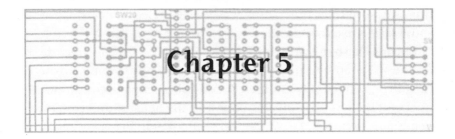

Chapter 5

THE M'HIR AND SPACE had something in common: you
didn't linger in either. Subjective time in the M'hir could be
measured in the effort made to stay whole. *Dissolving* was the eu-
phemism Clan used to describe the pulling apart of will and identity, memory spilling like blood, a mind to be lost, forever.

Space was no safer, in my newly informed opinion. The *Silver
Fox*, retired from patrol duty and destined to be scrap, had been
given a second life as a freighter. Keeping the venerable starship
whole took effort, all right, including walking outside on her hull
when necessary. Easy to imagine drifting away to be lost forever
in that endless dark.

Harder to do. Our suits had redundant safety features, as Morgan was fond of reminding me, and even if somehow I was
plucked bodily from the hull, there were beacons and tags to
keep me close to the ship. Worst case scenario, the suit came
complete with a stasis unit, so if I were to drift away and be lost
forever, I'd do it in my sleep.

That wasn't the comfort he thought.

Of course, in the event of real trouble I'd 'port my Chosen and
self, suits and all, back inside the *Fox*. Or to the nearest civilized
planet, nearest being defined, as always, by subjective time in the
M'hir. By how my strength and will endured—

If I failed—

"Stop that." I shoved the drawer closed and glared at it, that being easier than glaring at myself. I was fretting. The ship was fine, we were fine, our family was fine—I'd no conceivable reason, I told myself, to doubt the fineness of everything.

Except I'd so much to lose.

The link between my mind and Morgan, our Joining through the M'hir, still felt new, still felt incredible. I expanded my awareness of it below conscious thought and my heart acquired a twin, beating in harmony. He was well, I could feel it. Preoccupied, but happily so. In the engine room, I guessed. I could know for sure, could find him anywhere along our link or with a heart-search, but we were, after all, on a starship. Where else would he be? Morgan had wanted to recheck a faulty indicator once we'd gone translight from Plexis.

If satisfied, he'd run a strong callused hand along a bulkhead before leaving the room. If not, he'd curse the ship, with invention and considerable affection, and stay as long as it took to fix the problem. I'd be jealous if I hadn't come to think of the *Fox* as alive myself. Morgan's doing, that.

Almost done, Witchling.

I smiled. The Clan Chosen I knew maintained shields, keeping their thoughts private. Shipboard and alone, my Human left his mind exposed to mine, trusting me to respect his depths as he respected mine. I pulled the bed from the wall, waiting for pillows to fluff and blankets to soften.

Waiting for my love.

One day, I'd viewed the first teach-tape on alien sex. There were crates of the things and, after all, sex was an area of interspecies relations where any confusion in signals could lead to, well, unfortunate results. Or fortunate, depending on your interests.

Admittedly, I'd been bored. There were only so many hours one could spend reviewing ship procedure in the event of whatever-could-never-happen-because-we'd-be-dead-first. Or whatever-Morgan-wouldn't-have-let-happen-in-the-first-place.

In had gone the tape. I'd watched, tilting my head every so

often and squinting, struck anew with wonder at the lengths species went to procreate.

Morgan had, upon walking in on this activity, proceeded to turn an interesting color. Had I, he'd asked, been looking for something in particular? After all. Aliens. Sex.

Was there—with apparent concern—a problem he didn't know about? Our external anatomies were compatible, weren't they?

Nothing would do but we make sure, then and there.

Remembering, I licked my lips, savoring the flush of *heat* igniting my body. Hair, heavy and warm, stroked my skin in anticipation of Morgan's, and deep within my mind our link tightened, for whatever our flesh experienced would *burn* between us until we were one—

Not so done as I thought. Give me a minute. He became aware. *Or not.*

Laughing, I grabbed the blanket from the bed and concentrated . . .

From Plexis, we were on course for Snosbor IV, the *Fox* taking care of navigating at translight. After a full and highly satisfying, if sleepless, night, it was my turn to take first shift in the control room. I brought a book.

I hadn't read more than a page before a voice came through the comlink. "Sira Morgan."

I dropped my book.

I knew that voice.

"Sira Morgan."

I froze, not reaching to answer, unsure what startled me more, that my father was trying to reach me, that he used the com—

Or that my Human name had crossed his lips at last.

No, it was Jarad di Sarc, Clansman, using the com. He loathed technology more than most of my kin.

Is that your father *on the com?* Morgan's mind voice filled my thoughts with the same incredulity I felt. We shared an appreciation of my father as the ultimate example of Clan callousness and lust for power. I locked my shields in place, as Morgan's were. Jarad had been exiled for excellent reason.

If not for his Joining to my mother, Mirim, I thought coldly, he'd be dead; my well-known feelings on the subject likely why he'd not contacted me mind-to-mind.

"Sira Morgan. If you're there, answer me. Is Bowman with you?"

Footsteps from behind, then a light touch on my shoulder as Morgan joined me. A lock of my hair slid to rest over his hand, and I turned to look a question. He shook his head, no more able to guess than I.

I touched the control. "I'm here. She's not." About to end the connection, I paused as Morgan's grip tightened slightly. Curious to a fault, my Human. Fine. "Why would Sector Chief Bowman be with us?"

"You'd know if you'd accepted your obligation, Daughter, when you took the leadership from me. You're a dis—"

I may have hit the com with more force than necessary.

"You could have let him finish," commented Morgan. He went to lean against the com panel, hands in the pockets of his faded spacer coveralls. His remarkable blue eyes studied me. "Bowman implied she'd something to tell you."

"Jarad's in exile." Even to me, it sounded more excuse than reason. I fought the urge to twitch. "I know what he has to say. Jarad's disappointed I haven't donned the white robe and attended every Council meeting."

"Would he know?"

About to reply, I stopped, closing my mouth. Morgan had a point. Our race was nothing if not self-protective; of all the Clan, those who sat on Council knew the danger of exposing their minds to their disgraced former Speaker. Jarad's power was second only to mine.

"It's a mistake to engage with him," I said at last, sure of that much.

"Agreed, but to ask about Bowman, the day after she tries to talk to you?"

Morgan wasn't calm, I realized. Nor was this simple curiosity. "What's wrong?" I asked, abruptly certain something was.

"I'm not sure." He ran one hand through his thick brown hair, giving me a rueful look. "Maybe nothing. Just, when I heard Jarad say Bowman's name, I thought I *tasted* change. It's gone now." As if that would reassure me.

As if his gift, which wasn't mine, had ever been wrong. "What should we do?"

"Check on a friend." He tapped the com panel.

"What happened to keeping our distance, Captain?" I inquired. We'd discussed the ramifications of the sector chief inviting herself to the baby shower. The gift had been welcome.

But whatever she wanted from me? Not so much.

"That was before."

Real concern. For a Human who, last I checked, had her own full cruiser and troops. I drew up my knees in the copilot's couch, the back curling to support me in comfort, and regarded my Chosen. "Go ahead. You've her private code."

Another look, this sharp, but it was the truth and I saw no reason to deny it. There'd been a time when Morgan had reported to Bowman, for she'd been "sniffing around the Clan," as he'd put it, long before we'd met. My arrival hadn't diminished her interest.

For the second time in as many days, I wondered why other Clan had tolerated it.

"Feel free to tell her my father's been asking," I suggested, starting to enjoy myself. Not that I expected the information to rattle Lydis Bowman, who'd faced down Jarad at his most powerful; I doubted anything could.

The corner of his mouth quirked. "Let me find her first." Morgan turned to the com.

It should have been easy. It wasn't.

I'd lived on a starship long enough to value the small sounds the *Fox* made: the whoosh of air through vents, the bone-deep growl of lift engines, and the reassuring almost-whine that meant not only gravity, but that we were moving through subspace under power. Sound meant we were safe and all was well.

Silence meant the opposite.

Bowman wasn't answering. A troubling silence from someone who lived by communication, who was never without a scary abundance of personal tech to be sure she could always be reached—and reach out—let alone that possessed by the *Conciliator,* the massive ship she rarely left.

She'd received a message at the baby shower. Why couldn't we reach her?

I went to the galley for sombay while Morgan continued to try her code. He nodded his thanks on my return, but didn't touch his cup, eyes intent on dials I'd yet to learn. He'd flipped the main console, bringing up that legacy of the *Fox*'s early days as a patrol ship: tech an expert could use to search and find. I sat, sipping, watching Morgan come to a decision and begin to key in other codes. I could guess whose. Terk, first. Failing him, his partner, the feathered Tolian, P'tr wit 'Whix.

I'd no doubt Morgan could reach further. He'd contacts among the traders who plied the starlanes with us, as individuals or on family ships. I'd seen for myself how they'd put aside competition—temporarily—to act together at need. Morgan could well have others even I didn't know. How far he went, I thought, would tell me how serious this was.

I started as the com crackled at last. "Constable Russell Terk. Who's this? How'd you get this code?—"

Setting my cup on the side tray, I grinned with relief.

"—Hiding your ident's a Pact offense—"

"Shut up, Russ," Morgan broke in pleasantly. "Listen—"

"Why should I? Signing off in one—tw—"

"Kareen said to check in."

"—o." A longer pause than seemed necessary, then a bland, "Understood. She's with you?"

Even I, who still often missed Human subtleties, grasped that Terk didn't mean Kareen, his sometime lover.

Morgan's voice was a match. "No, not this trip. All's good, then?"

"Where have you been?" Nothing calm in that. Then, "News travels subspace. Keep up. Terk out."

While parked at Plexis, we'd picked up mail, including current news dumps. Our usual procedure was to send the *Fox*'s system through the unwieldy mass after keywords relevant to our next scheduled planetfall. Sitting together in our galley to go through the results had become a special pleasure for us both, except in those instances where what we'd brought to trade was suddenly the brunt of a new tax or banned. Or a local war was brewing. There'd been one of those lately. Better a lost cargo, Morgan had told me, than a confiscated ship.

Neither of us claimed a homeworld, not anymore, not to care about. Morgan had left Karolus and its failed settlement behind long ago. I'd owned property on Camos, where I'd spent far longer as a Chooser and scholar, but the building was Enora sud Sarc's home now. I supposed I'd kept the Clan attitude that whatever mattered to me, outside of trade, I'd learn from one of my kind.

I'd been wrong. "It's a lie."

"Is it?" Morgan froze the image. Instead of using the viewer on the table, he'd sent the replay to the wall that usually spun with stars. Words filled it, poisonous and wrong. Words that said Lydis Bowman, our friend, had an illicit fortune.

Words that said she'd taken bribes for most, perhaps all, of her career.

In growing horror, I skimmed passages stating she'd been suspended, was facing charges, that before she could be arrested, Bowman had failed to report back to the *Conciliator* and vanished.

The message she'd received last night, I thought, had been a warning. She'd walked out the door without a word.

And the hunt was on.

As Sector Chief, Bowman had ruled on treaty disputes among a dizzying array of races, including Human, sometimes in the open, before the Assembly of Trade Pact Board Members, but more often behind sealed airlocks, discretion being a hallmark of her command.

She'd done it for the Clan. For me. "I don't believe any of this."

Morgan shook his head. "Every agreement Bowman's touched will be torn apart and reviewed."

"Including ours." Not that the Clan was public knowledge, but the risk had to be acknowledged.

"Yes."

I swallowed. Nodded. "Well, then. We'll have to prove her innocence, that's all."

"Sira—" It wasn't often I surprised my Chosen. Or was it *dismay* he allowed past his shields?

"Don't we owe her that and more?" I jumped up to pace around the table, feeling Morgan follow with his eyes. "Bowman trusted us. Dealt more than fairly with the Clan. With me. You heard her. She told me we had something new. Trust. To hold on to it. She's a good person."

"Who has more secrets than anyone I know," he replied grimly. "Bowman's on the run." He shut off the screen, leaving the blank gray wall. "That tells me this is off our course and out of our hands, chit."

I stopped to glare down at him. "You don't mean that."

"If she wanted us involved, she'd be here."

"As Terk thought. And my father. They believed she'd come with us."

"Let's hope no one else does." Morgan stroked the table absently, as if to reassure the ship.

He was right to be concerned. On the realization, I sat and slumped. "I wish she had. One scan would settle this."

"Bowman has an implant."

I frowned. "You can get through it."

Morgan's face lost expression. "No."

Meaning he wouldn't, not couldn't. Morgan had learned the technique inadvertently, while repairing the damage caused when Ren Symon had ripped his way into a mind with a similar implant. Kareen's. "You've the skill to avoid harm," I assured him. "You could prove Bowman's innocence—"

"Or disprove it."

Not condemnation. When it came to the law, Morgan had

lived in the gray of society most of his life; that he'd made his own code to follow was to his credit.

Disappointment? I didn't *reach* to be sure, but he'd allowed Lydis Bowman closer than most.

Neither of us trusted easily.

"Regardless," he continued in the same matter-of-fact tone he'd use to order up a docking tug. "It won't happen. I won't scan Bowman."

A vow, despite that tone; one he'd not break. At times, I could wish my Chosen a little less virtuous.

But then he wouldn't be Jason Morgan, nor my Chosen.

So be it. I sketched an apology in the air between us, sending *warmth* along our link. "There's someone who might have answers."

"Jarad." Morgan glanced up; the galley's light caught in his blue eyes. "I admit I'd feel better knowing why he called."

"Then I'll ask him." But how?

I hadn't realized my fingers were cold till Morgan's laced between them. A lock of my hair slithered down to twine around both, as if to bind us together, but there was no need. Our thoughts met and merged, considering options all within a single, shared breath.

Not the coms. He called on an open link. With a certain scorn.

Humans were clever at subverting their own tech. I sent agreement. *Words are the easiest way to lie.*

The Watchers refused to let Jarad enter the M'hir. *I could bring him here.*

Denial! Wordless, that protest, and deep.

Answered by my own. This was our home, our place. My Chosen was right.

As I was right to flinch from the intimacy of contacting my father mind-to-mind.

Then don't.

The decision having made itself, we pulled apart on our next breath. "I'll go to him," I said aloud.

The corners of Morgan's eyes crinkled with worry, not disagreement. "Don't—"

The rest was lost beneath my lips, a kiss both urgent and necessary.

Besides, I thought to myself as his hands buried themselves in my delighted hair, I already knew what my beloved would say.

Don't trust Jarad di Sarc.

As if I ever had.

We'd planned to fill the *Fox*'s empty holds with nicnics, having calculated to the day when the region's fresh crop would arrive at Snosbor III's southern portcity. Without discussion, Morgan had popped out the course disk, replacing it with an intercept to Plexis. I understood. Coms couldn't be trusted and if anyone other than Jarad might know the truth about Bowman and the newsfeeds, it was Huido.

The *Fox* would arrive by shipmorning, hopefully giving Morgan time to figure out how to pay yet another docking fee.

My mode of transportation had different concerns. I finished dressing, then followed my *awareness* of my Chosen to where he waited in the control room.

Seeing me, Morgan's eyebrows rose.

I fought the urge to blush. Donning the robe of my "office" had seemed right in our cabin, its panels of embroidered white rich with history and significance. Standing here, amid the blinking lights and worn seats of our starship home, I felt—

Stuck, between what my kind expected and what I wanted to be. "I'm not going as his daughter," I said gruffly. In this robe, I was the First Chosen of the di Sarcs, holder of the Council seat for that powerful family, and, since defeating my father, High Councilor and Speaker for the Clan.

"Fair enough." He smiled suddenly. "You're magnificent."

"Not helping," I told him even as my hair responded, sliding over my shoulders in thick red-gold waves of approval and longing. Which was also not helping, but I'd yet to find a comfortable way to restrain it. Nor, to be truthful, did I care. "I'll be back in time to calibrate the coils." It being my turn this day-cycle and the coils being an excellent reason to keep my visit with my father brief.

Morgan's hands closed on my shoulders, the blue of his eyes darkening until I could have drowned in them. "And if you aren't?"

I didn't ask if he'd *tasted* change again. If we'd learned anything from our lives together, it was to plan for the unexpected. "I'll come here." I flattened my hands on his chest, feeling the strong and steady beat of his heart. "Home."

Before my will could falter, I formed the image of Jarad di Sarc as I'd last seen him. I could have *reached* for his mind, evaded the Watchers, and found that cold intelligence. I would not.

Instead, I poured Power into a heart-search, envisioning my father as he was, an image increasingly vivid until he might have stood between us, then . . .

. . . *pushed.*

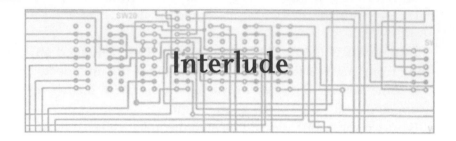

Interlude

TAUPE, NEXT. Morgan dipped his brush, tapping free a drop of excess, then aimed the tip where a new branch had begun its growth alongside the fresher stall. Painting was comfort and distraction, as much as a record of what he'd last found growing under an open sky, kissed by rain and wind. Pressed and dried bits of leaf and bark lay on the desk he'd pulled from the wall, welcome reminders of color and texture in a world confined and closed.

A world empty, with Sira gone.

From the ship only. He let himself *stray* into the warm golden space within his mind where she was, always, careful not to distract her. Their link was at its faintest—Sira's thoughts sealed behind formidable shields—but unbroken. It couldn't be, not while they lived.

A fact Jarad abhorred.

Morgan smiled to himself.

It still astonished him, the power she had. To think of a remembered place or known person, form a locate as the Clan called it, and simply will herself there.

Simply? Sira had taught him to move objects through that otherworldly dimension the Clan named the M'hir; he felt the drain on mind and body simply to push a pen from room to room. Not every Clan could do the same, he thought with some pride.

Though he'd lost more than a few pens at first.

But any Clan could move themselves, which he'd yet to do. Might never do, according to Sira, ever honest.

He'd taken the *Fox* through the M'hir. That had to count.

And be forgotten.

The brush trembled, marring the intended stroke; he wiped the paint from the wall. "Branch," Morgan reminded himself. Ruti had loved her gift. This would be for Sira, a welcome when she returned.

He'd surprised her here, in his cabin, shortly after she'd arrived on his ship, staring wide-eyed at the plants painted on every available surface.

She hadn't been the first.

"You were trouble then, too," Morgan murmured, pausing to remember.

There were risks, landing on worlds. Gravity was one. The other flashed badges.

Enforcers had boarded the *Fox* on Stonerim III, the officials ostensibly aiding the local Port Authority in a hunt for smuggled Skenkran eggs, a treaty-breaker if found in Human hands. Having that very morning closed his air lock behind a pair of passengers assuredly not on the *Fox*'s manifest, the timing had felt ever-so-suggestive of another kind of search.

As law-abiding traders—meaning any captain who wanted to keep their good rating and landing privileges—opened their ships and holds when asked, Morgan unlocked his air lock, allowing Enforcers and Port Jellies to spread through the *Fox* like a plague.

Then took a cup of sombay to his cabin to keep out of their way, trusting the locks on his control panels if nothing else.

Morgan was unpleasantly surprised to find one of the Port Jellies already there, not searching his belongings, but sitting at ease on his stool, surveying his artwork with a thoughtful frown.

Human female, short and sturdy, with glossy black hair gathered in a knot at the base of her neck and a uniform worn thin at cuff and elbow, as if she couldn't be bothered to requisition a new one. There was a noteplas on the table—his table—unopened.

Leaving a cluster of flowers, the woman's gaze found him. She didn't lose her frown. "Didn't expect this." She circled a blunt finger at the walls.

"Can I help you, Constable?" Morgan countered, standing in the open door.

"Depends." The finger beckoned. The back of that hand, her right, bore an angry, barely healed scar.

She was angry, too. No, furious. He *felt* it through the protections he'd learned to keep between his mind and all others, though her face showed only mild impatience.

Not a telepath, he concluded, who'd have protection as well or go mad, but a mind sensitive enough to *project*. Perhaps one made uneasy around any use of power.

Vulnerable.

He didn't believe that for an instant. Morgan came in, the door sliding closed behind him. His cabin was the largest in the *Fox*, making it roomier than a closet with the bed tucked away; he leaned politely against a wall so as not to crowd her.

That it gave him a clear view of the weapon she bore was no more than habit. With the *Fox* crammed with her colleagues, he'd no intention of causing trouble.

And every wish to avoid it.

The constable flipped open her noteplas and consulted it with a glance. "I know what arrived on this ship, Captain," she announced crisply. "Do you?"

"I'm no smuggler." Not this trip.

"You had passengers. I don't care about their documents," this before Morgan could protest again. "I'm interested in why they bothered with a starship. This starship."

A warning trilled along his nerves. To hide it, he took a slow sip from his mug, regarding her over the rim.

"It'll be worth your while."

He lowered the mug. "Offering me a bribe, Constable? Usually it's the other way around."

Her eyes narrowed. "You've joined a game bigger than you realize, Morgan of Karolus. Yes, I've done my checking," at whatever he hadn't kept from his face. "This isn't the first time you've brought the Clan to my planet in secret and I want to know why."

How did she—? Morgan didn't take passengers on the *Fox* if he could help it. Be confined with others, inflicted by the bedlam of unprotected thoughts and emotions? As it was, the moment the *Fox* settled on her fins he was ready to call up a tug, and stayed downworld only as long as it took to conduct his business.

Kurr di Sarc, and his younger brother Barac, were a pleasant exception, their minds soothingly invisible. They looked Human, but he'd known they weren't, not with the immense power he'd sensed *testing* his mind's protections at their first meeting. Clan, they had to be. He'd been certain they'd come to eliminate him. Wasn't that what rumor claimed Clan always did to Human telepaths?

Maybe it was. He couldn't say. He came to believe these two were more interested in the novelty of spaceflight—and not co-incidentally avoiding the notice of their kind—than in the thoughts of a ship's captain.

Didn't hurt they paid well and were decent company ship-board. One trip became two, then several. Kurr's passion was hunting artifacts in the ruins of Norval—whose Morgan didn't ask. It was a popular, if dangerous, pastime, the pancaked layers of the city having squashed its three earlier versions deeper into the marshy ground with no sign the collapse was done.

Barac wasn't interested either but tagged along, as he put it, to keep his brother out of trouble.

This constable was trouble. "I admit, I gave an archaeologist and his assistant a ride here off the books. They'd been robbed on Auord—" Plausible; who hadn't? "—and I felt sorry for them. I don't know anything about any 'Clan.'"

"Ah." She wrote quickly, then looked up with the smallest of smiles. "So you did have passengers this trip."

He wasn't caught often. "Who are you?" with real curiosity.

"Bowman. Lydis Kari Bowman." She snapped off a page and

closed her noteplas, tucking it in a pocket. "Here's my private code. Don't leaving it lying around."

Morgan, bemused, took the page. "And why do I need this?"

"You work for me now."

"Really." Bowman wasn't like any Port Jelly he'd met, he'd grant her that. He lifted an eyebrow, willing to spin the wheel a while longer. "Why would I do that?"

Bowman's smile vanished. "To keep this ship of yours. Seems there's a good number of eggs hidden in this cabin. I assure you I can find them all for my superiors before you locate the first."

Morgan stilled.

"You could use your Talent to stop me," she acknowledged dryly, shocking him to the core. "It's a family flaw, I'm afraid. Not enough power to be anything but weak."

"Which you aren't," he replied, sure of that much.

A chuckle; it wasn't humor. "No," she agreed and tapped a button on her shabby jacket. "A record's being sent to a remote and secure location. Meddle in my head, mindcrawler, and it won't be Port Authority after Jason Morgan, smuggler. It'll be the Clan after Jason Morgan, telepath. I trust you appreciate the difference."

Kurr had told him, one night over a bottle of wine, what the rest of their kind would do to him if they knew what he was. Mind-wiping was the least of it. Things suddenly made sense. "You work for them."

Then didn't, when Bowman shook her head. "The Clan watch me. Aren't shy about it. If they think to use me, my position, they're mistaken." Her face hardened. "Now I watch them. Seems only fair."

Fair wasn't the word he'd have used. Was she mad? "What do you want from me?" he heard himself ask in a stranger's voice.

She stood, straightening her uniform with a tug. "You're not their puppet, not yet; I've seen those." They were close enough he had to bend to face her. She tapped his chest with one finger. "I want eyes on the Clan. Eyes they trust—or at least tolerate." Tap. "I'll pay, don't worry." Tap. "As for the Clan, I strongly suggest you keep our arrangement secret." Then her palm landed over his heart. "Who knows, Morgan? This could be the start of a wonderful relationship."

A darker brown, Morgan decided grimly, if he was to work with shadows. Bowman never told him what she did with the information he'd provided; he'd never asked. That she mattered to the very aliens she spied upon was obvious, if only from their careful lack of interest in her activities.

Which wasn't true, he thought suddenly. Not all Clan. It had been Jarad di Sarc who'd known Bowman, maybe from the beginning. Who else? Sira hadn't, nor Barac. Not until their paths had tangled after Kurr's murder.

Or because of it. Jarad's doing, that death, and pointless.

Sira had defeated her father before all the Clan. Morgan didn't doubt she could manage him now. Nor that she'd learn what she wished.

Thinking of his Chosen, who'd managed to bring even Bowman around to her side, he reached for gold instead.

For light.

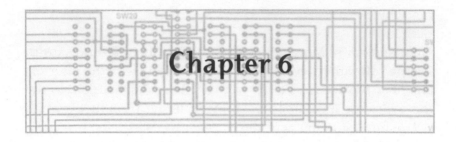

Chapter 6

. . . I found myself darkness within shadow, defined by Power and *will* amid nothing real or seen. The M'hir. The Drapsk called it the Scented Way; the Rugherans, home.

The Clan? Our proper name was M'hiray and part of us was here, in this otherworld, even when we were not. When we *pushed* ourselves fully into the M'hir, our passing etched bright pathways that could be followed by others.

Or we died. "Lost in the M'hir," we'd say of those who overstayed what wasn't in any sense welcome and *dissolved*. The M'hir was a whirlpool, to resist and escape, or be consumed. Distance here meant nothing; subjective time, everything. Misjudge your strength and what you'd been stayed in that darkness, consciousness swept apart and away.

The Watchers in the M'hir would inform Council of the loss.

Every so often, a remnant lingered, locked in place, its melancholy echo a warning to those who passed by.

A ghost.

Garatis 17, site of my father's exile, was a long 'port; coming from the *Fox*, I'd no previous passage of significance to ease the way, but my strength wasn't tested. I kept my sense of self as small as possible, as if that would hide me if the Watchers took an interest, and focused on my memory of a craggy, disapproving face . . .

. . . and became solid again, standing before my father.

Jarad di Sarc's hawklike nose and straight bearing hadn't changed. His eyes remained darkly beautiful, glistening beneath now-thunderous brows. If age or exile had touched him, it wasn't outwardly.

What surprised me was seeing him in dusty pants and shirt, as if fresh from labor. The pants had pockets on the outside of each leg, filled with small tools, and knees with pouches for cushioning. I glanced around to find out why.

We were outside on a loading dock, a pile of transport crates stacked nearby. A low brick wall separated the dock, with its aircar landing platform, from an ornamental garden. Beyond the flowers and trim shrubs was another wall, this of metalwork. Through its ornate openings, a city of red, yellow, and brown tile roofs sloped gracefully down to the sea, aglint under the morning sun. A warm breeze stirred fluffy clouds and carried the scent of flowers.

Jarad wasn't alone. Two Humans, both male and in similar clothing, had been unpacking the crates; after looking to Jarad to be sure I was welcome, they went back to work as if someone appearing from thin air was normal.

I *reached*, recoiling in disgust. Their minds held nothing but the task at hand and the need to serve. Only First Scouts were supposed to use their Talent to manipulate vulnerable Humans, and only by Council order and solely to defend us. This was the reality. Many Clan houses still had such unwitting servants. How long would the treaty hold if Humans knew we'd enslaved them?

The guilt wore on me; I was alone in it. Other Clan struggled to think of Humans as other than occasionally convenient. To all, they were disturbing. Too like us, too many, too unpredictable. Morgan's Power, proved to the Clan by our Joining, had more influence on the newfound good manners of my kind than fear of extinction or the treaty, not that I'd tell the Board Members.

The bitter truth was that we were too few to afford to admit our guilt, let alone make amends. I hoped for a better future, when we could.

Jarad knew my opinion; it mattered to him not at all. "What, no courtesy, Daughter?"

I gave a proper short bow, making the requisite gesture to recognize his lesser strength. "I'd have used the com, but I know
when such tech can't be trusted."

His hands remained still, not that I'd expected him to acknowledge me. "Well, you're here now."

As if I'd come at his behest. Temper wouldn't help, I told myself reasonably, my hair twitching in disagreement. To calm myself, I looked toward the crates just as the front of one was opened,
revealing an old and familiar trunk.

So much for calm. "That's mine!" Hair lashed my shoulders.
To be honest, the trunk—and the rest I didn't doubt were in the
remaining crates—belonged to the Clan Council and so all of us,
but I'd been the only one in recent times to study their contents.
I'd believed them safely with Enora. I tried not to shout. "What
are they doing here?"

Jarad smiled. "I've an interest."

The trunks contained parches, brown rolls of some forgotten
material inscribed with names. Those names held our history,
going back pre-Stratification, recorded as every successful Joining and result. Jarad hadn't been interested until I'd used them
to prove our kind was about to doom itself.

His smile dropped away and he gave my robes a dismissive look.
"If you'd been to Council meetings, Speaker, you'd know I peti-
tioned through third parties for access to these and other irreplaceable items. My request was granted. Our past must be protected."

Our past had led us here; I found myself heartily sick of it.
"Fine. I've other matters to discuss with you, Father. If you've a
moment?" Underneath I sent *NOW*.

And was pleased to see him wince.

Jarad led the way indoors, leaving his servants to bring in the
trunks. I sensed no other presence. I'd known my father retreated
here when frustrated with Council or family—or both—but hadn't
pictured such a sparse and simple dwelling, nestled in greenery.
Did he consider his exile punishment or convenient?

It could be both, I admitted to myself.

We went down a narrow hall into a room that stretched the width of the building, its screenless windows open to the air. My spacer instincts cringed. A bare worktable stood in the middle and there was space along the back wall where I presumed my trunks would reside. Above were cupboards fronted with transparent doors, the shelves within crowded with a multitude of smallish old things. I frowned at Jarad. "How much did you get from Council?"

"These I inherited." He walked to the nearest and opened the door, taking out what proved to be a wizened gourd. From the reverent way he held it up for me to see, it might have been his firstborn.

That being me, I was less than impressed. "Pre-Stratification." Our ancestors had brought with them what could be carried in hands and packs, most of it disturbingly primitive, none of it useful.

Replacing the gourd, he nodded. "The M'hiray began when the best of our ancestors left our Homeworld. We mustn't forget how far we've come, in every way." A sidelong look. "Your mother wants us returned to that life. Before the M'hir. Drinking from such husks."

"Mother isn't why I'm—" About to say "here," I stopped, turning back to the cupboards. Jarad hadn't these things on Camos. What inheritance?

No, I told myself, growing numb. He wouldn't have—

Of course he would. Power shaped into rage *rose* within me, clamoring to be released. Pushing it down, I made myself speak instead. "These were Kurr's. How dare you!"

Jarad raised an eyebrow. "You sound so Human."

Because Clan didn't mourn. We *pushed* our dead into the M'hir and did our best to forget all but the lineage of their power.

That my father—this monster—had arranged for Barac's elder brother to be murdered by Yihtor di Caraat?

That, I would never forget.

Jarad went to sit in one of three chairs by the window, waiting for me. The chairs were wood and painted, a crudity well-suited to the past he hoarded. I'd been wrong to come here. Wrong to think shields sufficient when dealing with him.

Having no choice, I picked the red chair and sat. Whatever else I might think, no doubt Kurr's beloved bits and pieces would be kept better here than anywhere else. I folded my hands neatly in my lap, relieved my hair had gone sullen and limp. "Why did you call the ship?"

He leaned back, palms together, long fingers meeting under his chin. "That's not what you want to know."

Fair enough. "Why did you ask about Sector Chief Bowman?"

"Something that—" Jarad stopped and aimed his fingertips at me. "Before I tell you, explain why you haven't opened to Those Who Watch."

I smiled without humor. "Because I choose not to." Di Sawn-da'at, senior on Council, had broached the subject once, calling it a formality so the Watchers could identify those presently in authority. I'd informed him that—as the mysterious entities had no trouble contacting me at their whim, and I'd no intention of being in authority again—I would do no such thing. He'd not pressed the point.

Death namers. Spies. Emotionless, bodiless, impossible to reason with or comprehend. Since our Joining the Watchers had become *interested* in Morgan. He couldn't sense their strange attention; I could. Not a threat. Not yet.

I'd let them no closer to us, to our link, than necessary.

"It's your Council duty—they have knowledge—"

And there it was, what he really wanted from me.

I lost my smile. Our history, as records, as remembered and shared, began on Stonerim III. We might have sprung to life there, if it weren't for the genealogy and relics now in my father's possession. Clan were taught that during Stratification, the M'hiray were freed from the memories of their before-lives to ease the transition to a new and better home.

Most of us, more cynically, believed those memories had been stripped to prevent any of us from returning to the old one.

Clan were also taught that the Watchers held those memories in trust, for the day—not that when, or how, or why was given—

we'd rejoin our former kin and live happily together. Reunification, scholars called it, when the Watchers would share their knowledge with the Clan Council, presumably including a locate for the Clan Homeworld so we could find it again.

"It's a myth," I told Jarad. "No one—Councilor or not—believes the Watchers capable of anything more than reacting to events in the M'hir."

I could show you.

"I can leave, and will." My turn to raise an eyebrow. "Unless you explain about Bowman and why—"

Tap. Taptap. Tap.

Distracted, I turned to the window, expecting a bird.

It was a hand, reaching from the shrubbery.

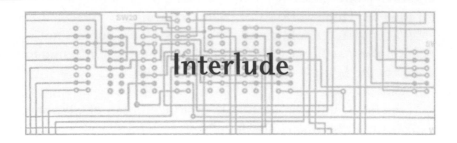

Interlude

PETALS CURLED LIKE FINGERS, their purple splashed with yellow, pink, and white at their feathered tips, encompassing a center ablaze with vermilion. The solitary flower sat on an arching green stem, other buds pregnant and waiting their turn.

The Clansman deftly collected pollen on the end of a brush, moving along to another orchid, this kept virgin within its glass dome. The art he practiced was older than civilization on Omacron, the world on which he'd decided to live. The species who'd evolved here might have had an interest in the beautiful alien flora within these greenhouses, but he'd discouraged it.

The majority of Omacron being mildly telepathic and so easy to *influence.*

Janac di Paniccia preferred his own company.

Is that so?

He smiled as he removed the glass dome. *I did, once.* He straightened from his crouch, looking around.

The image of a Clanswoman reclined atop trays of young plants as if lying on a couch. Thick black hair framed her lovely face and sent locks to stray across her breasts. A sheet of golden issa-silk trailed over her body; the sheet's end disappeared in mid-air.

For Rael di Sarc was on another world.

Janac held up his little brush, the glass dome within the curve of his free arm. *I need another few moments.*

I do not, my Chosen. In that other world, Rael smiled, then arched her neck, letting the sheet slip away. Revealed, her long legs were tattooed so that slender vines lipped the skin from inner thigh to toe and tattooed orchids embraced each proud nipple.

The orchids were a surprise.

Don't move, the Clansman sent, relishing the still-new, still-exciting *heat* flowing between them. He tossed the brush with its red dust aside and put the dome on the nearest surface, uncaring he'd just ruined the consummation of a years-long project.

Hadn't they waited longer?

Waited for the Clan Council to decide if their potential offspring would be of sufficient Power? Hadn't he—

Forget them. Rael licked the tip of her finger, stroking it across a nipple. *You know where I am. Come.*

Janac formed the locate in his mind and began to concentrate, something more difficult than usual as Rael began to—

The roof and walls imploded, knocking him to the floor. Shards of glass sliced cloth and flesh even as Janac *pushed* himself into the M'hir . . .

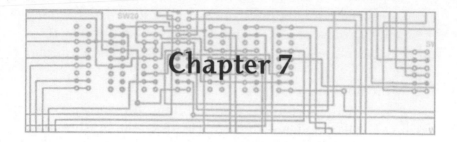

Chapter 7

I LEAPED TO MY FEET, Jarad doing the same. As his chair tipped onto the floor, there came a sound like drumming rain from behind. We whirled around to see—

My trunks. Marching into the room by themselves, their tops splattered with blood. Something was underneath, something running—

What is it? Morgan, worried by what he sensed along our link.

I shared what I saw.

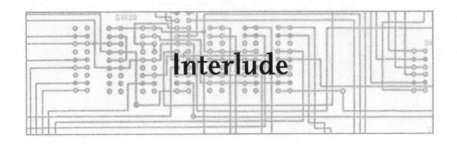

Interlude

WHAT THE . . . ? Worry became horror as he recognized—*Assemblers?!*

Morgan leaped to his feet and sent with the strength of fear. *Get out, Sira! COME!*

Then reeled with the sickening pound of *CHANGE* through his mind, the worst such premonition he'd ever experienced.

He shuddered free. "Sira, why would . . ."

The control room was empty.

Sira wasn't here.

"I am," he said aloud, seizing on that proof as though drowning. If he lived, she did.

But where was she?

Chapter 8

THE TRUNKS TOPPLED OVER, exposing a crazed mass of hands and feet and other parts—even heads—moving, glinting with metal, some coming together, all aimed at us.

Morgan's warning beating through me, I grabbed my father's arm and concentrated, forming the locate for the *Fox* . . .

. . . not there! HERE! HERE!

. . . I fought him in the M'hir, our Power streaming away like blood . . .

. . . A Watcher stirred. More than one. Their combined voices cut through what I was and wanted . . . WE FORBID . . .

. . . so I fought them, too. Let us pass! KNOW ME!

And . . .

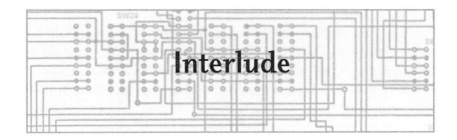

Interlude

P INCH ME.

Barac looked at Ruti, suspecting a joke. Sure enough, her eyes shone and she was smiling. *Why?*

Humans do it when something's too good to be true. To be sure they're not dreaming.

Ah. Barac gestured apology to their tolerant tablemate, Quessa di Teerac. "My Chosen thinks you're a dream."

Ruti turned crimson. Quessa smiled and took her hand. "I'm quite real."

The Clanswoman exuded calm the way another might excitement or tension. Even her white hair held itself in serene loops, emphasizing her long slender neck and dainty head, and her hands, when they moved, caressed the air. Most Clan of Quessa's rank and reputation dressed the part, but she wore a plain and practical travel cloak over a shirt and pants suitable for gardening, its hood draped over her shoulders, and a blue, not gold, air tag rested on her cheekbone, matching theirs.

Appearances could lie; not so Power. After theirs had *explored* one another's in mutual introduction, Barac continued to feel at ease. More than that, he realized. He felt cherished as an integral part of the small life they'd started. A life now protected.

So this was what a Birth Watcher did.

And more. Something *flowed* between Quessa and Ruti. Barac watched his Chosen's embarrassment disappear, her expression soften. "We're very glad you're here. Barac is, too," she added, smiling at him.

Wasn't it a bit early for their daughter to have an opinion, let alone express it? This, Barac decided, was the sort of question to ask their new Birth Watcher when his beloved was fast asleep.

There was one, however, he must—however awkward. If they were to lose her help, best it be before they'd grown to depend on it. "Do you have accommodations on Plexis, Quessa?"

"She'll stay with us," Ruti said hastily. "That's right, isn't it?" Her eyes fixed on the older Clanswoman, pleading in their depths.

Barac doubted Bowman had considered a houseguest when programming their voucher stick. "Ruti—"

"What's right is what's best for your baby," Quessa replied tactfully. "As it happens, I do have a place to stay, a small household my Chosen established in case his services were ever needed on the station. Level 5, as I recall. I've not visited Plexis before, but Cenebar assures me there would be room for you as well."

"Barac?" Oh, and if he'd thought Ruti's eyes shone before, now they glowed.

Level 5? No night life, no loud music. The stores were filled with unremarkable goods, of better quality than lower levels but of no interest to the wealthy. A blue air tag wouldn't rate a second glance.

He'd be suspicious of such good fortune, if it hadn't come through Sira. Barac began to gesture profound gratitude, only to find himself with a warm lapful of Ruti, her *joy* impossible to resist. "We accept and gladly," he told Quessa, holding his Chosen tight.

The Birth Watcher smiled. "Wonderful. We can 'port there whenever you're ready."

"But then you'd miss the *Yipping Prawlies*." Ruti twisted around, keeping an arm around Barac's neck. "We should stay for those. They're delicious!"

"Then we shall!" By the twinkle in Quessa's eyes, she was pleased to indulge the young mother-to-be.

Winning Barac's heart. Ignoring their audience, for the *Claws & Jaws* was packed as usual, he kissed his Chosen soundly, *happiness* soaring through their link.

"That's what I like to see," bellowed a familiar voice. Ruti scrambled back to her feet as, with a clatter, the giant Carasian arrived at their table, flower clutched in one great claw. A waiter followed, tray laden with three servings plus a pitcher of beer with what Barac recognized as Huido's favorite glass. Once the table was filled, and Ruti given her flower, the alien settled himself at the end.

Rows of shiny black eyes converging on Quessa. "You have the most magnificent grist, Fem—?"

"Quessa di Teerac." She nodded graciously. "You must be Huido Maarmatoo'kk. I've heard wonderful things about your restaurant."

A small claw waved airily. "I try not to poison any being."

"Quessa is our Birth Watcher," Barac said with pride, looking to Ruti.

A crease had appeared between her lovely brows. "I don't care how magnificent her grist is," she scolded, lowering her voice. "You can't just sit here, Huido, when the restaurant's this busy. The kitchen needs you."

"That's where you're wrong, little Ruti." Huido leisurely poured himself a beer. "The kitchen needs you."

"Don't tell me you fired the Zingy?" her eyes went round. "Why?"

"He/she walked out." The Carasian tipped his bi-saucered head to each shoulder. A shrug. "Apparently he/she couldn't tolerate the working conditions. Some nonsense about improper balloon storage. It's so difficult," to Quessa, "to find the right staff. That's why I'm grateful for my Ruti."

Who was ignoring her prawlies, eyes wide. "You're offering me a job?"

"Master chef of the *Claws & Jaws* is not a 'job.' It's a vocation." Huido's clawful of beer disappeared with a smug slurp. "You can start in the morning." Eyes clustered to aim at Barac. "You, too. Hom M'Tisri wants an assistant with shiny teeth. To smile at humanoids and the like. And you're pretty."

Why the old—Barac closed his mouth, aware the wily Carasian had backed him into a corner.

Fingers brushed his. *I do love cooking.* Ruti's sending was wistful. *And you are pretty.*

That did it. Barac burst out laughing. Who was he to argue with a conspiracy of such kindness? "Tomorrow it is."

"Excellent." Several eyes shifted to aim at the restaurant entrance. "I expect you to stop that sort of nuisance."

Hom M'Tisri, at his podium by the door, was surrounded by a sizable group of Humans with the gold air tags and innersystem clothing that meant privilege and promised attitude.

"Grandies." Ruti made a face. "They try to bully their way in without a reservation. Happens all the time," she assured Quessa, who looked uneasy.

Huido rose, snapping an irritated claw. "The curse of being the best restaurant in two quadrants. I'll handle this."

Change! Impossible to ignore that *taste*—or the urgent dread that came with it. Cursing inwardly, Barac slipped a hand inside his coat and wrapped his fingers around the handle of his force blade. "Careful," he warned the Carasian, rising to his feet. "Something's wrong—"

The Humans shoved by the protesting Vilix, entering the restaurant.

At their next step, fracturing into moving, scurrying parts!

Terrified patrons screamed or bellowed or vented gas, knocking over tables in their haste to be somewhere else.

They'd the right idea. "Ruti," Barac ordered. "Take Quessa."

Huido spared an eye. "Go to my pool. Use your Power!" Without looking to see if they complied, he charged forward, great handling claws snapping in fury. More screams filled the air as the patrons saw him coming.

Barac drew his blade, prepared to follow the valiant alien.

"No!" Ruti grabbed his hand and he felt the surge of her greater Power . . .

The restaurant *disappeared* . . .

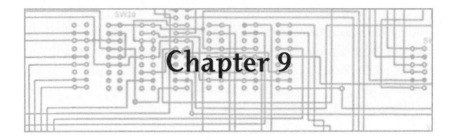

Chapter 9

...I became solid again, breathing in shuddering gasps, and looked around for Morgan.

Who wasn't here.

Of course he wasn't. How could he be? This wasn't home. Not my home.

Jarad had brought us to his instead.

Camos.

Snarling a curse, I dropped my father's arm.

Sira?

In answer, I sent Morgan reassurance as well as the image of where I stood.

I knew this place all too well. We were in Jarad's favorite room, deep belowground. The floor was rough stone, stepped in layers; the ceiling, shadow. Wooden pedestals stood everywhere, the items they displayed illuminated by portlights, each tethered in its place with rope. For this was the Hall of Ancestors, containing my father's most treasured scraps.

Are you safe? From the tone of Morgan's sending, he didn't believe it.

Inside a windowless room, built to be a vault, I supposed I was, but that wasn't the point. "This was your doing," I accused Jarad, letting him feel my growing *rage*. Needless to berate him for the deaths of his servants. He wouldn't care. "You used me to break your exile—"

Instead of gloating, my father staggered to the single stone bench and dropped more than sat, his face ashen. "We're safe here. We should be. What were those things?" His shields were whisper-thin. Through them, I felt something I'd never felt from my father before.

Fear.

"But if you didn't arrange this—"

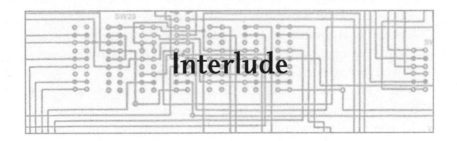

Interlude

THE SOFT, steady drumming sent those with legs scurrying up tree trunks or diving into holes. They thought they knew what came their way. There were heavy-jawed biters who ran in ground-darkening swarms, eating anything alive in their path. That this wasn't the biters' season gave no creature pause; better to hide than be wrong.

But what ran along the forest floor this night was deadlier still, if not to wildlife. Bodies shaped as hands or feet or grinning heads or thickened limbs or quarters of torso drove forward on thickened cilia. Whatever the shape, each managed to clutch a bit of metal or bead or tube. To those looking down, it might seem a machine had been their prey, its pieces being carried to some den.

But this was nothing so benign.

The Assemblers had dropped from space in a rain of boxes, too small to trip any sensors. When they succeeded, their ship would land and recover them.

They considered no other option.

Flowers, or their like, shone overhead, their pale light luring winged things and glinting on hard cold eyes. The horde ran and ran until the flowers were outshone by moons' glow.

The first halted before running into the clearing ahead. Those behind scampered overtop, a mix of disembodied parts heaving and pushing. From this apparent confusion soon appeared a growing structure as metal and beads and tubes came together.

A bead tumbled loose and the mass froze as one.

A finger and thumb stretched out at the last possible moment to snatch the bead, carefully, before it could strike the ground.

Movement again. They'd no time to waste.

Done. The mass of flesh spread apart to expose what was now a sinister device, with tube-mouths aimed toward the clearing.

To where a short road, striped in moonglow and shadow, passed between and around dark, quiescent buildings. There were no doors.

Those who slept within had no need.

Seemingly at random, feet found legs found torso parts found shoulders and arms and hands, hands plunging to acquire heads and snick them into place. Then two Assemblers stepped forward to take hold of what were now controls.

Their hands did what hands do.

Beads shot into the air like a tight flock of birds, their flight directed and sure. They sped low over the road between buildings, then rose sharply.

The Assemblers pressed forward, shoulder to shoulder. Fingers twitched out of synchrony and mouths gaped in breathless excitement.

The flock split apart, beads hovering over rooftops.

Then, all dropped.

What had scurried up trees lost their holds and fell as the forest shook; those in holes struggled for air as their homes filled with earth.

The Assemblers, knocked back and apart, didn't bother to link together again.

But every head wore a smile.

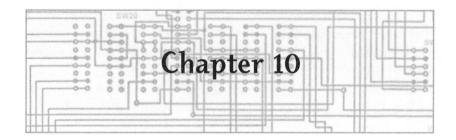

Chapter 10

SENSING ANOTHER PRESENCE, I looked over my shoulder. "Lord Jarad?" The young Chooser came out from behind a pedestal, dust cloth in hand. She grew still, eyes on me as if startled by more than our arrival, then swept a full and respectful greeting before I could be certain. "Lady Sira."

Camosians, being Human, used such titles; I'd noticed my father enjoyed them. "Sira," I corrected gently, bowing in return as I tried to think of her name. She looked Parth, with her straight black hair and almond eyes, wide-set and bright; something in the high cheekbones said Teerac to me.

"Assistant curator, Jacqui di Mendolar. Speaker," with a second and unnecessary bow.

With that, I knew her: a Chooser older than she appeared, her body holding its physiological age for the last nine years, awaiting a Choice that might never come. Another as I'd been. Our one meeting had been at the gathering on Camos during the treaty signing, when I'd been more concerned with keeping Morgan safe than my kind.

All at once, we were in the midst of another gathering. Seven more Clan appeared, their formal white robes a match to mine.

The rest of the Clan Council, the most powerful Talents of their families: Inva di Lorimar and Prega di Su'dlaat, First

Chosen; Clansmen Degal di Sawnda'at, Kyr di Mendolar, Crisac di Friesnen, and Cela di Teerac; and the lone Chooser, Tle di Parth.

No need to ask how or why, I thought, if anything surprised it had taken them this long to respond to the Watchers' protest. Their focus was Jarad, who remained seated, until heads snapped around to me.

Acknowledgments followed, deferential and profound; by their expressions, I judged all were more confused than pleased.

Not that they'd lower shields to me to share those feelings.

Sawnda'at took a deep breath, then asked very politely, as befitted someone of inferior Power. "May we ask why you've brought Jarad here, Speaker? The Watchers are unsettled."

"This crasnig can't be trusted," Tle di Parth said furiously, sending a sharp and insolent *disapproval.* "You shouldn't have—"

I silenced the rest of her outburst with an irritated *flick* of power. She lifted her head, green eyes narrowed, but remained silent. The young di Mendolar regarded us with growing concern. Those who found themselves trapped between more powerful kin didn't always survive.

Clan games. The attack must have rattled me more than I'd thought. I gestured appeasement to her and the rest, quickly *sharing* my memories. "There wasn't time to consult," I finished, then looked to my father. "What did you do to provoke them?"

"They attacked when you arrived!" He surged to his feet. "You're the one dealing with aliens instead of your own kind. This was your fault! I saved us." Oh, and wasn't that stern arrogance a return to the father I knew well?

Had it been me? Assemblers made even seasoned traders like Morgan queasy. He'd told me humanoids didn't visit Assembler planets. For their part, Assemblers away from home remained— I'd believed till today—in their linked form, meaning we could have mistaken them for Human. Unless the parts argued among themselves, how would we know?

I shook my head. No trade of the *Silver Fox* had gone so badly as to warrant violence. "It wasn't—what's wrong?"

In strange unison, the faces of the Councilors altered. Eyes went wide and staring. Mouths worked without sound. Inva staggered into Crisac.

I opened my mind to the M'hir, flinching at the chaotic howls filling it. Had the Watchers gone mad? About to retreat for my own sanity, the howls formed into words.

Names.

Names the Watchers were screaming, no two the same, names I knew, names pulling me deeper and deeper trying to comprehend a darkness seething with pain and shock—

"Daughter!" Distant, that voice, for all its attempt at command. Weak. Powerless.

Then, like a lifeline, strong and sure, *SIRA!*

I followed my name, the *caring* of my Chosen, back into myself.

In time to watch five of my kind crumple to the floor.

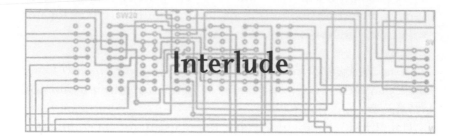

Interlude

...BARAC found himself standing by the tidal pool and imported coastal rocks of Huido's innermost sanctum. He wasn't alone. Ruti gripped his hand and Quessa's.

While in the calm, ink-like water, rows of shiny black eyes appeared.

"Where are we?" Quessa looked around, her once-tame hair writhing in a cloud. "What is this place?"

"Safe."

Not necessarily. The eyes belonged to Huido's wives, aroused and interested, and from what Morgan had told him, Barac hoped they weren't hungry.

"What were those things?"

Hearing the tremor in Ruti's voice, Barac turned his back on Huido's wives to hug his own. He rested his chin atop her head. "They're called Assemblers. I don't know what would make them—"

A muffled THWUMP!

An explosion. On a space station? "Make them insane," he muttered.

"Pardon?"

Another blast, closer. "Ruti, Quessa," Barac said hurriedly. "We have to go."

"No, we don't. They can't get in." Ruti pulled away. "Nothing can." She waved at the pool. "Huido built this to protect them and you know Tayno will be guarding the door. This is the safest place on Plexis."

Explaining why Ruti had been willing to 'port them here, if nothing else.

The eyes sank below the water until they might have been alone. Given their appetite for still-walking meat, Barac suspected the wives would be just as happy if the door was breached. So long as Clan weren't to their taste.

From the sounds outside, the restaurant must be rubble. He had to help Huido. "Wait here." Barac formed the locate of the dining area.

Ruti took hold of him, her fingers tight. "No!"

"Heart-kin. I have to—"

"NO!"

Barac stilled, turning only his head.

One of the wives, the source of the bellow, heaved herself partly from the water. Larger than Huido by half again, the black plates of her head and torso were scratched and dented; her left-most claw lacked a tip. Mating, the Clansman thought numbly, took its toll.

The creature couldn't have spoken. "They aren't sentient."

He hadn't realized he'd said that aloud until Ruti chuckled. "Of course they are." She smiled at the giant, now-silent creature. "They're the smartest of all."

"YES!" A different one spoke, crashing back into the water to submerge save for her row of eyes. Waves slapped the rock.

The first again. "STAYHERE!" She slipped underwater more tidily.

Ruti nodded and went to sit on the driest rock, patting a spot beside her for Quessa. "Hom Huido will handle those Assembler things," she said with touching and likely not-misplaced confidence. "Besides, Port Authority will be here soon. If we leave," this with familiar determination, "we won't know what all this was about. And," her final, telling point, "Huido will need help straightening the kitchen. I'm sure everything's a mess."

"You're very brave." Quessa managed a smile. "Such excitement!"

"It's not always like this," Barac started to protest, then shrugged. "Lately, maybe."

THWUMP . . . BANG! Like impossible thunder.

We're safe here. Despite the brave words, Ruti snuggled close when he put his arm around her, her hair sliding warm against his cheek.

Their Birth Watcher smiled gently at them both.

A smile that froze, then faltered.

With no other warning, Quessa di Teerac collapsed at their feet.

Barac went to his knees beside her, Ruti with him. He *reached,* only to recoil from emptiness. "She's—gone."

A soft breath passed Quessa's lips and it was over. Her white hair lay scattered like so much froth. Ruti touched it, picked up a limp strand. Her eyes met Barac's, tears overflowing to splash on stone.

Echoed by another splash. Another. They looked up.

The wives looked back.

Somehow, Barac didn't flinch, though he'd seen nothing so terrifying in his entire life as this uncountable mass of shell, claw, and eyes, and if any part had moved, he'd have 'ported with Ruti.

She trembled, but it wasn't in fear. "Don't eat her. Please."

A claw snapped dismissively. "We have no interest in the dead."

Not a bellow, which was a relief, but he couldn't tell which had spoken, couldn't tell one from the rest. Couldn't think, not clearly.

Except to remember how good their fortune had seemed, so short a time ago—

GRIEF surged through his link with Ruti, even as she gasped, even as her eyes rolled back in her head. *NO!*

To his horror, she collapsed in his arms. "Ruti?" *Ruti?*

"You shouldn't be here."

Barac's eyes shot to the wall of aliens. "This isn't about you." His Chosen was too brave for that—braver than he was—

"You aren't like us." Harsh, almost accusing.

"Of course we aren't." Save him from alien minds, especially ones as *scrambled* to his inner sense as these. He held his Chosen, desperately trying to grasp what more could be wrong. "We're Clan," he told the wives wearily. "Friends."

The word seemed to fill an eerie, lingering silence.

Eyes stared.

All at once, claws snapped, shells crashed together, and incoherent bellows echoed from ceiling and wall.

Ruti stirred, her face anguished. Wincing in pain of his own, Barac covered her ears with his hands, unable to concentrate through the deafening cacophony of sound. What were they doing?

Silence. Ears ringing, he raised his head.

Three wives remained above water. The first made a bell-like sound, then spoke quietly. "We concur. This was inevitable. The Clan shouldn't be here."

The second made the same sound. "The Clan don't belong."

The third heaved suddenly closer, menacing in its dripping black, and bellowed, "CLANMUSTGO!"

Barac swept Ruti up in his arms and *pushed* . . .

. . . walls formed around them.

They weren't nice walls, being streaked with grime and who knew what fluid. The floor was dry only because dust and grit soaked up the worst of what fell through the grates above. Barac sat gingerly, cradling his Chosen and the life she carried; afraid of her stillness, afraid to disturb it.

He'd tracked a Human down here, long ago: a telepath who'd caught Clan attention. She shouldn't have been where she was. What she was. Yet she'd begged him to understand.

Now, at last?

He did.

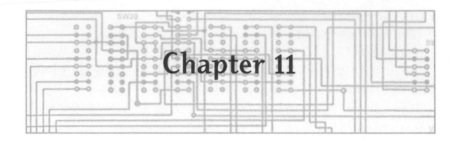

Chapter 11

JARAD MET ME at the nearest unmoving form; our eyes locked in an instant of terrible certainty. Nonetheless, I put my hand on Crisac di Friesnen's leg and *reached.*

Finding nothing. His body was an empty husk. "Gone."

Jarad checked Inva di Lorimar then Kyr di Mendolar, shaking his head. I went to Cela di Teerac and Prega di Su'dlaat with the same awful result.

Their minds had been *pulled* into the M'hir. Which meant for the five bodies at our feet, there were five more we couldn't see: those who'd died first, taking their mates with them. The link between Joined pairs was permanent and a sentence of death. "Their Chosen died," I said.

Or did I whisper?

"Their—you mean my grandmother?" Jacqui asked, then went terribly still.

Tle di Parth covered her mouth with her hands. *They weren't together. Each had stayed home. How could they die all at once?*

Jarad's face matched the stone around us. "It was planned. They were killed. Murdered!"

Degal di Sawnda'at stared at me, his eyes round. "Signy's at a play. She's asking what's wrong. What's happened. What do I tell her? Speaker, what do we do?"

Signy hadn't been home. "Go to her," I told him as realization struck, part of me startled by the flat calm of my voice.

Degal hadn't died because his Chosen hadn't been home.

Jarad'd brought us here believing this room safe. It wouldn't be enough against Assemblers.

Because they knew where to find us. We'd been—

I refused to think it, refused to think Bowman might have done this, might have taken credits in return for lives. I refused to think of anything or anyone, even Morgan, but my next breath and now.

"Jarad." I gestured to the bodies. It was our way, to send the remnants into the M'hir.

And I needed my Power.

Our homes are traps! My warning coursed outward, fueled by desperation, welling into a shout no Clan would miss. The Watchers joined me with their own. *FLEE!*

Even as I feared I was too late.

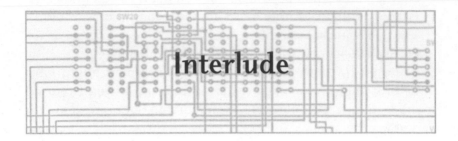

Interlude

*H*EART-KIN.

The greeting came with *connection* through the M'hir, deep and immediate. The waves of worry, fear, despair that had burst into Rael's mind with the horrific warning to *FLEE!* faded.

They weren't gone.

We're all right. Rael rested her hand on Janac's chest, as much for her own support as his. "It's Sira," she told him aloud, blinking away tears of relief.

She'd healed the most grievous cuts and slashes, carefully 'porting away each piece of glass violating his flesh as she'd done so. That he'd had the strength to come to her through the M'hir—

His hand covered hers, the pale pink line of new skin crossing red ragged cuts like some mad tattoo. "Ask her if others live," he said quietly.

Rael started, then nodded. *Are we all that's left?*

No.

The quick denial should have been reassuring, but the link between them thinned; her sister, keeping back the worst of her *grief* and *pain*.

She did the same.

Are you somewhere safe? Now with a tinge of distraction. The Speaker of the Clan, already thinking of who else needed her.

Rael's pride was mixed with sympathy. *Yes. Go. And Sira?* She lowered her shields, sending all her *love* and *belief.*

But their *connection* was gone.

"Rael. We can't stay here."

"And you can't move until I'm finished," she countered, trying not to shudder. Her Chosen appearing by her bed, covered in blood, falling into her arms . . . she would never forget it, nor the force of Sira's *warning.* She'd wrapped her arms around Janac, poured strength into his failing heart, and brought them . . .

. . . here. The tiny building was closed, shutters covering the gorgeous view of lake and mountain its windows offered in summer; the roof, which could open to the stars, sealed beneath plas. The bed had been stripped of its sheets and plump cushions, and snow had swept in beneath the door.

They'd discovered one another for the first time here, in this special place.

Now Janac sprawled on the bare, blood-soaked mattress, his eyes full of pain, and the only thing special about the building was its isolation. Gently, Rael reclaimed her hand. "This won't take long," she murmured, slipping back into the semi-trance of deep healing.

She worked urgently, disregarding lesser wounds. Janac was right to fear staying here. His clothing was in shreds, save for his boots; hers were on the other side of the planet. Already their breath fogged in the icy air and, though her hair did its best to cloak what it could of her upper body, Rael couldn't stop shivering.

Enough, beloved. He sat up with little more than a wince, then smiled up at her. *Nice orchids.*

She choked back a laugh and helped him stand. "Later. We need clothing. Credits." A safe place to hide until Sira righted the universe.

Janac's face tended to serious lines. They grew harsher, his eyes shadowed. "Other Clan will be targets. My servants—" he went to shrug and thought better of it, his back still raw. "The Omacron avoid unpleasantness at any cost. They'll have abandoned their homes, at least until things settle down."

His orchids. His home. Hers. Gone. Rael trembled from more than the cold and Janac pulled her close.

Here, she suggested, offering a locate.

Janac's *unease* fed her own, but he tightened his arms around her, equally aware they were out of better options. "Be ready to 'port away again and quickly."

And go where?

A question Rael didn't bother to ask.

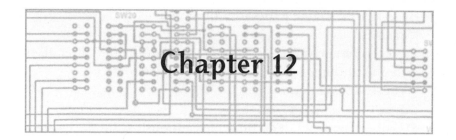

Chapter 12

*S*IRA.

More than my name. What Morgan sent throbbed with *love* and *compassion*, feelings I could hardly imagine as I contemplated what had happened.

Come home. We can do this together.

He meant what should come next, an accounting of who hadn't died in the last horrific hour. Assurance of safe havens, however temporary.

Finding who'd betrayed us, so it wouldn't happen again and again.

Finding a future, when the present lay shattered.

Soon, I promised.

As if I knew how to do any of those things.

I tightened my shields and opened my eyes. Tears spilled; I no longer cared. Perhaps I'd cry for the rest of my life. It seemed fitting.

Staying here a while longer seemed fitting, too, though I couldn't explain why to myself, let alone to my Chosen. Tle simply fled. I'd ordered Jarad to go to Mirim sud Teerac, my mother, despite knowing how little she'd appreciate his arrival. There was no question of his Power. He'd protect her, if only to save himself.

Cenebar di Teerac, who'd saved countless Clan with his Talent, had doomed his Chosen. I'd almost broken, *hearing* the Watcher's howl his name and Quessa's. Would have, if I'd heard Barac's and Ruti's.

By so selfish, so fine a thread, I hung on.

"Speaker?"

I'd forgotten poor Jacqui. Wiping my face—I cared after all—I turned to find her waiting by my side. "You should go."

"Where, Speaker?"

I didn't know what to say.

She tilted her head, regarding me cautiously from the corners of her eyes. "I wouldn't go home, even if I could. My family doesn't approve of this." She gestured to the pedestals. "They wanted me to be their next Birth Watcher." Her face changed and she looked as though she might be sick.

Because a Birth Watcher stood between the unborn and the fate of the mother, should her Chosen die.

I echoed her gesture and asked evenly, "Did you abandon a mother for this?"

"No!" Her eyes flashed, denial in every line of her small body, then she subsided. "I would not." Beneath, with even greater passion, *I WILL NOT.*

I excused the sending, though it stung. "Then I shouldn't worry." I stepped to the next level of the floor, granting her space to calm herself.

The step brought me to the focal point of the Hall, its great treasure. I rested my fingertips on the cool wood of the pedestal, staring down at the torn bit of fabric in its crystal, reputed to come from Naryn di Su'dlaat, my great-grandmother, who'd led the M'hiray to their new home. "What of the old one?" I asked, as if she would answer me. "How is this better?" Standing there, all I could feel was grief.

And foreboding. Assembler minds were hive-like and untouchable, putting them among the many species the Clan avoided. Why would they attack us? I knew what Morgan would say, as clearly as if he shared my thoughts. They wouldn't, perhaps couldn't, have acted alone. Who was behind this?

Worse, other species would take notice. Some might join the

Assemblers, while others could fear themselves the next likely target and strike. The Trade Pact would come undone.

Worlds could burn.

"Speaker. Sira?"

The softly anxious—innocent—voice roused me from that terrible vision. "I'm sorry." For still standing here. For so much. "It's time to go." I reached for the crystal.

"Please! You mustn't!" Jacqui started toward me, hands outstretched, then stopped as I picked it up.

Lighter than it looked. Hollow? Finding no seam or fastening, I tossed the smooth oval in the air and caught it again. The scrap within didn't move. I looked at Jacqui. "Did you think we were coming back?" I asked. "That anything could be as it was?"

Her mouth worked, then firmed. She gestured apology. "With your permission, Speaker, I'd like to bring what I can."

I wanted to refuse her outright; remembering a similar passion for the past, I relented. "Be quick. And, Jacqui?"

Already two steps down, she turned and looked around at me. "Yes, Speaker?"

"What might help us survive, young di Mendolar. Nothing else matters now."

She nodded, once.

My robe, however ornate and ridiculous, had discreet but sensible pockets. On impulse, I put the crystal in one.

And went to help the assistant curator of the Clan's Hall of Ancestors rob her own collection.

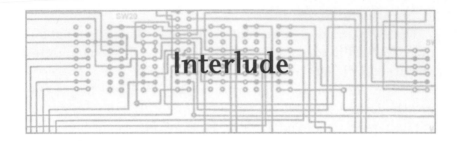

Interlude

THE TRADE PACT had grown too large, with species' interests too wildly diverse for any one bit of news to catch fire and sweep through; not so the Inner Systems. Morgan listened to the incredulous chatter of his own kind, sought what confirmation he could from any Human traders downworld, and tried to sift facts from speculation.

Incident reports. Assemblers destroying private property here. There. Assemblers causing disturbances in theaters and meeting halls. Assemblers rioting or going rabid or whatever their species did. Port Authorities on hundreds of worlds issuing travel bans.

As well ban rats.

No mention of the Clan, not by name, but he'd Sira for that sure and terrible truth. His heart ached for her, for all of them. He wanted her here, with him.

As if he could make this better.

A patiently blinking light caught his eye. Morgan pushed the button to open the link. "I wondered when you'd call."

"What's going on, Morgan?" For once, Constable Russell Terk didn't sound gruff or bothered.

"How secure's the line?"

A pause. Terk's voice filled the control room again, regaining some of its customary edge. "Should be tight. No promises."

Like that was it? Morgan tapped a finger on the panel, half inclined to end the call. No. He had to risk it. "The Assemblers targeted the Clan. The attacks were planned. They'd idents, locations, whatever they'd need."

Something short and profane answered, then the quiet question, "How bad?"

Morgan leaned back his head and closed his eyes, *feeling* along his link to Sira. *Preoccupation*. The layer of unshaken *calm* didn't fool him; it was a façade, maintained by dreadful will. "Some survive. That's all we know so far." He opened his eyes. "What's the official line?"

"What you'd expect. 'Classic Species Incompatibility.' Next they'll call in a bunch of fancy muck-muck experts to explain how these Assemblers were stressed out of their collective minds and had to kill people to feel better." A spitting sound. "All while our people are being grilled about the chief or out chasing her tail." A note of pride crept in. "Wish'm luck with that." Somber again. "So what can I do?"

Not what could "we" do. Catching that, Morgan pursed his lips, then nodded to himself. "Someone started this. There aren't many who could . . ." he let the rest trail away.

"Understood. My advice? Stay offworld, Morgan. They'll have your—wait." Terk didn't bother to mute his com; Morgan heard the rapid staccato of a coded report.

Terk came back on. "Bold little monsters. They went after your friend's restaurant on Plexis. Word is—are you sure?" to someone else. "Knew I liked the big guy," back to Morgan with dark good cheer. "There weren't enough bits left to question."

Why Huido? Morgan thought furiously, unless—"Was anyone hurt?" He refused to count the Assemblers.

"None reported, but it's Plexis. Most customers prefer not to talk to us." A considering pause. "I can get there. Check on Ruti and Barac."

"They're fine." He had to believe Sira would have told him otherwise.

Whatever had happened there was over and done. "Do your digging, Terk," Morgan told him. "Do me a favor and be careful when you turn over those rocks."

A grim laugh. "I'm touched."

Morgan forced a chuckle. "Just thinking of those beers you owe me. I plan to collect."

"You owe me," Terk corrected. "Terk out."

The control room fell back into machine silence, its soft, peaceful whirrs and clicks no longer soothing. Morgan dismissed the impulse to contact Sira again. She knew Camos wasn't safe. She wouldn't linger.

Even should this prove the sum of the attacks, with no more casualties, he feared the worst was yet to come. Karolus, the battles lost, the families destroyed. Hadn't he almost lost himself, after that? In grief.

In rage.

Sira mustn't—wouldn't. Whatever it took, whatever she'd need, he would be there.

Until then . . . Morgan picked up the disk that would send the *Fox* to Plexis, turning it between his fingers. He put it aside and reached for the com. He had to risk it. Huido would tell him what he wouldn't anyone else.

Pointless, maybe, but he wasn't going anywhere. Not until Sira came home.

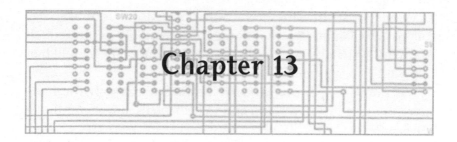

Chapter 13

HOME.

I stood in the main corridor of the *Silver Fox,* wondering why my feet refused to move.

Jacqui, who'd 'ported herself and her bags, was looking everywhere at once. *This is your ship, Speaker?*

Before I could correct her or draw another breath, Morgan appeared in the control room door.

He looked so alive. Hair mussed, his face bright and glad, even a warm glow to the tan of his checks. The once-blue spacer coveralls he wore were his favorite shipboard: faded to gray, with patches at elbow and knee. I'd given up trying to replace them. The collar stood open at the neck; the sleeves were rolled past his strong wrists. A stylo and wrench jutted from his pocket. My captain. My love. I was home.

And didn't dare touch him.

If I did, I thought desperately, if I let myself hold and be held, if I selfishly took any comfort now—

I'd lose control. I'd be useless to those who needed me.

"Captain," I said, putting that distance between us. Pleading for it.

Morgan stopped, out of reach, and nodded. "Chit."

His understanding surged through me like a stim shot. I

nodded at Jacqui. "Captain Morgan, I'd like you to meet Jacqui di Mendolar. Our new passenger." Any other time, I'd have asked him first; he'd understand that, too.

Master trader that he was, Morgan bowed his head as gracefully as any Clan, his hands miming the welcoming gesture suited to equals. "Whatever we can do, Jacqui di Mendolar," he told her, "we will."

Did the young Chooser realize he meant not only the hammock in the galley storeroom and shared meals, but the saving of the Clan?

"You're Human."

Without typical Clan disdain, which would have seen her no longer a passenger and lucky not to be spaced, but I felt *anxiety* leak through her shields. Had she not encountered one up close before?

It was, given her family and my father, entirely possible.

Morgan half smiled. "That I am."

Jacqui gave me, then him, that quizzical sidelong look. "Yet Chosen."

His smile widened. "That, too." He offered his left hand, palm up, well aware the right was fraught with meaning.

Between Clan, touch was an invitation: to mingle surface thoughts; to be sure of one another. It took courage to accept one from a greater Power.

While Morgan's shields, natural and trained, were a match for any of my kind, I wasn't happy to see him risk himself. Not today.

Courage she had, laying her left hand atop his alien one without hesitation.

An instant later, Jacqui let out a small gasp, her eyes wide and fixed on Morgan's, then her lips curved in the beginnings of a smile.

"The bags?" I said rather grumpily, picking one up.

Their hands parted, Jacqui coming to help; she took appreciably greater care with the second bag.

"Anything that needs special stowage, chit?" This said in his captain voice, Morgan ever-vigilant when it came to the safety of the ship.

Or its living cargo. Such hazards not having occurred to me while gathering what the assistant curator refused to leave behind, I looked to Jacqui. "Is there anything dangerous in here?"

"Knowledge can be," she said, more at ease. "But in terms of transport, no. Nothing reactive or biologic. These are," with a forlorn look at the bags, "were, simple belongings."

And her treasures. "There's room where you'll be sleeping," I ventured, giving Morgan a hopeful look.

He didn't quite frown. "See they're secured."

I nodded, relieved by so small a return to normalcy. "Come," I told Jacqui. "I'll make sure you're comfortable."

"Join me when you're done, Sira." Morgan turned toward the control room.

"Wait, please," Jacqui asked.

He paused and glanced back, an eyebrow raised.

"Are there more Humans here? Others like—" She faltered, looking at me as if expecting disapproval.

I knew where her thoughts had started to turn, having been a Chooser myself, longing for completion. Morgan's Power in the M'hir was a warm heady presence. "No. It's a small ship," I explained gently. "There's just us." Beneath I sent, *there is no other like Morgan.*

She kept any *disappointment* to herself.

"If that's all, then?" Morgan left us, but words formed in my mind. *Come as soon as you can.*

Piercing blue eyes searched my face when I stepped into the control room. I didn't attempt to smile. My Human would have seen through it even without our bond.

"How's our passenger?"

"Alive. Safe." I closed the door behind me. I'd gone to our cabin first, to change back into Sira Morgan. I'd stuffed my Council robe deep in a drawer only to pull it out again to retrieve the crystal with its scrap, for no particular reason other than it didn't belong there. It sat in a new pocket, where my fingers found it.

"I've asked Jacqui to begin the list." Of those she could *reach*. "Of survivors." It wouldn't be a long one.

Sira. What my Chosen shared with me was his strength and resolve, nothing of pity. Nothing of his own fury and outrage.

Morgan was perched on the copilot's couch, one knee drawn to his chest. I sat beside him, the position familiar except for the space I kept between us. My hair, having no willpower worth mentioning, slipped up his arm and broad shoulder to caress his cheek, curling around his neck.

As if I wouldn't notice. "I've heard from Rael." I kept my voice steady. "Pella—" our youngest sister "—isn't . . . She isn't," as if that made sense. As if the absence of family could be a stated fact and not a gaping hole.

I didn't have to look at him to feel his hard swallow, the effort made not to speak and interrupt what I would say.

What need did we have for words? I took hold of Morgan's boot, giving it a little shake.

Then closed my eyes, opening my mind to his, sharing it all.

So when the ghost came, it found us both.

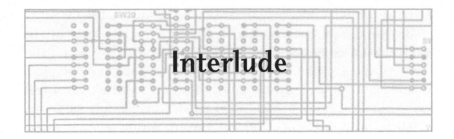

Interlude

NUDITY WASN'T UNCOMMON on Deneb, skin being considered the finest canvas, but was hardly normal attire for business.

At the office of *Michi and Booth*, the assistant didn't so much as blink when Rael and Janac materialized in front of her—the former naked and the latter looking as though he'd been through a meat grinder—merely coming around her desk with a professional smile. "Fem di Sarc. Hom," to Janac. "I'll let Fem Michi know you're here. May I get you anything while you wait?"

"Some clothes, please," Rael said promptly, her teeth still chattering. "And shoes. You have my preferences."

A nod. "At once. And for you, Hom?" Her eyes surveyed him.

Janac grimaced. "My shoes are fine. Anything conservative."

"Anything from *Flock*," Rael put in.

"An excellent choice. Please, wait here." She disappeared behind an ornate screen.

I don't like this.

The windows look out, not in, Rael reassured him. *We can't go anywhere like this, without funds.*

We won't be the only ones tapping resources. Our enemies will expect it. With a chilling certainty. *The sooner we're gone from here, the better.*

The assistant returned, followed by a pair of Tulis, one carrying robes, the other pushing a cart of covered serving plates, complete with steaming carafes and delicate cups.

"Fem Michi apologizes," the assistant told them. "There will be a very short delay. Please make yourselves comfortable."

"Very well," Rael said, having no choice. They let themselves be herded, courteously, into the waiting lounge.

When the assistant left, Rael helped Janac into his robe, then donned hers, hugging it close. The lounge, tastefully furnished complete with choice of easi-rest or padded bench, felt like a trap.

They chose the bench without a word, sitting so their shoulders touched.

Tell me about the baby shower.

She stared at Janac. *What?*

His mouth quirked. *It wasn't that long ago.*

It had been forever, Rael thought, feeling empty. Nonetheless, she *shared* her memories of what the Human had called a "family occasion" with her Chosen. Done, she leaned her head on his shoulder. *I'll need another gift for Ruti and Barac's daughter.* Easier to think of that, than of the future their daughter faced. If she had one. Rael rested a hand on her waist. New life hadn't quickened in her yet, that she could tell.

Good.

Balloons. I remember those. Here. Memories flooded her mind: a house beside an ocean, toes in warm sand, hitting balloons—larger and stronger—over a net. Laughter. *We had our occasions.* A bonfire on the beach. A voice. Music.

So much they didn't know about one another. *You sing.*

I don't anymore. Shields tightened, ending the moment of intimacy. *Does this Human usually make you wait?*

No. The firm handled Rael's affairs with the prompt dedication due a major client, whether investments or arranging the seamless care of her properties on Deneb. *I trust her discretion.*

'Trust'? Janac turned to face her, incredulous. *That's it?*

Rael flushed. *Michi's an excellent employee. I've never had to find one to* influence.

Which wasn't the whole truth. Before Jason Morgan, Rael had considered Human telepaths an abomination, the mere idea of entering such a mind repugnant. She could have invited a Clan Scout to do the work for her, but afterward, to deal with such a—a thing? She'd chosen to hire, as Humans did.

What if she'd been wrong? *Maybe we should go.*

Before Janac could respond, an older woman entered the room and closed the door behind her. Her hair was glossy black, sculpted to frame her face, and black had been tattooed on her heavy eyelids, elongating her oval eyes. Shell-like iridescence dusted the pale gold of cheekbones and brow, and more tattoos, done as a delicate amber lacework, crusted the skin of her neck and what showed of her arms and hands. A long straight dress of understated elegance completed the image of competence and wealth.

The Denebian bowed. "Fem di Sarc, Hom, my sincerest apologies. My assistant assures me your requests are being seen to as we speak." She took a seat facing them, settling a screen on her lap. "What may I do for you?"

Rael fought a shiver that had nothing to do with the cold. They'd discussed what to say, what not to say, what might work, what might not. Facing help at last, she abandoned it all. "Sell my properties, Janina. Everything. Put the credits in a fluid account, one I can reach wherever I go in the Trade Pact."

Careful. Don't sound desperate.

She made herself sit back, crossing her legs. "I appreciate it may take some time."

Michi nodded. "To obtain the best prices, certainly. If I may ask, does this have anything to do with the fire?"

" 'Fire'?" Rael echoed numbly. "What fire?"

They must have come after you—your home—too, Janac suggested grimly.

Her shoes. Dresses. Jewelry. Foolish to mourn things, but she couldn't help it. They'd been her outer self, her safety—

"My mistake." Michi consulted her screen briefly and looked up. "I could start by liquidating your prime investments. The funds would be available immediately, but I must warn you there will be some loss on the—"

"Yes. Please, do that."

The Human stood and brought over the screen. "I'll need an additional authorization, if you would, Fem. The sums involved are substantial."

This is too easy.

What do you mean?

You stand to lose more than half your worth this way, wealth that goes through this firm. She should be protesting.

Be glad she's not. Rael breathed on the device, then pressed her hand, palm down, where Michi indicated.

"That should do it." The Human smiled pleasantly, putting the screen on a sidetable. "Allow me to pour you a drink while we wait for your clothes."

"Something hot," Rael replied. "Sombay. With cream."

"The same for me," her Chosen said. "With honey."

When handed her cup, Rael quickly wrapped her fingers around its warmth.

"Wait, please." Michi knelt by the cart, opened a door, and brought out a bottle of Brillian brandy. "I'd like to offer a toast, in honor of our long association, Fem di Sarc."

Humans, Janac sent, with *impatience.* He held out his cup nonetheless. "By all means."

So Rael did the same.

Michi added a generous amount to each, then poured herself a small glass. She lifted it, light catching the rich brown liquid. "Thank you for letting us be of service. It's been a privilege."

They drank together.

Warm, the liquid. Soothing, the brandy's burn when it hit the back of her throat and traced a path downward.

Cold followed.

Rael's cup dropped, her fingers without strength. "I trusted—" Her heart seized as if gripped by ice, she couldn't breathe—

Out of the corner of her eye, she saw Janac reel and topple sideways. She couldn't move to stop him—tried to *reach* him.

Tried to 'port.

It was like slamming into a wall.

"Thank you for the funds, Fem di Sarc," Janina Michi said, tossing back the rest of her drink. "And yourselves."

Through their link, Rael sensed Janac's heart *stutter*. Weakened by his injuries, she despaired. Only partly healed.

His heart *stopped*.

"Hells! You—" Michi called out in gibberish. A Tuli came. Rael watched the alien lift her Chosen's head by the hair. Let it drop with a thud to the floor. Shrug its thick shoulders.

"Ah, well. I've you, Rael. They'll be—"

Sounds became nothing. Dark triumph surged through Rael di Sarc as her Chosen *called* her, *pulled* her mind after his. Into the M'hir. This was right.

This was how it should be. To die together, in that darkness.

A hiss. Colder, impossibly colder. Rael fought to *hold* their link. Tried to *follow*. But something interfered. Something *VILE*—

Their link *snapped*.

Leaving her empty. So terribly empty.

And here.

Her eyes couldn't blink. Couldn't. Rael stared her rage at Michi and understood, then. *You can't have me.*

As ice stole her sight, her heart slowing, Rael di Sarc *threw* herself into the M'hir, abandoning her doomed flesh.

Dissolving, as everything *ended.*

Alone.

Adrift.

A ghost.

Yet with *will* of a sort. What remained, reformed.

Coalesced.

SIRA! . . .

Sira . . .

s.i.r.a . . .

DON'T TRUST . . .

don't trust . . .

d.o.n.'.t . . .

There was nothing more.

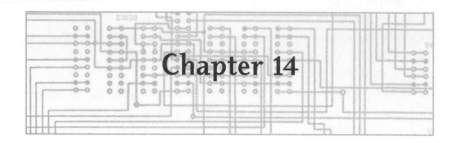

Chapter 14

S IRA!
    I grabbed for Morgan, feeling him take hold of me, both of us fighting to stay where we were, to resist that appalling summons.

. . . Sira . . .

It wasn't from a living mind. Not anymore.

. . . . . s.i.r.a. . . .

Already fading, *dissolving.* Soon there'd be nothing left. Of what?

Of who.

"Jason. I have to know."

Morgan tightened his hold. "I'll be here."

With him as my anchor, I opened myself to the M'hir and *listened . . .*

SIRA! . . . Sira. . . .s.i.r.a. . . .

Here, there was no mistaking the voice.

Rael.

Here, there was only the truth.

Ghosts, we called them. The brief flicker left within the M'hir by those lost in it. That she'd thought of me as she died, as her Chosen died, as . . .

DON'T TRUST THEM!

I fled the M'hir as the Watchers howled her name and her Chosen's, desperate for the gold and constant presence of my own, and buried my face in Morgan's chest.

Then warned my kind.

Muscle knotted along his jaw, Morgan's eyes were bleak. "Terk sent someone to the office. The place was stripped, but they'd left a body. I'm sorry."

I glanced at the image on the viewer and away again, uninterested in the flesh that had been my sister's Chosen. If Janac was gone, Rael was, too. That she'd managed a warning as she'd *dissolved* horrified me as much as its meaning. "Now we know," I said heavily.

Rael's wealth had been on Deneb, handled by one firm, run by Humans. Of course they'd gone there.

To die there.

I'd passed along her warning. *Stay away from existing contacts. Avoid anyone who knows you.* Been unsurprised to *hear* the Watchers echo what mattered in their hollow, unnerving way. *DON'T TRUST.*

The Clan, already on the run, were being hunted. Not only by Assemblers.

And not only Clan were targets. Morgan had told me about the *Claws & Jaws.*

"You're sure Huido's all right?" I asked, hunting what comfort remained. "That no one else died?" Tayno, Hom M'Tisri. Huido's wives. There'd been casualties among staff and customers, but fewer than might have been. The Assemblers had cared only to reach the Clan, attacking doors and walls built to withstand a love-struck Carasian. Some had gone mad with frustration before being killed.

Hopefully killed. The pieces had been collected in bins by Port Authority, then put in custody in case the species had regenerative abilities they hadn't declared on their forms.

Morgan hesitated.

"What?" I didn't need protecting.

"Huido can't find Barac and Ruti. My guess? They're hiding out on Plexis. It's a big station, Sira."

Full of beings I'd warned them not to trust. "Family," I said wryly.

His face lightened. "You can find them?"

I'd do better than that.

Once more I prepared a heart-search, this time of a mind I knew very well. My cousin had forgiven me for violently scanning him; since Ruti and their Joining, he'd might even have forgotten.

I'd do neither. I poured Power into my quest.

Sira?

There. A living voice, barely discernible amidst the roiling M'hir.

Heart-kin. I poured Power into our link to hold it, Barac's not equal to the task.

We felt your warnings. What's happening? Why is it happening? The M'hir was already unsettled, the Watchers on edge. His desperate questions drew them closer.

Instead of answering, I followed the bright path linking him to another, gathered all of my strength, and *PULLED* . . .

. . . Ruti gasped. Barac swore. Both stared at me in amazement. They were filthy, exhausted, and now—

Safe.

I closed my eyes and sagged. Arms slipped around me, plucked me from my seat with their own irresistible strength. "To bed, chit," Morgan said, his voice oddly hoarse.

I'd have protested—we'd no time for rest—but a feather's touch on my forehead sent me tumbling into a deep sleep.

To dream of names.

And a voice in the dark . . .

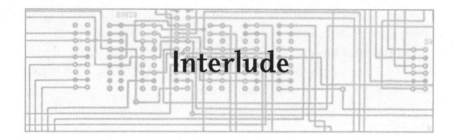

Interlude

THE OUTER ROOM of the Human Trade Pact Board Member was deceptively plain. Constable Russell Terk eyed the ceiling fixtures, furniture, and window coverings, making his own assessment.

Tech and plenty of it. Sneeze and your snot would be analyzed before it hit the carpet.

Ordinarily, he'd have approved. Protecting bureaucrats was best left to servos and gadgets, especially if those gadgets recorded what they shouldn't. He'd love to get his hands on records from this place—

A disembodied voice: "The Board Member will see you now."

Of course he would, given what he carried. Very few had the clearance; fewer now, with Bowman gone and her people under scrutiny. Terk rose, straightening his supposedly tailored-to-fit uniform. His featherheaded partner had assured him this one struck the right balance between seasoned and innocuous public servant.

If left up to him, Terk would have happily picked "don't mess with me" battle armor, but tact had never been his strong suit.

He'd need some, if the suspicion niggling at him since talking to Morgan was remotely on target.

Hells, what had Bowman set in motion?

One of three doors swung open on the far wall and Terk accepted the invitation, stepping into an office no fancier than a middling banker's, void of personality.

The suspicion went from niggle to itch. Yes, people did keep their private and public lives separate. He was one of them.

People who weren't politicians. They knew to at least plop a baby on their office vis-screen, even if it wasn't theirs. This office had been scoured of any connection.

The man seated behind the emptied desk believed himself alone.

"Constable. Please, sit."

Pleasant voice. Terk didn't have that version and didn't care. "Board Member." He handed Cartnell a plas sheet, standing at attention.

The man glanced over it, then looked up. "This Assembler business. You think you know what they're up to." He frowned. "Take a seat, please."

He could stand at attention for days. Had before now. "Sir. They're murdering the Clan. Sir." Bowman having advised him long ago to salute twice, given how hard it was to believe the sincerity of the first one.

"So your mysterious informant claims." Cartnell's eyes narrowed. "Sit, Constable. You're making me crane my neck."

Terk perched on the seat's edge, his back straight. "A reliable source, sir. I followed up on several reports."

"Did you." Neutral tone. Possibly a hint of impatience.

The itch grew. "Yes, sir." Terk let his satisfaction show. "The majority of the confirmed dead were previously identified as Clan. There's no doubt they were the intended targets."

"I know you." Cartnell leaned back in his chair. "You were at the signing. With Bowman."

Recognition—or something else? "Yes, sir." The constable nodded. "As were you, sir."

"A momentous day, to be sure." The politician came forward, flattening his hand over the plas sheet. "Good work, Constable Terk. I'll look into this. Thank you."

Dismissed, Terk stood but didn't leave. "Your pardon, sir. Until this is resolved, I'd like to reassign my people to protect the remaining Clan. With your permission." And didn't he already know the answer to that?

Cartnell frowned and shook his head. "Under ordinary circumstances, I'd agree, but Bowman must be found first. Too much is at stake. We can't risk destabilizing the Trade Pact. She remains your top priority." The frown was replaced by a sympathetic look. "If you're uncomfortable chasing down your former chief, I can make arrangements for your replacement."

"I'm uncomfortable seeing children murdered, sir. Are you?"

He'd hoped for a telling flinch or protest. Instead, Cartnell's lips twisted in a sneer and he shoved the plas sheet from his desk to land at Terk's boot tip. "Not if they're parasites. Not if they're guilty!"

"Is this a confession, Board Member Cartnell?" He'd have it on record twice over, both on his implant and uniform device.

"Constable Terk, really. This is my office. What's said here, stays here. You Enforcers made sure of that." All at once, Cartnell looked weary. "You'll find your weapons are useless too, not that you've need of them. Sit."

"Make me," Terk growled, curling his fists. Without weapons, was he?

"You are a tiresome person, aren't you. Oh, well." Opening a drawer, Cartnell pulled out a disk. He stretched to put it in Terk's reach. "You're what I've got. Here. Let's finish it."

He had the villain. Even without a recording for verification, his word would start suspicion flowing where it should.

It didn't feel like victory. Terk scowled at the disk. "What's that?"

"Surely you don't believe I did all this alone, Constable." A grim smile. "That's the evidence you'll need to convict the leaders of the Deneb Blues and Grays of collusion to commit speciescide."

"Real evidence? Or fabricated, like you did to the chief."

An eyebrow lifted. "This is real, I assure you. I'd act quickly. Once the Clan were dealt with, the syndicates planned to move against their puppets, those poor innocents." Cartnell rubbed a hand over his face. "Fry and Gayle will give up their accomplices. By then my work will be done. Humanity will be safe." He looked at Terk. "I suppose you want to know why I—"

"I'll go with crazy." Terk snatched the disk, his balance restored. A strike against the syndicates was long overdue and welcome. "You're finished, Cartnell."

A gentle smile. "I have been for some time, Constable." Cartnell seemed, if anything, relieved. "Bowman will pay, one way or another, for aiding those who preyed on us. As for my role? I suggest you consider the ramifications before doing anything rash."

Now the squirming. Predictable. Terk shrugged. "I don't do 'ramifications.' My job's to put you in a cell."

"An executive member eliminating a treaty species—do you think Humans will be allowed to stay in the Trade Pact if you reveal the truth?"

"Not my problem, Board Member." Putting away the disk, Terk took a set of restraints from his belt and rattled them at Cartnell. "Consider the ramifications of resisting arrest."

Cartnell rose to his feet, his face pale. "I've given you those with bloody hands and motive. That's enough! You've sworn to uphold the Trade Pact, not destroy it."

"Come as you are, or come in cuffs."

"The Clan deserve to die, all of them!"

Cuffs it was.

"I may not like the Clan much," Terk said as he secured his prisoner, "but an easy arrest is fine by me."

"You can't save them." Low and vile and triumphant. "The word's spread, about what they are, what they can do, have done. Some might be captured, used. The rest will run till they die."

"Save it for someone who cares," the constable rumbled, his big hand closing on Cartnell's shoulder to move the man to the door.

Fearing he'd heard nothing but the truth.

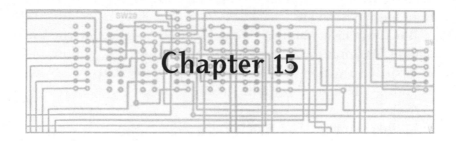

Chapter 15

"WE CAN'T STOP NOW. We can't—"

Gently, I pried the list from Jacqui di Mendolar's trembling fingers. "We are." Through the fleeting contact with her skin, I sent a pulse of *strength*. Little enough, but it eased some of the exhaustion on her face.

I'd slept, as I had many times before, on the copilot's couch in the control room. Morgan had sent Barac and Ruti to our cabin to use the fresher, then our bed. If he'd rested or not, I couldn't tell.

Jacqui hadn't. I'd found the Chooser at the galley table, stylo in hand, so focused she'd barely acknowledged my arrival, doing what had to be done. She'd let me take over, but refused to leave, writing down the names I gave her.

"It's been over an hour since the last new contact," I reminded her. Whomever wanted to be found, had been.

The list was handwritten, each letter flawless, each line numbered with a scholar's care. I looked to its end, finding the last name, the final number.

"Two hundred and seventy."

A number better than I'd feared. Far worse than I'd hoped.

Morgan, leaning against the kitchen's counter, spoke first, his eyes hooded. "How many are in immediate danger?"

Those who'd escaped were scattered, their shields as tight as their individual Talent permitted. Extending myself, I *saw* them as sparks and flickers within the M'hir's seething dark, some brighter than others, but nothing of identity or location. Those were hidden from me.

But I wasn't what hunted. "I can't tell. They've been warned, at least. They know to stay away from any—associates." A word encompassing any non-Clan help they might have had. "We could be more. There are those able to hide from me."

"Speaker, won't the Watchers know?"

I blinked at her. "The Watchers?"

"You can talk to them. Isn't that what the Speaker does?" Jacqui looked at Morgan as if summoning support. "Don't the Watchers know who's still alive?"

She was counted in that total, as were Barac, Ruti, and her unborn.

Not Rael or her Chosen, Janac.

Not . . . so very many.

"The Watchers pay attention to death," I explained, memory filling with the maddening echo of their ugly howls, my voice harsh even to myself. "Oh they told me who died. Every name. All at once. Every name since."

Sira. Like a hand, holding mine.

"I don't talk to the Watchers," I finished with a shudder, "I try to survive them." Giving myself an inner shake, I looked at the anxious Chooser sitting across from me and gestured apology. "None of which is your fault or knowing, Jacqui. You should get some sleep." I put my hand on the list. "Thank you for this."

"There is nothing to forgive," she replied with a wan smile, then yawned. "We all could use rest. You mustn't wear yourself out, Sira."

"I'll see to it," Morgan promised. I gave him a wary look, not the least interested in being put to sleep again.

Jacqui wouldn't need help. She had to steady herself after standing, and wove more than walked the handful of steps to the galley's storeroom, now her haven. She closed the door behind her.

Morgan lowered himself into the seat Jacqui'd left, turning the list around with one finger. The first thing he'd done when I'd arrived was drop the *Fox* into normal space. Drifting between systems was akin to a burrowing animal ducking into a hole, but we couldn't linger. The nearest sun was a red giant, spewing forth radiation already eating away the ship's outer protections.

Two hundred and seventy. Entire families from my great-grandmother's time lost, yet weren't, I supposed numbly. We'd mingled since. Crossed and recrossed until names might vanish.

But not the shape of an ear or—

"Two hundred and seventy," he said, echoing my thought. He gazed at me. Waited.

For me to snap out of it, because that wasn't a number, it was people, running out of time. My first deep breath had a ragged edge. My second was steadier. "They need help. Our help. But how?"

"The Enforcers who were chasing Bowman are now after the syndicates and stretched to the limit." His lips twisted and I felt the *anger* behind his shields. "It's not coincidence."

Terk had given us a name. I remembered Board Member Cartnell only vaguely and knew of no reason for his hate for us or Bowman.

"We're on our own, then." I reclaimed the list. No coincidence there either. Those who'd trusted the accord I'd made with the Trade Pact—with Cartnell—had stayed in their homes and died. Those who'd feared coming so close to Humans had quietly abandoned theirs and survived.

Clan like my mother. Her name was here, Mirim sud Teerac. She'd been granted the di Sarc upon Joining with Jarad. She'd refused it, along with anything to do with him beyond their scheduled couplings. She'd renounced the M'hir and our ways as well. What did she think of all this, I wondered suddenly. Would she feel we'd deserved it? That what we'd done to Humans had been our crime and this our just punishment?

Was it?

"Rael said there'd be a price to pay for joining the Trade Pact."

Sira. His hand covered mine. *Don't fly that course.* Aloud, "Bowman will be back. She's too slippery to be caught and too stubborn to stay away."

I looked at his dear Human face and did my best to smile. "You're right."

While between us, shared without words, a terrible understanding.

That even with Bowman back and all the help of the Trade Pact—even with the Assemblers stopped and those behind the attacks brought to justice—nothing would ever be the same.

Barac held his hand out for the list. I passed it to him, watching as the two huddled together, reading it in silence.

"There are none from Acranam," I said, unable to bear the wait. "I'm sorry."

"I know." Ruti sat back. She accepted a hot drink from Morgan with a grateful look, then sighed into it. "I didn't—I wasn't—" She composed herself. "I felt a great loss. I thought at first it was Quessa—our Birth Watcher—but it was more. My family. My friends. Everyone I'd known. They were part of me, unnoticed, until they weren't." Her round chin shook, but she steadied herself, taking a sip. "If we'd been there, we'd be dead, too."

She'll be all right, Morgan sent. "I let Huido know you're safe," he said aloud to the pair.

Who exchanged looks and more, from Ruti's stricken face. "What do you mean, they might be involved?" she exclaimed. "What haven't you told me?"

"Ruti—you were—" Barac gave a helpless shrug.

She half-rose to her feet. "Tell Morgan. If you're going to accuse Huido of something so horrible, his brother should know."

Morgan went very still. "Why did you leave the restaurant? Huido said you were safe with his wives."

"Here." Barac, white lines by nose and mouth, thrust his hand at Morgan. "Take it."

My Human's hand rose, clasping firmly. The two remained like that for an instant and it was all I could do to keep my *distance*.

Their hands pulled apart. The Clansman put his knuckle down

on the table, head hanging. "They said it was inevitable. That the Clan shouldn't be here—don't belong." He looked up, black hair tumbled over anguished eyes. "That the Clan must go."

"You have to be wrong," Ruti said fiercely. "Sira?"

I turned to the one who knew Huido best.

Morgan's face had developed a thoughtful look. "Interesting."

Interesting?

He lifted a placating hand. "The wives have been studying grist. Meaning the Clan."

"You knew?" I blinked. "For how long?"

"Impossible to say. The wives gather in a pool of their choosing. Their debates on a given topic can last standard years. I do know Huido's are considered exceptionally bright."

I did my best to merge "exceptionally bright" with the dangerous, sullen creatures I'd been shown. Or had I been shown to them? There was a thought.

"The Carasians," Morgan continued, looking at Barac, "are honorable beings. I promise you they're as horrified by what's happened to the Clan as the rest of us. After finishing off the Assemblers, Huido and Tayno scoured Plexis for you. Because they're family. Because they were worried."

Barac's mouth worked. He gave a slow nod. "I wanted to think that."

"Believe it. What Huido's wives told you are what they consider facts." Blue eyes shifted to me. "Can we really say, as things are, they're wrong? The Clan can't stay where they are."

Ruti di Bowart put her arms around her Chosen, her hair flowing over Barac's shoulders. "Then we go," she decided firmly. "Someplace safe."

We gave Barac and Ruti our cabin; it wouldn't be the first time we'd camped in the control room. I pulled my knees up under the blanket, unwilling to close my eyes. Morgan, no more eager to rest than I was, stood by the panels. He'd been studying a series of displays since we'd retreated here.

"We could warm the hold," I said suddenly. "Squeeze in another fifty."

"The math, chit."

I'd been in space long enough to know better, that meant. I fell silent, abashed. The *Silver Fox* had been built for a crew of five to six. Refitting as a freighter hadn't added air to her systems or capacity to her scrubbers.

To distract myself, I pulled out the crystal, trying to find an opening with my fingernail.

A flash of blue eyes. "What's that?"

"This?" I lifted the crystal so it caught flecks of light from the console. "A relic of my great-grandmother. We're taught she brought us here, to Trade Pact space. Jarad treasured it."

Morgan came over and I passed the thing to him. "From the Clan Homeworld." He looked at me, lifting a brow. "A planet none of you know how to find."

I nodded. A waste of a market, to a trader; to my beleaguered, now-homeless people, an irony too painful to contemplate. I took back the crystal, staring at the scrap of fabric within. "My ancestors 'ported here. That's real enough." I'd glimpsed the scar etched into the M'hir by the passage of so many at once. "The rest—why? From where? I don't believe we were meant to know." I put the crystal back in my pocket. "Or go back.

"Besides," I said more lightly, "this is home." I rubbed my thumb over a mended patch on the armrest, refusing to look at him. I had so much, when the rest had—

Breath warmed my cheek, followed by a swift, brief kiss. "A home that needs a shipcity and supplies, ideally soon. I'll get back to it." He stepped away before my hair could entangle him.

"Jason. There's no place safe, is there."

"No. Not yet," he qualified gently. "The syndicates have eyes on every Human world and likely beyond. The Assemblers? No telling how far they intend to take this."

"Or if they can be stopped."

"Oh, it'll happen. It's the beforehand we need to watch. Try to sleep, Witchling."

Dimming the lights, my Human went back to work. I watched

his silhouette pass back and forth, my mind busy with possibilities. Non-Human worlds—where we'd be all too obvious. Starships— they needed crews, crews that could be infiltrated. The Drapsk—

Inflict hundreds of "Mystic Ones" on the dear little aliens? Their social structure would fracture, maybe even collapse. I shuddered. Our list of allies was woefully short.

One bright spot lay on the horizon. When Jacqui di Mendolar woke from her well-deserved rest, Ruti and Barac would have a Birth Watcher again.

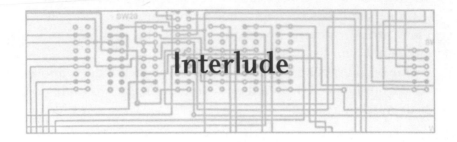

Interlude

"PASSAGE?"

"That's your business, isn't it?" Ambridge Gayle had lost her tattoos, or disguised them. She'd thickened her torso and changed her voice, adding the nasal twang more often heard on the streets of Ettler's Planet than Deneb. Doubtless the spacer coveralls she wore came with an array of hidden weaponry.

Manouya regarded her calmly, his thick ivory nails deftly peeling a fresh nicnic. "Where do you think you can go?"

"Auord. I've people there."

"With that much bounty on your head?" The Brill smacked his lips in appreciation, enjoying how the sound echoed. Stacks of white shipping crates made tunnels leading in every direction. At this hour, the servos were parked and staff gone home. He valued having time to himself.

And it could be a productive time indeed.

"Damn Cartnell. I've assets," Gayle snapped. "Name your price and get me to Auord. You can do it, can't you?"

The ex-Board Member wouldn't betray him, Manouya thought comfortably, not while so much of his plan remained in motion. After that, well, every prisoner was moved somewhere.

As for Gayle? "Move you without anyone the wiser? Of course." He'd dealt with Fry already, it being highly disagreeable to contemplate his name and face squealed to the Enforcers. Threems had such useful appetites. Gayle, however. She had a different reputation. A useful one. Popping fruit into his mouth, Manouya swallowed it whole, then licked his fingers. "My price is not negotiable."

"Name it."

So he did.

Later that day, a crate was loaded onto a ship bound for Stonerim III.

Shortly after, passengers boarded.

One of them wore a hat.

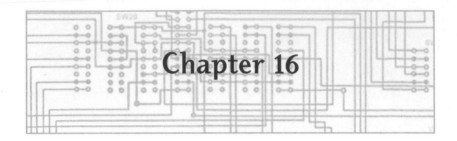

Chapter 16

REGARDLESS OF WHO'D SLEPT OR WHERE, Morgan declared the next meal to be breakfast, that being possible when time was set by chronos and had nothing to do with a sun. Ruti and Barac arrived as he began setting out plates, and were surprised to find another Clanswoman at the table.

"You two look like spacers," my Human complimented.

Ruti looked down at her overalls, plucking at the excess bunched over her belt. "It's comfortable."

"They never fit," I assured her. "Jacqui di Mendolar, my cousin Barac di Bowart and his Chosen, Ruti di Bowart. Sit," I added when all three prepared to bow and gesture in a proper Clan greeting. "Your food's ready. Nothing's formal on the *Fox*."

Nothing, chit?

There was that. I coughed. "Except for Captain Morgan's orders. You must obey them without question. For your safety and the ship's."

"Over yours, Speaker?" Jacqui said nervously. "Is yours not the greater Power? Meaning no offense, Captain."

Barac chuckled and Ruti dimpled. If I'd thought to let Morgan answer, one glance told me he was already enjoying this too much and I'd regret it. "When it comes to the *Silver Fox*," I said truthfully, "he's in charge."

"My first order," my Chosen said with a warm smile, "is enjoy your breakfast."

The *Fox*'s galley being compact at the best of times, I'd had no problem sitting Ruti beside Jacqui. Getting them to be comfortable that way?

I had my work cut out for me. While we ate, I studied the uneasy pair.

The Chooser's hair was thin and limp, her face and body still immature, in all ways opposite to Ruti's, but it wasn't that, I realized. In years, Jacqui could be Ruti's mother; in experience, the younger Chosen was by far the elder; and that didn't begin to address the edgy feelings between an Acranam Clan and one from Camos. One a disciple, no less, of my father.

They didn't need to be friends, I assured myself. Jacqui wasn't Quessa, but she had the Talent, respectable Power.

And was the only Birth Watcher we had.

Ruti quickly gave up, turning her attention to Morgan—or more exactly, to his painting. From her eager questions about the cabin and how to work on walls and furniture, I'd a feeling wherever she and Barac made their home, it would be similarly coated. As for the painting he'd given her, the "Night's Fire?" Barac produced the voucher. They'd left it in a room guaranteed with it. When next on Plexis—

Conversation faltered until Morgan began asking about the plant itself.

As for Jacqui, Barac did his charming best, but as the meal dragged on, the Chooser fell silent, eyes glued to her plate. I couldn't fault her shields; she might not have even been there.

I wanted to clear the table, it being one of my favorite tasks to throw dishes at the wall recycler, but Jacqui's tense silence spread to the rest. Worry creased Morgan's forehead. *She seemed better before. Is it all sinking in?*

He thought she suffered from what had happened, but it wasn't the past. I was certain of it. "Jacqui—"

Low and pained. "I can't be her Birth Watcher."

"You're a—" Barac's face lit until he saw Ruti's.

Hair lashed. Eyes glared. And if anyone in this room doubted the Power of Ruti di Bowart, they couldn't now, with it *storming* against shields. "She doesn't want to touch our daughter. Because I'm from Acranam. Because I'm not from one of the important families!"

"No." Jacqui's head rose, her expression full of dignity and regret. "Because I'm Sira's."

Morgan's cup hit the floor. *You're having a baby?*

My mouth having fallen open, I closed it with a snap of teeth. *You are mistaken, Jacqui di Mendolar.*

And if there was *rage* in the sending, I had that right. There was history, bloody and dreadful and mine, behind it. "You're wrong."

She shuddered but held herself straight, not dropping her gaze. *This is* my *Talent, Speaker.* Aloud, "I'm a Birth Watcher. There is no mistake."

Barac warned Ruti with a touch; the rising joy in her face faded to confusion.

I didn't look at Morgan. Couldn't.

I'll show you.

Neither of us moved, but it was as if her hand took mine and drew it low, pressing the palm over my flesh. A hand that became a conduit through the M'hir.

Touching . . . *life.*

"What is it?" My lips felt numb.

I'd been ripped apart, stuffed with alien seed, re-opened, and emptied. The damage done—I'd been told it was repaired, but I'd hoped to be barren. There mustn't be another like me, another with my deadly Power.

"What do you mean?" Puzzlement. Confusion.

Oh, the things this innocent young Chooser didn't know—in a perfect universe, would never have to know. "What kind is it?" I said grimly. "The species."

She swallowed, then gave a nod. "Clan. M'hiray. There can be no doubt, Speaker."

As I sagged with relief, that first dread passing, Morgan came close and I slipped my fingers through his, gripping hard. The emotions flowing between us were a confused blur. *Horror* was one. *Shock* another.

A whisper of barely felt, impossible-to-resist, *hope.*

So even as we pulled apart, dropping barriers to calm the storm, it was he who spoke first. "How is this possible?" Morgan challenged. "I'm Human. A different species. Biology doesn't go away."

"I don't care what you are," Jacqui replied with true Clan arrogance. "I'm a Birth Watcher. I cannot be wrong. There is a baby." She came around the table, offering us each a hand. "I can prove it. She'll have a bond to you both."

She. And didn't that one word make it real?

I turned my head, meeting my love's remarkable eyes. They'd darkened, holding a message as clear as if sent mind-to-mind. A Clan might not read the caution there, the concern.

My kind were often blind.

The slightest nod. Courage, that was.

We clasped hands with Jacqui, who closed her eyes to concentrate.

It began as the same sensation, made vivid by the physical touch, this time shared with one more, Morgan. *LIFE.*

This exploration went deeper and, suddenly, there it was. A bond through the M'hir, Power-to-Power, like mine to Morgan, yet unlike, for this Joined me to something calm, wordless . . .

. . . and *empty.*

"NO!"

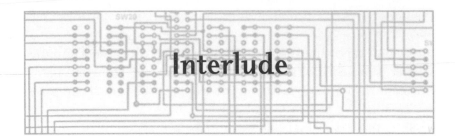

Interlude

SIRA'S DENIAL ECHOING through his mind as well as ears, Morgan didn't think. His Power surged, *tossing* the ashen-faced Birth Watcher away from them both. She slid over the table, taking the rest of breakfast with her, and missed the galley wall only because Barac was there first to catch her.

Ignoring the Clan, ignoring everything else, Morgan twisted to take Sira, gently, by the shoulders. "Are you all right?" He searched her face, dismayed when she stood passively in his hold, her eyes dazed, and he could *feel* only *pain*. Sira. He dared shake her, just once. "Sira."

A sharp intake of breath. A slow blink. Finally, she focused on him and he could breathe. "What did she do?" he demanded, though he knew it hadn't been Jacqui. "What's wrong?" Though he knew it had to be the astonishing new life within her. The baby. The word stuck in his throat, for there was nothing of joy here.

"It's a Perversion."

Sira's gaze hardened and went by him; Morgan turned, following its aim, his arm going around her as much for his support as hers. "Explain," she demanded.

Jacqui wrenched herself from Barac's hold, staring at Sira. "The Joining's to you alone." She seemed, all at once, more sorrowful than upset. "The baby is yours, alone."

"I thought—" Ruti hesitated, then went on, "—I thought Perversion was a myth. Something old Chosen would say to scare us."

"There hasn't been a case since the Stratification." The Birth Watcher hugged herself. "Perversion is a consequence of a Choice and Commencement without a proper Joining. I don't understand why it would happen now, to you, Speaker. I'm sorry. I can't help you. I don't know how."

Within his arm, Sira tensed. Morgan understood. Their Joining had been anything but "proper." A Chooser Joined with her Choice, their bond through the M'hir the trigger for physiological maturity, Commencement.

But Sira's body had matured first, in response to his Human power. Their Joining had been forged afterward; her will, their love, giving her the control to protect him from her greater Power until, at last, they'd found their way.

To this? When Sira didn't speak, he did. "What does it mean?"

"I don't know. But it's—it's not a good thing."

Morgan felt Sira stir. "How do we get rid of it?" she asked, calm only on the outside. "It" not "she." His heart hurt.

Jacqui's eyes widened. Ruti sank in her chair with a gasp, her hands over her unborn daughter.

"It's a simple question, Birth Watcher," Sira said. "Can it be done?"

The Clanswoman bit her lower lip. Finally, "Humans do that. We never have. I'm not sure we can. I don't know," this third time fiercely, as if to stop such disturbing questions. "The Speaker should ask her mother."

Sira made a sound like a choked laugh. "Pardon?"

"Mirim sud Teerac studies pre-Stratification Clan—"

"Because she wants us back there," Barac interjected. "Sira should go to Cenebar—" He shut his mouth, running a hand through his hair. Ruti leaned close. "I forgot," he said after a painful moment. "There's too many—"

Morgan's side chilled as Sira stepped away from him, shaking her head. "Even if Mirim had the knowledge," she said, an odd note to her voice. "I'm not sure she'd talk to me. My mother and I parted ways before the rest of you were born."

"At least you still have one," Ruti blurted, then buried her face against her Chosen. Jacqui closed her eyes, tears slipping down her cheeks.

Sira looked stricken. "I didn't mean—"

They were falling apart, Morgan realized, and knew what he had to do. "Do you know where she is?"

Her hair twitched unhappily, but she nodded. "Jarad does." Her eyes lost focus for an instant, and he sensed the *surge* of her Power.

Her gaze sharpened. *Here.* Something dark beneath it. *I should have known.*

"I'll set course," Morgan said briskly. A destination not his first choice—or fiftieth—but any decision was better, right now, than none.

Stonerim III. The southern hemisphere shipcity.

Norval.

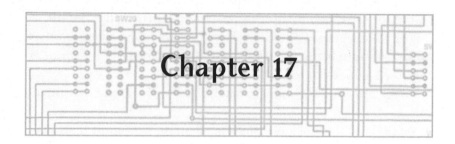

Chapter 17

WE WERE GOING SOMEWHERE. The low rumble within the *Silver Fox* as her translight engines came to life proved it, if nothing else. Going somewhere meant vital tasks, age and an unending sequence of second-third-fourth-hand parts having made those engines as cranky, as Morgan would say, as a starving Scat. I did my jobs and took on some of Morgan's, relieved to be busy while he pored through newsfeeds and reports: Huido's, possibly others, doing what we could not. As for the other Clan, Barac and Ruti had traveled in a starship before; Jacqui hadn't. The former had each other to pass the time.

Jacqui? Having admitted she didn't know how to help me, the honest Birth Watcher had asked to serve Ruti and her baby, to the relief of all.

Not that I couldn't feel her *interest* every time we passed one another in the confines of the ship.

Not that I couldn't feel the *life* within me, every time I took a breath.

It was that life I'd finally found courage to discuss with Morgan and a precious moment alone in which to do it, our third day in transit.

Only to find him ahead of me.

"Parthenogenesis!" The word greeted me as I entered our

cabin. Morgan tossed the reader on the bed to rattle atop a pile of tapes. "Knew I'd heard of it before. Females who have offspring without need for a partner. The Turrned do it. Who knows who else? Most species don't share their reproductive details."

For which I was, I decided, thankful. My hair twitched, unsettled. How much research had he done? "I'm not," I reminded him, "a Turrned."

"Well, no, but the same principles should apply. I've made notes—"

By the look of our table, masses of them. I thought he'd been compiling reports.

"I see." Not that I did, but such diligence was owed recognition. "Morgan—about the baby—"

"I know you didn't want this." He took my hands, sending *sincerity* and *love.* "Whatever you decide, I'll support you. But—" His eyes brightened and I realized with a sickening lurch of my heart that it was with hope. "—a baby, Sira. Something wonderful, out of all this. Our family."

And what could I say to that?

At my hesitation, the expression on his dear face changed, flickering through distress and guilt to pity; I felt something break inside me. "I'm sorry," Morgan said, who had no reason to, nor cause, and wasn't happiness better than grief—

Or fear?

"I shouldn't—"

"Yes, you should." Always I learned from my Human, his optimism and bravery today's lesson. "'Partheno-genesis.'" I had to admit it sounded better than Perversion and, after all, Turrned did it, who were pleasant, unremarkable beings, renowned only for their somewhat obsessive charity to others.

I bent to kiss my remarkable Chosen soundly, tendrils of hair tickling his neck. "Don't mind me," I whispered in his ear, following that with a nibble. "It's still a bit—" what wouldn't upset him further? "—overwhelming."

Pulling back, I unfastened my coveralls and let them fall, kicking off my boots. I tipped my head toward the fresher stall, hair sweeping over my shoulders like a silken cloak. As a collaborator, it had its moments. Morgan smiled.

"It's my turn," I reminded him. We'd a schedule for the use of the ship's limited resources. Sharing made sense.

And offered the illusion of privacy. I stepped inside, holding open the door.

Only to see Morgan shake his head and grimace. "I'd best tidy this and get back to the control room. The ship's not going to fly herself."

Certain even the *Fox* could wait a while, I sent a wave of *heat*, pleased when he let out a flattering growled "Witchling," less so when he chuckled and secured the door for me.

Swallowing disappointment, I keyed the timed spray.

Foam slid over my skin. My hands followed it, resting over my abdomen. Nothing had changed, not outwardly. Nothing would, according to Jacqui, for weeks yet. I dared follow that inner link.

Still nothing, beyond the strong, steady sense of *life*.

To Morgan, that was enough. But it wasn't. For all he'd filled me with hope, I knew better.

There should be more. A consciousness, however wordless at this nascent stage. Demands. Awareness. Words would follow. Some unborn were loud enough to be *heard* by those around the mother. I'd been one such, able to make the entire household feel my every twist and grumble.

Let alone what happened after birth.

Jacqui had said nothing; that didn't make her unaware. There was no hiding what was wrong from a Birth Watcher.

I took hold of as much hair as fit in two hands, pushing it into the foam. Engine grease was more than even a Chosen's hair could clean from itself, not that I could reason with the stuff.

More likely, I thought as locks squirmed, Jacqui was too kind to speak of what my baby lacked when she had no solution to offer.

Other than going to my mother.

I grabbed more hair, pulled, thought.

Morgan and I would deal with whatever grew in me, when the

time came. It—she—could wait. What couldn't? Safety for the Clan who remained. They were asking. What to do? What next? Some were quiet. Others demanding and querulous. The number grew with each hour.

Because all were afraid.

I didn't let them *touch* Morgan through our link; I didn't doubt he knew.

My mother hadn't been attacked. I went over my brief interaction with Jarad. He'd found her, decided she was safe, and left, speedily. If she'd found a haven, it would be temporary.

I'd *reached* to ask her. She'd rebuffed my contact, as I should have expected. Mirim and those with her distrusted the M'hir, relying instead on those Clan abilities free of it. It was rumored they refused to 'port, taking ships wherever they needed to go, as we did now.

Traveling at Human speed.

When I could be there in less than a heartbeat.

Couldn't I?

I stilled, letting my hair squeeze itself free of foam. I'd used the *Fox* as an excuse, hiding here with Morgan, pretending the ship's needs were greater than my kind's.

No longer, I thought, filled with *determination*.

The door opened. "Ready to go, chit?" Morgan asked, leaning in with a slow smile.

Why that— "Not quite," I assured him.

Taking hold of his coveralls, I pulled him the rest of the way, resetting the foam.

Without telling the others, after Morgan and I had made what plans we could, I left that shipnight . . .

. . . for Stonerim III.

Home, in a sense. I'd been born on this world, then taken from it as a child. I hadn't been back till now.

Feeling sentimental, I'd chosen a locate from my past, a favorite, private place overlooking the lake. Time hadn't been kind. I walked down a cinder path, my spacer boots crunching dead leaves. At what had been the shore, I stopped. "I'm back."

The words startled a few birds from a tangled scrub nearby.

So much for memory. I shouldn't have been surprised. The lake had been drained, the luxury towers taken down, all such materials of more use elsewhere, no one wishing to live close to calamity.

Stars crusted the night sky. Once, I could have looked from here and seen Norval rising on the horizon. A sparkling confection of a city, grown as a hill, I remembered it as bedecked with glass and light and gardens, surrounded at all hours by aircars, like flocks of birds, coming and going.

In reality, it had been a compost heap, rotting from within as the layers upon which each new version had been constructed began to fail. Its inevitable collapse had been both well documented and entertaining.

For those who hadn't lost home and livelihood.

Of course, the Clan had abandoned Norval before its ruin, choosing a province of wealth unconnected to events to the south. My mother had moved there, lived there.

>*here*<

And here, of course. My hair shifted uneasily. After our link, the binding of mother and child, had broken at last. After Rael and Pella . . .

Whatever grew within me, its future? Couldn't matter less at the moment. Morgan needed to know the whole truth; I wouldn't confide in anyone else until he did. He'd set course for my mother, as if there was hope here, and I'd seen how the others had reacted, gaining strength, gathering courage.

>*here*<

A direction did that. Movement did. I applauded my Chosen's wisdom and took it for my own.

Being here was a start.

>*here*<

I started, suddenly aware of the word I'd heard—felt—more than once. It wasn't a sending.

"Who's there?" Turning slowly, I scanned my surroundings.

Wind tousled leaves and pushed long waves through the grass. The sky was heavy with cloud and I could smell rain. Listening as hard as I could, I could hear my own heartbeat and nothing more.

>*here . . . here . . . here*<

Another ghost, I decided, firming my shields with a shiver, tied to this place. It felt like one: confused, demanding, no longer sane.

Impotent.

Even without the M'hir and the minds dissolving there, this world should be full of them.

No more, I promised myself. Time to talk to my mother. I formed the locate Jarad had sent, and *pushed* . . .

. . . finding myself in an alley.

I sneezed.

A filthy, stinking alley. Why were there no clean ones? What was wrong with civilization?

Something grunted.

My hand sought the handle of Morgan's spare blaster. He was many things, my Chosen. Careless was none of them. Having seen my somewhat creative choice of weaponry in the past, he'd made sure I could threaten with something actually deadly.

Until the Assemblers, I hadn't thought I would.

The grunt was followed by a rhythmic whistling snore as whatever I'd disturbed settled again. I relaxed, as much as I dared.

Most of the lights had been removed or broken, possibly by the alley's inhabitant. My boots squished and slipped through what I was just as glad not to see, and I guided myself down the middle by looking ahead. There, the alley met a brightly lit roadway wide enough for docking tugs and the starships they cradled in their arms, marking the boundary between Norval's portcity, a district of warehouses and hostels, and its more ephemeral shipcity.

While such was now-familiar turf to me, it was hardly a place I'd associate with any others of my kind.

Light rimmed the outline of a door to my left even as words formed in my mind.

Welcome, Daughter.

Times had changed.

Life clung to Norval only at its western edge, life that came and went in starships, life that scrabbled and dug like scavengers quarreling over a corpse. What any considered worth having was hauled offworld, legally or not; what wasn't, dumped. Decades of waste had begun to consume the portcity, filling its roads even as refuse piles swallowed row after row of abandoned warehouses. The few remaining buildings stood like a dam protecting the shipcity's landing pads. They'd be next. Ultimately, Norval would win.

My mother lived here.

Having expected a hovel, given the neighborhood, I was surprised to find a well-appointed apartment waiting behind the door. The furnishings were worn, but gently. I recognized a chair and rug, a piece of pottery and a lamp, and looked a question.

"I brought them from home."

Like her furniture, Mirim di Teerac appeared worn, but gently. Her hair was confined in the pre-Stratification net she'd used as long as I could remember, hair now more gray than gold. Fine lines rode her eyes and mouth, but she bore herself with quiet strength. A long table along a wall was covered with fabric and what I'd taken for a piece of art nearby turned out to be a torso with more fabric pinned to it.

Memory surfaced. My mother sitting, an embroidery hoop in her ever-busy hands. Singing to me as I played by her feet.

Mirim noticed my attention. "I do repairs and alterations. You'd be surprised how many from the shipcity need them. It's a good living."

Defensive.

A Clan—a "di Sarc"—working for Humans? It certainly explained my father's conspicuous absence. "I'll have to get your rates," I said, demonstrating how my sleeves, if unrolled, covered my hands. The ubiquitous spacer coveralls outlasted their original wearers many times over; I'd only seen new ones on crew from company ships.

She frowned. "You've changed."

How would you know? I might have asked, but didn't bother. The past was behind us. "Everything has." I looked around. "When did you move here?"

"The day you dragged me through that cursed dark."

To attend the treaty signing.

She waited for me to acknowledge how terribly wrong I'd been. As I prepared to do just that, I studied her face, finding Pella in her forehead, Rael in that expressive mouth and high cheekbones.

Then, in my mother's gaze, I found what we shared. A fierce and relentless will.

This was not, as my father believed, a Clanswoman who'd conveniently accepted her lack of Power and influence. Not, as I'd believed, one who'd withdrawn from a loveless family. Had I met Mirim sud Teerac while trading, I'd have put thumb to contract, as the saying went, with eyes open and an exit in sight.

I sat in the nearest chair rather quickly. The other thing about becoming a trader? Knowing when to gamble. I selected my next words with care and tossed the dice. "I've come for your advice, Mother."

Affront, plain and stark. "The First Chosen of the di Sarcs, come to me. The Clan Council's Speaker, come to me." Oh, no forgiveness there. She'd started civil, surprised to see me or curious. No more. "Why?"

I matched her bluntness. "We must survive."

An eyebrow lifted. "Why?"

I leaned forward, hands on the arms of the chair, and let the edge of my vaster Power brush hers. "Because I say so."

The Clan measured worth in Power, dominance by strength. Any Clan would have backed down.

Any Clan but my mother. "You?" Her lips twisted as though to spit. "I warned them about you. That change would begin with your birth, change to everything, and they'd regret wanting this Power of yours."

As hurts went, this was less than others and hardly a surprise. What was? That my mother *tasted* change. I'd not known she had that rare and disturbing Talent.

I put an edge into my voice. "You want the Clan to go extinct," I accused. "I think you're pleased Pella and Rael have died, that their Chosen have died, that the families on Acranam have—"

Her unClan-like slap stopped me.

Rubbing my cheek, I almost smiled. Trader trickery had its place. I had her. Understood her as I mightn't. Morgan would be proud.

"How dare you—"

"Mother." I stood to gesture profound apology and respect, saw her toss her head back in startlement. Before she could speak, I did, hearing my voice ring with the truth. "You've tried to save the Clan all along, but no one listened. This—" I glanced around her apartment "—is how we should have lived among Humans from the start. As part of their lives."

"We should never have taken from them," she snapped. "Never ruined their minds and used them. We could have renounced the M'hir and Power; been happy as we were. Greed took us down a path with only one ending. You—were inevitable."

Her one Talent of strength. It hadn't only warned at my birth. "You fled after the treaty because you *tasted* change coming. Why didn't you speak?"

"Who'd have listened?" Mirim turned away as if wearied by our conversation, walking to the tiny kitchen. "It's not as if I could point to any one danger. That's not how the gift works."

How many times had Morgan had such instinctive warnings, their true source clear only after the event?

"What about now?"

Mirim paused by the counter, then gave me a sober look. "It's not over. Not yet."

More change, I thought, my heart sinking. More chaos and disruption and death. I'd scolded Barac for losing hope; I came close to losing my own in that instant.

I clung to why I'd come—to find safe haven for those who remained.

It wasn't here. Nothing about the portcity, Norval, or my mother's apartment would be proof against the Assemblers or even a Human with an ax and a grudge. I was slightly astonished my father hadn't 'ported her away with him to save his own skin.

If not here, then where?

>. . . *here . . . here . . . here . . .*<

Instead of being startled, I froze. Was I hearing a voice, or was something deep inside insisting I listen to myself, to a hope I hadn't let myself believe?

Here. This place. Every Clan knew our history began on this world, Stonerim III.

Mirim had fled here for a reason. If I believed anything, it was that. She and her group, the M'hir Denouncers, were united in their intention to return to the pre-Stratification life of our ancestors. For all I knew, they'd started a colony elsewhere on this planet.

A dream not remotely big enough. Not to save the two hundred and seventy Clan left. Not to give them a future.

Not to keep the Trade Pact from weakening or worse.

We needed a world of our own.

"Mother," I asked, telling myself I was a fool, telling myself myth couldn't save us, "do you know where we came from?"

"Now you ask. Now you believe." Mirim leaned on the counter, her back to me, and I sensed *defeat*. "When it's too late."

"It's not. I don't accept that." I went to her. About to touch her hunched shoulder, I thought better of it and dropped my hand to my side. "I won't. Please, believe in me. We have to act."

Her hand reached back to capture mine, gripped, and all thoughts of the Clan Homeworld, of anything else, disappeared as Mirim *shared* . . .

Waiting. Waiting. Waiting. Years of dreadful patience. Years of wasted time and effort and disappointment. Waiting . . .

For me?

Waiting. For me to—?

I jerked free, shaken. "You wanted me to keep taking Candidates for my Choice. To carve a bloody swath through an entire generation if necessary! Why?"

"To save us! To be the first!"

We stared at one another. I didn't know what to say, what to do. All this time—"I did what I could," I said finally, desperate. "I found what was happening, that we were doomed—"

"Your work was meaningless. The M'hiray would not have gone extinct." Her eyes flashed with impatient anger. "We cannot." Suddenly, the passion left her face, leaving it old and tired. "What does it matter? Others have ended us. It's too late."

The *life* within me. A child outside a pairing. Commencement without Choice, reproduction without sex. Parthenogenesis.

The Turrned did it.

Not by Perversion. Nature. The past, the present, everything I'd believed shifted along that axis, disorienting—

—then, as abruptly, clear.

Jacqui'd been right to send me to my mother; she just hadn't known why. I'd never have believed this, any of it, if it hadn't already happened to me.

"It's not too late," I told my mother. "I am the first."

You agreed to this?

Oh, I knew that tone. It went with the look of incredulous dismay I'd see on Morgan's face whenever I'd had a "better idea" concerning the ship. The results weren't always disasters, but having been raised by technophobes, I, according to my captain, lacked several fundamental understandings. Admittedly, there'd been times I may have overestimated what I could learn from vistapes and going ahead on my own had, occasionally, caused a flood.

There'd been that almost-fire.

I'd ruined a—the point being, I knew full well Morgan was more concerned about possible consequences than angry.

They want to meet me. It wasn't as if I had a choice. Mirim had reacted with shock, then frenzied motion. She'd contacted her group. I hadn't expected she'd use an antique handcom to send coded messages.

Nor that we'd walk to our destination, within the towers of refuse.

It'll be fine. I infused the words with confidence.

I'll be there tomorrow. His presence faded.

Sooner than planned, that was, meaning Morgan would push the *Fox,* betting she wouldn't fail. He'd stay by those laboring engines, tools ready, until—

"Watch that puddle," warned Mirim. "It's corrosive."

I dodged in time, the green glow along the edges of the irregular pool promising nothing good. There were many such, oozing from the piles on either side of what was more path than road. "Thanks. I was distracted."

"By Jason Morgan." She said his name as I'd heard others do, the first time. Wistful, faintly unsure. As if he wasn't real and couldn't be, but how they wished he was.

For I'd shared everything with them, that day. My mistakes, my failures.

My love for a Human.

I glanced at my mother. "Yes."

"What you have—" Mirim fell silent, keeping her eyes on our path. Abruptly, almost angry, "It was like that for the M'hiray, before coming here. We formed loving pairs. A Chooser's Power-of-Choice was how we completed them, not a fight to the death."

Was it wistful thinking? Her Joining with Jarad had been imposed by the Council of the day and worse than loveless. They'd produced offspring to order, given them up when told, and hated each other as much as any two could.

I'd like to believe the Clan had been different once. "We're not taught that—"

"Why would we be?" Our path met a bridge, a flimsy thing of broken pieces. We crossed with care, the gutter beneath flowing with more of the noxious effluent of the piles.

Once we were both across, Mirim went on, not looking at me. "We're not to know anything was better then. We're to believe how we live now is the best choice, the only choice."

Choice. She used the word deliberately. "You could have taught me," I said, stung. "I'd have listened."

"Sira Morgan listens. Sira di Sarc?"

That silenced me. Perhaps her intention, perhaps not. The path narrowed and I followed behind, trying to keep from flinching as those around us turned to stare.

For we were no longer alone. Small groups—mixed by species, by age and health—foraged in the piles, filling bags and sacks. Having seen us, they returned to their work without a sound. A Trade Pact of the forgotten and homeless.

And desperate. A jointed arm reached from a cavity, seizing Mirim by the wrist. A body draped in garbage—or clothed in rags—heaved toward us, a wide head shaking free.

My blaster caught beneath the coat she'd given me. Before I could free it, my mother twisted loose. "Shame on you, Putzputz," she scolded. "You know who I am."

"Femmine. Femman. Fem." With a wheeze, it collapsed back into itself; its bulbous eyes remained fixed on me, their gaze hard and suspicious. "Who's he? Why's he? What's he?"

"With me. Are the rest here?"

"Some. Most. All."

Mirim nodded as if its babble made perfect sense, then tossed it the bag she'd carried over her shoulder. "Make that last, Putzputz. I don't know when I'll be back after this."

A moan. "Try. Might. Doubt." The bag disappeared within a cluster of eager arms. Membranes slipped over the eyes, turning them milky white, then the alien burrowed backward into its hiding place and disappeared.

"This way." To my disbelief, Mirim's finger pointed where it had gone.

No, worse. Above it. At the pile surrounding a dark-walled building.

I looked up, and up. The mess extended to the roof at one end. Small things with teeth looked back down, then scurried deeper within the loose structure.

"You're joking," I protested.

"Stay here, then." Without waiting to see if I obeyed, my

mother began to scale the pile as quickly as if she were one of the small things with teeth.

I discovered her trick only after slipping to flop facedown in the unpleasant mass for the second time. Mirim didn't climb at random. There were steps, disguised as bits of wood or plas. Handholds of rope or wire. This was an entrance, carefully constructed and as carefully hidden.

Guarded, at a guess, by the alien with those weaponlike limbs, now well below.

This wasn't in response to the attacks. Where I now climbed was an older section, the garbage weathered into something almost natural. To either side were patches of flat spiral crusts and little rounds of red or green. Growths like those Morgan had shown me, taking years to grow.

What was my mother up to?

I reached the top, only to find myself standing at a blank wall. Alone.

Mirim was gone.

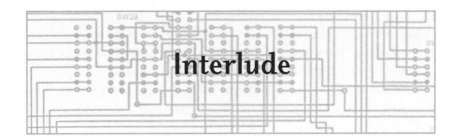

Interlude

"**Y**OU COULD HELP." Freeing his arm, Morgan used his sleeve to wipe sweat from his forehead.

Barac di Bowart crouched to peer into the mouth of the left air intake. He shuddered theatrically, moving back to let Morgan climb out. "Me, touch your ship?"

He'd thought he was too tired to laugh. Apparently not. "Good point."

The elegant Clansman pointed to the intake. "Are we going to blow up? I'd prefer some notice, so we can leave."

"Ship's fine." Morgan stood, working his shoulders. Been a while since he'd had to crawl in there.

To be exact, since Sira had become hindmost on the *Fox*. She'd the makings of a reliable mechanic, not that he'd dare tell her. She took enough on herself as it was, including what had taken her from the ship.

Add traipsing, at night, where the local Port Jellies refused to go—

Barac was a welcome distraction. "You've never come down here before." The Clansman had assured him, on several occasions, that he only felt safe traveling through space when he didn't have to believe in the machinery that drove them.

"You weren't coming out." Barac considered the stack of cups and e-rations, then nodded at the hammock slung between pipes. "Are you living here now?"

Morgan laid a hand on a curl of pipe, wincing inwardly. That vibration wasn't right. "I'm asking a lot of the old girl." With a pat. "Only fair I do what I can." And essential. The coolant system had been about to fail when he'd arrived; the quick patch looked ugly.

It would hold. It had to. "Why did you say you were here?"

"To keep you company." Barac looked for a place to sit, then leaned against the closed door. "Feels familiar. You and me. This ship. Even our course."

"Except for you being down here," Morgan pointed out dryly. The last time Barac had been a passenger on the *Fox* he'd been hunting Sira di Sarc. Easy to guess the reason for this "visit" was the same. "There's nothing to report yet. Sira's still with her mother." The good news that Mirim and her followers had knowledge about the baby was for Sira to share when she returned.

The rest? "What do you know about the Clan Homeworld?"

Barac's expression sobered. "Is that what's Sira's chasing? Call her back. Even if it could be found—we wouldn't be welcome there."

Not what he'd expected. "Time's gone by," Morgan said mildly. "Besides, I thought you didn't remember why the M'hiray left."

"Because we are the M'hiray." The Clansman turned the bracelet on his wrist, the etched design catching fire from the ship's lights. "Whether willingly or not, our kind split into those who use the M'hir and those who couldn't—or wouldn't. My unhappy aunt and her group have created their own version of our past. Don't expect reality from them."

The bracelet was of that past, pre-Stratification, its unusual metal shaped into a pattern reminiscent of water and stone. It had been a gift from Kurr di Sarc. Morgan found himself staring at it. "Did your brother believe Mirim's version?"

"No." Barac's shrug was bitter. "But he'd take her his latest box of discoveries. They'd spend hours poring over them, hours I'd be stuck with you and that deck of cards." His ever-charming smile was false. "I still say you cheated."

"I still say you're a poor loser." Interesting. To hear Jacqui,

Jarad di Sarc was the Clan's foremost expert on their past, yet Kurr had sought out Mirim. "Sira wouldn't waste time on a fruitless hunt," Morgan said more briskly. "You should trust her."

Barac's smile turned real, yet unutterably sad. "I do. It's the rest of universe that worries me."

"Don't flatter yourself." Tools secured, at least for the moment, the Human sat on a crate and stretched. "Most of the universe could care less."

"As most Clan are innocent," Barac countered. "I'm not."

So Sira wasn't the only one racked by guilt. The Human pushed a second crate away from the wall. "You didn't come to keep me company."

"No." The Clansman accepted the invitation and sat. He bent forward, elbows on his knees, and spoke to the floor. "Ruti isn't speaking to me."

A crowded ship wasn't the ideal place for the young lovers to find themselves. Morgan hid a smile. "What is it this time?"

"When I tell her what I've done, she's happy. She refuses to listen when I try to explain my—my regrets. It upsets her."

Being of lawless, independent Acranam, Morgan judged, wouldn't help Ruti's understanding. Nor would— "She's grieving and afraid, Barac. Right now, I think she needs to be proud of you."

"Proud?" Startled, the Clansman's face showed all his pain. "You know what I was. What I did. Finding telepaths like you. Manipulating their minds—erasing them if necessary. If not for Sira and her treaty, I'd be doing it now." A suddenly awkward *feel* between them. "And you'd be hunting us."

The treaty stipulated no action committed by the Clan before its signing could be prosecuted. Had that necessity tipped Cartnell to seek his own vengeance?

Morgan half smiled. "You couldn't have been any good at it, or you'd have won more games."

"I've never—you were our friend!" Realizing he was being teased, Barac shook his head but something eased. "I can't believe I said that."

"I won't tell." Morgan's smile faded. "None of us know what's ahead, Barac." He held out his hand. When the Clansman took it, he lowered his shields slightly, sharing his *compassion*, his *belief* in the other, before letting go. "Your regrets do you credit, but don't let them keep you from living."

Barac gave a slow nod, then sent, *Heart-kin.*

Still not letting you win. But their eyes met and held in acknowledgment of the bond between them, one stronger in many ways than mere blood. If only others knew the Clan as he did—

Or rather knew the Clan he did, the Human thought, who'd made the leap beyond their xenophobia. Could the rest? He shook off the despondent feeling. "Sira's looking for an answer."

"By chasing her mother's fantasy." Barac actually laughed. "We're that desperate."

"Finding options," Morgan corrected. Something he'd be doing up in the control room right now, if not for the *Fox*. He cast an eye at the nearest gauge. Running hot. He managed not to run his grease-streaked fingers through his hair, though odds were excellent he'd done it already. Grabbing a rag, the captain of the *Silver Fox* rose to his feet.

The ship could be at Stonerim III already, if the Clan on board lent him their strength. If he dared reveal himself. If that were in any sense a good idea.

And not a recipe for disaster.

"You'll let us know before we blow up, won't you?"

Morgan grunted an absent affirmative. "You could help."

The Clansman laughed again and headed for the door. "I'll bring you some real food. How's that?"

"Thanks."

Keeping his hand on the door, Barac glanced over his shoulder. "I've met them, Morgan. Once."

"Who?"

"Mirim's group. The M'hir Denouncers, or whatever they call themselves." He made a face. "I couldn't take them seriously. I hope Sira doesn't."

Alone again, Morgan patted the pipe. "If she does, old girl, I expect things to get very interesting around here."

If Sira found a new world?

"Very interesting indeed."

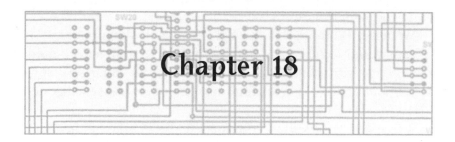

Chapter 18

*M*OTHER?
Two steps left.

My fist poised to hammer on the wall, for what good it would do, I stopped. *What do you mean?*

Take two steps to your left.

Where there was still a wall. A wall I could ignore, if I used my mother as a locate.

Ending what cooperation I'd gained. I took the steps, garbage shifting underfoot, to discover what had seemed a solid wall was a clever illusion. Someone had built a section, matched right to the flaking paint and stains, and set it in front. Between the false wall and real one was just room to walk.

And an open door, waiting.

Morgan had built a shelter on Ettler's Planet, its bulk disguised as part of the landscape; why and how were questions I'd not asked. He'd appreciate caution of such a Human sort.

And had given me enough that I didn't immediately walk forward, but crouched to examine the inviting space. Flat, clear of debris, and—I nodded to myself—easily hinged to drop an unwanted guest into an abyss.

Or holding cell. I thought abyss more likely, knowing what lay below.

Coming?

Assuming the best, I stood, brushed off the worst of what clung to my legs and stepped between the walls and through the door.

To squint and stare.

Whatever I'd thought to find, it wasn't a busy laboratory.

Counters lined the walls, 'port lights hovering where required. Cupboards with clear doors held objects—old things—of such variety and number that the four nearest put my father's ill-gotten collection to shame.

A massive work surface dominated the center of the floor, crisscrossed by light and crowded by a series of objects in various stages of dismemberment—or assembly.

There was, to my further astonishment, tech everywhere. The counters had stations, each with an abundance of custom consoles and panels, cluttered with devices I couldn't name. I'd taught myself data analysis and had a system installed in my former home no other Clan—I'd thought—could understand, let alone use.

What was here was beyond me. Quite possibly it was beyond anyone not a Trade Pact scientist.

The only problem? Those standing or sitting at the lit and active stations weren't Human. They were Clan.

Every one of them looking at me.

"Welcome, Speaker." Mirim managed to infuse her greeting gesture with irony, "to my vision."

Mirim's vision was shared by eleven others. They'd escaped the Assemblers the same way they'd escaped notice all these years. Their Clan lives were pretense, their homes maintained by servants charged with keeping their secret.

Servants who likely died for that obedience. These Clan weren't so different from the rest, I thought, but kept it to myself.

They were an eclectic group. Three Chosen pairs: Deni and Cha sud Kessa'at, Josa and Nik sud Prendolat, their daughter the youngest child, and Holl and Leesems di Licor, parents of two brothers. The brothers, Arla and Asdny, were on the cusp of becoming unChosen, voices about to change along with all else in their lives. The suds hadn't been authorized for children by Council, the same Council who'd labeled the Licor lineage highly suspect, it having proved impossible to breed out the faint dappling of their pale skin, like sunlight and shadow.

We had something in common. They'd broken the Prime Laws of our kind.

So had I.

The eight adults wore lab jackets over shirts and pants, Human garb on Clan; it made me oddly off balance.

Another surprise. My mother wasn't the only Chosen without her mate: Orry di Friesnen was here as well.

And, last and in no way least, a Chooser.

Tle di Parth. I'd respected her intelligence. I hadn't known she used it outside Council arguments. She wasn't glad to see me, but then, she never was.

The rest of my mother's group were. So glad, they rushed to make me welcome, the smallest child, Andi sud Prendolat, knocking over a stool in her haste to make the proper gestures and being quietly chastised. Mirim stood by, impatience in every line of her body, as a debate erupted over whether I should be shown this find or that first, and I honestly feared two of the older Chosen, Deni and Leesems, would come to blows.

They were impassioned, unworldly, and the most unlikely Clan I'd ever met. I found myself unexpected charmed.

My mother was not. "Friends." She had their instant, silent attention. "The Speaker," she continued, "has a question."

That attention shifted to me.

She'd told them about the baby. Why this? Their intent, unnerving gaze reminded me of Turrned Missionaries. I fumbled for a different beginning than I'd planned, forced to accept, for now, that Mirim had her reasons.

"Clan have been attacked." Obvious, but I felt oddly unsure of their understanding. Their faces didn't change. "We've suffered devastating loss. Barely a quarter of us survive."

A gasp. Tle. Was she thinking of her own future now,

wondering how many were unChosen? Most, I could have told her. We'd lost more Chosen, bound to their partners, and all of the infirm and aged, bound to their homes by care. The youngest children, already few in number . . .

I sensed *shock* racing mind-to-mind and gestured a sincere apology. "Those who survive are in hiding and at risk, their resources contaminated." It covered the point. "I've come to you, to my mother—" I'd no shame using our connection; the rest looked less upset. "—to ask your help."

Another shock, their unease more subtle. They'd worked in secret; that I could guess. It made sense they'd come to believe themselves separate.

No longer.

Nik di Prendolat looked around at the rest, then to me. She was a tall Clanswoman, with an air of gentle dignity. "We've room for you, Speaker. You'll be safe with us."

A round of now-cheerful nods. "And welcome. Most welcome. Please. Stay until everything's back to normal."

" 'Back to—' " I swallowed the word, unable to credit what I'd heard. This was no fortress. Mirim bribed their gatekeeper with what—scraps of supper? It was only a matter of time until the Assemblers—or some other enemy—found this pocket of Clan. Clan who wouldn't 'port, perhaps couldn't.

Clan with children.

"We're safe here," Tle insisted, giving me a defiant look.

She knew better. Knew better and hadn't told them. Why? *What's here that matters more than their lives?* I kept the sending tight and private.

Her eyes widened, then narrowed. *The truth.*

The truth. Words that haunted; words that held out—was it hope? I couldn't feel it, consumed by anger.

Secrets. Tle loved them. These people, so dangerously naive, could well die for them. What was I to do? Squander what time I had trying to save them?

Delay to unravel yet another puzzle?

All that, from the closet?

Morgan was smiling. I could tell, even if he was careful to keep *amusement* from his sending.

It's not a closet.

I'd walked away before losing my temper in what I'd feared would be an unforgettable and unforgivable fashion, choosing the leftmost of the two doors at the end of the big room. *Look for yourself.* I sent him what I could see. It wasn't exactly a closet, being a crowded storeroom no larger than our cabin on the *Fox.* Closing the door behind myself without slamming had seemed, at the time, dignified.

Barac says they're harmless.

He didn't accuse me of running away, of being unwilling to confront Tle in front of what was, in a real sense, her family. Harmless or not.

They don't accept using the M'hir. As we were doing now, our link through the darkness as sure and strong as sunshine. *Better in a closet,* I thought glumly, *than in front of them.*

Your cousin doesn't accept engines move the ship. His tone grew serious. *Talk to them, Witchling. You're their Speaker, too.*

I want to be crew.

Our link strengthened until I might have been within his arms and he in mine. When Morgan withdrew, ever-so-gently, I resisted the urge to keep him with me.

It not being dignified to stay in a closet, however tempting.

No one commented when I came out, though they must have shared the *PUZZLEMENT* Andi broadcast. Nik put an arm around her daughter. There was the faintest trace of *embarrassment*, then polite silence. Josa drew close, both parents looking at me as though expecting criticism.

Meant to reassure, my smile froze on my face.

These children.

>Here<

At their age, they should have been fostered to other homes, each stretched and tenuous link to a mother used, while it lasted, to reinforce a desired passage through the M'hir. But these links were here and intact; I could *see* them, like tightly woven braids. These were families who'd stayed together, in certain defiance of Council, their units closer to a Human culture like that of Stonerim III. Like Morgan's.

I'd imagined a colony. I hadn't been wrong.

"While you were away, Josa brought out some wine. This is an occasion." The way Mirim said the word wasn't like Morgan, yet was. These were her family, as I wasn't, but the realization held no sting. I'd my own, now.

What struck me more was how calmly they accepted the decimation of our kind, as if it were an interesting fact but little more. The Clan had rejected them and their ideas; I supposed it made sense for them to do the same. But it meant what I wanted and cared about wasn't going to be the same for them.

And that could be a problem.

I nodded graciously. "An occasion it is." I gazed around at their faces. "Thank you." With the words, I sent *gratitude* and *approval* and a smidge of *thirst*.

Andi giggled.

With impressive speed, stools were arranged around the now-cleared end of the table, a cloth placed, and a selection of glasses unusual in no two being the same filled with wine. The cloth looked more like a tarp and, after a sip, I suspected the wine of having been made in someone's kitchen, but there was no doubting the warmth in this room.

Warmth Tle protected. I could feel her *bristle* of worry.

She wasn't alone. When I opened my senses, emotions roiled and snapped at me from an unexpected source. My mother. Having borne Jarad's disapproval her adult life, I would have thought it unlikely she'd cared about my opinion.

Then again, these two, of all the rest, understood what had happened to the Clan, what could happen here.

If they were afraid, so was I. I could feel the hours slipping by, hours our enemies wouldn't waste, but instilling panic wouldn't help. There were times, Captain Morgan would tell me, when you went with the hand you were dealt.

"As my mother's said, I've a question for you. For all of you," I expanded, seeing their eyes light up. "Where's the Clan Homeworld?"

Eyes dropped. I could hear everyone breathing; nothing more. Mirim took a slow sip of wine, the only one to move.

What had I said? "Where we, the M'hiray, came from," I explained. "What can you tell me about it?"

"The Origin?" Andi smiled happily and turned to her parents. "We haven't reached it yet, have we, Father? But we're very very close—"

HUSH!

Was this promising or not? "Please explain." I did my best to speak quietly, but my hair lashed my shoulders. "Mother?"

She gave me a considering look, then nodded. "There's no more need for secrecy. Show Sira the orbs."

Mirim's command sent the young brothers rushing to a cupboard. They removed a box as long as my arm, a costly thing of wood and precious inlay, and brought it to the table. Others made room for it in front of me.

I might have been sitting at a trader table, trying to make sense of another species. Which I'd done before, I reminded myself. I went to open it.

"Don't touch it. You're pregnant!" Having frozen me in place with that sharp rebuke, Deni carefully undid the closures, one requiring the press of his thumb, and lifted the lid.

The inside of the box was divided into lined compartments. Slightly more than half of those were filled with oval crystals. Very familiar crystals. A couple were chipped, but most were in as fine a shape as the one in my pocket.

I bent to look closer. They were empty—or solid, I thought suddenly.

"We've had no way to test them," Mirim told me. She picked one up, holding it in the palm of her hand.

About to ask "What do you think they are?" I hesitated. Their serious expressions implied these were anything but simple hunks of rock; they'd the tech to know. "What are they?"

"They are repositories," Holl di Licor answered. "Meant to keep dying minds safe from the Great Darkness." Her strong dappled fingers rested on the lid. "We don't know if they've been used—if there are minds inside. The technique's been lost."

To their plain disappointment and my relief. I'd been in stasis, trapped within my body. To be trapped forever in stone? In no sense was that better than flowing away into the M'hir.

"We do know—I mean, we've postulated," Holl corrected at Deni's cautioning look "—that such minds could be retrieved."

And would be insane, I told myself, none too sure at the moment about the state of my hosts' minds. "Why would you want to?"

The others looked startled. My mother merely nodded. "These are pre-Stratification."

Staggered by the implications, as she'd intended, I let out a slow breath. "You think you—you want to talk to our Ancestors."

"They'll tell us how to reach the Origin," Andi said happily. "The best place in the universe!"

If this was how they'd been searching for our home planet all these years, I'd be better off trying for sense out of the Watchers.

>*here*<

Staying wasn't going to—I stopped, holding my breath, trying to listen. But it wasn't in my ears. It wasn't me.

"What is it?" Mirim sat, her eyes searching my face.

"I don't know," I said, suddenly terrified I did.

Not looking away from my mother, taking strength from my sense of her, of what was real and believable, I pulled out the crystal from the Hall of Ancestors and set it on the table.

All but my mother rose to their feet. Parents gathered their children close. The Chosen held onto one another, Orry moved back, and Tle di Parth . . .

. . . had disappeared.

Mirim's gaze dropped to the crystal. Reluctantly, I let mine follow.

The precious scrap of fabric had vanished. In its place, filling the crystal, was white smoke.

I'd 'ported with it before. It had been fine on the *Fox*. As if the thing might bring me badly needed luck, I'd slipped it in my pocket the way Auordians braided beads in their hair. I hadn't looked at it till now.

My hair drifted down. Curious. Attracted.

>Here<

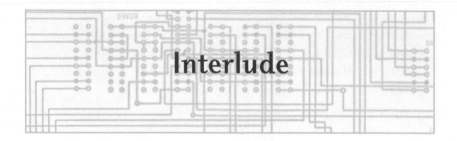

Interlude

HARD WORK, evading that questing, nosy mind in the M'hir. Almost as difficult as avoiding those foul creatures. It took Power.

Power she had. That the di Caraats had always had. So much, those jealous fools had ruled to excise her family's name.

Fools now dead or running, while she, Wys di Caraat, First Chosen of that potent House, remained. The future was bright indeed.

If she could find those she sought. Wys gave up, pulling free. The Watchers' continued *din* helped and hindered. Hiding her, yes, but also her quarry.

The opening of her eyes brought forward servants, one to offer a steaming cup, the other to kneel and rub the cramps from her feet. The Clanswoman accepted their ministrations without thought, her attention on what she hadn't expected to see. "What are you doing in my cabin?"

The Scat dipped its snout, regarding her out of one eye. They didn't like her or her kind.

She didn't care. "Well?"

"Your mate is-sss less-ss than content. He makes-ss noissse."

As if others among the pirate's less willing passengers didn't scream.

Wys dismissed her servants with an irritated gesture. "Put him in stasis if he's a nuisance." Would her Chosen ever stop being a burden? He'd protested their settlement on Acranam, protested leaving that overheated excuse for a world.

And would be dead now, if she'd listened.

Even now, Erad *pushed* at her shield. Doubtless wanting to complain about his treatment. He gave her nightmares when he could.

She'd tolerated his nonsense for the glorious child they'd produced, only to have Sira di Sarc destroy her son at the cusp of his ascension over all other Clan. The very cusp!

"S—stasssis-ss comes-ss with ris-ssk."

Wys glared at the Scat, the greedy creature well aware its final, and larger, payment required both Clan being alive and whole.

Was nothing easy? A shame she hadn't had Yihtor erase his father's mind and make him something useful. "Deal with him. Without damage—" she cautioned.

It chittered with pleasure, thin black tongue collecting foam from between its fangs, and left.

Wys snapped her fingers and the mindless Chosen pair who served her resumed their duties.

She'd lost a son and been disgraced. Things were different now. Opportunity unfolded like blossoms with every death of those who'd once opposed her.

She closed her eyes, going back to her careful, cautious *search*.

Acranam's Clan had believed they would one day rule over all their kind. That they themselves determined their own fate.

They never had been free—

And never would be.

Those who'd been offworld, who'd survived?

Were *hers*.

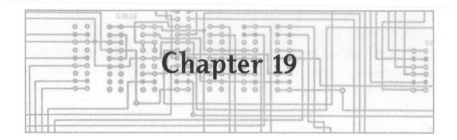

Chapter 19

>*H*^{*ERE*<} I stood and stumbled away as my hair went mad, stretching out longing tendrils, snapping those back at my face. I fought it with both hands.

Others joined mine, strong and sure. Together we twisted the locks into a heaving mass at the back of my head, holding it there, until, suddenly, it subsided. Warily, I let go, feeling the other hands do the same. As if it had never been anything but mannerly, my hair fell limp down my back.

I looked around, wiping tears from my eyes and not a little blood from my cheeks, to find Mirim there. "I don't suppose you have another of those nets, do you?" My hair gave a last little quiver, as if to apologize. I wasn't ready to forgive it.

"What happened?" my mother demanded.

About to ask her the same question, I gave a helpless shrug. "I don't know." The crystal, white and mysterious, sat on the table. The rest of the Clan kept their distance, their eyes shifting from it to me and back. "It didn't look like this before." I *shared* the crystal's original appearance with them all, impatient with words. "And it's talking."

" 'Talking'?" She said it in wonder, not disbelief. "Can it be? Leesems?"

"We supposed a Presence would make itself known at the—ah—appropriate moment," he answered promptly, though his face had gone sickly pale. I sympathized. "How was a mystery. There is the other—ah—requirement."

"For what?" I asked, doing my best to sound reasonable. "What 'Presence'?" Though that there was one, I no longer doubted.

>*Here*<

"It's true. I know it is." Andi tugged her hand from her father's and ran to me. She looked up, her gray-green eyes as serious as any adult's, and said what chilled my blood. "You carry a Vessel."

Vessel. What did it say, that this cold, hard word satisfied something in me, when "baby" did not?

I slammed tight my link to Morgan.

Her parents followed, putting protective hands on Andi's shoulders but not moving her away. "Our daughter has several Talents." The mother, with pride.

Birth Watcher among them. On impulse, I offered the child my hand. Little fingertips rested on my palm for an instant, their touch light and cool. A delighted smile dimpled her soft cheeks. "I feel her." Her eyes rose to mine. "She's strong."

As if they'd waited for the news, the others crowded close, reaching out to brush their fingers against mine, smiling. I made myself endure it, *sensing* nothing but goodwill and happiness.

Or else I was afraid of moving. Both, I thought stupidly, applied. A Presence, clearly aware. A Vessel, empty.

Waiting.

>*Here*<

Stay away from me, I told it, horrified. Stay away from mine.

My revulsion wasn't shared by my mother's group, busy murmuring with joy. "I never thought to see this day." "We're saved." "At last."

None of which eased my mind or helped me understand what was happening or stop it, but I nodded to keep them happy.

My mother, of course, stayed apart.

While that thing's >*Here . . . here*< crawled under my skin.

Deni sud Kessa'at put the crystal in a plas box, handling it with a pair of wooden spoons. Irrational, to be relieved to have the thing out of sight—

Especially as the >*here* . . . *here*< continued unabated, scratching, digging—

But it was an improvement.

More, the group lost their reticence, treating me as though I'd been part of them all along. Or belonged to them. The distinction was unimportant.

Tle had reappeared, tactfully walking in through the one door I hadn't. She gestured apology and sat, quiet and subdued, at the opposite end of the table. Her contrition wouldn't last; that she bothered at all made me wonder again about this "truth" of hers.

"Friends." Mirim rose to her feet. "In this terrible time for the M'hiray, it is tempting to believe we've found what we've searched for these many years. To believe my daughter's arrival and her condition are for our benefit and we have but to act, to succeed for all."

And didn't that sound unsettling? I prepared the locate for the *Fox,* just in case.

She glanced at me, a glint in her eyes as though she'd read thoughts I kept private. "It is, in fact, the other way around. Sira, we offer you our help. We are the only Clan who understand what you carry. We can help you survive its birth."

I focused on the key phrase—ignoring the highly alarming rest. An "offer" implied they wanted something in return. From me. "What do you want?"

The others stilled.

My mother smiled. "That you ask the Presence our questions. Chief among them, yours. Where did we come from?"

"The Origin," the others said in eerie synchrony. As if they said it often.

As if it were a prayer.

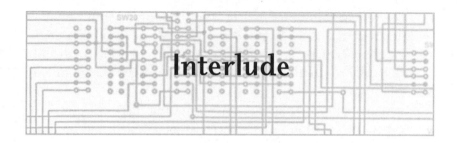

Interlude

YOU ARE MINE. Obey!

Morgan woke with a start, heart pounding in his throat, skin slick with sweat. Gods. He hadn't had that nightmare for months, hadn't relived that oily mind voice crawling around his thoughts, threatening, promising, full of lies and pain . . .

He'd had to retreat deep within himself to escape, so far he'd needed help to climb out again.

Yihtor di Caraat was dead.

And he wasn't the same. Since then, he'd been trained by the best, honed in battle, and had his Chosen's incalculable strength at his call, always.

"Lights. Full." Morgan sat up in the hammock, took slow, deep breaths. To his relief, the golden warmth along his link to Sira remained undisturbed. Not so his thoughts.

He'd *heard* Rael in the M'hir.

What did "dead" mean to the Clan?

"Captain. We have a problem."

Jacqui, not Barac, hovered in the doorway. Wan and anxious, she flinched at a rattle from the nearby engine. The rattle wasn't serious; what brought her here could be. Morgan rose to his feet. "What's wrong?"

"Can you leave—come to the control room?"

The control room he'd left locked, coded to admit only him or Sira. Not that locks stopped the Clan. Instead of answering, the Human went by her, half-running the corridor to the lift, pausing only to let her catch up before closing the door and sending it up.

He glanced down at Jacqui. "What's going on?"

"I—" She closed her mouth, looking miserable, then held out her hand as if words would be too difficult.

When he touched her, *fear* and *dread* poured through. *Ruti tried to do something to the ship. Barac's with her, stopped her. He sent me to bring you.*

He replied with *calm*, feeling none of it himself. The lift opened.

Five steps to the yes, locked, control room door. Morgan keyed it open and took a quiet step inside, waving Jacqui to remain where she was.

He closed the door behind him. Barac cradled Ruti's unconscious form in his arms. Her hair streamed down, limp and lifeless, but her chest rose and fell with steady breaths.

"The baby?" the Human asked.

"She's fine." The Clansman jerked his head at the console, then carried his Chosen to the copilot's couch, laying her there gently.

Blood cold, Morgan hurried over. Course disks were strewn everywhere, as if someone unfamiliar with their organization had tried to find a specific one. She had, he realized an instant later, spotting a disk on its own. For all her efforts—and there was sufficient damage to suggest Ruti'd tried some kind of hammer— she'd been unable to make the *Fox* eject what the ship's captain had installed.

He held up the solitary disk. "Plexis."

"It wasn't Ruti." Barac ran his fingers lightly over her forehead, his face bleak. "Someone dared enter her sleeping mind, Morgan. Dared control her. Who? Why?"

Because there were Clan outside any laws but their own, the

Human thought grimly, willing to take advantage of any disaster. He'd had that nightmare—or had it been more?

"First things first," Morgan stated, evading the question. "Teach Ruti how to protect herself at all times—and Jacqui." A First Scout would have that knowledge.

The Clansman nodded. "Of course. I should have—I never thought—"

"Why would you?" He should get back to the engines, but Morgan hesitated.

"What is it?"

"Why Plexis?"

"I think my brave one fought back the only way she knew how." Barac offered a finger to Ruti's hair; it rose, sluggishly, to wrap around it. "Wherever this invader wanted her to go, Plexis would be Ruti's choice."

Morgan hoped so, but the station could easily have been the invader's choice also, being a hub of transport, legal and otherwise. "Take her to the cabin and keep her there. I'll clean up."

"You don't trust her."

"Right now, do you?"

The Clansman's answer was to take his Chosen in his arms, then disappear.

"Thought as much."

Morgan collected the loose disks. A few had been dropped on the floor in front of the console, but one had been thrown clear to the wall, as if Ruti'd wanted it as far from her as possible. He picked it up, reading the coordinates with a growing frown. Snosbor IV. Had this been where the invader wanted to send the ship?

Troubling, if so. Before all this, an age ago, Snosbor IV had been listed on the trader boards as their next destination.

Or the disk had bounced. Still, it'd be worth asking Ruti. If she remembered.

Plexis, now.

Risking more time from the engines, Morgan keyed in the com and waited.

"*Claws and Jaws-Complete Interspecies Cuisine,*" boomed a familiar voice. "We regret we cannot take—"

"Huido, please."

"This is Hom Huido!" The voice paused, then asked coyly. "Can you not tell?"

Morgan almost smiled. "Hello, Tayno. This is Captain Morgan of the *Silver Fox*. I need to speak to your uncle."

"Captain Morgan." The deep voice resonated self-importance. "I'm to tell you, and you alone, that my esteemed uncle has left Plexis. I have assumed his place."

Huido, leave his home and wives unguarded? The Human was, to be honest, just as shocked to hear his old friend would leave the repair crews unwatched. "Where did he go?"

"Hom Huido did not inform me. He received a message, but I don't know from whom. That was when he left." A considering pause. "I could ask those in the pool. You can open their door, can you not, O most-trusted of allies?"

Why, the rascal. Morgan grinned. "Locked you out, did he?"

The clatter-clank of a heartfelt sigh. "He always does."

You had to feel for the lad. "I'm sure you're where your uncle wants you to be," the Human assured him. "Protecting the family during such perilous times."

By the uneasy rattle during the next brief pause, he'd given the young Carasian food for thought. "Do you really think so?" With dawning enthusiasm.

"I do. Huido's put all his trust in you, young Tayno. There could be more assaults. Be on your guard."

"I shall be Vigilant! I shall never leave my Post! I shall—"

"Let me know if Huido gets in touch," Morgan interjected before the bellowed exhortations could become any louder and alarm the restaurant's other staff. "*Fox* out."

Ominous, that a single message had made Huido haul orbit. Without contacting him first.

Who knew what had gone through that thick-plated head? Morgan snorted. Knock on that head when he saw him next.

If he saw him. Perilous times.

Impetuous Huido might be, but no fool. He'd take precautions. So would he, Morgan told himself. No one was going to steal his ship.

The *Silver Fox* had her secrets, among them the mental locks he'd added after a successful trade on Omacron. One released the scantech console that should have been removed when the starship was decommissioned from the patrol.

Another? Standing at the wall to the right of the consoles, Morgan concentrated, fingertips touching one another, *sending* a special command. A section of what appeared solid slid back and away revealing a cavity as deep as his arm. After putting the course disks inside, Morgan relocked it, waiting until the wall was featureless again.

A course could be manually input, but it would take a trained pilot and codes only he and Sira knew.

The ship safe, the Human went to check on his passengers.

A painful swell of *outrage* met him at his cabin door. Morgan knocked and entered.

Ruti was sitting up in bed, dark hair writhing around her head, her face flushed. Barac gave Morgan a grateful look. "She doesn't believe me."

"I had a bad dream—"

How he wished that were true. Morgan shook his head gently. "Someone used you. Look at your hands."

Ruti lifted her hands and gasped. Her nails were broken, a few severely enough that the fingertips bled. Her eyes went to Barac, filled with dread.

Then fury.

She swung her legs over the side of the bed and jumped to her feet. "I won't be a puppet! I won't!"

Barac held out his hand. "You won't," he promised, his voice thick with emotion. "I swear it." Without taking his eyes from Ruti, he said to Morgan, "I've summoned Jacqui. We'll do this together. Now."

Morgan left, heading for the galley. Jacqui passed him in the corridor. She didn't say a word, only gave a determined nod.

Well enough.

Passengers secure, he stuffed a pocket with e-rations and returned to the engine room.

Next stop, Stonerim III and Sira.

The *Fox* labored, pouring out her aged mechanical heart for him. Slowing would be as dangerous now as continuing with all speed.

It was going to be a long night.

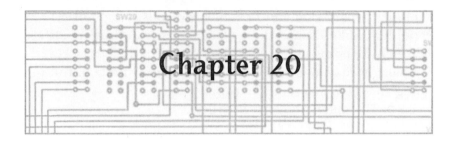

Chapter 20

"I 'VE TOLD YOU." Times without count, no matter how I attempted to contact whatever it was. "All it says is 'here.'"

And all it wanted was in. That I didn't tell them, certain they'd agree.

"Ah." Deni hummed to himself, then nodded. "Let me consult."

Again.

After their initial excitement, my mother's group had morphed into remarkably disciplined scientists, checking me—and the crystal—with instruments, consulting in small groups, their privacy assured by touch and mind.

Conversations I could overhear if I wished.

I didn't. Much as I wanted—needed—answers, time was running out. I'd heard from Morgan. The *Fox* was insystem, bound for the Norval shipcity, a docking tug called and prepaid. If I *reached* to him now, all I'd sense would be the depth of his concentration.

Much as I wished to be there, my more sensible self knew I'd be of greater help here, searching for answers. I accepted a cup of sombay and worked on my patience.

Deni returned. "We think the Presence might respond in a different environment."

I looked up at the lean Clansman, ready to suggest the ship, only to find him, along with my mother and others, ready for something else entirely. They'd summoned portlights to hover at shoulder height. Holl and Leesems had coils of rope over their shoulders, while Tle had slung a bag over hers. Mirim let me see her tuck the box with the unsettling crystal inside her jacket.

"What environment did you have in mind?" I asked. I wasn't going anywhere that required rope.

Until Tle smiled. *Ready for the truth?*

The first truth I discovered was that the laboratory sat on an upper floor of what had been a maintenance building. We went down a lift that moved with reassuring smoothness, each of us locked in our own thoughts.

Mine having more to do with why this was a bad idea and what Morgan would say this time, I rocked back and forth on my feet.

Andi took my hand. She'd waited at the lift door to join us, something everyone else accepted without question. "I won't leave you," she said quietly. "If that's all right?"

Birth Watchers. The instinct was stronger than I'd realized. This child was stronger. I looked down at Andi, thought of the strangeness inside me, and didn't hesitate. "Thank you. I accept."

She nodded, her face serious.

The doors whooshed open. A portlight flew politely ahead.

Just as well. I'd been in a parking garage before, just not one abandoned. Beyond the circle of light was utter black and the cold air entering my nostrils reeked of machine. With the tower of waste piled against the outside walls, I thought it safe to assume the lift behind us was the only working exit.

For Clan who refused to 'port, other than Tle, they were brave.

Or foolish. Both, in my informed opinion. I kept hold of Andi's small hand; if anything went awry, I'd no compunction about 'porting her to safety with me.

"This way."

Mirim and Tle went first and I followed, the others behind.

Our footfalls echoed, hiding any other sounds. The darkness folded in behind.

>Here<

As only I heard the insistent whisper, I did my utmost to ignore it. Ignoring my hair was less straightforward. It had become sly, reaching when I didn't notice for my mother—and the crystal.

Tle had braided her hair, it being limp and lifeless as suited a Chooser. My mother's behaved, immured in its net. I'd have threatened mine, for what good it would do, but knew better. There was a saying, "A Chosen's hair is desire's mirror." What my hair expressed came from me, however emphatically I disagreed.

Ahead, the lead portlight reflected from something long and lean. Two somethings, resolving as we came close into a pair of battered groundcars, their roofs removed. I turned to Mirim. "How far are we going?"

"Under Norval," she answered, lifting her light to reveal the opening of a dark tunnel.

It resembled nothing so much as a gaping mouth. Morgan wasn't going to like this.

"It's quite safe. We keep the system cleared, Speaker," Leesems said quickly. "As best we can."

Tle lifted a challenging eyebrow. "There are cave-ins. Rare, but some."

Morgan wasn't going to like this at all.

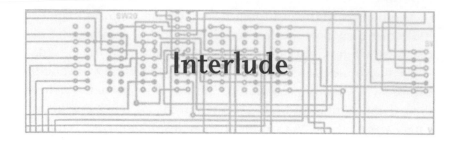

Interlude

FINGERS SCRABBLED, GRIPPED. They found the latch, fought it. Flipped it. As the lock released, the lid and case parting with a puff of chilled air, the hand dropped back to the ground. It subvocalized a complaint.

Then scurried out of the way of a frost-crusted boot.

Ambridge Gayle crouched and spun, weapons drawn. After a careful survey of her surroundings, she stood and allowed herself the luxury of a stretch, bits of ice shattering free of her envirosuit. She'd been glad not to be in full stasis; relieved to have weapons to hand and the ability to use them should her case be misplaced in shipping.

After a day, she'd changed her mind.

Done now. She'd arrived, alive and unseen. Time to get to work. "Hurry up," she told the Assembler, there being no point talking to pieces. Once the hat and head snicked into place, she snapped, "Where's Bowman?"

"Remember, we want the world, must have the world, must find the Hoveny world!"

"I'm aware," Gayle said dryly. The Brill had been clear on his payment: the location of the Hoveny world. In other words, capture Bowman, retrieve what information she had about the Hoveny, then dispose of the corpse.

Been a while.

She rolled a shoulder, felt a familiar, almost visceral anticipation. Not so long at that. "What resources?"

"You ask, we have." The Assembler wheezed with excitement. "After the Clan. Nest here. Burn it!"

"Your business, not mine."

"Our business. All! Hoveny world. Treasure. Clan. All!" An overstimulated hand fell off and climbed back up.

Gayle regarded the creature. "Like it or not—" and she didn't, but matters were as they were "—the Brill has the ships. Your job's the mindcrawlers. He's sent me after Bowman. He knows what I can do," with a slow smile.

At that smile, the Assembler known as Magpie Louli fragmented and scrambled in search of hiding places, larger pieces shoving aside the smaller in their haste.

"I see you do, too."

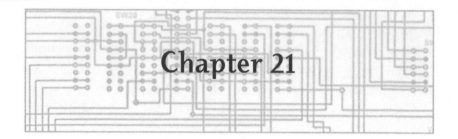

Chapter 21

THE TUNNEL PROVED to have a guidance rail down its center. Given we traveled beneath the collapsed rubble of an entire city—and familiar with aging machines—I distrusted my companions' touching faith in the system. On the other hand, staying down here any longer than we must was worse, so I hung on to the provided strap and endured a speed more suited to flying through open air without protest.

A protest I would have had to *send,* the whine of the ground-cars at full power deafening, let alone the grind of their track beneath. Fortunately there were airshields that rose once we were underway. They wouldn't save us from being crushed, but at least we could breathe.

Andi sat next to me, Mirim on her other side. Deni, who seemed to share her leadership, was in front, beside what would be the driver's seat, if anyone was driving who did breathe. But no, the group installed a boxlike servo in each 'car, revealing yet another chasm between these Clan and the ones I'd known.

The *Fox* was controlled by similar machines, tucked under her consoles and throughout her inner hull. I knew that.

I just didn't quite believe it.

Usually, it didn't matter if I did or not. Morgan had shown me how to communicate with the ship until, on my own, I could input commands with reliable results. Usually. Every so often, I suspected the *Fox* of being deliberately obtuse or worse, jealous of her master's affections and out to get me.

Not a suspicion to express aloud.

To my further dismay, we traveled through not one tunnel, but a series, expanding the possibilities for failure. Widened sections offered choices and, each time, our vehicles reoriented to enter a particular opening without slowing.

I eyed the servo box, guessing its true purpose was to navigate this maze. That should have been reassuring—after all, course disks took the *Fox* from world to world—but I'd no idea where we were going.

The Presence had an opinion. *>Here . . . here . . . here<*

The Presence being either insane or some ghost of the M'hir—or both—I kept ignoring it.

Andi squeezed my hand. *We're almost there.*

I wasn't ashamed to be grateful for her comfort. *What's 'there' like?*

A moment's concentration, then an image filled my mind.

Now I knew why they'd brought rope.

Granted the child viewed the world from a smaller stature; that didn't make her view of a gaping black hole any less terrifying. Keeping that reaction to myself, I did my best to understand what she shared.

No cave-in, this, but a carefully cut opening, with rings embedded around it presumably for the ropes. The nearby wall was intact; the floor clear of debris.

It was still a hole. I wasn't in a hurry to see it for myself, let alone go down it.

Of course, that's when the groundcar began to slow.

"We're here!"

Here, Norval was whole. Lights had flickered on, steadying when we approached. I climbed out of the groundcar, looking around in astonishment. Had I not known there was a mountain of compacted destruction directly overhead, I'd have thought the collapse a lie. Ahead of me stretched unbroken pipe and smooth floors, untouched.

Except for the hole carved in the floor.

"Everyone built on top," Holl informed me with a note of pride. "They depended on the superb construction done by the Second Wave—of alien colonists, that is—to support layer upon layer. It didn't fail."

"Yet," Tle pointed out, ever-cheerful.

I went as close to the hole as I dared and looked down. Sensing my attention, a portlight detached from the group and obligingly plunged into the depths.

To disappear below.

"What's down there?" I asked.

"What came before," Mirim supplied. She set Holl and Lee-sems to attaching the ropes. "You'll see."

Not if they expected me to climb hand-over-hand into what might as well be bottomless. They'd servos, why not anti-grav units?

A needless question, I discovered, for the Clansmen went be-hind a curl of pipe twice my height to return with the next best thing. I'd seen these before. Personal lifts, that attached to a guide rope but provided both security and power.

Tle came to stand with me.

I had to ask. "Why store those here"—I indicated the lifts—"and not the ropes?"

"To keep the more enthused of our group from descending alone."

I raised a brow. "That's happened?"

"Treasure hunting gets in the blood." A smug little smile. "The artifacts on display came from the Sarc tower or were passed through families. We've found more. Many more."

Down a hole. I gazed at her. "You found—or was it Kurr di Sarc?"

"He was first, yes."

Without hesitation or guilt. What was I missing?

Mirim joined us. "Kurr brought his discovery to me, Sira. Whatever he thought of my—our—beliefs, he knew we had the resources and time he didn't. And that we wouldn't squander this precious find for our own gain. He worked with us until—his loss was keenly felt."

By none more than Dorsen, his Chosen, and the child within her, dragged into the M'hir.

I calmed myself. Easy to credit Kurr, with his love for old things, had found allies here. But why here? "What's down there?" I repeated.

"The Origin," Andi exclaimed, then quickly gestured apology to her elders for the interruption, though her eyes shone and I wasn't the only one to find myself smiling at her *EXCITEMENT.*

>*Here*<

The reminder wiped away my smile. "Explain, now," I said tightly. Or I'd leave. Deny the M'hir all they liked, they had to know I could.

"The Origin is where we came into this world. That's where we thought the artifacts would lead us." Mirim gestured to the hole.

Deni spoke up. "Unfortunately, what we've collected had been scattered. By animals. Carelessness. Haste. We haven't found their source. Not yet."

"We all hope this—" my mother touched the box secured to her belt, "—and you, will show us."

"The truth," Tle said fervently.

The truth? The truth, I thought with disgust, was that they'd no more idea how to find the Clan Homeworld than I did.

It had been a mistake to come down here, to let their "treasure hunt" lure me from reality. "You can keep that," I told my mother, nodding at the box and its frightening contents.

I prepared to 'port—

"Sira." Mirim held out her hands as if she'd sensed what I was about to do; perhaps she could. We'd been linked once. "Give us a little time. You've only just come—given us our first taste of hope. Please."

Despite my better judgment, I hesitated.

"The next level down, Speaker," Holl pleaded, coming to stand beside Mirim. "Walk where our ancestors walked. The feeling is indescribable."

Curiosity wasn't a good reason. I'd other duties. *Jason,* I sent. *How is Ruti?*

Better, came his prompt reply. *Haunted, but determined. Jacqui's helped her sleep.*

So they didn't need me. Not right away.

Don't let anything blow up without me, I suggested with *affection.*

Deal. How's the search going?

I looked at the faces anxiously watching mine and sighed. *I'll let you know.*

"The next level," I stipulated. "No deeper." And no animals.

Curiosity being what it was.

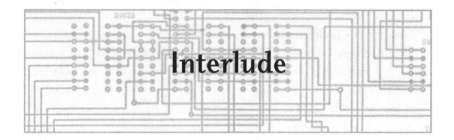

Interlude

FINSDOWN AND IN ONE PIECE. Morgan ran his hand along the corridor wall on his way to the galley. "New parts," he promised the *Fox*. "Newer, anyway." He'd worry about affording them when he'd time.

First things first. Real food, a turn at the fresher—he'd learned not to meet aliens smelling overly Human—and a change of clothing. He stepped into the galley, taking a loud and appreciative sniff. "That's not the ship's cooking."

Ruti smiled. "Some is," she admitted, waving a spoon at the galley's servo panel, admittedly limited in its food fabrication. A budget was a budget. "I added a few touches."

"My thanks for that," Morgan said fervently. Taking the plate she offered, he joined Jacqui and Barac at the table. "We're tucked in," to the Clansman's questioning look. "I expect Sira back sooner than later. Sooner," he complimented, "if she knew about this." He held up a forkful of omelet before tucking it into his mouth. When had he last eaten something not squeezed from a tube?

"Meaning Mirim's group can't help us." Barac pushed his plate away. "Now what?"

Ruti slid into her seat. "We eat," she told him, pushing his plate back.

"I would—" Jacqui began, then blushed. She gestured apology. "Forgive me. I'm—not quite myself. There's an unChosen here. I think. I haven't been this close to one for a long time."

Ruti chewed and swallowed. "Can you control it?"

Green eyes flashed. "I have before."

The urge to offer Choice, that meant. It wasn't Jacqui's fault; as a Chooser, her instinct was to find an unChosen and test him with her Power.

It wouldn't be her fault if she killed him, either. Morgan ate steadily, aware Barac was unsettled, aware they could have a problem. "How can we help?" he asked after a moment.

"It could be a good Joining." A lock of Ruti's hair strayed toward her Chosen. "They happen."

"There are too few of us left." Jacqui regarded her right hand, the hand of Choice. She drew her graceful fingers into a tight fist, lowering it below the table and out of sight. "Don't let me waste him. I would accept stasis."

When a Chooser's mind was put into an unreactive state. It hadn't held for Sira—

"Morgan has the Talent," Barac announced. "You do," when the Human merely stared at him. "You've healed minds. I should know."

Healing wasn't what they discussed. "I haven't the knowledge." Morgan looked straight at Jacqui, who'd gone pale. "Even if I did, we couldn't risk it. Not now. Not with what's happening. You'll have to control yourself."

She nodded, he thought relieved. "I understand. I will," firmly.

"You can't be the only Chooser feeling this way," Ruti said with her practical kindness. She put her hand on Jacqui's. "The baby and I will distract you. And—" a grimace, "—our training."

They're doing well, Barac sent with an undertone of *grim.*

Their would-be attacker being still unknown. One threat at a time, Morgan reminded himself, taking another bite of what was an excellent meal. Sweet. Sour. Salt.

No, he thought, going very still. That *taste.* The Human looked at Barac, saw awareness dawn in his eyes, for this Talent? They shared.

Change.

Barac surged to his feet. Ruti rose with him, taking his arm.

"What is it?" Jacqui demanded. "What's wrong?"

The warnings were never clear, never directed.

One this intense? Never to be ignored.

It hadn't come during landing, nor while the *Fox* had lurched in the hold of the docking tug to her destination within the ship-city. Not even when he'd shut down her engines, wondering if they'd ever start again. Even with repairs.

Thoughts like lightning as he sent an urgent, *Sira?*

Instant *reassurance.* She felt in no danger; her concern was for him.

His stomach sank. Because it was here, whatever it was.

Answering that instinct, Morgan looked to the Clan. "I want you to leave the ship, now."

"Our things—"

Barac and Ruti had only what clothes he and Sira could spare. Jacqui, on the other hand— "Safe here," he lied, in case she delayed.

Jacqui nodded.

"I'll take any suggestions," Barac said quietly. "Nowhere I've been on this planet will be safe."

Morgan put his palm against the Clansman's forehead. *Here.*

Barac blinked at him. "A closet?"

"With a door. You'll be with Mirim's group. You said they were harmless," Morgan reminded him. "Sira's there." In case they weren't.

Sira and the unChosen, no doubt, which couldn't be helped. Jacqui pressed her lips together and didn't object.

"This isn't right." Ruti was shaking her head. "One of us must stay. To 'port you to safety if there's trouble."

When, not if.

The Human gave her his best captain-knows-best smile. "I managed before the Clan. Ask your Chosen." Barac gave a tiny nod in answer to his look. "Go. If you so much as sniff trouble, pop back here. Understood?"

He held that smile until they'd disappeared.

"All right," Morgan said, his voice echoing in the empty galley and down the corridor. "Let's see what's wrong."

The control room first. Nothing new on the coms, other than Port Authority blustering for an inspection. With no listed cargo nor posted intent to load, he'd the right to refuse and had. No need to mention the *Fox* wasn't lifting again any time soon.

This time Morgan secured the door behind him, as he had the galley's. No reason, other than the continued *taste* in his mind and a dislike of surprises.

The engine room was in disarray, tools lying in pools of leaked coolant. He closed that door, too, with a sigh. Sira wasn't going to like the mess.

Or what it meant.

They'd been poor before; being so again was furthest from important right now.

The empty storage hold being still at hard vacuum, he left it. The *Fox* was set. Time to go.

Morgan opened the door to his and Sira's cabin.

To find he wasn't alone after all.

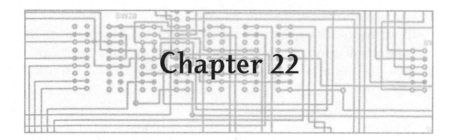

Chapter 22

A S I'D FEARED, Clan weren't the only living things down that hole. Every world had its city-loving vermin. Stonerim III's version, pox, infested the construction that supported the floor: orange reflections marking eyes before they winked away; the scritchscritch of eager claws, the creatures emerging once the portlights passed. I tried not to think of them calculating how best to leap and catch onto my rope.

At least all I had to do was hold on—not even that, according to Tle, the lifts safely secured to my feet—but I declined to experiment. Bad enough the rope vibrated to any movement by those connected below me. I'd thought one or more of the group would stay up top, but they'd all wanted to come.

Expecting me to provide some amazing insight. Well, not me, exactly.

>Here . . . hereherehere<

Excited was it? I held tighter.

The final drop involved the rope swinging, hands grabbing, and a grateful sigh on my part once I stepped on solid ground.

Rather, solid dust.

If not for the ceiling far above, we might have been outside. At night, since darkness was the most obvious feature, but the sense of space was truly impressive. To my right was—it wasn't a wall but a great cliff, its surface slanted and ribbed. A support, I realized, craning my head up, able to hold up a city, or what remained of one.

Hopefully for a good while longer.

Immense pipes rose up along the wall ribs, joined to others that plunged through the floor or flopped along it or looped lazily to the distant ceiling. They were everywhere, as if we stood inside a body among the vessels carrying its blood. White. Red. Black. Some oval, some round.

Between the pipes, paths scuffed the dust, leading from where we stood into the dark, so many and confused I might have stood at the center of a web; Mirim and her followers, exploring without guide or guess. I shivered. "Has anyone been lost?"

"We do use these." Deni smiled as he flipped open a handheld device: a placer, capable of generating a detailed map of anywhere it had been.

More unClan-like tech. I approved.

"Cha broke hers once," Andi said cheerfully, "I found her."

"You did?" That would have taken not only considerable Power, but the M'hir, yet the others nodded with pride.

My puzzlement must have shown, for my mother smiled. "Andi is always aware of the physical locations of others relative to herself, without exposing herself to the Great Darkness. A pre-Stratification Talent, extremely rare in M'hiray."

So rare, I'd never heard of it. What was her range? With such awareness, how had it felt to her when so many winked from existence at once?

Most importantly, could this small child tell me who was left and where they were?

Before I could think of a tactful way to ask, Deni beckoned us to follow. He'd selected a path no more trodden than any of the others.

And no more appealing. Planting my feet, ready to remind them coming down to this level didn't mean I planned to wander it, I found my head turning to look in a different direction, along another of the paths.

>*HERE* . . . *hereherehereherehere*<

Bother. "This way," I told them resignedly, now beyond curious. This voice wanted something; that, I couldn't doubt.

Did what it want have anything to do with my mother's expectations or mine?

Oh, I had doubts aplenty about that.

>*HERE*<

I halted. To my relief, the glow of the portlight we'd left at the hole was still visible.

"Why have we stopped, Speaker?" They'd followed without question till now, but this path and a couple parallel to it kept going into the dark—after a bend to avoid yet another giant pipe. Mirim and the others had explored here, at a guess quite thoroughly, and were right to wonder.

>*HERE*<

"How should I know?" I muttered. Or did I? The *Fox* had compartments that weren't obvious to the casual eye, some with secret mechanisms. Not that we were smugglers but, as Morgan put it, there was fair tax and there was graft and we weren't paying the latter if we could help it.

The floor, I decided. Borrowing Leesems' shovel, I gave the dusty surface a good thump, wincing at the echo. I changed to a quieter tapping.

Catching on, Deni held up a scanner, frowning with concentration. After a moment, he touched my shoulder, aiming the device at a spot on the wall. "I found a control panel, Speaker."

"Excellent," I replied as if I'd expected nothing less and returned the shovel.

The other five Clan stood waiting.

Looking at me. With an inward sigh, I ran my hands over the seamless section of whatever ancient metal had been used to make the wall that Deni claimed held a panel; not that I thought it would do any good. It didn't. This was Morgan's specialty, not mine.

"May I try?"

"Be my guest."

Deni put his hand *through* the wall I'd just touched.

I blinked.

"It senses the intent of a movement," Holl said with pleased surprise.

The Clansman nodded. "Pre-SW. Impressive tech."

And ridiculously old. "How can it still be—" We jumped back together as the section of floor I'd tapped parted with a puff of dust, replaced by a lift platform large enough for a groundcar.

>*Here . . . HERE!*<

I was not, I told it, going anywhere on that.

Before I could argue the point, Andi looked up at the ceiling. "Oh." She smiled cheerfully as she said what chilled the rest of us. "More visitors!"

My mother looked at Deni. "Check."

His Chosen had remained above. With a nod, he half-closed his eyes, then opened them with a startled expression. "Cha says they came out of the storeroom. They're looking for the Speaker."

Everyone turned to me.

As if it was my fault.

"That's the locate you gave him," Barac insisted, not for the first time.

Making it, yes, my fault the three of them had, in fact, made their entrance into the laboratory in such startling fashion. I touched Ruti's hand, then Jacqui's, sending a warm greeting. Back to my cousin. "Did Morgan say—what is it?"

Holl approached before he could answer, gesturing apology. "Mirim would like me to inform you that—"

"She can't talk to me herself?" I sighed. Of course not. My mother's fury at having more Clan arrive in her hitherto-secret laboratory had been exceeded only by her reaction when I'd re appeared a moment later with them here.

As if 'porting through her "Great Darkness" was contagious.

I supposed it might be. Any of her followers might see the ease with which we eliminated distance and begin to rethink their beliefs.

Which wasn't, I told myself, at all my fault. "Leave this to me."

I walked over to where Mirim stood at a distance, surrounded by the rest of her people. There was something to be said for their way of moving from place to place. By the fifth step, I'd let go of both temper and frustration; by the next-to-last, I'd stopped thinking of her and her kind as utter fools. Finally, I stopped in front of her and gestured my own polite apology.

"I meant no disrespect, Mother," I said, projecting *sincerity*. "I was concerned for my close kin and their Birth Watcher."

Andi's eyes widened with surprise.

Mirim's were like ice. "Why are they here?"

I told her the simple truth. "They have nowhere else to go." I raised my hand, indicating the lift in the floor. "And we do."

"All of us?"

>*HERE . . . herehereHERE!!!*<

I could *insist*, like the voice in my head. These might be Mirim's followers, but mine was the greater Power. What choice would she have?

Bowing my head to her, I raised it, hair slipping around my arms, for once in agreement. "With your consent."

She looked taken aback, then perplexed. Hers was a transparent face, unused to secrecy. Like Rael's, I thought, my heart sore. Finally, the tense lines around her mouth and eyes eased. "Kurr's brother," she said then, looking past me to Barac.

Who'd come, with Ruti and Jacqui, to stand behind me. At the acknowledgment, he bowed with impeccable grace. "Barac di Bowart. My Chosen, Ruti di Bowart."

The young Chosen bowed shyly at the introduction. "My mother spoke of your friendship with my great-grandmother. Ne sud Parth?"

Mirim's face lightened further. "We fostered together."

Though echoing their bows, Jacqui hung back. I sensed her *reticence*. Had the collection above overwhelmed her? With her training, the merest glimpse would tell her its significance.

Not that—or not only that, I thought with pity. She'd sense

Asdny—thankfully up in the laboratory—as almost ready for her Choice. Now, here, she'd be aware of Tle, another Chooser and competition she couldn't match. Not in Power, I added to myself. We were more than that.

We had to be. "Jacqui di Mendolar," I introduced.

"I know who she is." Mirim scowled and let a sting of *outrage* through her shields. "Jarad lured this one from her family to be his apprentice. Now he'd use her to get close to my grandchild."

"Jacqui's our Birth Watcher," Ruti countered. Mine, her tone said, and worthy.

A hand rested on Andi's shoulder. "This is Sira's. Leave how you came and take her with you." Mirim brought forth the milky crystal. "We know what to do."

"By bringing who knows what back to life?!" Jacqui pushed by Ruti and Barac to confront my mother, bristling like an outraged Skenkran. "You aren't the only ones who know about Vessels and what's used to fill them. What you're holding is a relic. There's no knowing if it even—"

"Excuse me," I interrupted, I thought with remarkable mildness under the circumstances. "What do you mean, 'back to life'?"

>*here*<

Mirim gave a harsh laugh. "No knowing? You've dusted it enough."

Which wasn't helping. "It's the crystal I took from the Hall of Ancestors," I clarified. "It changed when I 'ported it here." I braced for Jacqui's reaction. She'd been distressed when I'd simply touched the thing and now the treasured scrap had vanished. "It's been—talking."

Jacqui gasped with elation, her hands out and trembling. *Could it be?* She swept a deep bow to the crystal, gesturing the highest level of respect. "The great Naryn di Su'dlaat, Savior of the M'hiray, LIVES AGAIN!"

I found myself sitting rather abruptly on the dusty floor.

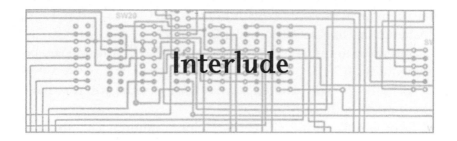

Interlude

"HOW DID YOU GET IN this time?"

Sector Chief Lydis Bowman tapped the side of her snub nose. "I'm good at opening things, Morgan. You know that."

Entering a locked starship—his ship—was as far beyond "good at opening things" as a moon over a planet, but he'd get no better answer. "Glad you aren't in custody."

He saw the wear of evading that custody: hollowed cheeks, an angry new scar-to-be along her blunt jaw, eyes as hard as he'd ever seen. "I'm on a clock," Bowman snapped. "You do realize this is the stupidest place you could have come?"

Morgan took the seat opposite hers at the small table, doing his best to appear calm even as his pulse raced. "You've set a trap here," he guessed. "With yourself as bait."

The corner of her thin lips twitched. "Of course. The rest can mop up; I'm after the Facilitator."

The legendary smuggler king? Morgan added that tidbit to Cartnell and the syndicates and didn't like the result. "Explains how the Assemblers could strike on so many worlds at once."

"Now the Facilitator's cleaning house. Fry's turned up dead. Gayle's missing, likely the same. I imagine the Assemblers will find themselves stranded when all's done, or worse." Bowman paused, fixing her eyes on his. Something stirred in their depths. "How many got away?"

"Not enough," Morgan answered grimly. "Tell me you didn't have a hand in this—that you didn't toss the Clan to Cartnell and his thugs just to catch a smuggler."

She gazed at him, no expression on her face. "And you'd take my word for it."

All in, he thought. There was no other way with Lydis Bowman; there never had been. "Yes."

Gods, a smile, however fleeting. "Good. I didn't. That doesn't absolve me of guilt. I've something they want, something Cartnell—" and the way she said the name sent a shiver down Morgan's back, "—used to set this in motion." Bowman put her noteplas on the table between them, by its shabby appearance quite possibly the one she'd had when they first met and always carried.

She cracked it in half.

A thin white strip dropped free, curled. A dataflash; one use.

It appeared to have her full attention. "Every family has some-one who stumbles, Morgan," Bowman said, almost idly. "Just not mine, you understand. The Clan don't let it happen."

The Clan? Questions crowded his throat. Knowing this woman, Morgan swallowed them and waited.

"I was on what you'd call a different career path when my mother decided the time had come to show me what's on this. Afterward, she sent me to meet the Clan Speaker, Jarad di Sarc. Law enforcement was his idea." Her bark of a laugh. "I believe he expected me to stay a Port Jelly."

"And when you didn't?" Morgan dared ask. "When you kept digging into their business?"

Bowman tapped the table with her scarred finger. "I open things because I don't like mysteries. The Clan were one. Still are. Accepting promotion gave me better tools to pursue my curiosity."

"A curiosity they allowed," he persisted. "Why?" Certain it mattered—that she'd come for this reason.

"Because I'm a Bowman." She readied her thumb over the wisp of white between them. "One chance to know what that means,

Morgan of Karolus." When he didn't reach for it, she shrugged. "Or not. Your call. As it happens, I'm also the last Bowman. There's no one else to show."

Before her thumb could descend, he'd picked up the wisp.

Change. Its taste disguised any the dataflash might have had as Morgan put it under his tongue. As it dissolved, he closed his eyes.

. . . Figures took shape. Human. Two women, two children. Their clothing was of a time before. The one woman had long red hair and held the youngest, a girl. The older child was a boy . . .

The image changed.

. . . A man's face, battered, bruised, with death in his weary eyes. A voice, halting yet determined . . .

"My name is . . . Marcus Bowman . . ."

There was more. By the end, Morgan buried his face in his arms on the table, his mind overflowing with a dead man's pained confession. No, whatever fault this Marcus took for himself wasn't deserved; by his actions, he'd proved himself a decent, good person, a hero.

If only to a few. "Marcus knew the consequences," Morgan said slowly, raising his head. "His reputation would be ruined; his family suffer for it. This was never about the Clan protecting the Bowmans."

"It was about us protecting the Clan." Bowman leaned back, arms across her stomach. "Now you know."

Something was different about her. All at once, he realized what it was. She'd lowered her guard, possibly for the very first time. Morgan wasn't sure if he should be flattered.

Or worried.

He settled for curious. "How's that been?"

"Easier herding toads in spawning season, let me tell you." She grew serious. "We knew their history, how they'd come to make this choice. Turned out they didn't. Something stripped their memories, and they arrived every bit as naive and vulnerable as

Marcus feared and made—let's say the Clan fell in with the wrong people and never looked back." A shrug. "We did what we could. Harder once they scattered, but a Bowman always had the ear of the current Speaker. Sometimes they listened. My time came." Her mouth twisted. "I thought I could change things for the better—that I had."

He'd been part of that change; looking back, knowing what he now did, so much more made sense. Morgan shook off the past. "That's why you came to the *Claws & Jaws* that night. To meet with the new Speaker. Why didn't Sira know about this?"

"Good question." Bowman picked up the halves of her noteplas, snapping them back together. "Each Clan Speaker is made aware of his or her obligation to Marcus' descendants. I'd assumed Sira had been, till Plexis. Afterward?" Her face hardened. "Cartnell'd poisoned most of the Trade Pact against me."

"You thought Sira believed the news reports." Explaining why Bowman hadn't answered her com, why she hadn't contacted the *Fox*. "You thought Sira—the Clan—had abandoned you."

"I had to consider the possibility." Her eyes chilled. "One thing I've learned about today's Clan? They aren't the same as those my grandfather helped."

They'd been, what had Marcus called them? Om'ray, once. The Om'ray of Cersi. Their world had had a name, not just a designation in a file.

Another name, spoken with aching tenderness. Aryl di Sarc. First to 'port through the M'hir; the one who'd gathered those like her, the M'hiray; and the one who'd fought to prevent her world from being destroyed by their very existence.

Whose descendant he feared faced the same terrible choice. "Sira."

"Sira," Bowman repeated, with sincere warmth. "Her, I didn't see coming. You'll tell her." With no doubt. The warmth left her voice. "As for the rest of it—you can guess what Cartnell dangled."

"The Hoveny site." The final piece: how the Clan had appeared in the Trade Pact with such wealth and power, how they'd kept their secrets so long, even why they'd feared Humans.

Anyone with that secret should.

"What of his records? The real ones." Marcus Bowman had feared sending the truth to those in authority; that hadn't meant he'd deserted his work. Part of his dying message had been the codes to retrieve his full reports.

Bowman tilted her stool back, her hand dropping out of sight. "Are you asking if I have the coordinates?" With a casualness that didn't fool him at all.

Morgan kept his hands where she could see them. "I'm asking," he said evenly, "if you still protect the Clan."

Her hand came back to the table; the needler in it safely in standby mode. "Someone better." Bowman gave him a keen look, then nodded. "Someone does. Well enough. There are no records. No coordinates to a secret treasure world. Kari Bowman, my grandmother, destroyed them. She understood how deadly that information could be—to us as well as the Clan. And was right. Look what mere rumor has done. That's everything," she announced firmly. "We're done."

Everything, from Bowman? Morgan frowned at her. "This isn't because you plan to throw your life away, is it? Because if it is, I'll get Terk on the com and lock you in the galley till he gets here."

"Such a suspicious mind." Bowman rose to her feet, pulling on a coat. She tucked the needler in an inner pocket, her noteplas in another. "My plan, Captain Morgan, was to stop by and warn you to get offworld, you and your lady and every other Clan here. Things are, I promise, going to get hot."

Standing, she came barely up to his shoulder, a stern-faced, middle-aged woman who made even a new dress uniform look scruffy. Dressed as she was now, she might have been a street merchant or custodian. Easy to overlook.

Easy to underestimate.

"What?" she snapped, giving her ill-fitting coat a tug.

And by far the most dangerous person he'd ever met.

"Good hunting," Morgan said blandly.

And hoped they'd meet again.

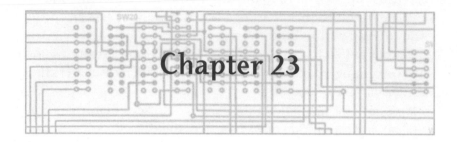

Chapter 23

THE OPEN SPACE AROUND US was a din of voices and their echoes. Loudest was my mother's. "Great? Savior?" Mirim snorted. "As I thought. Jarad's filled your head with his nonsense. My grandmother was bitter and Power-mad!"

As Jacqui responded furiously—something about ignorance and lack of scholarship, which drew more ire from the rest—Ruti offered me her hand. Meeting her earnest gaze, I accepted the help to climb to my feet, unsurprised to receive an urgent warning. *Some believe Perversion is a way for ghosts to be reborn. Don't let them do that to your baby, Sira!*

I squeezed her hand before letting go. However tempted I was to shout at the rest, it wouldn't improve matters. It appeared the more academic Clan were accustomed to arguing, loudly. So instead, to everyone but Andi, I sent what I hadn't yet shared.

My *grief*. At losing so many.

At losing Rael.

Silence fell, utter and immediate. Tle covered her eyes. Ruti pressed herself to Barac's side. He gave me a nod, his face working.

"Remember why we're here," I said very quietly. "The M'hiray will end if we fail." I looked at each in turn, waited for their nods before continuing, "Mother, explain to me how that—" I gestured to the crystal. "—can be of any help."

Jacqui made to speak, then closed her lips.

"This isn't only about our quest," Mirim said, her voice heavy. "If we don't act, you'll both die."

DIE?

Easy, I sent my alarmed Chosen, unsurprised my reactions were bleeding through to him. *Let's hear them out.* "What do you mean, 'cannot be born'?"

"Birth Watcher." Andi looked up; Holl silenced her with a gentle touch.

Jacqui swallowed, but answered. "Babies decide when to be born. Once ready, they loosen their link to their mother, allowing separation. Birth Watchers reassure them this is good and necessary." She paused; I'd the feeling I wasn't going to like what came next.

I was right. "An empty Vessel has no wants. No abilities. No way to let go. If it's not somehow filled before birth, the mother—" Her eyes evaded mine and she dropped her voice to a mutter. "There's no way to be sure. Such a thing hasn't happened since Stratification—"

"And won't happen anytime soon," Tle broke in. "What's urgent is to find the Origin. Naryn di Su'dlaat can tell us the way."

>HERE . . . herehereHERE<

Having a name to go with the eager voice made it no less horrifying. Long-dead relatives belonged that way.

Unless, I conceded reluctantly, they could be of use. "To ask, you need—her—in here." I put a hand on my abdomen. A round of mostly relieved nods. "How is it done?"

A disconcerting pause.

Barac laughed without humor. "There's your answer, Sira."

Wonderful. "Then we'll do this another way." I stepped on the platform. "Coming?"

Sira. Our link tightened until we might have been one mind. I held up a hand to stop the others, taking in what Morgan had to tell me. *Bowman's in action. Keep away from windows and doors. I'm coming to you.*

Do you want me there? Even as I asked, I felt his discomfort. *What's wrong?*

Stay where you are.

"What is it?" Barac, his breath on my cheek. "What's happening?"

"I don't know." *Jason.*

I'm bringing a few things.

As if we packed for a trip incountry. As if everything were fine. As if I believed any of it. *Jason?*

Almost done. Morgan closed off everything but the words. *I'll be there soon.*

Then I lost all but the faintest sense of him.

"Bowman's here and making a move," I told my cousin.

His hand dropped to where I knew he kept his force blade. Ruti stepped close. "What do you want us to do?"

"I—"

All at once, Mirim's face grew ashen and she sank to her knees. As the others exclaimed and hurried to her, I sent, *What is it?*

Her eyes met mine. There was horror in their depths.

"Change!" Barac was leaning on Ruti. "Stronger. Worse than before."

I didn't let myself doubt—or feel. Morgan wanted us away from windows and doors. Some weren't. "Barac, Ruti, Jacqui. Go to the lab. Get everyone down here, along with what supplies you can. 'Port them."

It was a sign of my mother's dismay that she didn't try to argue.

"What will you be doing?" Barac demanded.

"Finding someplace safe," I replied. "Safer. Go. Tle, you, too." She didn't pretend to misunderstand; whatever her group believed about the M'hir, Tle di Parth used it as willingly as any other Clan.

"Wait!" Mirim and her people averted their heads, covering their eyes. Andi did the same.

Ruti gave them a shocked look. *Go,* I sent impatiently.

Once they'd winked out of sight, I stamped on the platform. "Let's go."

Mirim, Deni, and Holl, with Andi, joined me. Leesems nodded to his Chosen. "I'll wait for our sons." He put his hand in the wall to access the panel. "Ready?"

In no way, but I made myself stop thinking of what might be happening above. "Yes."

Making the mistake of focusing instead on how old the platform was, just as it began to drop.

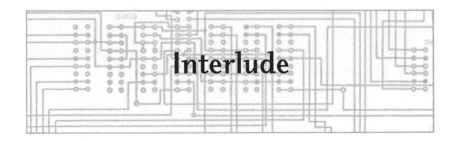

Interlude

"GET OFFWORLD, she says." With the *Silver Fox* grounded? The warning he didn't doubt. The moment the air lock closed behind his unexpected guest, Morgan jogged back to his cabin.

Sira. He felt the reassuring tightness of their mental link. *Bowman's in action. Keep away from windows and doors. I'm coming to you.*

Do you want me there?

About to agree, unease crawled along his nerves.

What's wrong?

What wasn't? He shook his head. *Stay where you are.* The *Fox* was a mess, he told himself.

That wasn't it. Something wasn't right, and he didn't want Sira here.

Stepping into the fresher stall, Morgan turned the top two jets clockwise, then put his shoulder against the tile and pushed. The wall sank inward in a smooth motion, revealing another dark cavity.

Inside was a pack and a loosely tied carryroll. Morgan brought both into the light.

Stripping off his spacer coveralls, he changed into clothes from the pack. A shirt and pants, vest with pockets, a belt. Last, a knee-length supple coat. The vest pockets were already full, as were the compartments of the belt. The coat? Body armor in disguise. Not enough to stop blasterfire.

Enough to let him take a return shot.

Jason?

I'm bringing a few things.

He stretched out the carryroll. Huido had packed it; the weapons were illegal on most worlds. And deadly.

As were these. After Morgan pulled tight the last strap, he tensed his arm and a blade dropped neatly into his palm.

Finished, he threw open the compartments Sira used for her things. There wasn't much room in the pack, but he shoved in what he thought she'd want.

Jason?

Almost done. He kept his shields in place; stuck to words. *I'll be there soon.*

Leaving the cabin, Morgan took the lift back to the air lock. *CHANGE!* The warning came with unrelenting force. The Human staggered to the door, keyed in his code and the relock sequence with a hand that shook.

Planet air rushed in, heavy with scent and humidity. He followed it out, down the ramp, slipping into his role. A trader with an appointment. A busy man.

Until a sound made him turn.

And look back.

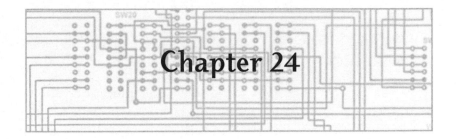

Chapter 24

SUDDENLY, the platform shuddered beneath my feet, as though trying to shake me loose. At the same instant, the ground *groaned*!

Another collapse? An explosion!? I heard commands. Shouts to stop, return the lift. It wasn't my voice.

MORGAN! Nothing. No answer. Even as dust filled my eyes and mouth, I concentrated with desperate speed . . .

. . . finding myself still on the platform.

When I should have been on the *Fox.* Why wasn't I on the *Fox?* I tried again, picturing the control room. *Pushed!*

. . . finding myself still on the platform. I stopped moving, stopped breathing.

Morgan?

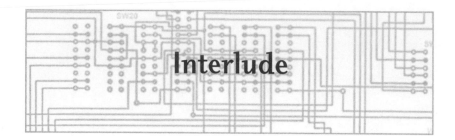

Interlude

BEFORE THE SHOCK of the explosion had died away, Barac scrambled to his feet. Above ground. Distant.

Not distant enough. He concentrated . . .

. . . finding himself still in the laboratory.

He didn't waste a second effort. *MORGAN!*

Nothing.

"What's happened?" Ruti, helping someone else up. The floor was littered with what had been on shelves or countertops, but they'd been lucky. No windows to shatter inward.

Stay where you are. Barac scanned the room. No sign of fire. The roof had held. When they'd first arrived, he'd taken a quick look outside. The waste pile had likely kept the building standing.

The explosion had come from the shipcity.

Bracing himself for the worst, for what it meant if Morgan was lost, he reached for another mind.

Sira?

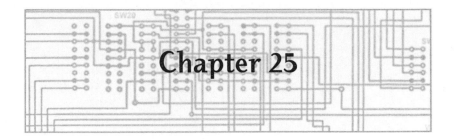

Chapter 25

*S*IRA?

Barac. I sent quick *reassurance*, feeling some of my own. That I lived, meant Morgan did.

For now.

It was the Fox. *Sira. It was the ship.*

I'd known.

I just hadn't dared admit it.

Only one thing mattered now.

MORGAN!

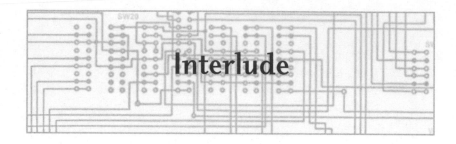

Interlude

MORGAN CRACKED AN EYE, closed it. The ground was still moving—no, he was.

Because he was being carried at a run, held by arms that felt more like steel clamps. "What's—"

There'd been blinding light, percussion. He should be deaf. He should be dead.

MORGAN! Desperate. Urgent.

Alive. They were both alive. Which was wonderful, if unexpected . . .

MORGAN!!!

He managed a faint *here.*

Where? Show me!

Being carried at a run by . . . Morgan rolled his head and looked up.

"Huido?"

An eyestalk bent over the rim of black shell. "You can thank me later."

Morgan?

Something stabbed him. Morgan's muttered protest vanished beneath waves of raw, reviving heat. A stim?

From the feel of it, more than that. He twisted. Another eyestalk joined the first. "Good stuff, isn't it? Want another?"

I'll get back to you.

His heart labored to keep up with the "good stuff." Or was it because the air was full of soot and acrid smoke, so he dared not breathe through his mouth? "S'nuff!" he managed to gasp. "Put me down!"

The Carasian came to a stop and lowered Morgan gently to his feet. The Human reeled, grabbing a large claw to steady himself.

A claw studded with—Morgan touched the nearest metal bit. "Is that my ship?" he asked, aware his calm state wasn't normal.

Eyestalks bent to consider the bit in question. "I think that's from a groundcar," Huido rumbled thoughtfully. "There were a couple parked nearby."

Nearby . . . "Where are we now?" Morgan craned his head around.

An immense pile of waste loomed ahead. Recent slides exposed darker, moister materials, already crawling with pox. The lively stench came close to overpowering the reek of the— "Someone blew up my ship."

"If a starship blew within the shipcity," the Carasian pointed out reasonably, "this would be a crater and we'd be glowing dust."

Morgan knocked on the claw. "Tell me what happened."

Huido sank down until rows of eyes regarded Morgan. "I came too late to do more than pull you out of range. It was set under her fins—" A hum of distress.

"You saved me, old friend," the Human said gently. "Tell me the rest."

A claw snapped. "A ship-eater."

A targeted explosion to crack the hull, followed by a reaction to melt the ship's components from the inside out. Within moments, there'd have been nothing but a puddle of cooling slag. A weapon, Morgan thought numbly, that shouldn't be on this world.

That no one in their right mind would use against a simple trader.

But against the Speaker for the Clan? The most potent of their kind?

"They wanted to kill her," he heard himself say.

"If you don't get out of the way, they still might." A different voice.

Morgan turned to meet his own reflection, then the visor disappeared to reveal a glowering Russell Terk.

The constable wore gray battle armor from head to toe. His partner stood on guard, blaster slung at the ready: the Tolian, P'tr wit 'Whix, identifiable only because feathers protruded out the back of his helmet.

Both were Bowman's.

Who'd tried to warn him, Morgan thought.

"Nice gear," Terk commented.

Huido clattered erect. "The pestilence!"

Morgan followed the claw tip the Carasian thrust past his nose to look up the pile.

Everywhere, pox were scrambling out of the way of a new and moving swarm. Hands and feet and disembodied heads and body parts in contrasting clothing . . .

Assemblers.

After Sira! *Danger!* Morgan sent. *Danger!*

Before he could free a weapon, a hand backed by servo motors clamped irresistibly around his arm. "Watch this."

Terk aimed the stubby rifle he carried vaguely toward the heaving pile, then squeezed. Three innocuous-looking globes shot into the air.

Pop . . . pop . . . pop!

They burst, one after the other, above the slope. Something yellow showered down, adhering to anything alive. Once touched by the mist, pox or Assembler froze in place, limbs or cilia stuck to the waste pile or one another. A chorus of outraged squeals and epithets filled the air.

Within seconds, nothing moved.

Terk holstered his weapon with a satisfied chuckle. "That was fun."

"It is not appropriate to enjoy the apprehension of—"

"You suck the joy right out of the job, 'Whix. Did I ever tell you that?"

Mournfully, "Often, Partner Terk."

Morgan ignored the pair, eyes on a slender figure who'd appeared at the top of the pile, no more than a silhouette against the wall. A force blade ignited, sketching a quick salute, then the figure and blade vanished.

Barac, returning to . . . *Sira,* Morgan sent, fighting back grief.

It was only a ship, with seized engines and worn upholstery. Not to mention the plumbing—

It was the only home he'd ever had or wanted.

Here. With such amazing *warmth* and *love* he took a deep breath, felt the world steady. The ship hadn't been home.

She was.

Sira. The threat's over. Come—

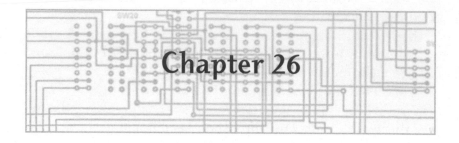

Chapter 26

'PORTING TO MY CHOSEN was as simple as answering my heart's greatest need . . .

. . . which was to be in Morgan's arms. He buried his face in my hair and I held him tight. *Don't. Ever!* I sent, half fierce, half terrified, and making no sense.

He understood. Somehow, he always did. *I will never leave you.* That promise made with all his *strength* surrounded me until I could unlock my grip and step back.

"The ship's gone." Morgan's voice was steady; his blue eyes dark but calm. A bruise covered the side of his face and I guessed there were others I couldn't see, a Carasian in a hurry being less than careful. I was glad of it. Flying debris had buried itself not only in Huido's armor plate but in the pack Morgan wore and one sleeve of his coat.

A pack and coat I'd never seen before, but questions could wait.

However steady and calm my love appeared on the outside, I knew better. *Loss,* heart-deep and weary, filled our link and at that moment I would have given anything to meet those who'd done this.

And drop them in the M'hir.

"Morgan, keep her back!"

The voice was familiar; the note of alarm wasn't. I looked up to find myself standing at the base of the pile I'd climbed mere hours earlier, presently covered in stuck and feebly squirming Assemblers. Two figures in enforcer battle gear stood midway up; if one was Terk, the other, taller one had to be his Tolian partner.

A massive black shape blocked my path even as Morgan took my hand. "I'm not going anywhere," I assured my too-anxious protectors. "Let me see!" I rapped my knuckles on Huido's shell until he shifted to one side. "What is it?"

"Dunno yet," was Terk's unhelpful answer.

'Whix pried something loose. He held it up to a device, then showed Terk the result. Scanners out, the pair searched the slope, a process made easier by how the bodies and waste were glued together, pausing twice more to collect whatever it was before stomping back down to us.

With whatever they'd found now sealed in a bag.

Sira. Barac, the tone sharp. *They're afraid down here. What's going on?*

I'm not sure.

Except that it wasn't good.

Possessing a Talent mattered, but so did Power, the strength to use it. All M'hiray could 'port themselves some distance through the M'hir. Many could 'port objects. Most could bring another person with them, even non-Clan, if in contact; a few didn't need to touch. I'd yet to find my limit; having come all too close on a number of occasions, I wasn't tempted to try.

It was no strain at all to bring Huido, Terk, and 'Whix with me, as well as Morgan.

Our appearance, however, stunned those already below.

Morgan spoke first. "Chit, introductions are in order."

Because manners were a trader's mainstay. I took an easier breath. "Jason Morgan, my Chosen"—though the Clan could *sense* our link—"and lifemate."—for those who couldn't. "Our—" What did I call faceless beings in full battle gear?

Vis-shields dropped. "Constable Russell Terk," the Human announced. "My partner."

"Constable P'tr wit 'Whix, at your service, gentle beings." The Tolian's great emerald eyes rotated, trying to see all the Clan at once. "I regret to bear bad news." He lifted the clear sealed bag, containing what looked like tubes of e-rations.

From the *loathing* Morgan shared with me, they held nothing so benign.

"Found them on three of the Splits we caught outside. Scan flagged aerosol toxin," Terk confirmed, his voice rougher than usual. "Reads noxious to theta-class humanoids, but I'm guessing deadly to—" His gaze fell on the child and he hesitated.

"To Clan," Morgan finished.

A custom poison. For some reason, this didn't appall me as it should; perhaps it was all the ways they'd killed us already.

Mirim shuddered, then gestured gratitude. "Thank you— thank all of you—for preventing a new massacre."

Her group, reunited, stood or sat in the dust around us, three portlights doing little more than creating a circle within the darkness and a glint from shocked eyes.

With our arrival, we numbered sixteen Clan, two Humans, one Tolian, and one unusually quiet Carasian. While Huido disliked entering the M'hir, claiming it affected his performance in the pool, my bringing him here wasn't what subdued him.

Nor had it been the *Fox*. The ship was a thing, no matter how attached Morgan and I had become to it; having saved Morgan, the proud being should have borne himself with deserved and noisy swagger.

I wasn't the only one to pay attention. I caught Morgan's considering glance at his old friend. Something was up.

Something we'd no time for, not now. *Ruti*. I sent, quick and private. *Check on Huido*. She gave a tiny nod and went close to the Carasian, speaking to him in whispers.

Satisfied, I raised my voice. "Where's Bowman?"

Terk hesitated; Morgan made a disapproving sound. The other scowled, then made a show of consulting a dial on his wrist. He pointed into the dark distance. "That way."

"She's wearing a tracer?"

"Look, Morgan—"

He stopped because Morgan had taken hold of his helmet and shoved his face so close their noses almost touched. "Why in Seventeen Hells didn't you stop her?" The shout echoed, and everyone turned to look.

"What's the matter?" I looked at Terk, who could have shaken free with a twitch, and saw the pure misery in his face.

I wasn't the only one. Morgan jerked backward, arms dropping to his sides. "I knew it," he snarled. "It's a setup."

"Only we can follow. The tracer's secure," 'Whix protested.

"I doubt that."

Terk stared at Morgan. After a long moment, he said grudgingly, "Can't say I liked who she picked to implant it."

Bowman using herself as bait was her choice. She could have done so, as far as I was concerned, on another planet. "Why here?"

Morgan's face lost all expression. "Why are we?"

My turn to stare at him, unwilling to believe what he implied. Would Bowman use us as well?

"Here's been her play all along," Terk interjected. "When she heard you'd arrived, the commander pulled us to protect you." His scowl appeared permanent.

The relief of that made my heart pound. "For which we're—"

"Why are we?" Morgan repeated, but in a vastly different tone. He looked around as if paying attention to our surroundings for the first time. "What's here, Sira?"

"Our destiny!" Tle di Parth had a way of appearing in a conversation. "The Origin."

For once, I welcomed her intrusion. Much as I trusted Terk and 'Whix, their first loyalty was elsewhere; knowledge of a Clan Homeworld wasn't something I planned to share. "The Origin's where our kind arrived in Trade Pact space," I explained before either Enforcer could ask. "We're looking for—" My hair lifted.

I knew what was coming.

>*HERE* . . . *hereherehere*< louder than ever.

Morgan started. His eyes found mine. *What was* that?

I confessed to a certain relief, knowing he'd heard it, too. *That, my dear Chosen, was my great-grandmother. According to them.* I tipped my head toward the cluster of Clan near Mirim. Aloud, "Excuse us, everyone. We need to talk."

By the speed with which he took my hand and led me aside, Morgan fully agreed.

But once outside the circle and out of sight?

We needed no words at all.

A stolen moment was all we could afford, as sweet as it was bitter. My hair lingered on Morgan's shoulders, loath to return to mine; our thoughts parted with greater reluctance. Separate again, I drew my hands down his arms and over his torso, offering strength; I was no Healer, to make his wounds vanish. "I don't remember this coat," I whispered, to avoid saying anything about the ship.

"I'd tucked it away. I thought for good." My Human pressed cool lips to my forehead. "It's from Karolus."

Explaining the aged suppleness of what might have been leather on the outside. I supposed, Karolus having been an unending war, it also explained why Morgan felt as though he was encased in metal. Finished with what I could do, I rested my hands on his chest. "We can't stay here."

"No. Not with Bowman on the prowl," he agreed. "We should get everyone somewhere safe—I'll check with Terk to see if the *Conciliator* is in orbit. What is it?"

I was already shaking my head. "Mother's people aren't like other Clan. Barac and the others had trouble holding them together long enough to 'port down here. They're afraid. They've refused to use the M'hir most, maybe all of their lives." I sighed. "The irony is they aren't wrong. Emotion unsettles the M'hir; panic turns it deadly."

>*Here . . . hereherehere*<

"Maybe we should listen to your great-grandmother."

He was amused. Morgan, I thought darkly, sometimes lacked

reasonable caution. "We don't know what's down there." Or what spoke, for that matter.

"Let's ask," he told me, with that grimly cheerful note signifying he'd a plan.

I followed him back to the others; a few were glad to see us, the rest gave me a worried look or hid their faces.

Terk muttered under his breath when he saw us coming. In the shadows, the heavy-set constable was more machine than man, the dull gray of his suit stealing what light reached them, while Morgan, in pack and coat, might have stepped from an earlier age.

>Here<

Had the voice? Not for the first time I questioned whose it was. Naryn? Perhaps. I'd learned to distrust the obvious.

"Whatever it is, Morgan," Terk rumbled, "the answer's no."

"He's miffed Bowman's given him guard duty," Morgan assured me. "Terk, my friend. We've decided to move these people to a less exposed position. What's on your scanners?" He pointed to the floor.

"Our equipment cannot offer reliable indications below this level," 'Whix volunteered. Soft down fluttered over his throat implant as he spoke, his beaked mouthparts unsuited to verbal communication. "It's puzzling."

"Only to a featherhead." Terk's armor scraped the wall as he shifted to lean more comfortably. "That'd be why the chief picked this hole for her game. You'll see. As for moving, we're waiting on an all clear." A grin. "Port Jellies are mopping up what we left for them. They'll send an escort to take everyone home or wherever."

My relief faded when I saw Morgan's face. "Call them," my Human said. "Be sure."

Terk's grin disappeared. "We can't break com silence for—" Perhaps he saw what I did because he changed his mind and snapped, " 'Whix, check what's going on upstairs."

The other nodded and walked a few steps away, raising his scanner.

Morgan's head lifted, his eyes looking elsewhere for the

briefest instant. Blood going cold, I turned to see Barac do the same.

And my mother. The three with the Talent to *taste* change.

The Tolian turned. "Partner Terk. I read approaching life-forms. Multiple."

"There. I told you. Should be the Jel—" Terk stopped, eyes dropping to his own wrist. "What the hells? It's the chief. Coming first, and fast."

He activated his vis-shield, a weapon dropping to his hand and coming live with a throaty whine. 'Whix did the same. They positioned themselves facing where we'd first entered.

"Move!" Morgan ordered, herding everyone back behind those with weapons.

All at once, Terk wheeled on a booted heel, the arm with the scanner rising to point my way.

A pox ran out from between their feet, straight at me, its fur flattened along its thin sides. Before I could dodge, it scurried past to where the others waited.

"Catch it!"

Huido's snap caught a tuft of fur. Andi threw herself on the creature. It squirmed free and clawed partway up a pipe, pausing to pant and spit at us before disappearing behind it and beyond reach.

Terk pounded by in hot pursuit. He staggered to a stop by the pipe, his arm swinging down, then over and up. "That—" the rest was impressively incoherent.

Morgan leaned over, hands on his knees.

Laughing.

"What's going on?" I demanded.

My Human pointed after the pox. "That—that—was Bowman."

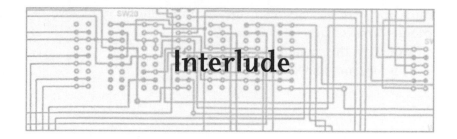

Interlude

"WHAT DO YOU MEAN? How can it be? Fifty of her?" Gayle tossed the now-useless device aside. "Clever." According to it, all fifty traces were not only Bowman, but moving, rapidly, in different directions. Ah, well. She hadn't expected an easy chase.

A hand picked up the scanner. Another poked at it. A third snapped fingers and grumbled. Soon the scanner was buried beneath aggravated body parts.

The Assembler named Magpie Louli ignored her kin. "What do we do now? How do we find her? Find the Hoveny?"

The creature tended to ramble under stress. Gayle amused herself by imagining how it would sound if she dropped it in a pot of hot acid. Still, they were allies.

For now.

"We're close," she pointed out. "You wanted the Clan, didn't you?" An instant's consultation of another, more ordinary scanner made her smile. "Even closer."

"Nice of them to come below." Louli smiled and tapped her hat. "I've a surprise, I do. Kills best in confined spaces."

"We're in those spaces," Gayle reminded the Assembler.

"That's the trick. The secret. The best!" Louli tapped her hat again. "This was made for them, not you, not us. Not field tested, not yet." Her smile widened, her semblance of teeth gleaming. "Soon!"

"Don't rush matters." Gayle's smile was cold. "Let Bowman think she's eluded me. Two can set traps. She'll try to save her friends. That's when we end this."

And when the screaming would start.

This job, she'd have done for free.

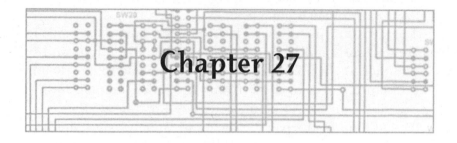

Chapter 27

"SHE MUST HAVE TAGGED every pox down here," Terk announced. He'd gone from swearing at Bowman to admiration. "Don't ask me how."

I looked at Morgan, reading the set of his mouth. "What is it?"

"If she's sprung her trap," he said grimly, "we don't want to be here."

>*Here . . . HEREHERE*<

Something did. I looked a question.

Morgan nodded and looked at the constable. "Well?"

"You want assurances, I can't give them," the constable replied glumly. "Something here—" an oversized boot thumped the floor, sending up dust, "—is mucking the readout. All I can tell's there's more alive that way than this." A nod to the dark. "And it's coming."

"The hole we made from the transit level is in that direction." They'd asked who knew the underground. To no surprise, it was Deni sud Kessa'at. "The tunnel we used from our building is one of several still open from the surface."

"This keeps getting better," Terk complained.

"But the hole is the only opening to this level," Mirim said.

"That you've found," Morgan countered.

Deni's lips tightened. "I assure you if there were another access, we'd know. I mapped this area thoroughly."

Terk's smile was without humor. "Then the hole's where we'll be. What about you? Sure about this lift?"

I grimaced. "It's worked once."

"And better than waiting here."

I agreed with my Chosen. This hollow empty space, with its shadowed curls and slanted walls, felt more like a trap with us inside than shelter. The constables kept looking longingly into the distance, eager to move. "Who'll operate the controls?" I asked, doing my best to sound as calm as the others.

Huido went to the panel, moving his spongy legs daintily to avoid the worst of the dust; Carasians disliked grit in their joints. He inserted a handling claw and the platform rose from the floor. "I will stand guard," he rumbled.

Ruti stormed up to the Carasian, her hands on her hips. "It's not your fault your wives said those things. They were only telling us the truth."

A claw snapped, the bell tone one of deep distress. "What they said sent you and your baby into danger, Ruti. I bear—"

"Bear it later, my brother. This isn't the time," Morgan said, coming over. "Barac, you and Deni go down first. Let us know if it's safe."

The former scout nodded, though clearly unhappy to be parted from his Chosen. For her part, Ruti hadn't taken her worried gaze from Huido.

The lift sank below the floor, taking the two and a portlight with it. My heart hammered in my chest as we waited.

Then, *Clear below. Send everyone down.*

"The rest can go," I said aloud, for those unable to *hear* Barac's report. While Morgan and Mirim sorted out the order of who went next, I went over to Ruti, still standing before the larger alien.

"What's the matter?"

She sent instead of speaking. *He's blaming himself for what his wives told us.*

Had Huido's coming to help us meant—*Are they in danger?*

No. Of course not. But I'm afraid this big idiot is looking to prove himself. I don't like it.

Neither did I. *Let us deal with him.*

With a final look at Huido, Ruti turned away, her shoulders hunched. Jacqui came and led her back to the others.

"I do not wish you gone," Huido said, as miserably as I'd ever heard him sound. "I do not believe something terrible will happen if you stay."

"We know that." Morgan frowned, coming close.

I rested my hand on the Carasian's great claw. Eyestalks bent to regard me. "Your wives could be right about us," I said quietly. "About the Clan."

An unhappy rumble. "They think all the time." As though that explained everything. "I never know what they'll say next. Magnificent creatures. I asked if they could have warned you." A clanking sigh. "They said time was a matter of philosophy and unreliable."

"We wouldn't have listened," I replied, falling silent. Not before tragedy opened our eyes. Not before we were reduced to grasping at myths to survive.

"Time to head down," Terk told us. "You're the last."

Morgan turned to face the constable. "I hold you responsible for him."

Terk eyed the giant being. Multiple eyestalks regarded him back. "Fine," the Human said. "But I'm not tipping next time we're in the restaurant."

"You call what you leave a tip?" Huido complained.

"Time," Morgan hinted.

"Mind you don't cross Bowman's plan," Terk advised gruffly. "Move out, 'Whix." Vis-shields activated, the two strode away into the dark, leaving a solitary portlight hovering beside Huido.

The rest of the Clan were below; I *reached*, feeling their anxiety. Stepping on the platform, I told myself this was a good idea.

I just didn't believe it.

About to join me, Morgan hesitated. His eyes went back to Huido. *Go,* I sent.

With a nod, he strode over to the Carasian and reached up. Eyestalks parted, needle-tips emerging to take his hand in a gentle grip. They stood like that, unmoving, long enough for me to imagine sounds in the dark.

The Carasian let go.

Morgan jumped lightly on the platform, taking my hand.

He didn't look back.

From beneath, the platform wasn't hidden, resembling a large door in the ceiling. The control panel was, but Deni had found it. That was reassuring.

That we stood in a narrow corridor, floored in hard-packed dirt, wasn't. "Are we at the bottom?" I asked, picturing the ruin of Norval overhead.

"Not necessarily." The Clansman had been on his knees, holding a device over the dirt. He stood. "There could be any number of layers below us. All I can say is this one was once exposed to open air."

The air entering my lungs was reasonably fresh, if you liked musty. Not musty, I decided, ancient. Mirim and her group—and Jacqui—could hardly contain their excitement.

Poor Ruti looked about to be sick.

Deni sent his portlights a short distance in either direction, revealing a sharp bend in one, a stretch of sameness in the other, without an opening or door in sight. "Which way, Speaker?" he asked, recalling them so we might have stood in a long narrow room.

>Here<

I ignored the voice and gave him a hopefully confident smile. "Neither. We're staying here till it's safe to leave."

"But we're so close!" Tle looked around for support. "We may never be back here again."

Not if I had anything to say about it, I thought, but kept that to myself.

Almost. The corner of Morgan's mouth quirked. "Make yourselves as comfortable as you can," he suggested. "We may be here a while."

Having no water and only whatever Morgan had tucked in his pack for food, his "while" couldn't be for long, but no one protested. The two Choosers, Tle and Jacqui, sat as far apart as the light allowed. Asdny, on the cusp of unChosen and so of intimate interest, wisely stayed with his brother and their parents. The rest settled in a tight group, by their furtive touches busily consulting one another.

I let them. Better preoccupied than wondering if Terk and 'Whix had found allies or enemies—if Huido was bored or defending our retreat with all his might . . .

I still taste *it. Change. Something's coming.*

"Not helping," I murmured, leaning my shoulder into Morgan's. I drew up my knees and rested my chin on top.

My hair took advantage to explore the edge of his collar and slip across his cheek.

Witchling. With *heat.*

Now, that was helping, I thought smugly.

"Daughter."

Mirim's voice made me jump. I'd been paying too much attention to my Chosen, I thought guiltily. "Yes?"

"Morgan," Mirim acknowledged. "I wanted to—"

"Stop!" Feet pounded down the corridor; Jacqui on the run. "Not like this. Stop!"

My mother's face changed. "We're out of time." She lunged before I knew what she intended, could believe what she intended.

Mirim pushed aside my knees, driving her fist into my abdomen.

Not her fist.

>HEREHEREHEREHEREHERE!<

The crystal.

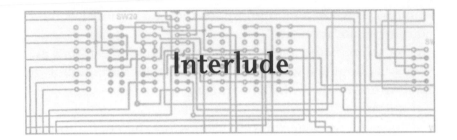

Interlude

TWO ROPES HUNG within the round opening. Neither was in use. Assemblers clung to the edge of the cut, scrabbled down until they ran out of holds, then dropped, landing with a thud and bounce.

Having retracted any features or digits first.

Others tossed down weapons, until the rain of rotund bodies and lethal hardware littered the floor below. Nothing stayed where it landed more than an instant.

The hunt was on.

Not that another hunt hadn't already begun.

A distance away, Ambridge Gayle eased between a curve and wall, careful not to snag so much as a thread of her scan-proof garment. Magpie Louli did the same, if less gracefully, having been apprised of the penalty for exposure.

Gayle raised a hand, then lowered it. Together, they sank behind the curve, holding still as two armored figures ran past. Only when certain the Enforcers were preoccupied with the new arrivals did she signal to move again.

She could have dealt with the constables, but the delay would have been tiresome.

The freshest tracks in the dust confirmed the initial scans. "This way," she whispered.

Then tracks proved unnecessary. A portlight hovered over an empty section of floor, the dust disturbed in a rectangular pattern. A lift.

When the Assembler would have continued, Gayle stopped her. She crouched on her heels, looking away from the light, waiting.

Something glistened. A reflection. Small and, yes, there were more, in a row about the height of an adult Human from the floor.

A Carasian. Gayle smiled. Thought to hide, did he? To ambush the unsuspecting.

A shame that was her specialty.

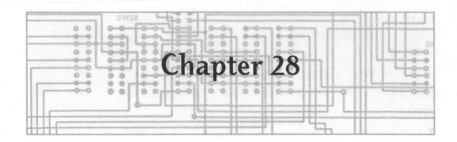

Chapter 28

THE CRYSTAL . . .
   So this is what it's like.

Around me were sounds, angry and alarmed. I lay on my side in the dirt, folded around my middle, and understood only the voice within. *What are you?*

A promise. Something *wry*. *Or a threat. It will depend.*

On what?

My Chosen vied for my attention. I felt his hands, his frantic *touch,* as though they were distant, unimportant things. They were.

He's strong.

So was—she, I realized. The *life* within me was no longer empty, but brimming with intelligence and . . .

Power. I felt her explore our link, follow it through to my thoughts, going deeper and deeper. I could have stopped her.

It didn't occur to me.

Whoever this was, whatever this was, I sensed no ill will or malice. As she learned me, I learned her. *Great-grandmother,* I acknowledged with a startling rush of *connection.*

Not Naryn.

This was she who had given birth to Taisal, mother of my father.

Aryl di Sarc.

Reborn.

SIRA!

I blinked at Morgan. "It's all right."

Eyes ablaze, his mouth soundlessly repeated the words as if he couldn't believe what I'd said.

"It is," I insisted, pushing till he eased his grip. There'd be bruises, I judged, feeling some responsibility for that. Only one way to fix this. I dropped my shields. "I'd like you to meet—"

Morgan didn't wait, plunging into my consciousness with deadly force.

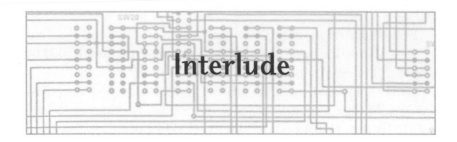

Interlude

HE TORE THE CRYSTAL from Sira's hands, flung it against stone, heard it fracture. Others grabbed the one who'd done this, pulled her away.

For her safety.

Sira gasped, convulsed. He took her in his arms, called to her, sent with all his might. As well throw himself against stone. Her mind was impenetrable. Morgan buried his face in her too-limp hair, tried to think what to do. There were Clan with knowledge, here. Clan who might help. His rational mind accepted the possibility.

His heart rejected it. They'd done this. They couldn't be trusted.

Movement.

Her hair first. It quivered gently back to life, rose in a silken cloud. He drew back as Sira's eyes opened.

She blinked at him. "It's all right."

How could she—?

"It is," gently but as if annoyed. She pushed and Morgan realized how tightly he'd held her.

He eased his grip, readied himself. Whatever had been in the crystal, he'd kill it.

His moment came! Sira dropped her shields. "I'd like you to meet—"

Morgan drove himself along their link, heedless of any pain caused or felt. Prepared himself for a quick and deadly strike, to rid them of . . .

Hello.

. . . he found himself standing in the M'hir.

To him, it appeared an unending beach, the sand beneath his feet at times soft and warm, at times rock hard or frozen. The ocean to either side could be wild and storm-chased, clouds filling the sky close enough to sweep him away, or filled with swells.

Or rarely, as now, smooth as glass, reflecting a featureless darkness.

He wasn't alone.

A figure stood a few steps away, bathed in golden light.

The light came from behind him. He didn't need to turn to know it was Sira, her glow resting like dawn on what wasn't a horizon but closer, the warmth of their link the greatest of joys.

And vulnerability. *You're not a baby,* he accused, facing the intruder, holding *disgust* between them like a blade.

No faces here, nothing real. Still, *amusement* trickled between them. *I am. And am not. You are not M'hiray.*

It wasn't a question, but he found himself answering. *I'm Human. Ah.*

Was that *satisfaction*? Morgan took a step, or tried. The M'hir refused to accommodate and held him in place. *You're dead.*

I am, she agreed. *And am not. It was my choice not to follow my beloved.*

Such *loss* filled him with those words that only the warmth at his back kept Morgan from fleeing the M'hir and that dreadful voice. *How could you?* he/Sira asked, united in their horror. *Why would you?*

Sadness became *resolve*. As it strengthened, as it grew into something deeper and primal, waves pounded against the shore and sand shifted under Morgan's feet.

To protect those who stayed behind.

He fell, her *WILL* a wave cresting high above him, blotting out the false sky and all light.

THE M'HIRAY MUST NOT RETURN.

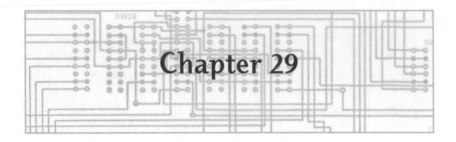

Chapter 29

. . . MUST NOT RETURN. The words chilled me to my core as I held Morgan together, fighting to pull us both from the M'hir.

Watchers tumbled close, one or millions, I couldn't tell. They *howled* and *gibbered* . . .

The M'hir *ROARED* in answer.

Whether protest or agreement, didn't matter. Chaos clawed at my edges, at my desperate hold on my love, frayed what sanity I'd left.

HERE. Not a hand, but I could grip it. That grip drew me, drew us, to a point of calm amid madness.

Before the strength giving us this chance failed, I *PULLED* . . .

. . . and was free.

Back underground, in the corridor beneath Norval. Morgan and I helped each other stand. The rest were on their feet, as much distance between us as the light allowed. *Aryl,* I sent.

Here. Faint but strong.

There was wonder in my Human's eyes. "Aryl. Aryl di Sarc. Alive—in there."

"There" being within my body, in the growing baby I hadn't expected or wanted. "She saved us," I told him, because it was true and I was grateful.

Yet was against us. Her words couldn't be mistaken: The M'hiray must not return. Aryl, who felt so *right* and *good* inside me, had torn her Choice and life apart to keep us from going home.

I had to know why.

"Aryl?" Mirim looked dazed. "Your father's grandmother?"

"She was no one," Deni objected. "Insignificant."

Tle nodded. "You must be wrong. The Presence must be the great Naryn!"

Naryn saw no danger in our path. A sending powerful enough that all heard. *She believed in it. I did not. Do not.*

Andi sidled close. "I feel her." She gazed up at me. "Aren't you happy? You're safe now. Aryl will let herself be born."

The earnest little Birth Watcher deserved a smile. When I couldn't, Morgan crouched to face her. "Give her a little time," he suggested.

Time we didn't have. Making a decision, I turned from the two of them and walked away, stopping when I could no longer see where to step. *Aryl.*

I sensed her attention.

She'd learned what I was; what I offered now was what had happened to bring us together, memories I relived with her, each pain and grief as fresh as if new.

Some always fall, she told me when I was done, her mind voice remote.

We are what you and the others began, I countered. But she couldn't know that, could she?

Hadn't Bowman told Morgan the M'hiray had forgotten?

Aryl—

Portlights flew past my head, their glow abruptly reduced to thin beams focused on the floor.

Out of sight. Quickly!

Before I could react to the warning, Morgan had my arm and was pulling me forward. I heard the others hurrying behind. "The platform's coming down," he whispered urgently. "Run!"

What if it were Huido or Terk coming to tell us it was safe? I swallowed any protest. Morgan said run.

I ran.

Beyond the bend the walls remained stone, the floor dirt, but
now that floor sloped slightly downward and rubble narrowed
the walkable path. I wasn't the only one to stumble; Morgan put
his arm around me and kept me on my feet till I steadied.

I glimpsed rust-coated wires atop the rubble along one side,
strung between antique lights. Beams had been used to shore up
a ceiling that I was frankly amazed hadn't collapsed with the rest
of the city.

The others crowded behind. I heard the snap and hiss of
Barac's force blade. Of no use against poison, I'd have told him,
but I was too busy watching where I stepped.

A hand brushed mine. *The Origin.* It was Mirim. *Ask her where it
is!*

I snatched my hand away. At least they knew better than to
speak out loud.

I knew better than to ask.

We hadn't gone far—not far enough—when we caught up to
the portlights, dancing haplessly in front of a wall.

A wall of loose stone and twisted metal.

And bone.

Without a word, Deni called back the portlights, tethering
them to his belt.

"We can't go back," Morgan said, no longer bothering to whisper.

He believed whomever followed would have bioscanners.
They'd already know where we were and who. And that we'd
stopped.

"What do we do?" I asked.

"We could start digging—" Arla suggested, picking up a loose
rock.

"With what?" his brother scoffed, but quietly.

Morgan didn't hesitate. *Get them out of here, Sira. Anywhere out of
sight.*

You, too, I ordered.

Always, with a heart-stopping look from those intense blue eyes.

Hold on, I told them, reaching out my hands. I'd take no chances. Andi took the left, Morgan the right. One by one, the others followed until we were linked, flesh-to-flesh. Their *fear* passed from mind-to-mind; I dared not share it. I felt *courage,* too, and *despair.* Emotions that would protect us in the M'hir, I encouraged, what would fight against us, I did my best to soothe.

When I judged they were as ready as they could be, I shared the locate for where I'd first arrived.

Where the Clan had once called home.

The Towers of Lynn. They're gone? Aryl's *dismay* rocked us all.

Not there, the others wailed at me, *terror* rising to fill every mind. *Not there!*

Morgan squeezed my hand. "Sira, go!"

If not there—where would be safe? Where would be safe? I couldn't think, couldn't picture anywhere . . .

Here . . .

An image formed in my mind, a place I'd never been.

Somewhere safe.

I *pushed . . .*

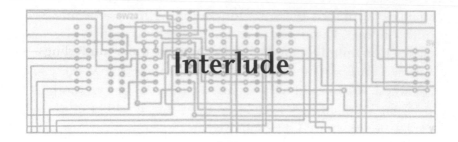

Interlude

"WHERE ARE THEY?" Louli patted the dusty stone as if feeling for a doorknob. "They were warned. They got away!" A wail.

Gayle chuckled. "Forget the Clan. Look." Bone protruded from the rubble. Bone and tools and weapons. "We're not the first."

"So. So?"

"Why did they come down here?" She gauged the rock fall and removed her wide belt. "For something worth having on the other side."

"Hoveny somethings?" The Assembler licked her lips. A hand twitched in time with a foot.

"It's worth a look." Worth more than that, if she was right. Gayle spread her belt on the floor, selecting components with care.

Fingers drummed on the hat.

She ignored it, snicking piece to piece.

Fingers drummed louder.

She glared at the Assembler. "Are you trying to blow us up?"

"It'll be soon," Louli informed her in a strange voice, fingers twitching near the hat, but no longer drumming. "Could be now."

Implying a part of the plan she hadn't been told. Perturbed,

Gayle lifted her hands and gave the Assembler her full attention. "What are you talking about?"

"We kill them all. Be finished and done." A finger tapped; the other hand grabbed the offending one and yanked it down. "You'll see. Time to dance, then."

She'd ice for blood, her underlings—former underlings—used to boast. Right now Gayle wished she had. "The Clan are scattered, in hiding," she said, keeping it light, dismissive. "It would take thousands—"

"We are billions!" the mad thing boasted. "Manouya has taken us everywhere Clan could be. This—" Both hands seized the hat and yanked it free with a *pop*, tipping it to show her the vials inside "—is species-specific-perfect. Clan breathe a trace, they die." The hat went back on the head. "We dance!"

And then what?

Don't ask, Gayle told herself.

And then what?

Don't even think the question.

She grunted something noncommittal at the Assembler and went back to work, unsurprised her hands wanted to shake.

There'd better be wealth beyond the wall. Was or wasn't, after this she'd end the little monster and head for the Fringe.

Before the Assemblers and that cursed Brill chose the next species to eradicate.

Cartnell'd been played. They all had.

This had never been about just the Clan.

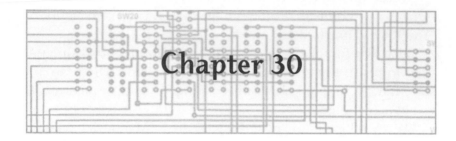

Chapter 30

I found myself upon a stage.

...And not alone. I took a startled breath, hearing others do the same. Hands fell away from each other.

Mirim and her group stared at one another in disbelief. At me. At where we were.

Deni roused, sending the portlights up and out.

They illuminated wide ledges of stone, like a three-sided stair, rising to where carvings met a domed roof. The carvings were huge. From where I stood, they appeared as figures, alien and interested, their bodies supporting the roof, the shadowed pits of their eyes gazing down in curiosity.

Down to where we stood, on what was—had been, I corrected—a stage.

"The Buried Theater." Deni stretched out his arms. "It has to be! We've found it. The Origin!" The word echoed, louder then softer.

Here. Aryl's mind voice was peaceful, almost content. *This is the safe place.*

Seeing Morgan's growing frown, I wasn't so sure.

"They 'ported once," Barac argued. "They can do it again."

I sighed. "They won't."

"We can't stay here," Ruti said. "Tell them."

Safe.

Aryl's strange contentment crept through me; I fought it, knowing none of my own. "Tell them?" I shook my head. "I'd have more luck with a sex-crazed Retian."

To Mirim and her group, this lost alien space was the culmination of years of searching. While I couldn't tell what they expected to happen, it was apparent they were ready for when it did. They bustled everywhere, taking measurements and readings, kicking up dust old before Norval had been built.

Some not so old. Morgan had done his own quick survey, returning with well-preserved bags and packs that even I recognized as ours. Pre-Stratification. We'd arrived here.

Why, none of us knew.

This was his place.

I sat straighter. Maybe one of us did. *Aryl, what do you mean?*

Marcus. This was his place. He gave it to us, to keep us safe.

"Marcus," I echoed aloud. "Aryl says this was his place."

Morgan knelt beside me. "I thought she couldn't remember."

Of course I remember.

"She hears, too," I said dryly. *Aryl,* I sent, choosing my words with care. *What do you remember of Marcus Bowman?*

I would never forget him. Fragments appeared: glimpses of a face, the sound of a voice, without words. With it all, a sense of *caring*.

But nothing more.

Morgan touched a finger to my belt, lifted an eloquent eyebrow.

That meant should he share with her?

We had to try something. About to agree, I saw Mirim coming toward me. "Later," I said.

Not realizing we were out of time.

Not understanding why my mother, who'd never been clumsy, was stumbling forward, her hands outreached.

Not until I'd leaped to meet her, taken cold hands in mine, looked into eyes abrim with despair—

—before they went blank.

Morgan helped hold her. I threw myself into the M'hir without thinking . . .

Stop!

. . . without thinking what would await me there.

. . . for the M'hir was full of the dead, their Joinings become chains, dragging down through infinite darkness.

I couldn't begin to find her.

Voices. Shouts. Sobs. Screams.

I couldn't begin to hear her.

So many. Were any left alive?

I couldn't begin to know.

A Watcher wrapped around me, cold and smothering. I struggled to escape.

Speaker.

It spoke?

Speaker. Summon.

Words that burned. That challenged.

Sira—call them. Save them.

He'd followed me here? My Chosen, in this nightmare? *NO!* The Watcher was a weight, on what I was, who I was, what I could do. I fought it, to *move,* to save him.

To be denied. *Save them, chit.* With familiar pride.

Misplaced. I couldn't begin to—

I have him. Aryl. Answer them.

The Watcher squeezed. Or had another added its embrace? *Speaker. Summon.*

Fine time to start communicating, I railed to myself.

Even as I did what they wanted, and *reached* for what lived with everything I had.

Here . . . I showed them, feeling Morgan's powerful echo . . . *Here!*

HERE! Aryl, with joy.

HEREHEREHERE shrieked the Watchers.

Or was it the dead?

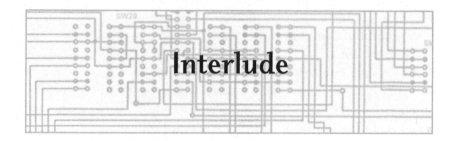

Interlude

COUNTING STEPS, Gayle came to a halt. "This'll do."

The Assembler kept edging back. "Further is better. Much better."

"Fine," she said mildly. "If you want me to go through first—"

Louli stopped where she was. "We go together. Partners!"

What "partner" meant to a being composed of spare bits, Gayle didn't bother to ask or guess. The creature would be out of her life soon. "We won't have long," she warned, growing cheerful. "The blast will draw attention. Grab what you can carry."

She crouched, the Assembler mimicking her position, and snugged the glove on her right hand. A press of thumb to palm would set off the explosives.

The glove had other interesting attributes, one in particular Gayle looked forward to showing her "partner" once they were safely away.

With Hoveny treasure. The words sang in the blood. If she was wrong, or even if she wasn't, there remained the extra pleasing chance the blast would kill some or all of the Clan—after all, they could well be on the other side of the rock.

With her treasure. With enough? Hells, forget escaping to the Fringe. She'd let Louli into her head. Best plan was to free herself of obligation to Manouya by paying for his assassination.

On second thought, why pay someone else to kill him?

Better yet, complete her mission, get paid, then kill him. In good time. She smiled. "Bowman next." Her thumb began to move.

Something cold pressed under her ear.

"Why not first?"

Gayle spun out from under, reaching for—

A heavy boot pinned her arm as a scarred hand twisted the needler free. "You're done, Ambridge Gayle," a calm voice told her. "Stay together, you." This directed at Louli.

Who crouched meekly to retrieve the arm and hand already on the ground. The reason for her obedience? A second needler with a tip set for wide dispersal, held in a too-easy grip.

Or was it something in those very cold, very sharp eyes watching them both?

"I've an offer, one time, for either of you," Sector Chief Lydis Bowman announced almost gently. "Give up the Facilitator and walk out of here. Or don't."

"Liar, liar." Louli snapped her arm in place and waved it recklessly. "You're an Enforcer. You don't murder beings."

"That's what you do," Bowman said, her tone making it abundantly clear how much she regretted having an "offer" to make. "I'm not an Enforcer today," she finished.

No, she was a Port Jelly, her uniform so faded and worn the elbows were about to split, with a noteplas and stylo, of all things, sticking from a tattered pocket. Passed over for promotion, that uniform said, loud and clear. Bitter and waiting to retire with a nothing pension.

A smuggler would know this Jelly would take a credit to look the other way.

And be wrong.

The disguise might have slipped Bowman past other eyes; not hers. "How did you get by me?" Gayle demanded.

"I'm good at opening things." Bowman's boot applied more pressure. "Especially when I'm aggravated. I don't like being used. You were, too, of course. Cartnell told you I could find the Clan's planet, didn't he?"

The amusement in her voice made Gayle want to find the Board Member and take him to pieces. Slowly.

"Time's up." The boot eased a fraction, though not nearly enough to allow movement. "I want the Facilitator. Ident, location. Who deals?" A tiny smile. "Who dies?"

Louli began spewing words like vomit. Gayle didn't bother to listen. Let the rest of the Trade Pact deal with Assembler ambition.

If Bowman had no worthwhile secrets, time was up indeed.

She moved her thumb the rest of the way.

BOOM!

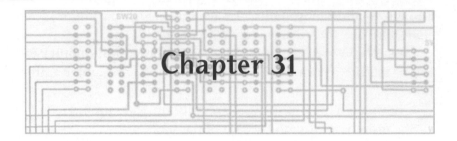

Chapter 31

... **I** came back to myself. Eyes closed, I savored the comfort of another heart beating in perfect harmony with mine. No, make that two, one smaller.

Disconcerted, I opened my eyes. Morgan rubbed noses, then kissed me soundly. "You did it," he assured me when we broke for air.

Exactly what, I wondered, had I done? Escaped the M'hir, yes. With Morgan, even better.

Then I saw his face, and the lines etched above the yellowing bruise, and how his eyes simply waited.

For me to remember the rest.

I closed mine again, briefly, soaking in his *love* and strength, then gave a tiny nod. When we stepped apart, my fingers twined through his, my hair around his arm, for we weren't alone.

An audience again filled the ledges of the Buried Theater, an audience once more of M'hiray.

Most stood. Most, like Morgan and I, held to one another: Chosen to Chosen. Parents to children. The few who stood alone must, being Choosers and dangerous to the unChosen—

Who clung to whomever they could.

Deni's lips moved. Counting. For myself, I couldn't bear to have a number. It wouldn't be enough. I'd been too slow, our enemy too quick, we'd—

Sira. Show them to me.

Aryl, calmer than I, as she'd been in the M'hir; stronger, in the purity of her *will.* Was it her age, for she was far from young, or the almost-death she'd endured for so long? Regardless, I was grateful. I *shared* what I saw with her, gazing up.

Only to fix my eyes in horror at a commotion near the top row. A Clansman slid to the floor, bounced down a ledge before anyone could reach him, landed lifeless.

I'd missed his Chosen. I'd missed—

It's every grief you've known, Aryl told me, with such understanding I shuddered. *Every grief you know will come. Some will always fall. You saved the rest.*

—missed . . . unbearable, that *grief.* To avoid more, I dropped my eyes to the stage.

There they were.

Mirim. Orry, her oldest friend. They'd left the bodies here, arranged side-by-side. They'd been friends since my birth—

A birth leading to this. I bent under the guilt, wondered numbly why I didn't break.

Jarad and Mies had disagreed with their Chosen, had sought safety elsewhere.

Had died first.

Who would be next—who?

Sira . . . Fingers tightened around mine. Not in protest; a support as tangible as Aryl's.

It was hard to breathe . . . why was it hard to breathe? I'd learned to think as a spacer. "We're running out of air!"

"No, Sira," Morgan said gently. "The walls are cracked. There's a good flow."

Cracked walls. All of us within cracked walls—

"It's held up this long," my Human soothed, ever-pragmatic. "But we—they—can't stay here."

Another small and hopeless cry. Another Lost. I stared up as the rest drew closer together, still silent, still trusting.

Me. A mistake, bringing them here, all in one place.

It had been that, or lose them. I forced aside my emotions, burying them deep. Mistakes, I reminded myself, could be fixed.

These lives, I would save. "We won't," I assured Morgan, my voice firm again. "What are our options?"

He'd waited for me to ask, I could tell, having trusted me not to wallow in what couldn't be changed. He rhymed off possibilities: out in the open, where there should be the rule of law and not wicked things. I found myself only half listening.

Hearing Aryl instead.

We are the same, you and I. You Joined with a Human to find a future for our kind. I let myself be put into that stone because when I thought of that future, I tasted *such change coming as might destroy worlds. I believed the M'hiray would be its cause. Believed I dared not let our kind return whence we'd come, or all of us would be lost. My Chosen, my Enris, believed in me and let me go.*

For naught. With terrible *remorse.*

Now I see the truth. That the change I foretold was this—that we would fall without the chance to fight back, that we would end, without knowing our beginning.

Sira, my heart-kin. I would save the M'hiray if I could—

"Jason," I whispered, tears slipping down my cheeks. "Aryl's going to help—"

—but I can't guide us home. I don't remember it. I'm of no use.

She'd saved us twice already. I shouldn't have expected more; I'd only hoped for it, like all those looking down at us.

You've helped—are helping. We'll do this together, I told her. Aloud, to Morgan, "Too many are already exhausted." He wouldn't like this; I didn't either, but the other choices were out of reach. "They can manage Deneb." Where we'd have to hope the syndicates had been cleared out by the Enforcers. I went on stubbornly, "There's a passage from this world through the M'hir." A passage forged, in part, by my father's fostering.

"Sira—"

BOOM!

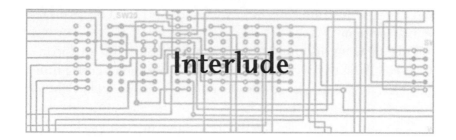

Interlude

THE EXPLOSION RINGING IN HIS EARS, Morgan checked Sira with a quick touch before jumping to his feet to scan the theater for its source. There. He'd marked the caved-in entrance with Barac as a weak point. It hadn't reopened, not quite. Another round would do it, given how much rock had shifted.

Dust dimmed the portlights, already hardly sufficient for so large a space; the last of the debris, pebbles, and sand rained down with light pings and clatters. Hearing nothing else, Morgan looked up.

None of the Clan had moved. None of them spoke or had cried out. Coated in dust, in their silent ranks they were like the carvings around the ceiling.

Inscrutable.

Inhuman.

The awareness crawled under his skin, prickling; sweat beaded his forehead, running down his chest and back.

A child coughed. A father bent to soothe her.

People, Morgan admonished himself, the spell broken. He wiped his face, smearing dust, then shoved his fingers through his hair and gave it a sharp tug. People who were telepaths, born to it like a Human to speaking aloud. Not hearing them react didn't mean they hadn't.

If he dared open his mind to them, he'd *hear*—but he didn't. Couldn't, was the truth. If it made him a coward, so be it, but he'd felt enough pain through Sira to last a lifetime, and that didn't begin to count his own. Any more and he'd be of no use to her or them.

One of Sira's mother's group approached: Holl di Licor, a Clan Healer as well as scientist. When she hesitated, giving him a troubled look, Morgan gestured to her to continue. Had she felt him? He tightened his shields.

"Captain, do you have medical supplies in your pack? We've some with cuts that need treatment."

Sira, who'd joined them, sent, *I've asked her to save her strength for what's to come.*

When things were worse, that meant. Humbling, the courage of his Chosen; Morgan took comfort from it as they all did. "I've a kit," he told the Healer, shrugging the bag from his shoulders. Like old times, that weight on his back, this coat. Not that they'd been good times, but what he carried had saved his life before now. "Here you are."

"Thank you." She gestured gratitude to him, then turned to gesture again, deep and profound, to Sira. "My family and I never thought to reach the Origin, Speaker. We never dreamed to fulfill our destiny. You've done that for us."

Morgan understood the faint desperation to Sira's "I'm glad for you." The last thing she'd want was to be thanked for the present situation.

When Holl left to join the others moving among the newcomers, he put a hand under his Chosen's elbow and leaned close. "Anywhere but Deneb, chit. Trust me."

"I do." Soft warm strands followed the line of his jaw, toyed for an instant with the beginnings of bristle. Sira pulled her hair back with a muttered, "I'm trying to think," that wasn't for him, so he carefully didn't smile.

She chewed on a full lip, her gray eyes clouded. "It's the strongest passage from here."

Which mattered to how they traveled. He understood that, even as he marshaled arguments against it. Syndicates had ruled Deneb since settlement; the world's wealth merely a crust of civility over one of the most corrupt governments Humans could claim. He'd never trusted the *Fox* there. To take the Clan's refugees—?

"Surely it's not the only passage."

Her nose wrinkled at him; the sign of impending disagreement. All at once her face changed. "No. No, it wouldn't be. Not from here." She looked around as if seeing where they were for the first time. "We're at the Origin. Jason. We're at the Origin!"

"And now that's a good thing?" he ventured, mystified but willing.

"If I'm right, it is, but—" Sira searched his face. "I haven't asked you," she said, her voice inexpressibly tender. "Not once. About any of this. About—trying to leave the Trade Pact."

"Because you know better," Morgan replied airily, hands cupping her cheeks. "If you're talking about a new world to explore, chit, as I recall you owe me one."

At last, there it was. The smile that never failed to send his heart and spirit into orbit. He bent to kiss the tip of her nose, refusing doubt. *Together, always.*

Hair billowed around them as her lips found his. *Always.*

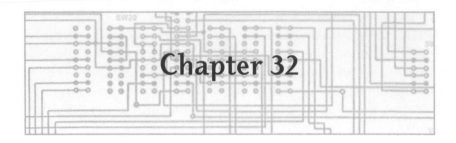

Chapter 32

I GATHERED MY PEOPLE on the stage. We'd gleaned everything useful from the leavings of our ancestors: bags, a few blades, an ax, bits of leather still intact; adding those to what little we had. The husks of our dead we sent into the M'hir to be with their Chosen. Now, it was our turn.

Morgan joined me, having left a note beneath a fragment of stone. I didn't ask who it was for or what he'd written. We were, if I was right, leaving. A farewell was only fitting.

As was this.

"The Origin," I told them, "isn't a place." I let my awareness expand into the M'hir, not moving, simply touching.

Here.

When 'porting, wounded and at the edge of my own existence and limit of Power, I'd glimpsed a distant brilliance, a path once so wide and great its passing burned an echo in the M'hir itself.

Here, Aryl agreed.

Before me, before us, was its end. A true passage—no, I corrected, the Passage—etched by the migration of the M'hiray from their world to this one. End? Beginning.

I *showed* the others, waited patiently, sensed them find it, feel it; learn how it extended *away* from here—and only here—reaching out and beyond.

What do we do? they asked then, wary. Weary. Afraid.

We follow.

Like children learning to 'port, we would have to trust those who'd gone before and left us their road. Let ourselves go . . .

And believe in a destination.

A home.

Home. More than a word. *HOME!* A desire, a need, feeding from one to them all, echoed within me and without.

Now, I thought. Across this gulf of time and stars, to whatever awaited.

I took my Chosen's hand, looked deep into extraordinary blue eyes that trusted, that loved, that dared all things—

and *leaped* . . .

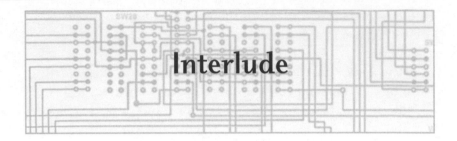

Interlude

A SOLITARY FIGURE limped across the stage, a small hand-light carving a path through blasted rubble and forgotten things. Her footsteps echoed from unseen walls and a distant ceiling. The air tasted of dust and endings.

The light caught the edge of what was neither dust nor stone.

She crouched, freeing a piece of plas. Turned it over with gloved fingers. Read its message.

"Interesting."

She folded the piece once, twice, again, before tucking it in a pocket.

Then stood and walked out.

Leaving darkness behind.

M'hiray and Their Associates, in Trade Pact Space

M'HIRAY

Andi sud Prendolat, child, Birth Watcher, M'hir Denouncer

Arla di Licor, brother of Asdny, M'hir Denouncer

Asdny di Licor, brother of Arla, M'hir Denouncer

Barac di Bowart, Chosen of Ruti, former First Scout, cousin of Sira

Cela di Teerac, Chosen of Sey, Council Member

Cha sud Kessa'at, Chosen of Deni, M'hir Denouncer

Crisac di Friesnen, Chosen of Serena, Council Member

Dasimar sud Annk, Chosen of Pella

Degal di Sawnda'at, Chosen of Signy, Council Member

Deni sud Kessa'at, Chosen of Cha, M'hir Denouncer

Erad di Caraat, Chosen of Wys, father of Yihtor, of Acranam

Holl di Licor, Chosen of Leesems, mother of Arla and Asdny, M'hir Denouncer

Inva di Lorimar, Chosen of Bryk, Council Member

Jacqui di Mendolar, Chooser, Birth Watcher, Curator in the Hall of Ancestors

Janac di Paniccia, Chosen of Rael

Jarad di Sarc, Chosen of Mirim, father of Sira, Rael, and Pella, former Speaker/Council Member

Josa sud Prendolat, Chosen of Nik, father of Andi, M'hir Denouncer

Kyr di Mendolar, Chosen of Zidi, grandfather of Jacqui, Council Member

Leesems di Licor, Chosen of Holl, father of Arla and Asdny, M'hir Denouncer

Mies di Friesnen, Chosen of Orry

Mirim sud Teerac, Chosen of Jarad, mother of Sira, Rael, and Pella, Leader of M'hir Denouncers

Ne sud Parth, Chosen of Ubanar, great-grandmother of Ruti

Nik sud Prendolat, Chosen of Josa, mother of Andi, M'hir Denouncer

Orry di Friesnen, Chosen of Mies, M'hir Denouncer

Pella di Sarc, Chosen of Dasimar, Sira's sister

Prega di Su'dlaat, Chosen of Neri, Council Member

Rael di Sarc, Chosen of Janac, Sira's sister

Ruti di Bowart, Chosen of Barac, formerly of Acranam.

Signy di Sawnda'at, Chosen of Degal

Sira di Sarc (Sira Morgan), Chosen of Jason Morgan, crew of *Silver Fox*, Speaker and Council Member, sister to Rael and Pella

Tle di Parth, Chooser, Council Member, M'hir Denouncer (on occasion)

Wys di Caraat, Chosen of Erad, mother of Yihtor, of Acranam

OTHER SPECIES

Ambridge Gayle, Human, Syndicate Head, Deneb Grays

Hom M'Tisri, Vilix, host of *Claws & Jaws*

Huido Maarmatoo'kk, Carasian, owner of the *Claws & Jaws*

Jason Morgan, Human, Chosen of Sira, Trader, Captain of the *Silver Fox*

Janina Michi, Human, Senior Partner in Deneb firm, *Michi and Booth, Consultants*

Lydis Bowman, Human, Sector Chief, Trade Pact Enforcers

Manouya, Brill, smuggler known as the Facilitator

P'tr wit 'Whix, Tolian, Constable, Trade Pact Enforcer

Russell Terk, Human, Constable, Trade Pact Enforcer

Sansom Fry, Human, Syndicate Head, Deneb Blues

Sarran Coffler, Human, Trade Pact Scientist

Tayno Boormataa'kk, Carasian, nephew of Huido

Theo Schrivens Cartnell, Human, Trade Pact Board Member

Cersi

Prelude

THE WIND SWEPT DOWN the mountainside. The M'hir, it was called, and had its beginnings half a continent away. Wet once, dry now, it seared as it passed. What needed moisture hid itself in the lee of stone or clung to the edges of fitful streams. What hunted rolled itself tight and waited.

Others took to the sky, for the M'hir was both opportunity and signal. The great rastis unfolded their tops, exposing seed pods ripe and ready to open. Touched by the hot, dry wind, they cracked, their interiors uncurling in spirals of red, wings unfolding.

As happened every M'hir, Sona Om'ray took to the canopy, hooks ready.

For the M'hir would end, and only while it blew could they harvest what they needed to survive.

To endure.

For whatever time they had left.

Chapter 33

*S*LIDING . . .
. . . Childhood it was, this letting go, this heedless joy . . .

Which part of me resisted. The Passage didn't carry us; we fell, and I'd never cared for that sensation.

But we—for I was far from alone—were going somewhere, and the M'hir couldn't stop us. Falling was less than effortless; it would have taken more Power than I had or all of us together to leave the Passage now . . .

Which part of me distrusted. The Passage didn't lead us; we were taken, and I'd never allowed another force to rule me.

But the weakened and weak could use their strength to hold together and stay safe . . .

So I let myself fall and be taken.

Though I did wonder what Morgan thought of it all . . .

Interlude

*...D*ROWNING... His mind knew he didn't breathe, didn't need to breathe.

What the mind knew was irrelevant. There was no doubt he was *drowning*...

... what had been a beach underfoot having vanished, replaced by this ferocious boiling sea. Did it sweep him anywhere or merely suck him down? No way to know ...

No way to stop ...

... *drowning* ...

Something *bumped* him. Curiosity or hunger? His mind knew—too well—there was *life* in the M'hir.

Bad enough he was drowning—he'd no intention of being eaten at the same time. He twisted and kicked, or whatever was the equivalent here. Nothing.

Bump.

He welcomed anger, it being safer than fear, and kicked again and again.

Nothing. He'd driven it off, he thought, wondering why he felt afraid again.

Then ...

That crawling sensation, as if something *watched*, as if he'd gained the attention of what he most certainly didn't want to meet.

... *drowning*...

Might be best.

Chapter 34

...H*ERE.*

As my heart resumed beating, I strained to see anything but darkness. Had we left the M'hir or been immured there?

"Lights, anyone?" Nothing could have sounded so good at that moment as Morgan's voice, however breathless.

I heard a fumbling.

And there was light, low and gentle, increasing as our eyes adjusted. I'd not appreciated portlights before, I told myself, feasting my eyes on my Chosen's dear face. "We did it!" I noticed the pallor of his skin, a wildness in his eyes. "Are you all right?"

Morgan's lips quirked, and the wildness faded. "Glad to be breathing. Now," he went on briskly, "comes the fun part. Where are we?"

"Where are we?" echoed someone else, with a hint of fear.

I looked for myself, more than curious.

Whatever I'd imagined, it wasn't this. Scraps of leather, gourds and knives, rope—nothing brought to the Trade Pact by our ancestors belonged in this place. The gleaming floor beneath our feet appeared metal yet felt resilient. It was banded with color, the result as beautiful as it was unlike anything I'd seen before.

The portlight strengthened and rose, revealing more floor and more bands, drew walls from the shadows.

"How big is this—?"

"Big," I heard someone answer.

Finally, the dimensions of the chamber became clear. Five times our number could have stood here. Longer than it was wide, the room curved along what must be an outer wall, for our images reflected in tall arched windows. Black, beyond those windows, as though the M'hir pressed against them.

"Night," Morgan pronounced it. Whatever had unsettled him having passed, he looked around with the same avid curiosity we all shared.

No furnishings, but close at hand a narrow raised dais was centered on the windowed wall. It looked oddly familiar.

"For a Council," Tle exclaimed. I supposed she was disappointed there were no chairs.

Instead, something unfamiliar stood in the center of the dais. The tall smooth pillar was featureless and green—no, more than green. At a closer look, I could see other darker hues in it, as if pieces of a—

"A machine," Morgan stated. "It fits in this slot." He pointed to the base, then indicated similar shapes marked by texture in the surface of the dais. "There's room for more." He looked around the chamber. "Nothing that's here."

Here being . . . where?

Near the pillar's base lay an incongruous pile of brown fabric, like laundry forgotten. Morgan glanced at me and I nodded gratefully, unwilling to touch whatever it was. Whoever it had been.

My Human stepped up on the dais, the soft tread of his boots and their echo the only sounds other than our breathing. We were drawn closer, those with burdens setting them down. He went on his heels by the pile, moved some of it gently. "Just clothing," he reassured. "A robe. Shoes. This." Morgan stood, holding up a pendant and chain. He came back, bringing it to me. "Can you tell if this is Om'ray?" he asked.

Because we didn't know, yet, where we were.

What did he find?

I shared what I was seeing with Aryl. The pendant was pale and green, its shape organic, like a hardened leaf. There were markings etched into it, more like lettering than adornment. There was a chain, implying it went around a neck; the links were sturdy rather than delicate.

There's something—I've seen this, Aryl said suddenly. *But where?*

That was promising. I held out my hand.

"Heavier than it looks," Morgan advised, letting the pendant and chain drop onto my palm.

The lights went out.

Interlude

THE INSTANT THE NECKLACE touched Sira's palm she went limp. Morgan hurriedly caught her in his arms, easing her down. "Sira!" He *reached* along their link.

She was—she was asleep. That was all.

He looked around to find the rest of the Clan lying where they'd collapsed. Their faces were peaceful, despite their awkward positions. Asleep, too, he guessed, swallowing hard. Why?

The pendant seemed harmless. Nonetheless, he gave it a grim look and left it where it had fallen. "Witchling, wake up," he coaxed, running his fingers through her hair. The locks quivered, recognizing his touch, then went still.

Honest exhaustion, after the Passage and all else, he'd have understood. This was something else. Making Sira as comfortable as he could on the floor, Morgan went from one Clan to another to do the same. With each, he tried a gentle shake, then *reached*. All were in a deep sleep. To his dismay, none had shields in place, leaving their minds open and vulnerable.

Not everyone was a stranger. He was overjoyed to find Enora and Agem; less happy to see Degal di Sawnda'at, head of the old Council and among those made uncomfortable by a Human's presence.

He'd leave the past behind if they would.

None were aware of him. Eyes roved behind closed lids, flitting side-to-side in uncanny unison. They dreamed; he couldn't help but believe it was the same dream.

A quick perimeter check revealed one door, its ornate panels immovable by any means at his disposal. Cupping his hands, Morgan pressed his face to one of the windows. Outside wasn't completely dark. A faint glow marked what might be a rail running parallel to where he stood.

He spotted a cluster of lights, barely discernible in the distance. Another building? The edge of a city?

Sunrise would tell him. About to turn away, a flicker of light caught his eye, closer.

Too close! He spun around.

The pillar was no longer green and black. Brighter areas moved and pulsed beneath its surface. Fleeting sparks coursed from side to side, met to spawn more, then faded.

The machine was alive.

Morgan grabbed his scanner from his pack, running the device up and down the pillar, walking around to cover every part of it. Unknown material. Unknown energy source. Unknown function.

How wonderfully useless.

He hurried between sleepers to reach Sira, setting the scanner to its med function. Her vitals were normal, for Clan, something his inner sense had told him. He'd have been entranced by readings for the baby within, if not for it being Sira's great-grandmother.

Who'd been here before. In fact, she'd left with the M'hiray from this very spot, if he understood anything about passages through the M'hir. Morgan stared at the pillar. Had their return activated it? Was this unnatural sleep some sort of defense?

He'd ask Aryl, but as far as he could tell, she slept, too.

His thoughts darkened. He could destroy the machine easily enough; hadn't he brought what he'd need? No. Not unless it became clear they were being harmed. Nothing for it, the Human decided with a heavy sigh, but to wait—wait and hope they'd wake up and be able to explain.

Morgan positioned himself to face the door, using his

belongings to support his back, his chest and arms to cradle the one who mattered most. It was night. There'd be day.

He'd stood watch before, if not like this.

Surely there'd be day.

Before dawn, Morgan came alert. Some of the M'hiray were stirring, their sounds reassuringly peaceful. At last. He checked Sira. Was she waking? He couldn't tell.

One change. The junction between the walls and ceiling had begun to glow. The illumination grew in intensity until the chamber might have been bathed in sunlight. Because the sleepers were waking?

Or, Morgan tensed, had someone noticed their presence?

It seemed so. After a moment, a section of wall farther down spun silently on its length, letting through a single figure. She uttered an astonished, "~@#~%. ^!^~!" before noticing him.

And heading his way.

The long knife—make that two knives—belted at her side gave him pause, but she didn't draw them as she approached. Leaving his own weapons where they were, Morgan slowly spread his arms in greeting. "Hello."

Her limbs were tightly wrapped in white gauze; more hung in folds around her neck as if otherwise used to cover her head. Her thigh-length leather jerkin was coated with overlapped black scales. Clothed to a purpose, though for what he couldn't imagine. She moved with light, fluid steps. Morgan modified his opinion: a hunter.

Chosen, by the net confining her black hair and the proud set to her scarred, still lovely face. Her skin was dappled, not as a Human would bear freckles, but with splashes of rich brown on cream. Unusual coloring. He'd seen it before only in the di Licor brothers and their mother, though much fainter.

Making this the Clan Homeworld, if he'd doubted, and this his first Om'ray. Success of a sort. Maybe she'd know why the new arrivals slept. *Sira. We've company.* She snored gently, oblivious.

The Om'ray spoke another string of fluid, incomprehensible syllables. Her tone, if related at all to the Clan he knew, expressed extreme displeasure. The comlink in his pack had a translate function, the best he could afford—there being those species who'd switch to their language at the trade table to discuss an offer, thinking to be secretive—but it required data; at minimum, a dictionary with rudimentary grammar. A dictionary Marcus Bowman probably had included in the records his daughter had destroyed.

Another planet. He had to deal on this one.

Where the situation couldn't look good to a stranger, Morgan admitted. Helpless recumbent forms, himself the only one awake and armed. If she could tell he wasn't Clan, well, that made it worse, didn't it?

More words, slow and menacing.

An ultimatum.

When you don't know what not to say, went the Trader axiom, say nothing at all. Or—on impulse, Morgan made the Clan gesture of greeting between equals.

Her eyes widened, then narrowed in consideration. She spoke again.

A lock of hair wound around Morgan's thigh; Sira, beginning to stir.

Faster than he'd have thought possible, the longer knife was out. The Om'ray indicated Sira with it, swept to include the others, then aimed the tip at him, flicking the blade to one side.

Move away, that meant.

Morgan shook his head. If Om'ray couldn't *sense* their connection as Chosen, maybe a demonstration? He brought his hand to his leg. Strands of living red-gold slipped up and around his wrist.

Sira wasn't the only one rousing, he saw with relief.

The knife tip came nearer. Businesslike weapon, that, with a well-maintained edge, runnels for blood, and a small, very nasty hook at the end. "^!^~!"

"~@#~%?" The same language from—Morgan tore his eyes from the very nasty hook to stare down at his Chosen. Though Sira's eyes were barely open, she was struggling to her feet, as were others. "~@#~%?" she repeated sternly, looking at the Om'ray as he helped her.

He sighed with relief. There'd been no hint his Clan spoke anything other than Comspeak, the common tongue of the Trade Pact, and how Sira understood this new language was something he'd love to discuss—later. First, "How do you feel—"

The edge he'd admired rested against his throat. Morgan ignored it. *Sira. Talk to me.*

~%. ^.

Their link was intact. The feel of her voice in his mind hadn't changed. Why couldn't he understand her? He saw her pick up the pendant. *SIRA!*

She grimaced at him. @`^^~%&/^

Again, he *heard* only gibberish. "Sira. Please. Speak to me."

Sira took a step back, her wide gray eyes filling with unease.

At him?

The edge pressed. Morgan tensed, ready to rid himself of the distraction, then felt the *snap* of a powerful connection through the M'hir.

Human Chosen. It was Aryl. *What's happened?*

As quickly as he could, he supplied the image of the pillar machine and the roomful of Clan overcome by sleep, then, *Sira's talking like an Om'ray.* A word Aryl didn't remember. He sent the image of the Clanswoman holding a knife to his throat. *This is an Om'ray. We've arrived to an interesting welcome.*

Other Clan—M'hiray—were rising. They spoke to one another instead of sending, which normally he'd have taken for a sign they felt safe enough to be social except that they, too, were speaking in the other tongue.

Sleepteach. Feeling his surprise, Aryl seemed almost amused. *We lived on your worlds, Human. I don't remember this machine, but perhaps it's the Om'ray version, to help us settle in our new home.*

It made sense. Of course it did. He should have been the one to see it. They'd dreamed to learn, though Human-made sleepteach only added to what was already learned. Certainly being fluent in the local tongue would be a huge advantage to newcomers.

As not having a clue put him at considerable disadvantage. *Do you understand it?* he asked her hopefully.

No. With a touch of asperity. *This body has but begun to grow. I'm fixed within its potential.*

Information Morgan tucked away to consider later. When he didn't have a knife at his throat.

And Sira looking at him so strangely.

What need for words between them? Confident, he sought their link, poured *love* and his own *concern* along it.

Only to slam into a shield stronger than anything she'd put between them before.

The closed panel door opened and more Om'ray poured into the chamber. Two grabbed his arms, and Morgan let them, too stunned to fight.

Watching Sira turn away, as if she no longer cared.

Chapter 35

THERE WERE TASKS TO DO, proper for an Om'ray and important. I was the Keeper, responsible for . . .

. . . *itch*. Why did I hold the Speaker's pendant in my hand? I was the Keeper, my role to stay in the Cloisters and guide the dreams of . . .

. . . *itch*. My Clan—Sona—who stood around me, well rested, their eager faces filled with smiles. Why was I confused? I'd guided their dreaming and mine. We were ready to start our new lives.

. . . *itch*. Here? Not here, of course. I shook my head at the thought. Only myself, Sona's Adepts, and those needing their care—the aged or Lost—would spend our lives within the Cloisters.

. . . Cloisters? Another *itch*. It was becoming maddening, this *prickle* of discomfort as I thought of what was right and proper, such as proper homes for the rest of my people. We, the Sona, would build them, with help from our new neighbors. We'd brought everything necessary.

None of which were here, I realized with sudden alarm, seeing only a few scattered bags. "Where are the materials we brought with us?"

The stranger Om'ray who'd greeted me eyed the pendant in

my hands, then replied diffidently. "Speaker, we do not understand. What materials?"

I had no idea. *Itch.* I wasn't the Speaker. *Who is our Speaker?* I sent urgently, to my people.

Confusion.

You hold the pendant, said one. *You must be.* Dozens more added their *agreement.* From others, *Weren't you?* as if they struggled to remember . . .

. . . *itch.* Had I been? Having no better answer, I accepted their will and put the chain over my head, settling the pendant between my breasts where it could stay until Council chose . . .

. . . *itch.* We had no Council. How could we have no Council?

"Speaker?" the stranger Om'ray prompted.

"What we need for our homes," I said, fighting a growing uncertainty. "We brought—there should be materials."

"I assure you, nothing's been removed—"

"Stop this nonsense, Destin." Another stranger Om'ray spoke to the first, pointedly ignoring me, his voice low and angry. "I tell you these are Vyna. Thieves—"

"With children? Impossible!" countered this Destin, as quietly but without the anger. To me, "Forgive my impertinence, Speaker, but who are you?"

I drew myself up. "Someone with the right to be here which you do not have. Let us leave—" for a couple had taken up posts at the doors, refusing to let any of us out, "—and begin our homes!"

Something I'd said startled them speechless. The angry one recovered first. "It's truenight. Whatever you intend must wait for dawn." As if I was a fool.

"Then we will wait," I replied evenly.

"Should we remove the *not-real?*" asked a third.

The term meant nothing to me, but I knew who they meant. I *felt* what wasn't my name, but me, an identification more complete than any word could be. *Itch.*

Trying for my attention. Again.

My eyes went to the dais and the "not-real." They'd stripped him of coat and shirt. Discovering the clever knives strapped to his arms, they'd searched the rest of him thoroughly, taking both footwear and belt, then tied his arms and pushed him to sit by the now-quiescent Maker. This, instead of killing him, because we were Joined.

Despite it being impossible. I was Om'ray. He was not.

"Leave him here." *Itch.*

The link, however implausible, was there. I could touch it; I would not. The link made us a pairing. Another proved us fertile. Sona's Birth Watcher had fussed over me upon waking, assuring me the baby was in fine health.

Despite being impossible, too.

Itch.

I tore my eyes from him. "While we wait, please bring us food and drink. My people have traveled a great distance."

The strangers exchanged troubled glances. "Surely you brought your own, Speaker," the first ventured. "Better than we could offer."

Itch.

"There wasn't time," I replied. My people shifted closer, smiles fading.

"Something for the children, at least," insisted Nik sud Prendolat.

"Why? You are all fat. You won't need to eat for days."

It was true, the strangers were the thinnest Om'ray I'd ever seen; if muscle hadn't corded their limbs, I'd have thought them struck by some wasting illness and near death. "I am Speaker for Sona." Though the reminder should have been unnecessary. *And more POWERFUL.*

Perhaps that, they'd needed. The two male Chosen left without a word, including the one who'd thought we could wait.

It left a foul taste regardless. My eyes wandered back to the dais.

He wasn't fat either. Healthy muscle crisscrossed his chest, defined strong shoulders and arms. Healing bruises covered his ribs with yellow. His otherwise pale skin was tanned at the wrist, face, and neck.

As was mine. *Itch.*

His eyes, an unusual blue, locked on mine. His face bore the same expression I'd seen on his face since they'd sat him there: calm concentration. He was powerful; I could feel him against my shields.

Where he belonged, I told myself, looking away. I considered the stranger Om'ray, unsure where they fit in all this. "Why have you come here?"

"When we sensed your presence, we came to—" the one named Destin hesitated briefly, "—meet you." A gesture of apology. "Forgive our surprise. We weren't expecting—"

"Visitors," another supplied, when she hesitated again.

Whatever was wrong here, at least they hadn't interrupted our dreaming. "We are not visitors," I corrected as graciously as possible. "We are Sona!"

My people stood straighter, smiling. "Sona!" they repeated cheerfully.

The strangers looked aghast. "But—we—"

Their fingers brushed, doubtless a sending. I hoped it encouraged better behavior.

It seemed so when the one called Destin bowed and said, "A matter for our Speaker and Council, who will wish to greet you as soon as possible. I am Destin di Anel, First Scout."

Itch.

These Clanless Om'ray claimed a Speaker and Council? A First Scout? A ploy of some kind, and only now a name, when they'd refused that common courtesy before. I wasn't inclined to share mine. I sent a quick summons. "This is Barac di Bowart, Sona's First Scout," I introduced blandly when he joined us, not needing touch to send my message. *They have secrets. I want them.*

My able cousin gestured a polite greeting. "I look forward to sharing any information you have on our new home, Destin," with his charming smile. "And to having your guidance outside, come daylight."

"You can't go out." Flat and rude, from the as-yet unnamed male. As I stared at him, he flushed, then muttered, "Gurutz di Ulse, Speaker."

"The *not-real* could leave," Destin qualified, gesturing apology. "The Tikitik won't count him."

"They count everything—"

"Which matters not to Sona," I interrupted, wondering what they were talking about. "The Oud are to be our neighbors, not the Tikitik." A Clan didn't establish without knowledge of its neighbor. Who were these Om'ray, to be so ignorant?

Itch.

If I turned my head, I'd meet the regard of those impossible eyes.

I did not.

Interlude

THEY'D SPRUNG A TRAP—or he had, picking up the necklace, giving it to Sira. Something in the simple action had triggered the machine, in turn changing the M'hiray. How could wait. What mattered was getting free again.

Morgan had an idea about that; fortunately, it did not rely on recovering the coat and other belongings they'd piled on the far side of the green pillar.

Sira's eyes found him, each time with a puzzling in their depths. He'd seen that look before, when he'd reinstated the blocks in her mind. Then, they'd worked together to restore her full memory and self.

This time, she had the ability to keep him out and used it. Painfully so.

That didn't mean he was alone. *Aryl.*

Grumpily. *What makes you think you can fix what's been done to them? For all we know, this change is permanent and they'll never remember us.*

Because he wouldn't accept that. Couldn't.

Morgan flexed his wrists, keeping blood flowing to his hands. The bindings the Om'ray employed were disturbingly like those used to truss prey. The old Clanswoman was just as trapped, not only in flesh but equally unable to communicate with anyone else.

Aryl di Sarc neither wanted nor deserved pity. Like him, she wanted freedom.

The M'hiray arrived on Stonerim III without memory of this world and its language, he sent. *Without memory of why you had to leave.* From this very chamber, with its abundant evidence of sophisticated technology, alien and potent, from the pillar machine to the lighting.

If not the dress of those native here.

A question for another time. *Marcus Bowman knew why the M'hiray left. He sent a recording—his legacy—to Stonerim III with you. Do you remember?* He held his breath.

Silence. Then, with great weight, *I remember giving it to his daughter Kari. I remember how the Bowmans had suffered for our secrets. I made it the Speaker's role to watch over them. We owed Marcus that and more. What do you mean, he knew why we left? How do you know any of this?*

The Bowmans have been watching over you. Here. Morgan brought forward his memories of Lydis Bowman, of their meeting.

Then, he allowed Aryl di Sarc to see, once more, the friend who had died saving her.

Naryn feared death. Feared entering the M`hir alone. I don`t know where or how she learned the method to put herself into a crystal instead, only that Sira`s birth was part of her plan. Naryn wanted to produce a Vessel of immense Power in which to be reborn. She didn`t care about the consequences, not by the end. Enris and I—we talked about my foreboding, about Naryn`s ambition, about where she was taking the M'hiray.* Wry affection. *Always ready to charge ahead without looking, my beloved. It was his plan to stop Naryn before she could instill herself in that rock. Neither of us guessed this would be the only way. That I'd take her place. That we`d lose each other, forever.

At some unremarked moment, she`d become as real to him as anyone else in the chamber. Closing his eyes, Morgan could believe this special Clanswoman stood before him, unbowed despite her age, as strong and beautiful as his Sira. As determined and brave. *I`m sorry this happened,* he told her, going on honestly, *but I`m glad you`re here.*

The M'hiray were my mistake. I haven`t fixed that, not yet.* A glimmer of *warmth* directed at him. *I`m glad of your company as well, Jason Morgan, if not what you've told me. A pause, then. *You believe my memory was altered, my life here stolen, by this machine.*

I do. And now it's done the same to Sira and the M'hiray, Morgan assured her. *It can't be coincidence. I've been able to free memories before, Aryl. Let me try. If this doesn't work, at least we`ll have that answer, a start.*

The *warmth* grew, soothed. *You won't give up.*

He shared the merest hint of his *determination.*

Well enough. Let us do this now, before they move us apart.

Having only done this when in physical contact, Morgan knew they could be too far apart already; a detail not worth mentioning. Confidence, he reminded himself. How many times had Sira encouraged him, saying "Limits should be given a nudge."

Along with a terrifying wealth of cautionary tales about that nudging, mind you, but he was in no mood for those.

So when Aryl lowered her shields, Morgan immediately *sent* himself along the connection between them.

A shock, as if he'd plunged into ice water, yet all around was clarity, clarity and space.

She welcomed him into the core of her thoughts, keeping nothing back. Beyond the order and calm intelligence he glimpsed a curtain red as blood, rippling with menace. *Do not go there,* Aryl warned gently.

Her Chosen, Enris—his loss—lay behind it, Morgan guessed, and obeyed. He began his search elsewhere . . .

Swimming back through a lifetime of memories, acquired before he'd been born. Tantalizing glimpses at what had been, of history lived . . . but he dare not pause.

There.

Do you see it? he asked, for she'd come with him, standing by his shoulder.

The mind interpreted what was unseeable. To Morgan, what he'd found appeared to be a round container, the span of his arms in circumference. Its fine weaving was coated with a clear gloss, as if intended to keep water out.

Or memories in.

Tidy, Aryl commented, a new *edge* to her calm. *How do we get inside?*

Sira's blockage had appeared a smothering, as though portions of her mind were wrapped in thick blankets. In a sense, he'd pulled those aside.

Morgan studied the container, finding nothing to show how to open or break it.

So be it. For the first time, he risked imposing his *will* on what he saw. A lid, *here.* A handle to grab it, *here.*

Draining, that effort. Finally the image obeyed, showing what he wanted, but no matter how he tried, he couldn't *touch* the handle or *lift* the lid.

My turn, Aryl said.

And did.

Morgan left her alone, respecting the Clanswoman's right to her own past. He pulled back into himself, the arduousness of that return a warning. Limits? He'd shattered them.

The Human shivered as the sweat coating his skin began to dry, stealing what heat he'd left. A shame they'd distrusted his clothing, though in their place he'd have done the same.

He looked for Sira, found her by one of the windows, standing with a pair of the Om'ray. She was easy to spot. Faded blue spacer coveralls. Hair like a red-gold waterfall to her waist.

Rare grace.

Unconscious dignity, be it the lift of her head, her posture, or in the careful regard of eyes that had beheld far more than the age she appeared would suggest.

Yet forgot him.

He refused to believe it was permanent, that anything could separate them after all they'd been through together, were together.

Aryl?

No reply. Had he found a cache of stolen memories, or

exposed Aryl di Sarc to what she herself had hidden, for her own protection? Every time he entered another's mind to heal it, he feared causing more harm than good.

No choice, Morgan told himself. He'd know if he'd made a difference soon. If what he'd done for Aryl di Sarc would work for his Chosen.

Or if he was now truly alone.

Chapter 36

*I*TCH!

The *prickle* in my mind kept intensifying. If I could have pulled open my head like an aged Eifla and scratched, I would have.

An Eifla?

. . . *ITCH!* A Keeper knew how to dream safely, how to open minds to receive what the Cloisters needed its Clan to learn so gently most non-Adepts wouldn't even be aware. How could I have failed so badly?

"—Oud aren't welcome."

I gave myself an inward shake, focusing back on what these strangers were trying to say. While making no sense, they appeared in deadly earnest.

Destin agreed with Gurutz. "Oud may not come here."

Appearance was all I had to go by. Their minds were behind shields of unfamiliar configuration; I somehow doubted these knife-bearing strangers would grant me the moment to discover how to breach them.

"What we live near is not for an Om'ray to say," I cautioned sternly. Or even think. The neighbors who awaited our arrival were in every sense independent of us. Ours was to be a relationship built on mutual respect and collaboration. We were farmers—

ITCHITCHITCH!

—though I wouldn't have believed it, to look at us. None of my people looked to have worked outside or hard, surely what farmers did. We'd adapt, I reminded myself. That's what a Cloisters did: prepare us to thrive outside its walls.

Protect us when we couldn't.

As I might have predicted, the two exchanged yet another look. Destin said, as she'd said a tedious number of times already, "Such matters are for Council. They will come in the morning, Speaker, to meet with you."

They'd be awake now, by my estimation, and doubtless well-briefed, but the hour had nothing to do with the availability of their so-called Council. Power struggles I understood, even such petty ones. Unfortunately, short of attacking our hosts and forcing our way out, this struggle was one I couldn't win. We all knew it. They were polite; I would be no less in return. "I await their convenience."

They bowed, I thought gratefully, and left me, taking the other strangers with them. Barac checked the door that turned closed behind them, shaking his head as a signal when it couldn't be reopened.

The rest of my people had made themselves little nests along the windowless wall, families and unChosen clustered. I'd asked a silent question; the answer had taken some of the joy from our safe arrival. None of us having seen another part of the Cloisters, we'd no locate for a 'port. Despite our marvelous Talent, despite our long journey to this new home, we were trapped in the Council Chamber until one of us stepped through a door, or the sun rose to reveal what was outside the windows.

Which shouldn't be.

. . . *itch.* Why couldn't I picture another place? Even if we didn't know Sona, yet, we'd come from—from somewhere. Straining to remember intensified the *ITCH* until I had to pace or scream; it didn't stop my efforts.

Nor could I stop glancing at the not-real. He should be miserable, shivering and bound, but he sat without moving from where they'd pushed him, his gaze steady and ever on me.

Was that pride on his face?

Destin and Gurutz judged him dangerous. He was, I'd no doubt. But to whom?

The stranger Om'ray kept us prisoner, too, as surely as if they'd tied us with ropes. They did this though we belonged in Sona and they did not. As for their Council?

I recognized no authority but the entitlement of my greater Power. If what these strangers would say after this needless wait didn't suit me?

They had strong shields. We'd see how long they lasted.

Uneasy, such thoughts, ones I shouldn't have; my growing outrage was even less helpful. My hair writhed around my shoulders in unseemly display. With no other outlet for my anger, I let it.

Seeing my mood, my own people carefully avoided me.

I needed a task. The strangers had provided gourds of water, distributing those along with flat disks of bread studded with bits of dried meat. I'd taken my share more to appease my Birth Watcher than because of appetite.

Nothing had been offered to their prisoner—my Chosen; cruel to him, potentially deadly to me.

Two could play that game. Gourd and bread in hand, I strode to the dais with an air of confidence.

An air harder to maintain as I approached him, caught by what I couldn't name. Was it the darkening of the blue in his eyes, fixed on me?

The tiny creases at the corners of his lips, as though ready to smile?

Heart pounding, I knelt beside him, offering the water. Though unable to understand my voice or inner speech, he grasped my intention. When I lifted the gourd to his mouth, he swallowed eagerly.

My eyes wouldn't leave the movement of his throat. My hair, ever-willful, sent a curious lock to touch it . . .

Finding the pulse of blood beneath skin . . . exploring the curved junction of shoulder to neck . . .

Sliding down his chest, as if drawn by lines of drying sweat.

I tore my eyes away, meeting his again. They contained a

message, intense, powerful. But what? I took a frustrated breath and the scent of him, sharp and *familiar,* filled me.

ITCH ITCH The gourd dropped from my numb fingers.

I drew closer still, because I must. Shut my eyes and pressed my face into his neck, because I must. Felt my hair cloak us both, because this was where I had to be.

And tasting the salt on his skin was beyond me to refuse.

Interlude

SIRA! Feeling her lips on his skin, Morgan closed his eyes, his heart singing.

Now!

Aryl. He fought to think. She was back and that meant—

A tongue tasted, the nip of teeth following. Hair, heavy and smooth, heated his bare shoulders and he reeled with a flood of desire even as hands—

Sira hasn't remembered you. *Chosen mate.* Dry and cold. *Is that what you want?*

No. Yes. How could he not? This was Sira! Blood boiling with anticipation, he sought their deeper connection, the one that let every sensation flow back and forth in exquisite, maddening harmony until—

—there was none. Her shields were locked against him. Instead, *NO!* What she was doing, in front of—she pushed him over on his bound arms, straddled him—

Now. Or lose her.

Morgan used the agony in his arms and hands, his revulsion, his overwhelming fear of, yes, that loss, to regain control. He would do this. Save Sira. But how? Aryl had let him into her mind.

Sira guarded herself against him.

Not against us, Aryl said. *Jason, thanks to you, I do remember; every-thing, to the beginning. Sira deserves no less.*

Trusting her, Morgan drove himself against the most powerful mind he'd ever known.

Hoping to find the person he loved.

Chapter 37

IT WAS SAID HATE was no barrier to Choice and Joining, that Om'ray life pairings must be managed with care or this would be the result. Rutting as loveless and driven as fish spawning in their season.

I didn't hate the *not-real*. I just didn't care. So when the attack came, part of me refused to disengage from what was more urgent than defense.

But when the attack came, it wasn't one mind against me, but two.

Interlude

IF EVER HE'D WONDERED what had changed in the generations of M'hiray culminating in Sira, Morgan was answered now. What Aryl sent against her great-granddaughter's precise and layered protection had never been structured by training or honed in Clan duels.

It was raw, unadulterated *FORCE*.

Morgan rode it—or was he part of it? Sira's defenses parted as if they were gauze and he a knife—

Finding himself in a stranger's mind, one where he existed solely as an object of lust.

He wouldn't look. Wouldn't *feel*. They didn't have time. Already, he sensed her surprise at their invasion turning to rage.

She might not remember him, but he knew the shape of her thoughts better than his own.

The shape, if not this. Morgan ran on floors banded with color he couldn't name, along corridors that rose and fell as if breathing. He closed what weren't eyes, trusting he knew the way.

RAGE!

He ran faster, knew Aryl did the same. What pursued them couldn't be fought or escaped. Not if they were to succeed.

There'd be no second chance, no second moment of surprise.

So he ran, and ran . . . until he crashed into a wall.

Morgan opened what weren't eyes. Not a wall, a door, like those in the chamber. One that hadn't been in Sira's mind before arriving on Cersi.

Locked, of course.

Morgan! Aryl shared the image of a hidden latch. *Hurry!*

Try as he might, he couldn't *touch* it. Couldn't *affect* it.

The wrong door, he realized. *It's the wrong door!*

The mind around him shuddered. *ITCH!* The body pressing against his was gone, as if Sira had thrown herself clear of him, but that ominous *RAGE* closed in—

What do we do?

Show her the right one, he thought.

Morgan looked at the Om'ray door, rejecting it with all his *will*, accepting Aryl's strength, adding it to his. Not *this!*

Not this . . .

This.

The cargo hold door from the *Silver Fox.*

Chapter 38

*R*AGE!!!
     How DARE they!? I pursued the interlopers. They may have tricked their way into my mind, but mine was the greater POWER! Mine, the WILL! I would tear their minds apart, scatter them in the M'hir.

They fled; I chased. I almost had them when—

I came to a stop. What was this?

ITCH!!

The mind showed what it knew.

How could I know this?

A door, tall and wide, like a flat panel. No handles, no—there was a pad with symbols to the side. There was a—

The minds I'd chased faded before I could grab them. Ah! They'd put this image here to trick me, to hide behind.

All I had to do was open the door. I punched symbols at random.

A second panel slid down in front of the first, equally impenetrable, and a sound roared in what weren't ears, like wind.

DANGER!

How did I know? How did I know time was running out, that the air around me was venting into—venting into—

Not a trap. I'd made a mistake. It wasn't the first time. I'd survived by—by—there was a sequence, a code. I'd known it once.

ITCH!!! Impossible. How could I know this door or any code to open it? I'd never seen such a thing—

The pad softened at the edges, began to sink into the wall. The door stretched, as if growing taller.

I couldn't seem to fill my lungs now, no matter how I tried. Could barely stand, if I stood at all. Ridiculous, that their illusion could defeat me.

I would solve this.

With what weren't fingers at all, I keyed in the code I shouldn't have known and couldn't forget.

The wind stopped. Reversed. No air could be better than what I breathed in great gasps, feeling my strength returning.

One panel whooshed up. The first still barred the way, more solid now. Tantalizingly familiar.

I keyed the code a second time, the pad now bright and glowing. The panel lifted more slowly than it should, resisting my will.

What was behind it? Who?

. . . *itch* . . .

There was only one way to find out.

The moment the door opened, I stepped through.

Interlude

"SIRA?" Morgan rolled over.

There, on the dais near him, her hair spread like sunset. He worked his way to her, leaving skin on the floor as he squirmed, fighting to see her face.

There.

Her eyes were closed, but expressions played across her features, emotions passing like flickers of firelight, too quickly for any one to be read.

Morgan let his head drop, content to watch and wait.

Please. Show her to me. My great-granddaughter.

He did.

Why—she has his brow, his—her pleased surprise faded. *I'd felt Naryn in her—something of myself. Enris would be proud of her—and of you, as I am.*

It may not have worked, he cautioned, to himself as much as Aryl. *We'll know soon.*

Chapter 39

MY FIRST COHERENT THOUGHT was I should have lubricated the hold door when I did the galley's, the *Fox* being a thirsty ship.

I opened my eyes on the second. "Morgan!?"

We were lying, face-to-face, on our sides. He smiled, not lifting his head. "Hello."

Which would have been fine if we'd been in bed, and possibly led to something delightful, but we were lying on a floor, in an alien building, with him trussed like a fowl and me—

"Oh." I couldn't have blushed any hotter. I sat hurriedly, drawing together my clothing along with what dignity I could muster, the others in the room studiously looking elsewhere. What had I—

First thing, free my poor abused Chosen.

The next being to apologize, forever, I focused on the first.

Morgan drew on his shirt, closing the fastening one-handed while I finished putting medplas over the abrasions. I felt him watch me; felt his smile.

Morgan . . . I choked on *remorse*.

Hush. He bent and kissed me. *Remember that?*

How could he tease me, after I'd abandoned him to strangers, after I'd—

Witchling, you weren't the only one to have your past stolen by this thing.

"It's called a Maker." I traced the line of Morgan's jaw with a finger that caught on stubble, gazed into eyes showing the strain of the past hours and events. I imagined mine looked no better.

My restored memories hadn't erased those forced into my mind; I supposed I should be grateful and not simply nauseous, but the sensation was deeply unpleasant. "I am—I remember—" I fought for words. "I believed myself the Keeper, the Adept assigned to the Dream Chamber. But this is the Council Chamber and the Maker shouldn't be here, not according to—" I tapped my head. "The Maker's a Healer's tool, used to stop a damaged mind from contaminating those Joined to it."

By severing what binds Om'ray to one another, Aryl told us both. *The M'hiray brought it to the Chamber to sever our binding to Sona, so we could leave this place and prevent further harm. We didn't realize it would cut us from our past.*

"Which makes me wonder if its original function was forgotten."

I blinked at him.

Morgan shrugged. "The Maker left you believing you were newly arrived and where you should be, ready to build the Sona Clan. Complete with a new language and roles. Recruiters would love it."

'Recruiters' being slavers who trafficked skilled labor to other worlds, kidnapping and stasis boxes being their methods of choice. "Is that what this is?" I asked, horrified.

"I doubt it's anything so simple, Sira."

I rubbed my face, then looked to the silent throng around us. Tle should have accused me of being unable to lead by now—Barac showing concern over my very odd behavior—Degal making disapproving faces. Our Birth Watchers, young and adult, should be fussing over Aryl.

None should be sitting, eyes absent of thought, lips relaxed in gentle smiles as though the prospect of building shacks on the ground and farming was the best of all possible futures.

I'd no problem with shacks, ground, or farming. This? This I would not abide.

You know what to do. We'll help.

Great-grandmother. Private from Morgan, I added, *thank you.*

Amusement. Then, her mind voice turned grim. *Repay me by finding out what all this means. It can't be to the good of Om'ray.*

Night—truenight—leaned on the windows still, but it couldn't be much longer before dawn and the return of the Om'ray who—as I now knew—did belong here. "Let's get to work," I decided, pulling away from my Chosen.

At the same time, I widened my awareness of him, and his of me, until our hearts filled as one and I knew beyond doubt there was no need for guilt or forgiveness.

Though, knowing my Human, I could expect to be teased for an interminable time.

Morgan and I went from person to person, freeing the section of memory the Maker had suppressed. We began with those most able to help us: the three Healers, including Holl di Licor, and their Chosen. Two of the six went aside to be quietly and thoroughly sick. I managed not to join them, but it was close.

To my relief, the Healers took over the task, one of them sharing a technique to ease the blending of imposed and restored memories, while keeping clear which were which. Morgan and I left them to it, sitting together on the edge of the dais. Possessing a refined ability to nap anywhere, my Human leaned against me, eyes soon closed.

Parents helped their children, their shields one and the same. The older Chosen stayed close, as we did. I watched awareness enter each face, troubled to see what had been joyful—if false—acceptance turn back into confusion and dread.

We were all affected, regardless of Power or Talent, I told them, with undertones of *confidence* and *hope. The machine sought to make us into farmers.* With a note of *wry humor* that brought heads my way and won a few rueful smiles. *We've gained knowledge and a new language to help us understand the Clan already on this planet.*

Then, because those Clan had mistreated him, I added, *We survived this first test because we did not come to Cersi alone. We came with Jason Morgan, a Human these Om'ray dismiss as "not-real." What would you say to him?*

They rose to their feet. As the outpouring of *trust* and *gratitude* reached him, as Morgan stood, his face pale and working, the M'hiray bowed, offering him the gesture of deepest respect, holding it—even the ones who'd wanted him dead in the past—longer than I'd ever seen.

And, for the very first time, we were one.

We waited, more or less peacefully. Many busied themselves comparing their rather uncomfortable new knowledge, however old that knowledge might be.

"Anything to eat?" Morgan asked brightly.

I broke my bread disk, offering him the larger piece. "Try this."

"And turn all purple and die?" he chuckled, taking it.

I nibbled mine as he rummaged through his pack, unsurprised when he pulled out an older model scanner to run over the bread. Careful, my Human. Sure enough, he sat back down with a tube of e-rations in his hand, returning the bread to me. "Definitely in the 'all purple and die' category."

I stopped chewing.

"For me." Morgan grinned, wagging the tube. "It's fine for you and Aryl."

Chewing once more, if with less appetite, I considered the significance of what he'd done. We'd arrived with resources of our own, and expertise. Some of it stood nearby, my mother's group having reformed.

"You're thinking."

I leaned my shoulder into his. "What I've been—taught—about this world is limited. I imagine it's the same for all of us.

This—" I patted the dais, "—is a Council Chamber. Every Clan has a building like this, called a Cloisters." A building any Om'ray could enter, the "di" designation part of every name regardless of Power; it was a change from the past that made Aryl uneasy, not that she'd explain.

"With tech you don't understand."

I nodded. The sud Friesnens had named their home "The Cloisters." At the time, I'd thought it because I'd come to live there, sequestered from any unChosen. Now I had to wonder how often a buried memory had resurfaced, out of context and beyond comprehension. But some hunted those secrets. "They might." I indicated Deni and Holl. "And you."

His eyebrow rose. "Curious I may be, but we've seen the danger here. My preference is to get everyone out, as soon as possible. Trade for supplies and guides, then make our own home, away from here."

We cannot, Aryl sent.

"I didn't say it'd be easy," Morgan began.

"That's not what she means." I rested my hand over his. "The Om'ray share their world with two other intelligences, the Oud and the Tikitik. Resources aren't simply divided between the three, they're controlled, down to the number of Om'ray and where they may live. And to them, we're Om'ray."

His face lost all expression. "Go on."

Aryl answered. *Only unChosen ready for Choice may take Passage between Clans. Other travel is forbidden. This is* why *the M'hiray couldn't stay on Cersi. When we—when I—learned how to move through the M'hir, we changed the Balance among Clans. Om'ray died for it. The only solution was to leave.*

"Generations ago," Morgan pointed out. "The situation could be different now."

I shared with them what Sona's First Scout had said.

Clans change neighbors, Aryl replied. *Sona was Tikitik before it was Oud. When we left—*inexpressible grief—*the Tikitik had begun to reclaim it.*

I aimed a thumb over my shoulder at Maker. "This thing prepared us to live with the Oud. Why?"

"Interesting question." Morgan rose and went to the pillar, walking around it. Shaking his head, he lifted the brown robe. "No clues here."

I shared what I saw with Aryl.

My mother's. Free of emotion. *Someone had to stay to operate the Maker. Why—shouldn't there be a husk?*

Morgan had *heard.* He ran his scanner over the fabric, then around the pillar's base. "No trace of remains. Maybe she left these behind."

No. I felt Taisal's death. If she didn't die here, she went—with wonder, now—*she went into the M'hir. I wouldn't have believed it.*

Gently replacing the robe, my Human waved me to join him. "What is it?"

He turned his back to the others in the chamber, speaking quietly. "This—" he shook the device "—isn't much use on inorganics. I can tell you we're alone in this building. Out there?" He nodded to the still-dark windows. "Life off the scale."

Confirmation, if we'd needed any, that Sona was within a grove, dependent on the Tikitik.

We'd come seeking refuge.

This was about as far from safe as my combined memory contained.

Interlude

BARAC DI BOWART, once sud Sarc, former First Scout of the M'hiray Clan of the Trade Pact and now First Scout, apparently, again—though of what, was debatable—gazed out the window and waited.

Waiting he was good at. Sira'd set him here, as she'd set the scientists from Stonerim III to use instruments from their packs, as she'd set ten others to inventory supplies, as she'd—

"Anything?" Ruti came to stand beside him.

What he could see were their reflections looking back. They'd dressed to meet Quessa on Plexis an eternity ago, clothes they'd cleaned on the *Fox* and donned to leave the ship.

The minor addition of Morgan and Sira's extra coats and, in Ruti's case, flat slippers, didn't make them ready for what was waiting outside. Nothing, he feared, could. "The Sona live over there," he pointed. "You can see their lights if you put your face to the window." In trees, if he was to believe it.

He didn't know how to live in trees or with Tikitik. The machine that raped their minds had been tragically wrong, preparing them for fields and brick homes and Oud. Ruti could repair a harvesting machine she'd never seen. His mind was stuffed with details about brickmaking, of all things. Brickmaking and foods he *remembered* tasting—and had never put in his mouth.

Barac's stomach roiled. All he knew for certain was that outside this Cloisters, anything could be deadly.

"You worry too much, my dear Chosen. I grew up in Acranam's jungles," Ruti reminded him. "I know all about them."

"And that will be helpful," he replied gently. "But this isn't Acranam. What might look the same, won't be."

She made that little, you-haven't-convinced-me, sound that reserved her right to argue, ever brave and determined.

A combination ripe for danger. "Ruti—"

"Our pardon, but are you the First Scout?"

Not if he could help it, Barac sighed to himself, but nodded at the two who'd approached.

"Our parents sent us, First Scout. To be useful."

Enjoy yourself, Ruti sent with a grin as she left them. *Jacqui needs us.*

He'd no right to feel deserted. That there'd been no incidents—yet—was remarkable. The shock of their arrival had helped. The three unChosen stayed together, surrounded by family, waiting with that delicious blend of terror and urgent need Barac had no trouble remembering.

Having been drawn, time and again, to the alluring Power-of-Choice of a Chooser. He remembered knowing he'd die; it hadn't mattered. Such was the nature of their kind.

He'd been lucky. The only thing saving these unChosen was the unnatural self-control of the Choosers forced to share the chamber.

Full credit to his Chosen, keeping Jacqui apart and preoccupied. Tle di Parth, thus far, had shown unusual good sense, avoiding Jacqui and remaining in the midst of the Chosen of her group. As for the third Chooser swept to Cersi? Ermu sud Friesnen's minimal Power, an embarrassment to her father Crisac, made her no threat to the others. Ironically, if not for the presence of Jacqui and Tle, her lesser strength would guarantee a successful Choice.

Perhaps with one of the youngsters waiting respectfully for him to speak, the elder brother as yet oblivious as to why the eyes of all three M'hiray Choosers followed when he passed by. He'd pay attention soon. He'd be unable to help himself.

"Call me Barac."

"I'm Asdny di Licor," the elder introduced himself with a very proper bow. "This is my brother Arla. How can we be of use? Barac," he finished, greatly daring. His brother looked at him with admiration.

Barac carefully didn't smile. "You've skills? Of your own," he added, not ready to trust the rest.

Arla stood straight. "I've studied—"

"He means for out there," his brother interrupted. "We're good climbers. And Arla's a Looker."

Blushing accentuated the dappling on Arla's cheeks. "Not much of one," he muttered.

"Arla's always right," Asdny boasted. "You can't trick his Talent by switching what he's seen, not even once."

Doubtless a trick he'd tried to play, often. Barac was intrigued. Lookers of substantial Power were uncommon—just as well, their intense memory of a place or person at odds with the slightest variation in it. He'd heard it said they dared not visit anywhere subject to change more than once. Putting Plexis definitely off limits.

No one here would be going to Plexis any time soon, he reminded himself. Not with the Assemblers waiting.

Would any of them, ever again?

"Will you teach us to be scouts, Barac?"

"Please?"

He'd been this young and eager once. Barac smiled. "If you'll teach me how to climb. My brother said I was hopeless at it." The words came out free of pain. He supposed it was all the new losses.

"We will," Arla promised, eyes aglow.

"And soon." His brother pointed out the window. "Look!"

Dawn.

Chapter 40

WHAT DAWN REVEALED, rain mercifully hid behind a curtain of gray.

Aryl was the only one who'd responded with joy to finding ourselves engulfed by giant trees, their girth rivaling a starship's, their whorls of mighty branches overlapped to leave no room for a sky. Branches coated in vines and other growth.

Most with thorns.

Looking down hadn't improved matters. Aryl remembered Sona's Cloisters as sitting half buried in the ground. Now it drowned, water like ebony lapping against what had been the railing to an upper level.

Things lived in that water, she assured us, her *fear* ample warning not to ask what.

The Maker having programmed us to be farmers, the lack of ground was disconcerting. My people busied themselves as best they could, a little too casually avoiding the windows in case the rain let up.

I chewed and swallowed the last of my bread. "Here's hoping they realize we'll need more than this."

"You said they weren't happy to share." Morgan gazed at the rain-slicked window. "I wonder why. It's not as if they don't have enough out there to eat."

Everything out there, I judged wryly, busy eating everything else.

He went on, "This much biomass? If the population is as clever at living here as Aryl describes, I can't see food being a problem."

"It might be." Holl joined us. Her delicate features were drawn with worry. "I've analyzed what they've given us. Several key nutrients are missing. If our diet consisted solely of this bread, we'd starve to death, and quickly."

Dresel.

The word came with such *longing* my mouth filled with moisture. A special food, moreover a necessary one, that the stranger Om'ray hadn't offered. "Something else for their Council." A growing list. I shrugged. "That's if they're in a talking mood."

Let me deal with them.

I glanced suspiciously at Morgan. He'd not shared his reaction about being tied up by the Om'ray; not sharing didn't make him in a forgiving mood. There were weapons in his pack, as well as those returned to his clothing.

His mouth quirked. "We're traders, chit, remember? Negotiation's our specialty."

When had I started thinking more like a Clan Speaker than myself? "One problem. You don't speak the language." Yet, I added to myself. Morgan had begun to add Om'ray words and phrasing to his comlink. On noticing Andi's interest, he'd enlisted the child to walk around and collect as much as she could. The M'hiray might not have employed such tech, but they quickly understood its importance to Morgan.

Having remembered Morgan's importance not only to me, but to all of us.

"I'll be in your head," my important Chosen said, smiling at me. "Here's what I suggest we put on the table to start."

When he told me, I smiled for the first time since dawn.

"You want to—to live in our Cloisters?" The words barely made it through Teris di Uruus' tightened lips.

I spoke to be heard by everyone. "All we ask is living space until we find another home." Aryl's memory of how they'd housed a bulging population in this same building had been extremely helpful. "The upper levels would be sufficient. You'd be welcome to keep using the rest, of course."

" 'Of course,' " echoed Sona's Speaker, Odon di Rihma'at, with the beginnings of a thunderous scowl.

Sona's Council had been late, suiting themselves. I'd greeted them graciously, the extra delay suiting me. We'd need the time to prepare, as best we could.

They were five, including their Speaker, and all Adepts: three female, two male, Chosen and elders of their families. Elders? Eand di Yode and her Chosen Moyla were shockingly aged, faces so deeply wrinkled they were impossible to read, hands gnarled into claws. Whether advanced in years or worn by life, they moved with much the same vigor as the rest.

Other than the robes and their bearing, they were as diverse a sampling of our kind as I'd ever seen in one place. Nyala di Edut was the tallest, the irises of her eyes and her netted hair colored like a rainbow. Teris and Moyla had the heavier builds, neither as tall as Ruti, but the former's skin was as dark as the lake outside. At a younger age, Eand could have passed for my father's kin, having the same hooked nose and angular jaw.

None claimed the role the Maker had assigned me, to be Keeper and in charge of dreaming. It might be they had none, Aryl thought, or considered the matter private among their Adepts. Regardless, it was high on my list to find out; we wanted nothing more to do with those automated memories, helpful or not.

Sona's Speaker, Odon, wore a pendant identical to mine on his chest. His finely drawn features and thick black hair would make him strikingly handsome, I thought, when he didn't look ready to strike someone.

As for the extra finger on each of his elegant hands? I reminded myself I had dear friends more alien than this and managed not to stare. Harder to ignore were names I'd seen only on parches, families left behind on this world when the Om'ray and M'hiray divided one from the other.

Sona's Council had dressed for the occasion in white ceremonial robes that might have hung in Tle's closet or mine. The robes made their desired impression. My people had bowed with respect; now they hung on every word with rapt attention.

Words they could only understand because a machine had reset their minds to take Sona from these people.

Other Om'ray had accompanied their Council, bringing wooden stools for them and one for me. Tables and cups for them, nothing for me. The stools were arranged, not on the dais, but directly in front of the door they'd used. The Council sat in a curve with me at its focus.

As planned, Morgan stood behind me, as did Tle di Parth, from my brief *reach* by far the most powerful Chooser in the area, and Barac. First Scout, I'd learned from Aryl was a highly significant rank here.

By their glowers when they'd sat, we weren't what the Om'ray expected to face.

Good.

As any Clan might do, during our introductions we'd acquainted ourselves with one another, the discreet *touch* of Power to Power widening their eyes as they assessed mine.

I hadn't known what to expect of them. When the M'hiray left, they'd stripped Cersi of Om'ray with Talents that used the M'hir. From what I sensed of the Sona, that hadn't diminished the strength of those who remained. Did they possess Talents now rare or extinct among us? I looked forward to learning more about them.

If they let us stay.

Odon was the strongest Sona by a slight margin, the aged Eand second. Sona's First Scout, Destin, rivaled them both. I'd given her a nod of recognition, making her shift uneasily at her post behind the Speaker.

Then I'd made what Morgan called our opening offer, and no one had been at ease since.

"The Cloisters belongs to Sona." Odon made a dismissive gesture. "You are not Sona and not welcome. Use your foul Vyna tricks and leave!"

" 'Vyna'?" I echoed.

"Do you deny it?"

Aryl supplied an image of beings I could scarcely credit as Om'ray, letting me feel her *repugnance.*

A Clan who lived apart, refusing Choice, reproducing without mates. In Aryl's time, the Vyna prevented contamination by killing any unChosen lured to their Choosers. They stored the minds of their Adepts, pouring them into their empty unborn. Vessels.

Here was the source of the myths.

Anaj di Kathel lived in Naryn's womb until—Aryl's sending stopped as though cut. When she continued, quickly, it was of something else entirely. *The dream of how to enter the M'hir would have reached their Adepts,* she said, *dread* beginning to grow. *None of them joined the M'hiray. Sira, what did they become?*

A problem for us, apparently. "I say use your eyes as well as your Talent. We've Chosen here. Families. We are not Vyna." I spread my arms. "We are the M'hiray, yes, and strangers, but the blood in our bodies is the same as in yours. We've lost our homes. What we ask is a chance for a new one."

Though we were carefully keeping our inner distance from one another, I'd sat at trade tables. Attitudes were shifting— some, anyway.

Moyla's pale eyes shone, as if close to tears. His lips worked. "Our families, too—"

"Hush," his Chosen snapped. "We agreed to dispense with these intruders. I say they leave now or be removed!"

"And the Tikitik?" I countered.

Teris regarded me through lowered eyelids, her restless hair white against the dark of her skin. Her attention shifted to her fellow Councilor. "A valid point. Eand?"

"What happens within these walls is of no concern to our neighbors."

Aryl had been translating for Morgan. He leaned forward, an urgent hand on my shoulder. *Sira, she's threatening to have us killed.*

Who wasn't? I thought wearily. "Are there so many Om'ray here," I argued, keeping my voice even, "you would waste our lives?"

"See? Proof! She doesn't know our number. A Vyna would

know. Anyone would." Eand looked at the others on Council. She climbed to her feet, voice rising. "We feel them. Can these M'hiray not feel us? Are they blind to the world? Are they *not-real?*"

The others erupted from their seats, the First Scout not the only one dropping hands to knife hilt. Shouts overlapped. *ANGER* and *FEAR* drove outward. "These are all *not-real,* like her Chosen!" "Don't belong!" "Be rid of them!"

"Thirty-three!" A child's voice rang out, high-pitched and unexpected. As the others fell silent, in and out, Andi looked at me in triumph.

"Thirty-three," I repeated as calmly as possible. *What's going on?*

An Om'ray trait, Morgan told me quickly. *They sense one another at any distance. They*—an incredulous pause—*Aryl says they navigate by it, that the shape of their world is defined by where Om'ray exist. A sense those who became M'hiray lost.*

Andi's antiquated Talent, to know at all times where another was without expending her strength. Thirty-three Sona. Fewer than I'd thought.

Aryl says it was rare in her time.

Clearly rare no more.

"M'hiray you call yourselves," Odon proclaimed. "Om'ray you are."

Eand stayed on her feet. She was the key, I decided. Protective of those in her care. Ruthless, yes, but not needlessly so. We were alike in that, and more.

"I want what you do," I told her.

The wrinkles of her face deepened. "And what do you think that is?"

"A future for our children."

She huffed at that, eyes locked with mine. After a long moment, she settled back on her stool and gave a curt nod.

"Then allow us to live here, within your Cloisters, for a time." I looked from one to the other. "We can help one another, as Om'ray do."

Approval, from Aryl, if tempered with a certain *skepticism.* Our kind, I gathered, hadn't changed that much.

"Even if we agreed," Odon said heavily, "we haven't lied. We cannot feed you. The harvest was a poor one—"

"Be truthful, Odon," Teris interrupted. "We can't feed ourselves. We'd too few to ride the last M'hir Wind. After the Tikitik took their share, we've glows enough, but we'll starve to death before the swarm takes us."

Nyala's gesture of apology seemed meant for her people, not mine. "You picked the wrong Clan to join, Sira. Teris is right. Sona won't last the rains."

Their *despair* was as sincere as it was mute. A great deal became clear to me in that moment. These were proud people, facing a situation they'd no hope of surviving alone, ashamed at what they viewed as their failure.

However we'd come here, this was the right place, at the right time, for us all.

Holl, I sent, *are you certain? We can't be wrong about this.*

Confidence came back. *We can find what they need—what we need. I promise, Sira.*

Good enough.

"We should be able to help with that," I told Sona's Council, and proceeded to explain.

Sona's First Scout lingered to see her Council safely out of our clutches. Not that I believed she considered us a threat, but distrust seemed her nature, one Aryl approved.

Something's on her mind. I'd say it's not good news.

Morgan was right. The door closed, Destin di Anel came to us, her expression an interesting mix of reticence and determination. "Can you do what you say?"

"Yes," I said, equally blunt. "How soon depends on what you bring us to *analyze.*" The word came out in Comspeak, so I clarified: "Test with our devices. The more the better."

"Your samples are coming." Her eyes went to Barac, I thought assessingly, then settled on Morgan. "These two have weapons."

"Which they haven't used," I pointed out, unsure where this was going. I translated for Morgan, felt his *curiosity*. "Why?"

"Weapons and the Vyna's cursed Talent. When were you planning to rob us?" Destin whipped out her longknife, resting the tip against my neck, then froze—

—Morgan's blade resting along hers.

The chamber fell silent. I sent *reassurance*. "We call what we do 'porting," I said as matter-of-factly as possible while not daring to move. "We travel through the M'hir to any place we remember being. We can use someone else's memory of a place. Some of us can 'port to a person, especially heart-kin."

Her brows met. "You have heart-kin?"

Of all I said, that caught her attention? I thought quickly. Om'ray were connected, one to all. Deeper connections would be significant. Unable to share that sensation, I did the next best thing.

I stretched out my hand.

Careful. From Barac. My Chosen merely waited.

Destin's eyes shifted to Morgan, then back to me. Suddenly her palm, hard and callused, met mine.

Power she had, along with a control as finely honed as the blade still at my throat. I lowered my shields, giving her room to explore what I was, what we were, without exposing Morgan or Aryl. When I felt the knife move away, I sought her mind in the M'hir.

There. A wisp of light within the darkness, steady and calm, beating like a heart. Connected, like a heart. To her Chosen, to others. I let them be. *Destin.*

This is the M'hir. Without fear.

We mustn't linger, I informed her, pulling us both back.

Between breaths, that moment of distraction, but enough for Destin to have lowered her weapon and Morgan's to have disappeared again up his sleeve. She stared at me. "You—I could hardly look at you."

Barac nodded. "Sira's like that."

You are, you know, my Chosen sent softly.

What mattered was how Destin saw me now. "We mean Sona

no harm," I told her. "We are what I said, looking for refuge. A home."

"I know." Almost a smile, then she turned serious again. "Our Council wasn't wrong to warn you about staying here. It isn't just the lack of food." Destin lowered her voice. "The Vyna know our number's increased. They're cowards and few, but this—" she gestured to the chamber full of M'hiray "—will tempt them beyond reason. They'll come. For your supplies." Quieter still, "most of all, for your children and unChosen."

I found myself speechless, my hair coiling like snakes. Barac and Morgan exchanged grim looks; likely more.

My cousin spoke. "Go on."

"There's no more Passage. No unChosen go from Clan to Chooser. The Oud put a stop to it and the Vyna grow desperate." Destin paused. "You may be safe in here. I've never heard of a Vyna appearing inside a Cloisters. It may be they can't."

I wasn't reassured. Cloisters were for Adepts and the infirm, unlikely to attract such raiders as Destin described, until now. "What can we do?"

The First Scout dropped her hand to her knife hilt. "What we do. If any Vyna appear, kill them. You won't have a second chance."

Kill Om'ray? Aryl's *distress* mirrored my own.

"Understood," Barac said curtly. From the look on Morgan's face, the two were in full accord.

How was I to tell our people we faced yet another threat?

Worse, that it was from our own kind?

I took it as a mark of their desperation that the mystified Sona had voted unanimously to supply samples of plant and animal life for Holl to analyze, choosing to believe our claim of being able to find an alternative to—what had Aryl named it?—dresel.

They weren't the only ones. *The Tikitik said there was a food—a favorite—like dresel for each Clan.* Aryl appeared entranced. *We'd no way to discover which it was for ourselves, even if we'd thought of it. This is wonderful!*

"It's a start," Morgan replied, ever-cautious. As a gesture of goodwill, we'd promised the Sona to feed ourselves. A fair number of M'hiray had been traveling with what emergency supplies they'd been able to pack; combining those, we had sufficient concentrated rations to last our group for three days.

Three days ago, a lifetime ago, I'd been on the *Silver Fox,* learning I was pregnant. "We've time," I said, forcing cheer into my voice. "That's what counts."

My Human lifted an eyebrow. "Stuck in here for another three days?"

"We're more comfortable." Thanks to Destin, the Sona had brought bedding and some furnishings, having those to spare. The decline of their Clan was written in hands that placed a chair just so, or gently unfolded a blanket. They brought us clothing as well, better suited to the jungle than ours; a gesture that boded well.

"I had to promise. We outnumber them three to one," I reminded him. "They've every right to be anxious about us roaming freely." We'd worries of our own. *And what of the Vyna?*

We're ready.

I stopped trying on boots. Morgan and Barac had had a series of murmured—or utterly silent—conversations since Destin left us, with, now that I thought about it, the most physically capable of the M'hiray.

And weren't those blue eyes just brimming with innocence?

An innocence I knew better than to trust. "Do I want to know?"

Witchling. With a world of *regret.*

Meaning I didn't. I went back to fitting a Sona boot against the sole of my foot.

Because Morgan knew and Barac—and now those others—how to kill another person. They hadn't taught me.

Knowing there was no need. I'd defend my people if it came to it, my way.

Barac stood watch by the door the Sona preferred to use, offering his smiling help with each new load for the M'hiray. That this let him see outside the door each time it turned open hadn't bothered the Om'ray. I'd a feeling Destin had arranged it, realizing that view, now shared, would allow us to 'port from the chamber at will.

It wasn't quite freedom, the still-wary Sona having insisted we promise not to leave without permission. Deni, eager to explore the Cloisters, refused to talk to me. Tle di Parth had proved disturbingly agreeable, given there was an unChosen of respectable strength on the other side of the door, a better Candidate for her Choice than any here and doubtless eager to meet her. Her easy cooperation puzzled me until I noticed her attention to the older of the di Licor brothers.

The pair had been assigned the unused door by Barac, a valid duty, if one unlikely to be dangerous. Asdny seemed unaware, as yet, of Tle's interest or that of our other Choosers. When ready, instinct would step in. If Tle's Power-of-Choice roused, he'd be drawn to it over any other.

If? When. Then the fireworks, as Morgan would say.

Jacqui and Ermu would rouse as well. Three Choosers, four unChosen, five if I counted the Sona, all in one place.

Om'ray unChosen left on Passage. Or did, Aryl informed me. *Choosers would call to them. Guide them.*

It sounded like a romance-vid until I considered the landscape and neighbors between. *How many died?*

A pause. *Most.*

There were reasons the Clan Council had rules governing Choice. Saving unChosen from themselves—and Choosers from one another—among them.

Asdny was the youngest and weakest. Tle's Power was too great for him to survive. What was she thinking? If she was, I decided grimly, having had my own brush with that instinct lately. I supposed I'd have to talk to Sona's Council on this issue, too. Or, I brightened, I could have Enora sud Sarc do it. Who better than—?

"We've a visitor," my Chosen announced. We watched Barac speak briefly with whomever stood outside. When the conversation ended, he waited till the door closed, then beckoned to

Asdny to take his place. "With news," Morgan added. For my cousin was heading our way in some haste, dodging what were becoming minor encampments.

When Barac came close, I could see his frown. "Now what?" I grumbled. Cersi was becoming a bit unfair.

Morgan stretched lazily. "Nothing's wrong. That I can *taste*."

I eyed him. "You aren't always right, you know. Remember that time on Pocular—?"

He grinned. "All of them. Happy you do."

Incorrigible, that's what he was. I found myself grinning back.

Arrived, Barac shook his finger at the pair of us. "No more of that." Before I could blush, he gave the news. "They want Morgan outside to choose the samples we need."

And didn't those blue eyes light up at that?

"I said we weren't putting any of our people at risk," Barac continued, giving me a look as plain as any sending. He knew Morgan, too. "They insisted I tell you of their—request."

"Good thing," Morgan said briskly. "Perfect timing. The rain's stopped."

As if that could possibly make the notion of him outside, with these Om'ray who considered him *not-real*, not to mention the threat of Vyna, any more palatable. "Check the samples," I told him, "and come right back."

"Check the samples. Take a look around. Then come right back." Morgan lifted his arms, palm up. His signal for the final offer on the table. "Come get me if there's a problem."

"There better not be a problem," I threatened.

"That's the spirit," he applauded, growing improbably more cheerful.

While he and Barac went over the necessary preparations, Aryl contributing advice I did my best not to overhear, I considered the Sona and this change to our arrangement.

Wanted Morgan—my Chosen—did they?

Fair enough.

There was something I wanted in return.

Interlude

MORGAN LOST HIS SMILE and tightened his shields the instant he passed through the door. Much as he'd like to view this as an adventure, it was as far from it as any action he'd seen on Karolus. The Sona had been willing to murder them.

He was more than willing to find out how.

"$#@*~"

Destin, the First Scout herself, gesturing for him to follow her down the hall. Three more Om'ray stepped up to flank him. Instead of moving, Morgan brought up one hand, fingers spread, then slowly reached into a pocket. Her pale eyes tracked the movement, flicking to his face, then back.

He fastened the comlink to the collar of his coat. "Repeat." A burst of fluid sound came from the small cylinder.

The Om'ray nearest him grunted, "(*#&@S"

The 'link rendered that as: <u>Oud tricks.</u>

They weren't surprised by his tech. "Not Oud," Morgan replied earnestly. With the barest rudiments in the 'link, he couldn't trust it with anything complex. Unfortunately, this was, if he understood Cersi at all, a crucial point. "Not Oud. Mine." Morgan pointed to himself.

"$#%"

That one he'd figured out already: "not-real." "Not Om'ray," he corrected firmly. "Chosen."

Destin studied him for a silent moment. <u>Come.</u> She paused, then added, <u>Chosen</u>.

Translator's working, he sent in triumph. Morgan didn't look back at the sound of raised voices. Sira'd told him what she planned to do; the Om'ray, he thought fondly, didn't have a hope of resisting. Still. *Don't trust them.*

I won't if you won't. A rush of *affection* . . . something *wistful.*

He wasn't the only one who relished exploring. Morgan hid a smile. *Next time, chit.*

Once he'd determined this new world's risks.

Chapter 41

BEFORE THE DOOR COULD CLOSE after Morgan, I stepped into the opening. "Move aside, please."

Gurutz's attention had wandered after Morgan and the others. He started at my voice, leaking *astonishment.* "What did you say?"

I chose to ignore his lack of manners. "Risking my Chosen outside has changed our arrangement," I informed him. "We're going to examine the levels we'll be using." I smiled. "You're welcome to come along."

"I can't leave my—" Flustered, he looked around for support. It having left with Morgan, he deflated. "You can't. This is a matter for—"

I moved forward.

"—Council." The poor Om'ray hesitated, eyes dropping to my pendant, then backed out of my way. Attitude, my Human would say, was half the battle with aliens. Not always the better half, but I'd taken his point. Trusting those behind me to follow my example, I sauntered down the hall of Sona's Cloisters as if I'd lived there my entire life.

I'd left Barac in charge, much to his chagrin, bringing with me those most likely to make sense of what we might find: Jacqui, Deni sud Kessa'at, Nik and Josa sud Prendolat, and—after some thought—Degal di Sawnda'at.

Morgan wondered what had changed since Aryl di Sarc walked these halls. So did I; so did she, though her memories of this place were filled with loss. I could wish to spare her further grief.

I respected my great-grandmother's courage too much to even try.

Degal, like most of the others, didn't know Aryl existed. I hadn't felt inclined to share that a "ghost" inhabited my father-less baby, there being a sufficiency of strange for them to face at the moment.

What Degal did know were the Prime Laws, the guiding principles set in place, I now suspected, not by the M'hiray but by the Maker in this Cloisters. Degal's familiarity with the finer details as well as resulting Council decisions might not seem immediately of use.

I was betting it would. There were deeper reasons here. Implications that teased at me—or was that terrified? I wasn't the only one to question this world. Morgan could name several within the Trade Pact where more than one intelligence had evolved in tandem, but those were either combined as obligate symbionts or isolated by adaptation to physically incompatible environments.

If Cersi was the Om'ray homeworld, where had the Oud and Tikitik come from—and why?

The first mystery to solve, however, was this building. My new memories told me something of its structure, as did those of the other M'hiray the Maker had intended to serve as Adepts, yet there were gaps not even Aryl could fill. As for the Dream Chamber?

It held a fascination I thoroughly distrusted.

The corridor was illuminated by light emerging from the curve where walls met ceiling, as we'd seen in the Council Chamber; unlike that space, this floor was less resilient underfoot and pale yellow. The outer wall was broken by a series of large triple arches, the inner being a metal door, the two outer being clear windows. Opposite those, on the inner wall, were smaller doors. Aryl showed me the trick to opening them, but I stopped after looking into the third identical room, each empty and too small for living quarters.

We passed framed art at intervals, none of it comprehensible. Deni grew so intent on whatever his device's display was telling him, I waited for him to walk into a wall. He certainly wasn't observing for himself.

Jacqui was, eyes round with wonder, head turning each time we passed a window. The Chosen pair divided their attention between the device Nik held in one hand, and where we were going.

With occasional dark looks at Degal.

Forget him, I wanted to tell them. Forget what Degal's Council had forbidden that had driven them to my mother and her lonely lab, starting with a daughter they hadn't allowed to be fostered. I wanted—but wouldn't. We'd forgotten too much recently.

You can't protect them from their choices.

I smiled at Aryl's crisp advice. *I but follow your example, Great-grandmother.*

Deni stopped at one of the frames and we gathered around him. It looked like all the others, to me, of the same gray-green metal as the pendant weighing on my neck. Like the pendant, its disks and squares bore symbols. Not identical, I judged, comparing the two, but similar enough to have been made by the same hands.

If hands had been involved. Nothing about the Om'ray suggested they were capable of such construction. Another mystery.

Show me. After I did so, Aryl replied, *I never knew what they were. Marcus*—a poignant pause—*I wondered if his clever devices could have told me, but he wasn't allowed inside.*

"Deni?" I asked for us both, for he'd brought up his own.

Only to put aside one instrument to hurriedly fumble out another, repeating the same motion over the metal. He reached along a section of bare wall.

"I—a moment, please." He touched Nik and Josa, consulting in private, as was their habit. Before Degal could be offended by this breach of manners, Deni dropped his hand, staring at the framed symbols. "It's a control panel—or input of some kind." He looked down the hall, mouth moving as if counting those in view. "They're connected within the wall."

I asked what I thought a sensible question, given we stood in an otherwise ordinary hallway. "What are they for?"

His smile was rapturous. "I have no idea."

Om'ray technology? Aryl sounded fascinated. *Enris always claimed it was so, that we were more, once.*

But what? I might not *taste* change, but this left a sick feeling in my stomach. Rows of empty rooms. Panel after panel of controls across from them. Storage?

Or a prison.

Maybe I had another clue to offer. I passed Deni the pendant, pointing out the symbols. "Do these mean anything?"

The three huddled over it, scanning and muttering.

Sira. It was Barac. *Andi says more Om'ray have entered the Cloisters. Coming to you.*

We'd been noticed. My point made concerning Morgan, I saw no gain in further confrontation until I'd reason for it. "We've company," I advised the others. "Let's see as much as we can first."

"We concur." Nik wasn't answering me. She handed back the pendant. "It's a transmitter."

I paused, the chain over my head. Not was, is. "It's still working?" My voice had a regrettable squeak.

"If you'd put it on, please, Sira?"

And why would I do that? But the three gave me such earnest looks, I finished the motion, feeling the pendant thud into place. *The Tikitik can detect the metal of the pendant—and of tokens,* Aryl ventured. *Is that what they mean?*

I don't think so.

Heads went down over instruments. Then up. Nik spoke, "Increased signal emission, both strength and complexity. I'd say it's intended to be worn."

By a Speaker, Aryl qualified, her mind voice as troubled as I felt. *They all wear one. Om'ray, Oud, Tikitik. Only Speakers may communicate with another race.*

Making the pendants the perfect way to overhear that communication.

What was this world?

Interlude

THE WIDE SURROUNDING PLATFORM and its low-railed wall, he'd glimpsed from the Council Chamber windows. Morgan hadn't expected the bridge.

It joined the platform at a pair of massive beautiful doors, their surface worked in intricate color and patterns, abstract or simply too alien to grasp. They'd been turned on centered-hinges, allowing him to see how the bridge threw itself up to meet a wooden platform built around the nearest of the gigantic trees. The bridge itself was of cunning construction, gray-green metal slats for a floor and more of the metal woven into a tight mesh, forming walls and a curved roof.

The wooden platform at the end, with its rope ladders, however well crafted, were light-years distant from the technology to create the bridge or the building behind him.

As arriving Om'ray arranged their bundles of foliage and bags of what he was to inspect, Morgan studied the Cloisters.

Aryl had shared an image of the one at Yena, her home Clan. That had sat high above its swamp on a three-sided tower, coated in vines. From below, the building had resembled two giant bowls nested one atop the other. From above, it was more like an opened flower: two walled platforms encircling a curved inner core—always curves, Morgan noted.

Sona's tower and lower platform were submerged in its swamp. Though water edged the remaining platform, diligence by the Om'ray, or some feature intrinsic to the structure, kept the walls free of moss or other growth. Luckily for him, it also kept away the abundant flying life, the volume of that frustrated hum and whine as much warning of what waited beyond as the gauze wrapping the heads of those Om'ray crossing the bridge.

The Cloisters' round outer wall was broken by a series of arches, within each a set of three more: centermost a door, outer two windows. Or clear doors. There were upper floors, smaller as the building rose to a dome, marked by a rising spiral of windows and what resembled white petals. Artistry or essential function? Both, Morgan decided, as impressed as he was mystified.

He chose the nearest Om'ray. "Who built this?"

The Clanswoman shied at the sounds from his comlink as if he'd struck her, returning to her work only after Morgan gestured apology and moved away. It was the same with the next he tried.

The question or who asked it?

<u>These are ready for you.</u> Destin indicated a table assembled from planking and collapsible legs. It was covered in platters of a red gleaming wood, each with a portion of some foodstuff to test.

Morgan nodded, bringing out his scanner. Already set for Human standard, Holl had provided markers for the compounds required by M'hiray and Om'ray, substances readily available from a Human-sourced diet. Had they not arrived on Stonerim III, a Human world, the M'hiray might have come to a quick and unpleasant end.

He hadn't told Holl the scanner also contained Huido's latest, extremely comprehensive list of toxins. By adding as many of Cersi's organics to its database as he could, Morgan hoped to flag anything dangerously similar. Chemistry being chemistry. It'd be a shame if their new friends were like the Assemblers and tried to poison them.

Not that he believed the Sona planned to murder their guests. That they were capable of it, to preserve limited resources and save themselves, yes, but the interest of Destin and the others who knew if what he hunted was palpable. If he lowered his shields, he'd *feel* it. They wanted hope above all.

Morgan set to work. The first offerings turned up negative. The table was cleared without comment and replenished.

Nothing. As the table was cleared a second time, Morgan didn't need Talent to read their disappointment. Some moved away in disgust, communing with others who gave him wary looks.

Destin waved over an Om'ray, taking the pouch from his belt. Putting her back to Morgan a moment, she turned to face him again, holding out two closed fists.

Demanding a demonstration—proof their technology could do what was promised, find a new source of what they needed.

Morgan set the scanner to audible, brought it over her right fist. Nothing. There was an unhappy murmur from those gathered to watch.

Over her left.

The scanner gave a loud cheery *WHIRR-PING!*

The First Scout uncurled her fists, showing them to the Om'ray. On her right palm rolled a little brown nut, on her left, a wizened bit of purple. Dresel, she told Morgan with a satisfied smile, returning the precious scrap to its owner.

A shame Destin wasn't on Council. That being hardly political to say to her, he gestured to the table. "More."

More, she agreed, snapping orders to the rest.

They weren't paying attention. Heads had lifted, turned to face away from the Cloisters, into the undergrowth.

A shriek rang out, long and shuddering, sending a visceral chill down Morgan's spine. The sound was repeated. Whatever made it was coming closer—and nothing good, by the now-grim quiet of the Om'ray.

"Destin?" he whispered.

Tikitik. She gave him a distracted, then calculating look. Wrong time—bad time—"@#$%#@^^"

The translator garbled the rest. No matter. A surprise visit so soon after their arrival? It couldn't be coincidence.

Another shuddering shriek, as though something died horribly. Or celebrated such a death.

Morgan?

Sira, sensing his tension.

We've company. Stay there.

Time to meet the neighbors, Morgan thought. Whatever they were.

Chapter 42

*S*TAY THERE.

My Human was curious—and no fool. I swallowed my worry, though I tightened my awareness of him. Should these Tikitik be dangerous—

They are. Before I reacted, Aryl added, *But they love to talk.*

Talking, in my experience, could be dangerous too. In this, however, I trusted Morgan.

If not what I wore around my neck.

I fussed with the pendant as Deni, Nik, and Josa took the lead, festooned with instruments taken from their packs. A transmitter implied a receiver. A receiver implied—what? Someone or something paying close attention to Cersi's Speakers.

Maybe once, long ago; after all, the pendants were ancient, like the Cloisters.

The lift below Norval continued to function, though the city above had failed and crumbled. The thought made me want to toss the pendant into the next empty room—

As if I could afford to lose an object with meaning to the Sona, granting rank even among the non-Om'ray. I was, as Huido would say mournfully, stuck in sand.

The floor became a ramp, rising evenly as we went to circle the building's outer rim. Doors became less frequent, windows more so. Outside was a dark wall of muted greens, mauves, and browns, interspersed with mist-filled shadow. It might have been twilight. I'd hoped for sunshine.

The canopy doesn't let it through. Aryl shared a dizzying image of rounded treetops and a brilliant blue-purple sky. Things flew there, with black-and-white wings or clear ones. Flowers like giant twists of candy—I used my names while learning hers: wastryl, flitters, nekis, and fronds. The mighty rastis. In the distance, Aryl showed me the dusty jagged edge of a mountain range.

The source of the hot dry M'hir—namesake of that other space—the seasonal wind that freed the rastis pods—my heart beat with her *love* of this wild and terrible landscape, her *pride* in having lived here.

Beyond the mountains, a void.

At the incongruity, I slowed my steps. Beyond the mountains stretched the rest of this continent, or would be an ocean or—

Aryl had followed my thought. *It doesn't matter. Marcus could go there. We could not. Our world ends there.*

She shared the memory, of flying in what I recognized as an antique aircar over those mountains. I felt the echoed urgency, Marcus Bowman's, his need to warn other Triads of the attack.

Attack?

I saw a ship bristling with weapons, landing.

Pirates?

Meaning someone else had found Cersi. Distracted, I was swept into the moment with Aryl—*reaching the world's* end *to be torn from all other Om'ray and cast adrift. Knowing the only hope was to find our way home, to 'port through the M'hir—abandoning Marcus, who'd trusted us, saved us—*

—*seeing him suffer for it, until I took my knife and*—

"Sira. Sira di Sarc!"

I hadn't realized I'd stopped, that tears poured down my cheeks. My hand shaking, I wiped them away. It hadn't been my hand granting mercy to my dearest friend.

It might as well have been.

Taking a breath, then another, I managed to give Degal a

wavering smile. "Must be the baby." It wasn't a lie. Aryl's grief tore at mine, reopening still-fresh wounds.

"You're pregnant?" He looked toward Jacqui.

And must have sent her a private message, for she stopped at once, turning back to us. "Is everything all right?"

"How can she be—? Baltir said—" Degal gestured a hasty apology, well aware what my reaction would be to the name of the Retian who'd carved out my insides in hopes of making more of me. At the order of the Clan Council, no less.

While I no longer cared, I couldn't resist. "Jason and I are happy he was wrong."

"Why—that's—" the former Council member blanched, perhaps considering the unthinkable. Was my baby half-Human?

I sighed inwardly. In no way did this Clansman, who'd been willfully blind to the truth for so long, deserve it now.

Our people, who'd listen to him, did. "Our child is mine alone. Apparently," I showed my teeth, "it's common here." Among the Vyna, but that, he didn't need to know.

Oblivious, Jacqui stood moving her hands in front of my abdomen, squinting in concentration, her posture so like Nik and Josa with their scanners I wanted to laugh. I closed my lips over what I feared would sound more like hysteria.

Forgive me, Sira. Aryl's presence had returned to its normal, soothing self. *I didn't expect—it won't happen again.*

You weren't to blame. Then or now.

What had happened—however painful—was in the past and not my concern. What was? Why Aryl, an Om'ray, had been unable to leave this part of the planet.

Could the Oud or Tikitik?

Could we?

I'd enough disturbing questions to last a lifetime without these. I shifted my attention to Degal, who'd changed the subject. "—thought the Sona were right behind us. Where are they?"

The Clan must show itself to the Tikitik.

"They've other visitors," I stated, letting him assume I'd heard from Morgan. "Let's hope they keep one another busy. I want to explore as much as possible."

A light brush of fingertips on my wrist, a gentle *protest. Let us continue,* Jacqui sent. *You could go back. Rest.*

About to argue the night of dreaming had been more than sufficient, I was struck by inspiration. We could cover more of the Cloisters if we split up and 'ported to different locations; I was willing to trust Aryl's memory, if not the one imposed by the Maker. No one would know—

The Om'ray will sense where you are, she disagreed. *If not who. That was the rarer Talent—in my time.*

Making it possible it was no longer rare, and any Om'ray could track any of us.

Between that disquieting realization and the pendant, I began to feel back on Plexis, tagged and monitored. With Huido and Huido's restaurant and real food—

And Assemblers, I reminded myself. Not Plexis, then.

Not yet.

Not, I told myself, ever.

When had I known we weren't going back, that there was only forward and this world?

When you met the Om'ray, Aryl sent gently. *When you learned these few survivors were not the last of our kind. When you found hope, Sira.*

Older, yes, and occasionally wiser, but she was wrong, that wasn't it, that wasn't—I stopped myself.

Of course it was. I *felt* Morgan smile, reacting to the *peace* within me.

I could no more help caring what happened to the Sona than I could the M'hiray, and by extension all the Om'ray on Cersi.

Except the Vyna.

No, including the Vyna, though I probably should meet them for myself before pronouncing judgment either way. Every family had its problem child. I pressed my hand below my waist. *Thank you, Great-grandmother.*

I put aside the notion of 'porting inside the Cloisters. Given the First Scout's feelings about the Vyna's 'cursed Talent,' we'd be wise to be circumspect in its use. For now. We'd teach those who could touch the M'hir, if they wished.

"Sira?"

Jacqui, waiting patiently.

"Let's continue till someone stops us," I said, rewarded by smiles from Deni, Josa, and Nik, a nod from Degal.

I spared a moment to hope Morgan was getting some answers. And not, like me, alarming new questions.

Interlude

THE SONA BURST INTO ACTION, abandoning the samples they'd brought in order to hurry across the bridge. Morgan stood to one side as more ran out from the Cloisters. In the distance, he could see others arriving, climbing down the trunks of trees, dashing along branches. He was forgotten.

Almost. The First Scout paused at the doors to the bridge. An Om'ray had been assigned to stay there. After a quick exchange with him, Destin came back to Morgan, pointing meaningfully at the door to the Cloisters.

Smiling, they had in common. Morgan smiled his very best and pointed to the bridge.

Destin's answering smile was anything but pleasant. Go back #@#$^^

Another shriek, close enough to raise the hairs on his neck. Seeing her tiny flinch, the Human put a hand to his chest. "Speaker is my Chosen. Her right to hear this."

She understood, he could tell. Moreover, he thought she was inclined to agree with him, Sira having made an impression.

At last, Destin tapped her knife hilt and gestured to the bridge. Hear only.

Morgan tried not to walk too eagerly.

The slats were strong, not bouncing underfoot, nor did their footfalls make any sound. He resisted the urge to scan the structure, Destin being right behind him and likely glad of any reason to send him back. The air pulsing up was thick and fragrant with rot, warm enough that he'd regret the coat soon.

If not its protection and the contents of its pockets.

Metal met wood, and Morgan stepped up, careful of his footing. The Om'ray didn't believe in handrails. Nor that ladders— he discovered with a dismayed peek over the side—needed to be more than sticks and braided rope.

Fine for them. He watched Om'ray slip over the edge of the platform—not only here, but from others he could now see— hooking toes and fingertips to descend so quickly they might have been falling.

Falling not being a good thought, with what was below, though at least they weren't climbing to the ominous black water but to floating docks secured to the buttresses of this and nearby trees, taking up positions on benches and slings.

Go back? Destin offered pleasantly.

In answer, Morgan lowered himself over the edge, shifting his coat out of the way. Work on the *Fox* had entailed its share of ladder climbing, ladders properly fastened to walls and not swaying through the air with each movement. He took his time, uncaring if the First Scout followed impatiently.

Until fire shot through his hand! He almost let go.

Destin chuckled as more bites made Morgan abandon caution for speed; whatever'd found him feasted as greedily on face and neck as hands. He let himself drop the final length, hurriedly reaching inside his coat to activate his persona-shield.

He sighed with relief as the cloud of disappointed biters flew off. The sting of their attack subsided; just as well, his med-kit was in the Council Chamber.

Morgan found himself on another platform. Below, along the network of docks, the Sona Om'ray had finished arranging themselves. Counting quickly, he'd reached thirty-one—thirty-two—as the First Scout landed lightly beside him, her gauze net lowered as if flaunting Om'ray immunity.

No, to show him the seriousness of her expression. Destin

tapped the platform with her toe. Stay here, she said in a low voice, frowning when the 'link's translation was louder.

Understanding, Morgan set it to a whisper. Better?

Better none, she warned. Only the Speakers talk. Understand?

For they weren't alone.

A tall narrow form emerged from the darkness, a shadow come to life. It rocked toward them on six long and armored legs, broad feet lifting in measured step, each dropping with a splash. The neck was elongated, with two deep bends, and the head carried low, sweeping from side to side. Four large eyes, paired nostrils, and a line of bristled hair running from snout to neck implied ample senses. The mouth gaped, revealing twin rows of needle-sharp teeth.

However exquisitely adapted to the conditions of this swamp, the fearsome-looking predator wasn't here to hunt. Overlapping black plates protected the lower half of its body but the thick hair of the upper half was dyed with red-and-white geometric forms and bore riders. One sat astride, two more clung precariously to their mount's sides, gripping its hair.

The mount halted a distance away, as if the riders awaited a signal to approach.

Tikitik, Destin said in his ear.

The neighbors. Morgan studied them. Bipedal, with a thickened knobby skin, the torso was concave and thin, as were the long arms and legs. The arms had a second joint, as well as short spines along their back edge. The neck, like the mount's, curved down and forward so a Tikitik's head hovered before the midpoint of its chest. Or, like those clinging to hair, extended to aim.

Wider at the back, that head, framed by two pairs of eyes set on fleshy cones, the front pair a quarter the size of the rear. Thick finger-like cilia covered where Morgan guessed would be a mouth.

The ankles and wrists of all three were wrapped with cloth patterned in complex symbols, while belts around their thin middles supported longknives identical to that at Destin's side.

Speaker.

The one sitting astride. It wore a white sash from right shoulder to left hip, ending in tasseled braids that hung to its dangling foot. On that sash was a pendant.

Putting a hand on his shoulder, Destin pressed down. Stay, that meant. Morgan sank with the pressure into a comfortable squat, nodding.

Her eyes darted to the foliage around them, back and forth, up and down, then she looked at him and tapped her knife hilt.

Things in the bushes, Morgan interpreted. Lovely. He gave his wrist the tiny twist to drop a throwing blade into his hand and showed her its grim shine.

Destin grinned, putting a finger to her throat. There was a great deal to like about the First Scout.

She dropped over the platform. The Human watched her take her post by Sona's Council.

White-robed, standing with their Speaker centermost, they formed a line between their people and what approached.

Morgan couldn't help but admire their courage.

Odon spoke, his tone formal. We see you.

After bobbing its head twice, sharply, the Tikitik sent its mount splashing to the dock. They'd waited to be acknowledged by the Om'ray Speaker, Morgan noted. Why? Good manners between such different neighbors? Or simple prudence, by those considered "not-real."

The beast crouched at a command, sinking into the water to allow the Tikitik Speaker to step onto the dock, then rose, water dripping from its hair like rain. The eyes of the two Tikitik still mounted swiveled to lock on the Om'ray.

The Tikitik Speaker darted toward Odon with such speed Morgan tensed, fearing an attack, but it stopped short of the Om'ray. Though twice his height, the low hanging neck brought the Tikitik's face to the same level. Eyes turned on their cones.

Providing multiple images or differing information?

A three-fingered hand stretched out toward the Om'ray Speaker's pendant but didn't quite touch. "@#$%# $#@#%^^^" A guttural voice, differently pitched, but the same language as far as Morgan could tell.

Confirmed when the comlink, after a slight delay, rendered: <u>Where is the other one?</u>

As if it knew about Sira, but how—

"#$@%>"

From behind.

Morgan turned, slowly, tightening his grip on the little throwing knife. <u>I think you know,</u> whispered the 'link.

He shared the platform with another Tikitik, the textured black and soft gray of its knobby skin superb camouflage. This one wore a black sash, narrow and with its excess secured to a low belt so as not to impede movement. The fabric around its wrist was red, marked with symbols, the largest being a wavy pair of lines above three widening circles. It squatted at seeming ease, knees over its head, neck outstretched. All four eyes bent to regard him, the movement making a meaty sound. <u>Do you not?</u>

No obvious weakness, Morgan calculated. Longer reach—he'd seen the speed—and at home in the trees as he was not, to come up on him like this.

Only Speakers communicated with other races, and they wore pendants. Did this Tikitik want to trick him into breaking that rule?

As if he cared. *Look what's come to visit,* he sent Sira, *sharing* an image of the creature. Morgan smiled. "I'm new here. Who are you?"

The head bobbed, then the body moved with that blinding speed, the alien winding up so close he could smell the faint spice of its warm breath. The cilia around its mouth worked the air between them as if tasting his. <u>Not Om'ray,</u> it concluded.

That again?

Before he could reply, the Tikitik eased back. It uttered a soft husky bark the translator didn't try to render.

Then a word it did.

<u>Human.</u>

Chapter 43

A THOUGHT TRAVELER!
The naming came with incoherent torrent of images and emotions. I staggered as if struck; felt Jacqui's hands steady me.

Aryl—but she was frantic and wouldn't stop. I shielded myself against her until all that could pass was *DANGERDANGERDANGER!*

Shaking myself free, I followed my link to Morgan and *pushed* . . .

Interlude

SIRA APPEARED ON THE PLATFORM, hair thrashing, her expression boding ill to anything in range. The Tikitik scrambled back—

Morgan opened his mouth—

Too late. Sira took one look down and . . .

Morgan found himself standing inside the Cloisters, with his Chosen. They were in a room he hadn't seen before, no bigger than their cabin on the *Fox* and empty of any furnishings.

It did, however, contain one extremely unhappy alien.

Chapter 44

MORGAN AND I DODGED in opposite directions as the creature bolted dizzyingly from side to side in the small room, throwing itself against walls while *KEENING* so loudly I wanted to cover my ears.

The racket prevented any chance to reason with it. *Aryl?*

An unhelpful *confusion* along with intense *disapproval*.

My first Tikitik and I'd driven it mad. Huido abhorred traveling through the M'hir; it was entirely possible I'd done this alien harm in my desire not to have a conversation perched in a tree.

We were outside?

I shared my impression of shadows, wet wood, and that appalling too-near drop, feeling her *disapproval* change into *amusement*.

I refused to feel guilty for preferring solid ground. Bad enough watching the gangly being rebound from yet another wall. "I'd better put it back."

Before I could, Morgan managed to intercept the Tikitik. He wrestled the larger being to the floor where it subsided in a curl of misery, hands pawing at its eyes.

He took off his coat, easing it over the creature.

The *keening* stopped.

"It's this room." Morgan looked at me. "We need somewhere with windows."

Here, Aryl sent. *It's private.*

Because bringing a not-Om'ray inside a Cloisters was forbidden. I'd received that message from her already.

And ignored it.

I would not be bound by Om'ray rules, especially those in the category of "not helping."

I *pushed* . . .

Interlude

THE CLOSET-LIKE ROOM gave way to one of natural light and airy space. They were at the top of the building, Morgan realized with delight. The large white petals he'd seen from the outside formed the walls, folding inward to meet—or was it allow—a view of the sky through an irregular slice of transparent ceiling. Rows of elongated benches curved along one side, facing an open space; seating for a hundred or more.

He dropped to his heels beside the huddled Tikitik, gently tugging on his coat. The creature resisted, clawed fingertips digging into the fabric.

Sira joined him. Feeling her *remorse,* Morgan shook his head. "We need to talk to more than the Om'ray. You did the right thing." He feigned a shudder. "Besides, things bite out there."

The start of a dimple. "I can speak its language," she said. "What do I say? And don't tell me 'hello.' We're past that."

"True." He was guessing, to be sure, but he'd relied on instinct in stranger circumstances. The Tikitik had been confident, arrogant even, in its own environment, one unlikely to include closed buildings. It could be, Morgan decided, that simple. "Tell it to look up. That the sky's back."

She did.

Its fingers unclenched, but he left it his coat. After a moment, cilia pushed out from under that protection, wiggled cautiously, to be followed by the tip of its head and two smaller eyes. Those bent sharply on their stalks to regard the ceiling.

Unwise, Aryl sent, no doubt to them both.

Morgan agreed with Sira's shrug. Unwise was staking the future of those waiting below on the chance they could find food for all in three days. This was a remarkable opportunity, if they could reassure their guest.

The Tikitik unfolded, shedding the coat. Its large eyes drank in the sky, then rotated to bear upon him.

Then found Sira. It rose to its feet, not taking an eye from her.

Morgan stood with it, knives loose and at the ready beneath his shirt. A small eye cocked his way for an instant, then bent to the coat, then returned to Sira.

You shouldn't have come back.

Chapter 45

CALM AND DIGNIFIED, our Tikitik, given a view of the sky; Morgan had been right, as he often was. Now he gave me a warning look I understood completely.

How could this being know of us?

Fair was fair. We knew something of it, too. "Thought Traveler," I greeted, bowing my head; Aryl a grim silence in the background. "My name is Sira Morgan. This is my Chosen, Jason Morgan."

"Names I do not know. Intriguing." Cilia clustered, then spread. Its voice came from somewhere within them. "Your heritage is plain," it announced suddenly. "Descendant of Sarc and Mendolar, Parth and Serona." An eye considered Morgan. "Human—yes. We do not forget your taste."

I translated that ominous phrasing for Morgan. He looked more intrigued than worried. "Sorry for the rough ride." The comlink spouted something more like "regrets-bad-too-fast-walk" but the Tikitik grasped his meaning without difficulty.

"It was a pleasure." A guttural bark—a laugh. "You travel as the Vyna. I've been interested to experience the sensation, but not so foolish as to wish for it. You realize the Vyna use this 'badtoofast-walk' not only to visit other Clans without invitation but to—shall I be delicate?—remove unwanted visitors from their own."

Aryl supplied a rather bloodthirsty *satisfaction*.

Morgan gestured to the benches. "Shall we sit?"

Tikitik, it turned out, didn't sit, preferring to squat so its "face" was reasonably level with mine once I took my seat. Morgan, as I might have expected, retrieved his coat and stood behind me.

The coat being full of weaponry, the point he made wasn't for our unwilling visitor but me. "Don't provoke the alien" had been a regular part of our pre-trade session briefings; this time, any mistake would cost us this potentially valuable source of information.

Unless it lied.

It won't lie. Grudging advice. *But it won't give away the truth for nothing.*

Understood. I settled myself, unperturbed by eyeballs that moved. Though this wasn't Huido. This, I decided, was more like a Scat. A predator.

Showing it weakness would be a mistake. "Yes, we're back," I said bluntly. "With questions. There've been changes on Cersi while we were away."

Cilia groped in my direction—*tasting* according to Morgan. "In you as well, Far Traveler. Your age—quite remarkable."

As a starting point, it seemed harmless. "How so?"

"Our Om'ray burn faster."

And wasn't. *Aryl?*

Marcus said we had rapid reproduction. Sixteen-year intervals. He was surprised.

So was I, though this would explain the multitude of generations recorded in the parches the M'hiray had brought with them. I'd assumed a longer—much longer—period of time had passed, our generations being closer to Human standard. I'd been wrong.

"We've learned not to rush life," I said evasively. To Morgan, *Is such a difference even possible?*

"Life is the point." A finger, thin and supple as well as clawed, aimed precisely at what I bore.

It knows.

A large eye rotated to stare at Morgan. "Not yours." Then back at me. "Yours. Like the—"

"Vyna. Yes, I've heard." I leaned forward, wincing as my hair pulled itself back in a rude knot of aversion. "You're right. We aren't like the Om'ray who stayed on Cersi." Time to press. "We've technology to tell us this—" I held out the pendant "—is a device to send information. A transmitter."

The head reared back and up. "Speaker pendants are not devices," with scorn. "They are what *sing* to the Maker's Gift. Here." With a painful-looking motion, it tilted its head to expose the softer, gray skin of its upper throat and touched a clawtip to the tissue between its jaws. The head dropped to its normal position, eyes locked. "Any Tikitik has but to *listen* in order to *hear* the pendants being worn, no matter where in the world, just as we once *heard* the tokens of unChosen."

'Maker'? The Cloisters' machine? It couldn't be the same, yet— was it coincidence? I translated for Morgan. *Aryl?*

It has nothing to do with Om'ray, she replied testily. *The Tikitik call many things 'Maker,' including the smaller of Cersi's moons.*

If we accept the Tikitik have such a sense and the pendants were made to take advantage of it, the transmitter must be for another audience. "Oud listen, too?" Morgan asked out loud.

"The Oud are blind and deaf and thoroughly ignorant." The Tikitik rose to his full height, his head awkwardly high so I had to lean back—not that I could read its expressions, but eye contact was a habit. "Why would they listen? They consider themselves to no longer need Speakers." His head lowered, all eyes on me. "They consider themselves beyond any limits. The last time we tasted *Human* was the last time Oud accepted their part in the Balance. Is this why you've returned, Far Traveler? To see for yourselves the great hurt you did this world?"

No! An image appeared behind my eyes, a mug smashing on a floor, the liquid within spreading like blood.

I didn't need to ask what it meant.

After such dire news, any questions we had for Thought Traveler were no longer ours alone. I invited Sona's Council and the Tikitik Speaker to join us.

"Invited" involved disrupting the meeting already underway, a breach of custom, law, or whatever established for all I knew before the mountains rose to the west.

Making them too old to matter, in my opinion.

Fortunately, the shock of being 'ported silenced the Sona before they could be outraged by my breaching another: the presence of Tikitik in their Cloisters.

The presence of Thought Traveler, meanwhile, quelled the Tikitik Speaker into a humble posture, squatting while the other stood. Comparing the two, I saw the differences in their clothing. The fabric around Thought Traveler's wrists and across its chest was finer than that of the Speaker, the symbols more carefully applied. I judged the former older as well, if thicker knobs on the skin and more faded scars measured age in their species and not just personal history.

Even without those clues, Thought Traveler carried himself like someone above the rest of his kind.

Apart, Aryl corrected. *They observe and carry information between factions. The ones I knew had a dangerous curiosity and didn't hesitate to stir trouble to see what would happen.*

The Tikitiks' eyes watched the Sona, who sat, exchanging bewildered looks, on the benches.

"Thank you for coming," I said, seizing the initiative before Odon, who'd begun to rouse, could open his mouth. The Sona left in the jungle would know where their Council had reappeared; they'd be coming in a fury, I thought, especially Destin. "When the M'hiray left Cersi, the world was in Balance." Use the Tikitik's terms. "What happened afterward?"

Nyala di Edut answered for the rest. "The past isn't real," she snapped. "Why would you ask?"

I paused, dumbfounded yet again. How could the past not be real?

Because those who die can no longer be felt, Aryl explained. *Ask about Clans instead.*

Which these Om'ray assumed we could *feel* for ourselves. I sent a question to Morgan, received his answer. *Give to get.*

I hid a grimace. "You suspected we were different," I told them carefully. "We are. The child, Andi, possesses what we consider an old, very rare Talent, the one all Om'ray appear to have kept: the ability to sense where others are."

"As you do not. I thought so!" Eand exclaimed triumphantly.

"I do not," I admitted. "Of the M'hiray, only Andi does. If I *reach* through the M'hir, yes, I can find other Om'ray, but it is not the same as your gift." I gestured at the Tikitik. "Times change. What came before does matter. Let me show you the world as we remember it, so you can tell me how it is now. How it has changed."

Doubt was the least of the emotions leaking into the room, but Odon gave a slow nod.

I *shared* with the Sona Aryl's memory, her final "view" of her world as defined by Om'ray minds, speaking aloud and pointing as I did so for Morgan's benefit and our "guests."

Seven Clans plus Sona, the reborn. From Sona, I pointed south to Grona, nestled at the foot of the mountains and last to see the sun each day. North, to Vyna, deeper in the mountains, smallest in number. North and east to Rayna, one of the larger Clans.

I pointed east: Yena, Aryl's birth Clan, came before Amna, the most populous. South of Amna, bordered by the same ocean, Pana, the next largest. They first saw the sun.

Last, but not least, Tuana, south of Yena.

The grimmer naming. Before Om'ray returned to Sona, Oud claimed Tuana, Pana, and Grona; the Tikitik: Yena, Amna, and Rayna. Oud, having taken Sona from the Tikitik in the distant past, intended to keep it. To restore the Balance, they prepared Tuana for the Tikitik, killing most of its population—Om'ray and Oud—in the process.

But the Oud of Sona were destroyed by the pirates who'd tortured Marcus Bowman, and the Om'ray of Sona became the M'hiray, and abandoned it.

"Sona lives again," I finished out loud. "And is Tikitik," I nodded to the creatures. "Thought Traveler accused the Oud of no longer caring for the Balance, of no longer having Speakers. Is this true?"

The Tikitik's head bobbed up in annoyance; it didn't interrupt.

Odon rose to his feet. "The Oud," said as if spat, "claim Cersi."

He echoed my gestures, finger stabbing the air. "Amna and Rayna are theirs. The Tikitik cling to what's left of Tuana and Sona, for however long they can keep them."

No reaction this time from Thought Traveler.

"There is no Yena Clan. No Pana or Grona. If there ever was," he finished, and sat.

Aryl's presence vanished from my mind; I let her be. "Is this true?" I repeated, but to the Tikitik.

"Regrettably, yes. The Oud did not reshape Yena, Grona, and Pana," he replied, eyes fixed on me. "They obliterated them, burying their Cloisters as well."

Gasps. *Horror.*

Numb, I asked Morgan's question. "Why?"

"The Oud remain inscrutable. Perhaps they thought to smother those inside. Perhaps they expressed frustration. Oud have been unable to penetrate these structures." With a certain grim satisfaction, Tikitik having managed just that.

"What does it matter? Without a Cloisters, no Clan could survive," Teris said fearfully, her fellow Councilors nodding, faces ashen. "Will they do this to us? Is that what the Oud intend for Sona?"

The Tikitik Speaker's eyes moved frantically, as though looking for Oud under the benches. Thought Traveler bobbed its head again. "First they would have to drain the Lay Swamp. I suggest you save your panic until its water begins to disappear."

The poor Sona looked ready to run down to the platform and start measuring the water level.

Pre-Stratification, Cersi's three species had abided by the Agreement: that none should change the Balance between them. My implanted memories, as well as what Aryl had shared, suggested this Balance was more about the Oud and Tikitik dividing the Om'ray Clans—and land—evenly, with any change being "balanced" by another. They'd traded Clans, back and forth, at terrible cost to the Om'ray.

However dreadful that sounded, what I was hearing was worse. "If the Tikitik still value the Agreement," I said slowly, "why haven't you stopped them?"

Thought Traveler's eyes rested on me. "You misjudge the situation, Far Traveler. There is no Agreement left to value. As for stopping the Oud?" That guttural laugh had nothing of humor in it. "These," a three-fingered hand indicated the Council, "descend from stock we plucked from Amna as we ran for our lives. That any Om'ray still exist there astonishes me." Another laugh. "Perhaps the ocean contains more water than the Oud can remove."

I translated for Morgan.

"Descend from stock." A grim pause. *You're sure that's the meaning?*

*Yes. They think of these people—of us—*for I saw less and less difference between Om'ray and M'hiray with each moment together—*as animals to be raised.* I didn't doubt the Tikitik had picked those Amna to be saved based not on compassion but something else entirely. *Where have I brought us?*

With the aching depth of *despair* I'd show no one else.

*You've given us options. But we need more. We need—*with *conviction—to hear the Oud's side.*

I looked to where he stood, relaxed to less knowing eyes, waiting at the door where we expected the next arrivals. *You think they had some reason. To kill all those—*I couldn't bear to say more.

He shook his head at me. *Sira. You should know by now. There's always a reason. It's finding it—comprehending it—that's the challenge. What do the Oud want? What could they possibly think to gain by killing so many Om'ray?*

They may not know that's what they've done. Aryl to us both, her mind voice like ice. *Marcus believed Oud didn't know to count individuals. To them, a Clan might be a single thing. Also,* with hesitation, *I heard an Oud once say Tikitik die to become Om'ray who die to be reborn in their shape. "Best is."* That, more firmly, *I won't believe.*

What matters is what they believe. Morgan was firm. *Remember the Drapsk, Sira. We can't rely on what others say about the Oud. We have to talk to them.*

Alien communication being our specialty, no one else's, not here. I hoped my Chosen also remembered that the Drapsk, dear as they'd become to us both, hadn't stopped being a particular nuisance.

Though they didn't, as a rule, kill others.

Morgan was right. I said firmly, "We want to talk to the Oud."

Thought Traveler took a step closer to me. Or away from its fellow, I reminded myself. Alien ways. "To what gain, Far Traveler? Believe me, in our desperation we invited the Oud to Tikitna. To 'talk.'" It came closer still, closer, until I felt the soft brush of its cilia against my lips.

Don't open your mouth. From Aryl.

Sira! From my Chosen.

It's all right, I reassured Morgan, mouth firmly shut.

"The Oud, predictably, died of that conversation." The contact added a vibration to its low voice that rang through my clenched teeth. "Imagine our consternation when their Workers tunneled up from below and Tikitna was laid waste."

Aryl supplied images of a thriving city made from living things, of walking on water, of hard-won understanding . . .

She finished with *loss.*

"Since the destruction of our sacred meeting place," Thought Traveler continued, "no two factions of my people have met without blood spilled. That, for 'talk' with the Oud. Will you still risk this?"

I waited, lips closed, for it to retreat before answering.

Before I could, its head bobbed up. "I see you will."

"I must," I agreed.

"You must not!" The Tikitik Speaker leaped to its feet. "Makers protect us! You cannot interfere with Their Design! What will be—" A blow sent it scrambling.

Thought Traveler smacked it a second time to be sure. "Factions living near a Maker's Rest tend to be superstitious," it apologized calmly. "Ignore its ravings."

The Hoveny site. Marcus' find. I saw Morgan start as he received Aryl's sending, too. *The Tikitik name any such place a "Maker's Rest."* Dismissively. *I told you they liked the word.*

Morgan's face settled into an expression I knew very well: the one that usually preceded an unexpected—and often profitable—shift in our plans. *We're not treasure hunting,* I warned him, quick and private. Not yet, anyway.

We aren't, he agreed, only to add disconcertingly, *Who else might be?*

The other Tikitik was cowed, but not silenced. A small eye appeared in the crook of an arm, glaring up at Thought Traveler. "Our 'Rest was desecrated by the diggers! Desecrated!"

"As have been all such ruins, fool." Thought Traveler held out his hands in an almost Human gesture of exasperation. "Does no one listen? The Oud have—"

The door spun open, admitting Destin with five of her scouts right behind, weapons in their hands. Morgan lifted his, empty, and backed out of their way.

Odon stood. "What's the meaning of this interruption? Your Council is in session!"

The First Scout came to a stop, her mouth slightly agape. Snapping it closed, she gave me an accusing look.

As this was—most definitely—my doing, I gestured apology.

Certain Destin di Anel would like what I planned to do next even less.

Interlude

SOFT GRAY FEATHERED the undersides of airy fronds, their tips wider than Morgan's outstretched arms, the rib down their center strong enough to bear his weight. Whorls of the fronds girded the mammoth tree fern the Om'ray called a great rastis, but weren't used for climbing. Instead, healed scars formed a ladder up the straight stalk, a ladder leading—"How much farther?" he called up, again.

"You don't want to know." Sira was above him, a pleasant view in Sona clothing if not for the unfamiliar ease with which she climbed.

He suspected Aryl asserted herself.

If she gave his Chosen confidence, fine; if she'd any to spare, he could use some. With rare unanimity, the Sona and Tikitik had agreed this was the only possible place to find an Oud in the Lay Swamp.

At the top of the canopy.

Which the Oud flew over, to Morgan's relief, in proper aircars. The Oud—other than being mass murderers, tragically confused or not—were gaining promise as allies. All they had to do was attract an Oud's attention to this one tree, and them.

Deni sud Kessa'at, the closest they had to a communications expert, was certain he could do just that. He and Holl di Licor were on the ladder above Sira, each accompanied by a Sona charged with making sure they didn't fall. Food remaining their greatest concern, Holl had come to expand her search.

When they weren't offering the Clanswoman samples, Destin's nimble scouts used the fronds to move beyond those confined to the ladder.

Sentries, Morgan had guessed and asked against what. When Destin replied "Everything," he regretted leaving his coat—and its persona-shield—in the Cloisters. True, it would have made his climb a misery, but could have warned of things larger than the ever-present biters.

The First Scout came last, behind him. She hadn't assigned him a helper; the Human might have been flattered, if he hadn't been sure there were no Sona left to spare.

When he glanced down, he could no longer see the swamp through the intervening foliage. His shoulders burned, his arms were weights; sensations he ignored, drowning in scent and sound and color. The canopy of the Sona was another world, one of grays and browns and brilliant green. The higher they climbed, the more colors appeared. Flowers, some plant, others mimics that took flight or folded into balls. Other growths hung from the bone-white limbs of different types of trees. Vines wrapped and hung and twisted—

Forget his coat. He needed his sketch pad—and time. Everywhere he looked, Morgan found something else he ached to study, something new to paint.

Forget the Hoveny's dusty relics. This was treasure.

Well, he could do without the biters. Fortunately, here they were hunted in turn. Small winged not-quite-birds snapped them from the air, sometimes pausing to hover near him, gemlike eyes intent.

Sira disappeared through the next platform. It was built to take advantage of the rastis' own strength, the ribs of fronds supports for the floor. A gap left room for climbers on the ladder; there was a hatch the Sona closed behind them, as if to prevent something following.

Rope bridges linked the platforms to others on neighboring

stalks, for this rastis was one of many, a grove harvested in season. The plants, he'd been told, were a source of many materials for the Sona, most importantly, dresel.

While young rastis functioned as a birth cradle for Tikitik, the details of which Aryl refused to share.

As for the Tikitik?

They belonged here. Thought Traveler, having invited itself along, promptly disappeared the instant Destin had indicated the rastis to be climbed, leaping up and away with fluid speed.

A ladder was fine with him. Morgan heaved himself up and onto the platform, cheered to find Sira and the other M'hiray sitting on the floor to share a gourd of water. He planted himself by his Chosen, accepting a drink with a smile, and waved at Deni.

The Clansman heaved for breath, sweat pouring from his face, but managed a wan smile in return. "They—stopped for—me," he panted, gesturing apology.

"My thanks," Morgan assured him. "I need the rest." He rubbed a shoulder and made a face. *Sira, he won't make it to the top and down again. Not sure I will.*

I'll 'port them back to the Cloisters, she promised. *And us.* "We're almost there," aloud. "Look. The crown."

Above, the stalk widened into a giant bulb. Thin vines hung like hair from its outer rim, dense and coiled. Some were pale, oozing a white sap. Others were beaded with yellow galls Morgan didn't want to see any closer. Nor did he trust any of those vines to support a climber.

He wasn't the only one with doubts. Holl frowned, "How do we get past that?"

"You climb." A familiar triangular head appeared, upside down, in the midst of the vines. Familiar, except that Thought Traveler's skin was pale green, the knobs scattered throughout now brown. It bent one eye in their direction, the rest busy with its surroundings.

Arriving on the platform, Destin motioned vigorously at the Tikitik. Don't disturb the "##$%$#@!"

Stingers. They nest in the galls. Aryl's sending turned *amused. She's calling it stupid.*

Thought Traveler barked its laugh and faded from sight. Destin glared at where it had been, then shrugged. "This way."

She led them around the platform to where a ladder hung waiting. It was, Morgan saw with resignation, of slats and braided rope. Any vines close enough to touch were being tied back, with care, by the other scouts.

The ladder did lead past the width of the bulb.

To where?

Vines trembled; the hanging ladder swayed. All at once, the platform tilted!

Holl cried out. Morgan resisted the urge to grab Sira and hold on to whatever wasn't moving only because everything was.

Sira glanced up him, a dimple in her cheek. "Just a breeze."

He'd have to talk to her great-grandmother, he would. And would, Morgan realized suddenly. Aryl would be born—when would she be born?

Climb first, Aryl suggested.

Good idea, Morgan told himself, not at all ready to think about Aryl di Sarc as a baby in his arms.

The platform steadied again.

"I want to set this before we get to the top." Deni pulled out his comlink, newer and more powerful than Morgan's. Those from Mirim's group had been the only M'hiray to bring such tech.

The Sona who'd been helping him made a disapproving sound.

"It will only take a second."

"Watch—" Morgan began as the preoccupied Clansman stepped close to the edge, but Destin was quicker, grabbing him back by the arm.

As vines trembled and the ladder swayed—

The platform tilted again, this time farther and farther over.

DOWN! Aryl and Sira ordered as one.

The Sona moved first, grabbing the less experienced and pulling them to the floor. They drove their short knives into the wood, holding to the hilts with their free hands.

Over . . . over . . . then back again even faster—

"Catch it!"

The comlink rolled and bounced by, dropping over the edge. To reappear in a black three-fingered hand.

Thought Traveler landed on the platform, balancing with artless ease. Its frond-mimicking camouflage extended across torso and limbs; the neck and hands alone remained black. "You really should be more careful," it chided.

The rastis settled, once more vertical. Deni scrambled to his feet, snatching the proffered 'link from the alien's hand. "You might have broken it!"

"I assure you—"

Change!

Morgan looked around to see black fingers reach through the opening in the platform.

But it wasn't a hand.

Chapter 46

STITLER! I passed Aryl's warning to the others as Morgan moved in front of me, drawing his weapon, and the Sona pulled their knives.

Thought Traveler? Gone.

As usual.

While climbing, I'd lowered any barrier between Aryl's mind and mine. I'd instinctively done so again, feeling a rush of memory and awareness. My hand curled: her desire for a knife. My breathing steadied.

Her courage.

What looked like fingers proved fiercely hooked claws. Even as Aryl/I wondered why an ambush hunter that lurked deep in its trap would be attacking in full day, those claws dug into wood, pulling its body through the opening.

A nightmare rushed forward, jaws open.

A male. This must be mating season, when solitary males willingly risked exposure in their search for the traps of waiting females. That their dance of desire would see them eaten alive didn't matter.

While searching, however, they were fiercely territorial. *Big one,* Aryl/I admired. *I've seen bigger.*

Who'd want to?

The thickened black body likely outmassed mine. Worse, it was quick, spinning on a multitude of jointed legs, spikes rattling. It hissed with fury as the Sona struck at it, gave a sharp cry when Morgan shot off a limb.

A cry repeated by another. A second—yes, bigger—male squeezed through the hatch, jaws snapping.

They'll fight each other.

Part of me had her confidence.

The other, more sensible part clung to Holl and Deni while our protectors formed a ring around us, the stitlers circling—hissing as much at each other as at us—and wondered why I hadn't already 'ported us anywhere but here.

Because we can deal with this, Morgan sent. His Power *surged* and one of the beasts disappeared. It reappeared in midair, falling out of sight with a surprised wail.

Knives buried themselves to the hilt in the body of the second.

"We did it!" Deni shouted, then stopped, staring down to where a black hooked claw protruded from his stomach.

Before anyone could move, the claw ripped up and back, slicing him open. Blood and entrails spilled on wood, on our hands—

What had been a third stitler died with a shudder.

Deni sud Kessa'at was gone.

I hadn't seen Tekla di Yode die. Morgan told me she'd spotted the last stitler before anyone else. Her blade had been trapped within the body of the second beast, so she'd used her bare hands to try and protect Deni.

The grieving Sona stripped her body of anything that could be used, then tossed her husk over the side of the platform.

Food for what scavenged. Aryl approved.

I was numb.

Holl clutched Deni's corpse when they came for it next, giving me a pleading look. "He wouldn't want that."

"Would he want what hungers to find him here and wait for you?" Thought Traveler wasn't tactful.

He wasn't, I knew, wrong.

"We can't leave a husk," Destin said grimly.

"I'll take care of him." I waited for Morgan to gently separate Holl from her friend's body, watching when he knelt to go through Deni's pockets and gear, collecting what was now irreplaceable.

On Cersi.

All too easy to be sick of this deadly world, of trying to survive it.

All too easy to believe peace and order restored in the Trade Pact, that we—the Clan—could go back as if nothing had driven us—

Home, I finished bitterly, and *pushed* Deni sud Kessa'at into the M'hir, to join his Chosen.

To become another of our ghosts.

The crown of the rastis was topped with barren stems, their pods swept clear by the hot M'hir Wind long before our arrival. The rope ladder met one of sturdier construction, leading with two others up to a central deck.

To the sky Aryl remembered, brilliant blue, arching overhead like freedom.

I'd sent Holl back to the Cloisters along with Destin's people, glad to have them safe. The First Scout sat cross-legged, sharpening her knife. She'd represent Sona when we met the Oud.

No, I corrected to myself, Destin di Anel would represent Cersi's Om'ray, a claim I couldn't make.

The Tikitik, black again and gray, curled a leg around a rail. It stared out over the canopy. Another time I would have been curious. Did it see beauty?

Or a map drawn in blood.

"Signal's going out," Morgan announced. He came to stand behind me, arms around my waist. "See, chit? There's room for us."

Mountains rose, jagged and forbidding, to the west and north. To the south and east, the land of Om'ray and Tikitik and Oud. "Over the sea," I said, attempting the same lighter spirit. "We just need a ship." I drew a sharp remorseful breath only to feel him chuckle.

"That we do. I'm tempted to ask the Oud if they've a spare lying around."

"The machines of the Oud fly through the air, not water," the Tikitik replied without turning from whatever had its attention. "Neither can they fly through the Maker's vast emptiness, though they persist, the fools, in that ambition. The Makers put us here to fulfill Their Design, not our own. We are none of us free. We can never be."

Risky, assigning emotion to a being so fundamentally different, yet in that moment I believed the Tikitik was gripped by a despair as deep and dark as my own. I translated, ending with *Morgan?*

I felt his *agreement*. My Human stepped away from me and went toward Thought Traveler, stopping well short of the platform edge. "Superstition?" he challenged. "I thought you a rational being."

Its long neck unfolded, bringing head and eyes to bear on Morgan. "There is a past to Cersi, Human, as there is a now. Within that past existed a was-once of my people and of the Oud. Perhaps—" as if making a great concession, "—of Om'ray. What we were is not as we are, but some of us—fewer, now—remember more truth than others. Because our Makers are outside your remembering does not make my truth 'superstition.' The Makers are there." All eyes aimed to the horizon. "Watching."

The smaller of Cersi's moons had risen, pale against blue. The other, Aryl told me, would rise behind it. The Makers, the Tikitik called them, reusing that maddening word for what some considered the dwelling place of those who'd made the world—made it for the Tikitik, other races being "flaws."

Morgan's brows drew together as I relayed that. I waited for him to question how anything could be watching from a presumably airless moon. Instead, he asked, "What do the Makers watch?"

Supremely confident of its balance, though a leg hung over empty air, Thought Traveler swept out its arms to include the canopy as well as the distant mountains and sea. "The dance of life across the world. Its glorious Balance." Its head moved like a snake's on that neck, flowing to stare out again. "Or lack thereof," it finished grimly.

"Here they come," Destin exclaimed, rising to her feet.

I shielded my eyes, searching.

Morgan spotted them first. "The Oud."

Interlude

THE VEHICLE BLOTTED OUT THE SUN as it descended in uncanny silence. If this was Oud tech, Morgan thought with admiration, things had indeed changed since Marcus Bowman and Aryl di Sarc last stepped on this planet. This well-designed powerful craft would not have attracted a second look on a Trade Pact world.

Except by those concerned for their own safety, for as the Oud airship—there being no other name for anything this huge—slowed its approach, ports dropped open to emit hollow-mouthed tubes. Aimed at them.

In addition to what had to be weapons of some kind, clusters of small craft were attached to the airship's longer sides. That the Oud had sufficient power in those silent engines to flaunt aerodynamics was his worrisome first thought.

The second being a speculation of what might be in those craft and their intention should the Oud feel threatened, Morgan had Sira pass a silent warning to the Sona First Scout. Destin sent him a sharp look, but kept her hands away from her knives.

Thought Traveler appeared bored. Something Morgan doubted.

The Oud airship sank lower and lower, sighing to a stop just above the point the Human had marked as too-close-we're-leaving-now.

The tube weapons retracted at seeming random, each door sliding in place at a different speed. Crewed, not automated, that
told him. The airship's belly was a mass of such small doors, implying a significant number. The rest of the underside was composed of wide fused straps of metal that looked more like bands
of muscle than any construction method he'd seen before.

The metal itself? He'd need another look at Barac's bracelet to
be sure, but if he was right, they were the same, making the relic
a connection between Oud and Om'ray, Oud and M'hiray. It
could make the head spin.

Two of those doors were much larger—access ports, at a guess.

Sira stood beside him, her shaded face inscrutable, her emotions equally muted, other than the stir of *curiosity*. A lock of hair
rested briefly on his arm. "Tell me this is a good idea," she whispered, staring up.

"That depends on the Oud."

A sideways glance. "Must you be so honest?"

Morgan half smiled. "Only with you, Witchling."

The farther of the doors he'd noticed opened, one end dropping to reveal a ramp. The ramp's end hovered the length of his
arm from the wooden structure, as if aware it was fragile.

He hoped that meant those inside the airship were also aware
of the fragility of the guests they'd just invited inside.

Chapter 47

DESTIN DI ANEL JUMPED on the ramp and ran up a few steps. She came right back. "No one's there."

Morgan jumped up with equal ease. When he turned to offer his hand, he looked past me. "We may have a problem."

Thought Traveler hadn't moved from the rail. I walked over to the creature, waiting until two of its eyes bent to me. The others remained fixed on the dark opening of the ramp. "We don't go into their tunnels," it confessed. "Other than to die there."

Was that why the Tikitik had panicked in the windowless room?

"You've seen what I can do," I assured it. "Say the word and I'll 'port you away from the Oud, into the open."

Another eye joined the pair. "You want me with you—in there. Why? Do you not trust yourselves to understand the Oud, Far Traveler? I doubt I can aid you better than the Human's talker."

Why did I? I nodded to myself. "You've a right to hear what concerns your people. Where my Chosen and I come from, there are not three kinds of beings, but thousands, living in peace." Recent events excepted.

"Not all on one world," it guessed shrewdly.

Plexis had to count. "Sometimes on one," I stated. "We share ships, common interests. Equitable trade. Security. We get along."

Recent events excepted.

"Very well." Thought Traveler descended from its perch. "I will walk this path with you. Let us see if the Oud understand this concept of 'get along,' Far Traveler."

For all its bold words and prancing walk, I noticed the Tikitik stayed close enough to grab me if necessary.

The ramp tested its courage at once, rising underfoot as we climbed. The Tikitik's two smaller eyes rotated in their cones to watch the brightness behind us disappear. Before it could bolt, I put my hand on its wrist.

My fingers encountered dry pebbled skin, felt a pulse racing beneath. Its arm was as rigid as stone, but the contact must have reassured it, for it gave a faint bark. "Did the Om'ray warn you of the Oud with Power like yours, Far Traveler?"

"We're aware," I replied, not mentioning the Om'ray who'd warned us was Aryl di Sarc. Torments, she'd called them, able to cause a *sound* in the M'hir; she'd cautioned their presence could disrupt the workings of the more powerful. Aware and careful. I'd let a tendril of thought into that other space the moment the airship had dropped its ramp.

So far, nothing but the warm gold of my Chosen, Aryl's comforting presence, and the shielded *grim* that marked Sona's First Scout. I withdrew.

With a soft vibration, the ramp became floor. The four of us stood waiting in a fetid darkness. A darkness in which something moved. What was in here? I stifled a cough and felt the Tikitik tremble. Impossible to tighten my grip—or hold it. I called out rather desperately, "We need light!"

Regretting it the instant my request was granted.

Interlude

"THERE'S NO ONE GUARDING the door."

Though tempted to point out that yes, he was, Barac di Bowart simply raised an eyebrow. "We agreed to stay here."

Tle di Parth would ripen once Chosen and Commenced, her body maturing, hair becoming full and opinionated, even her face rounding into the beauty promised by her bones. If not, he supposed she'd stay as she was, with lines at mouth and eyes etched by years of regarding the world with suspicion and disappointment. If Sira had been like this—

"Let me out!" Tle's Power *surged*.

Barac shrugged off the *sting*, well used to Clan intimidation. As sud, he might have given way. As Ruti's Chosen, he'd the right to call Tle before—who? They'd no Council.

As First Scout, however, Tle was his responsibility, awkward as that was. "You aren't the only one tired of this place, Tle, and of each other. My orders are no one leaves this chamber until the Sona—or Sira—gives permission. Hopefully, it'll be soon." He grimaced. "I, for one, could use a bath."

Worse was not knowing what they waited for, and few here had faced such uncertainty. Life as a sud, he thought ruefully, had given him practice.

Her eyes narrowed. "You mock me?"

Barac gestured apology. "I understand."

How can you? With real pain. *I can't stay here. I can't.* She whirled and stalked off, other Clan moving out of her way.

Ruti came to his side, gazing after Tle. Barac sighed. "I can't make an exception."

"You may have to." *It's starting.*

What?

The Power-of-Choice. Ermu is twitchy. Jacqui no better. Tle's afraid she'll be next. She wants to get away from the unChosen. "Being upset makes it worse," she said aloud. "The sud Kessa'ats are—were Tle's friends. I don't think she has many."

Cha's fate shook everyone, Barac thought. Deni's Chosen had stopped speaking mid-sentence, her eyes going vague. She seemed healthy enough.

Until Sona scouts had arrived, with Holl, to tell them about Deni's death. They'd taken one look at Cha and pronounced her "Lost." Some of the mind, enough for life, too little for personality, remained trapped in the body. The Om'ray had taken her with them, accustomed to dealing with the condition.

M'hiray died with their Chosen. This—this living death was a new horror.

And a drain on resources already stretched, but he kept that opinion to himself.

The Sona had their own Lost, the Chosen of the scout who'd given her life trying to save Deni's. To their credit, the Sona didn't bother blaming Sira for putting their people at risk. Barac supposed they always were, in this harsh place.

Now they had to fear their own Choosers? "Keep an eye on them, Ruti." *Let the Healers know they may have to impose stasis, but do it quietly.*

Ruti shuddered. Stasis bound Power, there was no way around that, making the three helpless. "I will," she told him, then gave the closed door a longing look of her own. "Would it be so bad if we went out, just into the hall a little?"

Heart-kin.

She reached up to kiss his cheek. "Don't worry. I'll follow orders. This time," with a hint of the mischievous grin he loved.

His own self-control was wanting. Yes, he'd rather be with Sira and Morgan, guarding them instead of this door, but that wasn't his duty.

Making himself relax, Barac leaned against the wall. Ruti leaned against him, her hair soft against his cheek. He wrapped his arms around her, hands over the tiny swell of their daughter-to-be. *We'll have quarters soon.* He breathed in her scent. *Sira promised.*

I'll settle for Sira and Morgan back here and safe. All of us safe. She shivered and he tightened his hold. *Barac—are you sure about me?*

Sira herself couldn't enter your mind now. An exaggeration, but he'd do anything to comfort his Chosen.

That's not what I meant. Somehow, she squeezed closer. *I don't know who it was. What if they're here, with us?* Beneath, a layer of *dread* that hadn't existed in her clear thoughts before, like a stain.

Then they'll wish the Assemblers had found them first. They'd suspects, starting with Yihtor's mother; to his relief, neither Wys nor any of her ilk had come with them to Cersi.

If it was someone else? Well, that was something he planned to discuss with the redoubtable Morgan when the opportunity came. The Human had, Barac thought grimly, an interest.

Good. With a shocking amount of *bloodlust.*

Or not so shocking. *Sometimes I forget,* he told his fierce and capable Chosen, adding *love* and *admiration.*

Smug. He sensed her relax. *This is a new world,* she said. *We'll make it a home.*

Resting his chin on her head, Barac surveyed those who'd share it with them, heart easing to see his mother sitting with the three young children. Enora had always, he remembered fondly, been a gifted teacher.

Only three children. His ease faded. The Sona were daunted by the number of M'hiray; they shouldn't be. Of the nine hundred and thirty-three Clan on Trade Pact worlds, a mere hundred and eleven had made it to Cersi. Sira's magnificent effort to bring them to this refuge couldn't undo that loss.

Or guarantee a future for the survivors.

They'd been culled by the Assemblers like a herd of Brexx, he thought bitterly, losing more than the weak or infirm. Only three Choosers. Three—soon to be four unChosen. Two-thirds of their Chosen long past child-bearing age, in a race already in decline. How many of the rest were even fertile?

Ruti had followed his thoughts. *We are,* she declared, her mind voice determined. *We'll have five more babies. Six. Not while you're on duty,* she added primly.

He hugged his irrepressible Chosen, grateful beyond words she had hope.

Few here did, Barac thought, knowing better than to lower shields. The M'hiray were trapped and desperate. Whatever Sira and Morgan accomplished, even he couldn't see a future coming from it.

Not here.

Not here, he repeated to himself, then began to smile. *Ruti, start everyone packing.*

But—Sira's orders—

These are mine. Barac di Bowart stood a little straighter. *I'm First Scout. It's time I acted like it.* For Tle. For Ruti.

For the good of his people.

He put both hands on the door of the Council Chambers, turned it open, and stepped outside.

Chapter 48

I'D MET MY SHARE of physically unappealing aliens—who hadn't—but the Oud threatened to make me lose what little was in my stomach.

The glare of lights revealed we were surrounded by what looked like giant slugs, their pale bodies hunched as if in shock. Dozens, maybe hundreds of little black limbs, were clustered under their bellies, disturbingly like those of the stitler. I couldn't distinguish anything like a head. When they began to uncoil and move, I supposed the front tapered end had to be—

No, I was wrong. Two collided "head" to "head," sending thick ripples along their flesh, but the Oud simply switched to moving in the opposite direction.

They avoided us, milling along the outer rim of what was a hollow space the size, I judged, of the entire airship. While most stayed on the floor, an unsettling number climbed the walls and scuttled across the ceiling.

"These are workers and mindless," Thought Traveler said in a ghastly whisper. It had either forgotten I was holding its wrist or couldn't bear to have me let go.

While I'd rather hold Morgan, I could *feel* him, strong and sure, through our link. "How do we attract—" my Chosen started to ask, then looked up. "Here we go." He sounded pleased.

Hatches cracked open above us, letting in beams of sunlight. The Tikitik pulled, very gently, and I took back my hand. Then I saw what the worker Oud were up to and couldn't help myself. "I'm not doing that."

The ones on the ceiling had somehow glued themselves by one end to the edge of the centermost hatch, the rest of their bodies extended to quiver like obscene fruit. The ones below climbed one atop the other until they touched those hanging.

As if cued to a silent command, every Oud froze in position, forming—I shook my head in denial. "That is not a staircase," I said firmly.

What it was—to my dismay—was climbable. Destin grinned fiercely and ran up, her feet sinking ankle-deep in squishy Oud flesh.

At least their little limbs were on the other side and out of sight.

C'mon, chit. Morgan took my hand, the Oud-stairs being wide enough for us to climb side-by-side. I tried to ignore how the stench intensified each time our feet sank into the creatures.

Halfway up, I stopped in guilt. "Morgan—the Tikitik!" We looked down in time to see Thought Traveler bouncing forcefully on the bottommost Oud. Each bounce brought him higher—and hopefully wasn't harming the poor Oud—until a final effort saw the Tikitik sail past us like a gangly bird to land above. Waving.

My Human laughed.

I was up to the ankles in cloying flesh—cold cloying flesh at that—and he was laughing. I dropped his hand and climbed the rest of the Oud on my own.

Hearing Morgan chuckle behind me.

Interlude

A S HE TOOK IN their new surroundings, Morgan drew fresh air into his lungs with relief. If they traveled with the Oud in future, best make sure the accommodations weren't belowdecks.

Besides, the view up here couldn't be better.

The upper deck of the airship was surrounded by a clear cowl barely taller than the Tikitik, allowing a perfect view in all directions. No other structure rose from the textured floor. Even the hatches closed to be flush with the surface.

He lifted his face, impressed to feel no wind from their now-rapid movement through the sky.

Sira noticed, too. *Shields.*

Good ones. Standard option on a Trade Pact rental aircar, but on Cersi?

Destin stayed to the middle, her feet braced as if ready for the airship to tilt like a rastis. This wouldn't, Morgan judged.

One figure stood on the deck at the bow, facing the mountains where the airship was heading. A slender figure, Sira's height, dressed in a sky-blue hooded cloak.

Thought Traveler waggled its mouth cilia, tasting the air. "Oud. Though—what kind? How unexpected."

When it went to walk toward the figure, Morgan stopped it with a gesture.

Eyes bent to him. "Among Tikitik, any delay in greeting would be unwise."

"Do you know this about Oud?" Morgan asked, the translator rendering his Comspeak after a slight hesitation.

The figure turned and beckoned.

Because of what he'd said—or how?

Only one way to find out. Morgan walked forward at a pace that to another Human would say willing but not too eager. Sira came beside him, Thought Traveler stalking behind—maybe his question about the Oud had hit a sore point and the creature had decided to accept his lead. Or to put them first, in case the Oud meant harm.

The Sona First Scout, though she was clearly uncomfortable being in flight, didn't hesitate to come with them.

A cloaked limb lifted a second time when they were about five paces away. Morgan stopped at once. The garment engulfed the figure from head to toe, assuming there were those structures. Up close, the blue fabric was something else again, far more intriguing, akin to an extruded or formed material like plas. Designs like circuitry were embedded within its surface and visible, for the outermost layer was transparent, while beneath that was blue and opaque. A garment that no more belonged on the Cersi he'd seen so far than—than he did, he supposed.

No smile, not until he knew more of it. *Sira?*

A blend of *confidence* and utter *trust. You're better at this. Go ahead.*

Staring across a table or blanket or over a rock at eyes as varied as the goods being traded might have given him more experience, Morgan thought, but Sira had the knack. Still, there was the classic opening gambit. He spread his arms, hands open.

"Hello."

Chapter 49

HEARING CAPTAIN JASON MORGAN say "Hello," his deep voice followed by the echo from the comlink, was reassuringly familiar. I'd lost count of how many times we'd done this— granted, never while flying through the air on a giant airship full of slugs—but the whole scenario of first contact, of opening a fraught, hope-filled conversation with such a simple greeting? That hadn't changed.

The stakes had. We bargained for more than the latest batch of truffles or used parts. He knew it; he just wouldn't show it. Another very good reason to let Morgan lead what I hoped would become a negotiation, a profitable one.

"Speak more." The Oud's voice was husky and low-pitched.

I blinked. Morgan didn't hesitate. "My name is Morgan. This is the Speaker for the M'hiray, Sira, and First Scout of the Sona Clan—"

"Speak more other."

Morgan began to spout numbers, then a sequence of random-seeming words, his comlink scrambling them into nonsense. I quenched Destin's *alarm,* glaring at Thought Traveler in case it planned to speak. My Human had his reason.

The limb gestured. Enough, that was. Morgan stopped.

What's going on? I asked, a little perturbed myself.

Wait for it. With a *confidence* bordering on *glee.*

"Matched. I have corresponding data," the Oud announced then, in accented but perfectly comprehensible Comspeak.

Its robe split down the middle, edges rolling neatly aside to reveal the Oud.

"What kind is this?" hissed Thought Traveler.

What kind indeed. Aryl's memories? Those imposed on me?

Neither held this strange and elegant being.

Exposed, its flesh was translucent, the blue of organs and delicate vessels showing through skin that glistened in the sunlight. Down its middle was a dense line of black appendages set in neat rows, like a toolkit. Very much like tools, I realized, for the tips of each were extraordinarily specialized. As far as I could tell, no two were alike. A few formed a cluster close to what my humanoid self persisted in calling its head. Those would be what the Oud used to make sound.

The appendages weren't empty. Metal objects gleamed in their grip, dozens of them and all in dizzying motion. They were being passed from one to another, touched and passed along again, for all the world as if the Oud wore tech like adornment and fidgeted with it as I might the pendant.

Or as if what I saw was as much machine as living thing.

The rolled edges glittered as well. Glittered and bulged. Suddenly, hordes of small round things erupted from under the fabric, flying around the Oud in a cloud until it made an annoyed sound.

The cloud fell to the deck with a clatter, reforming into a struggling mass within the Oud's narrow shadow as the things climbed atop one another to fit. They made little *whirr/clicks.*

"A new caste," Thought Traveler mused, taking a step closer. Its eyes moved over the Oud. "How is this possible?"

"Tikitik ignorant." The Oud spoke the language of Cersi, a higher echo repeating in Comspeak. "Maker, I."

The other being's head bobbed up and I waited for it to object, but Thought Traveler merely said, "An impressive accomplishment."

I could have sworn the Oud preened, the way its appendages

quivered. "Maker, new is. Maker, best. Hear this?" It fluttered several appendages.

A blast of *noise* filled my head. I saw Destin instinctively cover her ears, but nothing would keep this out. It was as though the M'hir had become a drum and the Oud somehow beat on it, driving this *sound* through us.

"You're hurting them," Morgan shouted. "Stop!"

He was unaffected?

Though startling, the Oud's assault—or demonstration—was primitive and relatively weak. The instant I comprehended what was happening, I set in place what would reflect its *noise* back at it.

"Yesyesyesyes!!!" It dropped to its belly and began spinning about, whirr/clicks scurrying out of the way, whatever it used for feet making a *clickity-click* of their own on deck.

"I see your 'best' has no better manners," Thought Traveler commented.

So it is a Torment, Aryl sent wonderingly, *but one with control.*

The Tikitik scooped up an errant whirr/click, fingering the body and wriggling legs with the cilia around its mouth before tossing it aside. "Interesting," it murmured. Catching my attention with a small eye, it barked its laugh. "Our host is one of many. It appears this is the shape of the Minded now."

The Oud reared again, standing perfectly erect. "More than. Yesyesyes. Have purpose. Now have Om'ray, best is!" Its appendages snapped into a blur of motion, conveying some devices down, others up.

And something different, from its base. Something with a jewel-like sparkle. Having reached below the talking cluster, an appendage thrust forward, offering it to me. "Make work. Best is!"

Careful. Morgan moved to intercept. The Oud protested, "NoNoNO," and turned its dorsal surface to him. "Sira. Best is!"

I'd underestimated the creature. The *noise* had been a test, I thought with disgust, gauging our Power in the M'hir. "If you want me to have it, give it to Morgan first."

Its base stayed where it was, its body coiling to aim the top half at my Human. I noticed the jeweled object was nowhere in sight. "Why not function?"

Did it mean Morgan's lack of reaction to its *noise,* a question I had myself, or something else?

Something else, according to the more experienced trader, for Morgan grinned and unclipped his comlink. "Needs data. Here." He held it out.

The Oud brought the rest of itself around. An appendage with a pincer-like tip reached to take the device and bring it close. "Bad is. Not function," the Oud dismissed. Other appendages attacked the comlink, tearing it apart, the pieces ferried in opposite directions.

"Hey!" Morgan ran a hand through his hair, giving me a rueful look. *So much for my instincts.*

"Don't be so hasty," I told him, nodding at the Oud.

The appendages hadn't stopped their rapid motion. All at once, a spot of activity formed.

An appendage thrust out from its center, offering the now-reassembled comlink. "Better than."

Morgan took it, pressed a few controls, then looked up with a grin. "A full vocab with grammar! Better it is, my friend, indeed. My thanks."

Every word rendered perfectly, without lag. Destin looked impressed.

"Maker-I. Good is." Out came the jeweled object. "Sira."

"Me first." Morgan held out his hand. This time, the Oud passed him what I could now see was a stubby cylinder, the "jewels" attached to its sides. After running his scanner over it, my Chosen handed it to me. "Haven't a clue," he said cheerfully.

It was warm from his hand—or from wherever the Oud stored things. Moving past that concept as quickly as I could, I turned the cylinder over. The faceted jewels, though colorful, didn't seem to be decoration, or were that and more. Each sat in a small depression. Depressions that, yes, fit the thumb and fingers of my two hands, for it took both to hold it. I pressed, cautiously. Each sank in and stopped, rising when I eased the pressure, but nothing happened.

"Bad is," the Oud said, as if agreeing with the result. "Sira do."
Do what?

The jewels reminded me of the antique pistol our father had given Rael as a child. A toy, he'd believed, having no moving parts or mechanism; its age and strange design were of more interest than the gems. Pella had waved it as a pretend-weapon, coming to my aid with Rael. My sisters . . . gone . . .

Sira.

I chewed my lip. *I'm fine. I will be,* I told him, more honestly. For now, we'd a job to do. The Oud's trinket was wasting time. "You're right, it doesn't work." I went to give it back.

The Oud clenched all its appendages and refused. "Nonono. Sira do."

"Do what?"

That *noise* again. Before I could react, the cylinder *warmed* in my hands.

"Do better," the Oud said smugly.

I managed not to drop it. *Morgan. It responds to Power. To the M'hir!*

"Do nothing!" Thought Traveler loomed over me, shading the sun, but its eyes were fixed on the Oud. "Where did this come from?"

For the first time, the Oud wasn't quick to answer. Its append-ages fussed at bits of metal, at other small devices.

Stalling. Morgan clipped the comlink to his coat. "We can't help unless you give us more information."

Appendages paused. "More than." Something appeared to re-assure it, for the appendages began to move more easily. "Yes-yesyes. This Om'ray. What do?"

Show me. When I did, Aryl replied, *an Oud brought something similar to Enris. Mindtouch activated voices he couldn't understand. He—the experience was unpleasant.*

"Difficult to say what it does," Morgan said blandly, after I shared that with him. "We need to see other such items. You do have more?"

"Nonono."

"Then we can't help you." Morgan motioned me to return the cylinder.

The Oud reconsidered its answer. "Yesyesyes. More than." A wavering appendage pointed to the back of the airship. "Go there. See more than! Say what do! Make do! YESYESYESYES!" with unnerving enthusiasm. Something had occurred to it. Something I'd a feeling we wouldn't like.

The Tikitik hissed in displeasure. Morgan gave it a quelling look; to my surprise, the creature subsided. Maybe it remembered I was its only way off the airship, other than dropping over the side. "We need more information, first."

The Oud went perfectly still. " 'First.' " A brief pause. "Then go there. YESYES."

Smug, that was. A quick study or not as naïve as it had seemed? Either way, I waited to see how Morgan dealt with this turn of events.

Interlude

"FIRST, information that answers our questions," Morgan replied comfortably, "then we'll consider your request." The words echoed.

Perfect, Sira sent, a smile beneath the word.

About time, he thought. Nothing worse than feeling unable to trust what came out of your mouth—or translator. Working with Trade Pact species had made him complacent. No more. Tonight he'd run the sleepteach and be able to talk for himself from now on. *Let me know if it fails.*

He'd like to know if the Oud's clever trick relied on a database started during the time of the Triads, perhaps by Marcus Bowman himself, or if they'd had more recent access to those fluent in Comspeak. Could be both.

The Oud vacillated, as the Human interpreted its appendages dithering aimlessly. At a guess, it wanted to press for a commitment but rightly feared pushing too hard would cost it their cooperation. Sira's cooperation, he corrected to himself. The Oud had been clear on that.

She stood by, watching him, her hair blazing in the sun like molten gold. That was how she appeared in the M'hir too, apparently something attractive to the Oud as well.

Why?

"Not all questions," the Oud admitted grudgingly, "answers, I."

The Tikitik gave a soft bark. Amused, was it?

Fair enough. Where to start? Oud and Om'ray. Tikitik and M'hiray. He flew above the land they all inhabited, Morgan thought suddenly, but which of them belonged?

"Who was here first?" he asked. "Oud, Tikitik, or Om'ray?"

Appendages tapped, eyes rolled in their cones, and Sona's scout scowled. Finally, the Oud spoke. "Old Ones first here."

Not helpful, Sira sent.

"Brought Oud. Brought Tikitik."

That could be. "Did the Old Ones bring the Om'ray?"

Thought Traveler remained still. Morgan suspected it was equally intrigued to learn the Oud mythos. Not superstitious, this Tikitik, or defensive. Intelligent, curious. Dangerous. That, too.

"Nonono." The Oud tapped urgently, then ceased. "Old Ones Om'ray best is."

Maybe his Oud-modified comlink wasn't working after all. Morgan looked at the Tikitik. "Did you understand that?"

Its eyes were locked on the Oud. "It believes the Om'ray brought us here. That they were the Makers."

The Oud jiggled in place, appendages rattling. "YesyesYES! Sira Om'ray best is!"

"I believe it is mad. We should leave—"

"NonoNO. Not mad!" Bits of metal rained on the deck as the Oud flailed and shouted. Destin rose from her crouch, hand on her knives. "BEST IS!! Tikitik ignorant! Badbadbad—"

"How do you know the Om'ray were the Old Ones?" Morgan shouted, lowering his voice when the Oud quieted to listen.

"Nothing old works." The Oud sank down by thickening the lower portion of its body and began picking up what it had dropped as though embarrassed by the mess. "Old bad. Old broken. Not for Oud. Not for Human." Done, it straightened, objects flowing down and disappearing, tidy again. "Old works for Om'ray."

"Making this our world," Sira said bluntly.

"Nononono. Old Ones come here, too." Its demeanor altered. Was that pride? "Cersi Om'ray not, Tikitik, NOT. Cersi Oud. Om'ray best is, stay." As if a concession.

Or was it an offer?

Thought Traveler gave its barking laugh. "So I've heard your kind say before, Oud Maker. You would reshape Cersi to suit yourselves, ridding the world of everything else. If you ever succeeded, what then? Have you given thought to that?"

"Cersi best is. Oud more than!"

"Oh, there'd be more of you. Your mounds would burst open and the ground boil with the more of you." Its head rose sharply. "A ground no longer fertile, no longer moist. How long do you think you'll have before all there is to consume are your own offspring? How long before you make yourselves less—and then gone?"

"Gone first."

Did it mean the Tikitik, or could it mean—

The deck vibrated beneath his boots, twice.

"No time." The Oud dropped to its belly, this time moving by humping its midsection and then thrusting its body forward a considerable distance. It sped toward the bow of the airship, Morgan and the others following at a run.

The Oud rose at the clear canopy, tapping what sounded like glass with a single appendage. "Hereherehere."

Morgan tested the transparency with a finger. Firm and cold, it bulged outward, allowing him to look straight down. They were passing over the last of the canopy. Ahead rose a deeply scarred and folded ridge, beyond that another, each rising higher until the sky met a line of ragged peaks. Nothing green or living, as though the jungle slammed against an implacable desert.

"Aryl says the Hoveny site was there," Sira said, pointing. *Morgan, it's taking us out of Cersi.*

Chapter 50

THOUGHT TRAVELER PATTED the clear canopy with the cilia covering its mouth, rearing back with disgust in every line of its gaunt body. "All I taste is Oud!"

The smell of too many Oud in one place being something I hoped to forget, the creature had my sympathy, but I was too preoccupied with the view to comment.

What are we doing here? Aryl wasn't happy. *We shouldn't be here!*

Fingers brushed mine. Destin, even more upset. *We're leaving the world, Sira. We mustn't. You must take us back!*

Yes, take us back!

The light fingertouch became a punishing grip. *Who are* you?

Not when I'd have picked for them to meet, but it was done now. *Aryl di Sarc, Sona's Former Speaker, meet Destin di Anel, Sona's First Scout.*

I tightened my shields against them both, twisting my arm from Destin's now-slack hold. Aryl could explain her existence; maybe it would keep the pair of Om'ray from noticing what lay below.

Starting with the Hoveny site. Or rather, where it had been.

I shared Aryl memory with Morgan: the wide stairs, unearthed by Oud diggers, as well as the curve of a wall and an opened door. There was nothing left to show it had ever existed. From this perspective, I couldn't tell if the Oud had filled in part of the valley or somehow drawn the ancient building underground.

"Why destroy what was here?" Morgan asked.

The Oud appeared distracted, answering in a mutter. "Minded Oud ignorant. Decide not function. Decide bad. No what is. Minded Ignorant. Minded bad. Maker best is. Decide other."

"How very disturbing." Thought Traveler bent an eye its way. "Would I find any 'Minded' Oud in your mounds and tunnels or are they gone, along with all reason?"

"Reason Maker best is," the Oud retorted calmly. "Decide other. Find more than. Goodgoodgood. Be more than. Best is."

"Which is not an answer." The Tikitik barked. "Arrogance, 'best is.'"

It wasn't wrong. But not helping.

"What's that?"

At the shock in Morgan's voice I looked forward again.

To be shocked myself.

What I'd thought another ridge was not.

Twisted wreckage and boulders formed a line between us and the lowest gap in the mountain range ahead, as if something had built a barrier.

Or had they found one?

Interlude

THE OUD AIRSHIP entered the shade of the nearest mountain and eased to a stop. They weren't over the line of wreckage.

And weren't far enough from it. Morgan stared down, trying to comprehend how many flying machines had to have crashed here to create a ridge of such magnitude. Though it wasn't all of metal fragments. Rocks surrounded the newer wrecks—from large boulders to fist-sized—as if they'd been attracted there. Which made no sense . . .

Unless those weren't rocks at all. "Are those . . . ?" he began, shutting his mouth as, yes, he spotted several of the boulders quiver, then start to roll toward them. "Those aren't rocks."

"Oud young," the Tikitik answered. "The small ones are tasty. I can show you the trick to it."

"I'll pass." Scavengers. Wreckage. "What happened here?" Morgan demanded.

"Happened? Show." The Maker Oud began tapping on the canopy.

"What's it doing?" Sira whispered.

"I don't know." But he'd an idea, much as it turned his stomach. Morgan went to look over the airship's right side. He'd been right. The line of small vehicles he'd seen from below were quickly being filled, a worker Oud emerging to settle its bulk on each one. The first detached, sprouting short wings as it banked away.

Aimed at the ridge of wreckage. More detached, in meticulous order.

Morgan rushed to the bow in time to see the first of the Oud aircars pass beneath, their flight slow and noisy. More "rocks" began rolling uphill in expectation.

"You're sacrificing your crew!" He managed not to grab the Maker Oud, much as he wanted to shake sense from it. "Why?"

"Cersi more than," the Oud answered calmly.

The Om'ray feel this as the edge of the world. They can't pass it, Sira sent urgently.

Thought Traveler turned to stare with all eyes at the Oud. "The Makers set Cersi's limit. Who are you to challenge them?"

"Best is." With chilling confidence.

They were about to find out. Morgan reached for Sira's hand, slipping his fingers through hers.

When the first Oud dropped from the sky, the Tikitik began to laugh.

Chapter 51

I HELD MORGAN'S HAND, making myself watch as aircar after aircar suddenly wavered as if out of control, then fell. Oud tumbled free of their craft to strike the ground. Strike and split open like sacks of jelly—

I jerked my eyes upward, but it wasn't easier to watch them waver and start to fall—

"Stop this," Morgan ordered, his voice low and deadly. The comlink might not convey his tone, but the weapon in his hand, pointed at the Maker Oud, surely did. "You have your answer. Enough have died."

How many must have been sent out like this to make the ridge? Did the Oud come every day, day after day, year after year, hoping for a change?

The Oud tapped the canopy. I felt the vibration beneath my feet again and held my breath until I was certain the remaining aircars had turned about.

Thought Traveler gave a final bark. "A shame. Just when Oud finally prove entertaining."

Kicking it would hurt my toes more than its armored shin, I decided. Not to mention it probably fell under the heading "don't provoke the alien." Something Morgan could get away with, in my experience; my results had been more problematic.

Morgan, weapon now out of sight, stayed focused on the Oud. "What causes them to crash?"

It shuffled to "face" him, appendages twitching. "Minded all say goodgoodgood. Minded all go stupid, crash. All Minded, bad is. All Minded, gone."

"Gone indeed." Thought Traveler no longer sounded entertained. "You wasted your most intelligent individuals on this fool's pursuit. No wonder you've no sense left."

"Intelligent, most I. Maker, best is. Tikitik fool." The Oud uncoiled and tapped vigorously.

Destin cried out as the airship threw itself forward!

Before I had to choose between joining the pile of crashed Oud machines and 'porting away without answers, the airship tipped violently left. Somehow I held onto the cylinder and grabbed Morgan at the same time, somehow not surprised to see the Om'ray and Tikitik keep their balance.

It leveled out, speeding east over the canopy.

"Where are you taking us?" I demanded.

"Stop, did," the Oud said primly. "Go there. First, now."

Meaning it was our turn.

Interlude

THE JUNGLE PASSED BENEATH, an impenetrable carpet of browns and vibrant greens broken by the occasional taller growth. Clouds were building to the south; a promise of an afternoon's drenching. A rainbow or two. It could be any world, Morgan thought. Why couldn't he shake the feeling it wasn't?

Because something's wrong here, Sira agreed, following the thought. *Should I 'port us home?*

Using the word didn't give the Sona Cloisters the feel of the *Silver Fox*. Too soon, he reminded himself. He was adaptable. What good was a starship here anyway? What they could use was one of the Oud's airships—maybe he should negotiate for that.

He hadn't been as careful as he should be. *Beloved,* Sira sent, her mind voice as soft as her skin. *I could take you back. To where there* are *starships and old friends and—*

Morgan captured her fingers and brought them to his lips. *And miss all this?* Underneath, his *determination. We stay together. That's the deal.* "Time for a new course," he said lightly.

She'd risk it for him, would launch them into the unknowable distance between this world and wherever they could go. Risk them both dissolving in the M'hir if she exceeded the limit of her amazing strength.

Then what? If they survived the 'port, she'd leave him to

return here. He knew the quality of his Chosen, of his partner and crew. She'd never abandon her people. Neither would he.

A lock of hair slipped along his cheek. *I love you, you know.* She sent the emotion coursing between them, meeting his response, *love* becoming, for a heartbeat, all there was or need be.

"Human."

Until they were interrupted. Morgan let her fingers go and looked at the Tikitik.

"Come with me," it said. "I would speak with you. Alone, if I may," with a curious twist of its head at Sira.

Who nodded back. *Wonder what this is about.*

So did he. Morgan followed Thought Traveler to the rear of the airship's deck. Their departure was noted by Destin, who stepped closer to Sira, but the Maker Oud appeared oblivious. It hadn't spoken since declaring they were now to complete their part of the bargaining.

The Tikitik stopped, cilia and eyes moving restlessly. Morgan waited for the other to collect itself. Finally the small eyes fixed on the treetops below, the large rolling to meet his.

"You accused me of superstition once," it said quietly. "After seeing proof of Cersi's limits and of the punishment inflicted by the Makers' for trespass beyond them, I find myself perilously close."

"There's an explanation," the Human suggested. "These devices the Oud wants Sira to activate, the Old Ones, your Makers, somehow they fit together."

A faint bark. "You persist, as does the Om'ray's shining achievement, Sira. Is it because you see a future?"

Morgan chose his words with care. "It's because we'll make one."

A thin-fingered hand reached out, rested almost tenderly on Morgan's shoulder. "If you ask those who worship the Makers and their Works, they will tell you there are but two imaginable futures. Either the Balance continues for all time, with Om'ray, Oud, and Tikitik walking the path together between life and death—"

"Or?" Morgan prompted when the other fell silent.

"Or the Makers restart the world."

That *taste*. Change. He'd pushed it aside, assumed the inner warning a sensible one about climbing giant trees, fighting monsters, and flying with strange aliens. Sensing it *flare* with the Tikitik's grim pronouncement, Morgan realized the warning was for nothing so simple. "Are there any details about that?"

Fingers tightened, then released. "You can ask the Oud what their version of the end is, though I'd be astonished if it wasn't just 'Oud, best is,' or some such nonsense. The Om'ray of my experience have no concept of a future or its lack, just as they've no true grasp of the past or change. A kindness, I would suppose." A pause. "Ours is simpler. The Makers send fire."

"The Oud claimed the Om'ray were the Makers."

Thought Traveler's eyes gazed outward. "I would not say this to my kind, Human, nor would I have considered it before the return of those who style themselves M'hiray." Its fingers toyed with the fabric on its wrist. "But it is my purpose to doubt and question. We are not now what we were. Perhaps the Om'ray were more once." The fingers gestured downward. "It is time. This is why I brought you here. To see what Oud and Tikitik have seen. I am—interested—in your opinion, being what you are."

Morgan looked down, half curious, half wary.

To see what at first looked so familiar, he might have been anywhere but here.

Then he realized what he saw . . .

It couldn't be. He put his palms flat on the cowl to steady himself, dizzied by the *taste* of change.

Morgan?

It's all right. The Human gathered his wits. *I'll explain later.*

He hoped. What he was beginning to imagine—no, it couldn't be.

Unless it was.

He knew that shape, even viewed through trees, even half drowned. There were constraints to design, Human or alien; certain economies.

Physics ruled.

Morgan straightened, turning to face the Tikitik. Could the creature hear the pound of his heart? "Are they all the same?"

"Identical." Its neck flexed, moving the head close, eyes fixed in rapt attention. "Your opinion?"

He had to say it. "That was once a starship." "That" being Sona's Cloisters.

Cersi wasn't the Om'ray homeworld.

Chapter 52

WHEN THOUGHT TRAVELER and Morgan rejoined us at the bow, my Human's face was set in the mask of outward calm that meant "don't ask" and all he allowed through his shields was a confusing *sizzle*. Whatever he'd learned or seen, I'd have to wait until he'd thought it through.

Whatever it was, I'd a feeling I wasn't going to like it. The Tiki-tik's head was tucked tight to its chest, as if deep in its own thoughts.

Sira. The First Scout no longer hesitated to contact me mind-to-mind. I'd have taken that as an indication she'd welcomed me into Sona, if I wasn't reasonably sure it was Aryl she considered to already belong. *The end of the grove.*

With an undertone of *dread*.

I paid attention, sharing what I saw with Aryl.

The grove ended in a long narrow lake bordered on its near side by thick mats of a reedy grass. Across the lake, the land couldn't have been more different. Towers of earth rose at regular intervals along the shore, their tops domed in a clear material. Between them, beyond them—nothing but dirt.

Not the rich healthy dirt Morgan put in the rooftop planters he'd maintained on Pocular, nor even the black muck prone to stick to everything on Ret 7; this was dead, dry, and pale. Where wind scoured, gravel showed; in the lee of the towers and along any furrows, dust collected.

Furrows. They weren't furrows, I realized all at once. I'd not grasped the scale of what I was seeing. These were mounds.

They stretched to the south and east as far as I could see, their course seeming random, but each parallel to the others.

And there was nothing else. Anywhere.

"Oud, is." With sickening pride. "All."

The Tikitik's larger eyes retracted into their cones; it kept staring out with the smaller, plucking its wristband as if seeking reassurance of what it was.

Show me!

You don't want to see this. For Aryl-memory placed Yena before me. Yena and the vast Lake of Fire, with its sunken city. Beyond should be grassy fields, with proper furrows. Not these endless mounds of sterile dust. How many would have died?

Show me. Please, Sira.

So I did.

A long moment passed. Then, at the edge of sensation, bordered in red *agony,* a question formed.

What have they done?

So I asked it. "What have you done?"

"Goodgoodgood!" The Maker Oud dropped and spun around, *clickity-click,* then rose again. "Goodgoodgood! Done. Do!" It paused, an appendage tipped with a sponge waving at me. "Sira, see?"

I glanced at Morgan. He saw only the Oud. Muscle knotted his jaw and his eyes—the last time I'd seen that look in them, it had been the instant before he'd killed the pirate captain who'd ripped a hole in the side of Plexis. Then something flickered in his face and he met my gaze. He nodded, once.

"Show me," I told the Oud. Morgan was right. M'hiray and Om'ray had died for this meeting. We couldn't turn back now.

"Sira, see." It spun back, tapped the cowl.

The airship lost forward momentum.

Then began to rise.

Interlude

THE MOUNDS WERE LEAVINGS from subterranean excavations; Morgan had seen the like on other worlds. Easy to conclude the Oud had been digging tunnels here.

Harder to conceive how digging alone could have accomplished what they saw as the airship gained altitude. The scale toyed with the eye, made it seem they flew over a vast ocean with waves, not mounds of dirt, rippling the surface of the world.

Sira watched with him, silent and too quiet.

Looking toward the setting sun, he made out the rich green of Sona's grove against the mountain range, shaded by rain clouds. A glint of water. Dangerous, yes, but life-sustaining. Real, as this no longer was. He spoke to the Tikitik. "I don't have the Om'ray sense. What are we seeing?"

"Rayna, once Tikitik." Thought Traveler drew their attention to the northeast, indicating a tidy patchwork of gold-and-brown fields, then to another, due east. "What remains of Amna."

Taptap. "Oud, are."

"Disagreeable creature. Yes, Oud. Now." A flick of its hand northwest, to where the mountains clawed higher. "The Vyna."

A more restive *taptaptap.* "Oud, not. Never."

"On that we agree." The Tikitik put its back to Vyna, hand rising again. "Pana."

"A Clan we don't know." Destin stepped up to the Oud. "Pana. Yena. Grona. All empty, these names, without meaning. What did you do to them?" she demanded harshly, her face set and grim. "Why are they gone?"

"Done," the Oud replied readily. "Goodgoodgood."

Almost losing its life. Morgan got there first. He interposed his body, stepping forward to force Destin back, her knife hand falling to her side. She glared at him, eyes brimming with fury. "It says this is good. How can killing Om'ray be good?"

Her gaze shifted abruptly to Sira, then fell. She gestured apology with her free hand. "I acted unadvisedly."

His Chosen, or Aryl? It didn't matter which. Morgan eased his guard, knowing Destin wasn't going to attack the Oud again.

Not that he blamed her.

They kept climbing, the land below falling away. The air remained warm, but there'd be an upper limit. Morgan couldn't believe the shielding of the Oud airship capable of dealing with reduced air pressure, not after seeing the hatches and ports of its underside.

The Tikitik, having waited to see if the Om'ray would kill the Oud, resumed its dire orientation. "Tuana is there." To the south, a faint smudge of green, mountains beyond. "And remains ours."

More *taptaptap.*

"Ours," Thought Traveler insisted.

"There's Amna," Destin interrupted, her tone full of longing. She stared east where a section of fields met the shore of a real ocean. "The edge of the world." Her voice quivered for the first time, *dread* slipping her shields.

Behold Cersi, Aryl sent. *Within its walls.*

Morgan turned in place, taking in what was, from this height, an area defined by a half circle of ridges rising to join the mountain range, that range meeting ocean at its tips, an ocean stretched to the darkening horizon with no other land in sight. Within the half circle, those "walls," the plain of the Oud dominated, the stray bits of color from field and forest squeezed against its outer rim.

The Maker Oud roused, giving itself a shake. Whirr/clicks flew from its robe only to dive back under its cover. "Amna, bad," it announced. "Sira, best is."

"So this is your version," Thought Traveler said, a meaningful eye on Morgan. "You pick your favorite Om'ray and discard the rest. What then?"

From Sira and Destin's wince, the Oud made its *sound* in the M'hir. "Sira lives, Oud. Old things, all work. Om'ray *frequency*. Sira, Power. Best is. GoodGOOD—"

"Bad." The Oud's cylinder in her outstretched hand, Sira turned her wrist to let the object fall to the deck. It bounced, then rolled away.

"What do?! What do?!" The Oud coiled this way and that, torn between chasing it and staying with Sira. When she spoke again, it stilled.

"I say no." Hair lashed her shoulders and back, but her expression was icy calm. "This meeting is over. Take us back to Sona."

"No, I!" The Oud squeezed itself down, appendages in frantic motion. Bits went downward. Up from that hiding place came something else.

As Morgan realized it now bristled with what had to be weapons, the Oud sprang high in the air.

At Sira!

Chapter 53

I FOUND MYSELF covered in goo.

Shaking and covered in goo. I knuckled it from my eyes, spat what I tried hard not to taste, and peered out to find that yes, I was covered in what was left of the Maker Oud.

So was Morgan, who held me tight. *Are you all right? Are you hurt?*

"I'm fine," I muttered. Why did aliens have to be full of goo? It wasn't the most rational of thoughts, but I preferred it to replaying the moment when the creature's attack had so utterly surprised me I couldn't even 'port out of its way. "Need—to breathe," I reminded my Chosen.

He eased his grip, leaving an arm around me, and looked up. "Thank you."

Thought Traveler barked its laugh. It wasn't covered in goo. Then again, it had moved to strike at the Oud with such speed all I'd seen was a flash of black against the sky.

Before it rained goo.

That hadn't gone well. I shouldn't have dropped the cylinder. Or not said "no" quite so emphatically, though the mere thought of being confined in an Oud tunnel had given me an entirely new appreciation of why Thought Traveler hated windowless rooms. Still, always leave a prospective client an alternative, Morgan had taught me. Before they become goo.

Any time now. His arm squeezed, then let go.

Pull myself together, that meant. I nodded, taking a steadying breath, and considered our changed situation.

Climbing in a now out-of-control airship full of Oud. "Can you fly this thing?" I asked hopefully.

Earning an incredulous look. "Maybe with time and a manual—time on the ground." My Human wiggled his fingers in the air. "I think we should leave. Coming?" he said to the Tikitik.

"The Oud destroy the Balance." Its head twisted, eyes aimed up. "The world will end in fire."

Morgan?

I'll explain later. Aloud, "Make your own future."

The larger eyes dropped to regard Morgan. A listless arm encompassed the landscape below. "I see no room for one."

"Preserve the Balance another way," my Human proposed. "If the Oud want to be alone, let them. The Tikitik and Om'ray can live apart. Separate."

Destin was appalled. "We can't survive alone. What of glows? We wouldn't last the first truenight without them. Blades. Supplies!"

"We'll all live in the Cloisters," I told her. "Come out by day."

"That's not how—" she closed her lips over the protest.

"The way things were done has already changed," I finished gently.

"You weave an interesting tale, Human." The Tikitik moved closer. Now I saw goo, dripping from the claws of one hand. "Where would you put us in it?"

A Thought Traveler told me the world was bigger than this. They know it is. The image of a great winged beast filled my mind, a basket hanging from a harness. *Esans,* Aryl identified. *The Tikitik can fly.*

"The Oud—do they fly over the ocean?" I asked quickly.

"Never. They abhor water, other than what they steal to bury within pipes. Why?"

Morgan nodded, understanding at once. "What if the Makers relied on the ocean itself to confine you to Cersi. What if, my gloomy friend, you could leave?"

"And go where? There's nothing," Destin protested, her face gone white. "The world ends at Amna!"

"Peace, Sona." Something had changed about the Tikitik. Its large eyes bent toward the horizon. "It's true. Wind and wave would bring gifts to Tikitna. Living things of different taste than here. Of different—potential."

"You told me your purpose is to doubt and question," Morgan said, pressing the advantage. "Consider this one. What have you to lose?"

Thought Traveler brought its clean hand near my face, as though cupping my cheek. Its spice-filled breath warmed my skin and I braced myself, lips closed, but it came no closer. After a moment, a lock of my hair wrapped itself around a long black finger. "This," it said very quietly. "The Makers put us here, together in Balance, for Their purpose. I begin to glimpse what it was. Why all of this was." It pulled back. "The Tikitik remain with the Om'ray."

Fair enough. We'd climbed, in my estimation, too far already. I spared an instant to pity the worker Oud about to die below-decks.

Then thought of the Cloisters, and *pushed* . . .

. . . to find things had changed in our absence.

The Council Chamber was deserted, its colorful floor neatly swept. One hundred and ten M'hiray, plus one Human, might never have arrived or lived in it. Shocked, I *reached*—immediately reassured by the feel of M'hiray minds, nearby and . . . content.

"They're still here," I said aloud, then frowned. "Only not."

"They're in the Dream Chamber," Destin told me, her tone matter-of-fact. "Oh." I felt her awkward *pity* as she remembered I couldn't sense that for myself. "The level below. It's where I'd thought you might want to stay," Destin continued more briskly. "Council must have authorized the move."

I'd a feeling it hadn't been the Sona who made the decision. Fair enough. "Please add my appreciation to what you have to share with Sona's Council."

Of which none was good news. I sent *encouragement*.

Thought Traveler aimed its eyes at the windows; dusk had

fallen, to my surprise. I supposed it must grow dark sooner under the canopy's shadow, not to mention the remnants of rain clouds overhead. "Firstnight," it intoned. "We must leave now, Om'ray."

The First Scout glanced outside and frowned. "We can't. We won't make it before truenight."

My imposed memories didn't hold any particular dangers in the dark, other than walking into things. *Truenight?*

The swarm.

Thanks to Aryl's vivid sharing, I could almost hear the masses of insatiable appetite climbing from the swampwater, feel the slice of their jaws through flesh as they began eating me alive.

Nightmares as long as I lived were likely. "Stay here," I urged. "Till it's safe."

"The swarm is no threat to me. Observe." The second bend of the Tikitik's neck expanded into a ball, its textured skin stretched smooth and taut. At the same time, the black of that skin leached away, leaving behind—a glow. Bright enough even with the lighting of the chamber I had to squint or look away. "Let us go. I, too, have much to convey to others of my kind, concerning the perfidy of Oud and a variety of futures." That faint bark. "I knew you'd be interesting, Human."

"As were you," Morgan replied. "Wait. Before you go. You said you've 'glimpsed' the Makers' purpose. The why of everything. Of Cersi."

Four eyes locked. "I need not tell you, Jason Morgan, what you already know. Good-bye. It may be that we see one another again. It may be that we will not."

I bowed, Destin following suit. The Om'ray left with the Tikitik, the door turning closed behind them.

Leaving Morgan and me alone, mostly.

I turned to my Chosen and waited, hearing our breaths echo in the empty chamber.

The corner of his mouth lifted in a half smile. "What if I told you we were standing in a starship?"

Rasa lunged over the oval bed, arms outstretched. Before he could tag Andi, she squealed and disappeared . . .

. . . reappearing in front of Degal who let out a "Woompf!" of surprise and dropped a stack of blankets . . . disappearing as Rasa appeared in her place. The older child sketched a hasty apology then disappeared . . .

. . . Andi in hot pursuit.

'Port and seek. Children played, their elders smiled indulgently, and my people seemed happy for the first time in—

For the first time. "You're an idiot."

Barac chuckled, then quickly resumed his so-serious expression. "I mean it. I'd punish me."

I eyed my cousin. "Just as well you aren't in charge anymore, then."

Another shriek of laughter brought back his grin. Completely unrepentant, that's what he was. Along with disobedient.

And wise. "You did very well," I assured him. "This is wonderful."

Morgan was beside me, reclined on a lazy elbow. "I'd stop praising him," he advised. "His head's big enough."

We shouldn't be here, Aryl sent. Ever since learning of the M'hiray's new quarters, she'd been like a thorn inside my head. *Nothing good happens in a Dream Chamber.*

Other than being as large as the Council Chamber, with enough well-padded beds along its walls for twice our number and, most wonderful of all, five doors on each of the longer walls leading to separate and ample facilities dedicated to cleanliness. The bliss of that discovery, given the goo?

I'd raced Morgan for the first shower, only to happily share.

Sira—

We're not primitives, to activate what we don't understand.

Silence.

Harsh and hardly true. I asked her forgiveness, but Aryl had locked herself away. I sighed.

The fingers working that tight muscle along my spine paused. "A dispute?" my Chosen asked.

"She doesn't like this place." My Keeper-memories resisted us being here, too, though that made as little sense as Aryl's vague misgivings. The chamber had been designed to house a multitude in comfort, if not privacy. Paired doors in the shorter end walls granted access to the corridor circling the Cloisters, putting this room at its heart.

No, I corrected, putting this room at its core, the safest location in case of radiation. Radiation as in a hazard of space travel, this not being a building at all.

Morgan's notion about the Cloisters, all of them, was something I thought the M'hiray would accept, being well used to starships—especially the more lavish ones. The Sona?

I wasn't sure where to even start. "The Sona will be here in the morning," I said, which he didn't know. Destin's sending had been of respectable strength and clarity.

Barac nodded. "Another Council meeting? I'll start the preparations."

"They've already met and decided. They'll be joining us." I patted the mattress. "Here."

Morgan resumed his attention to my back. "Good idea."

Especially if—or would it be when—the Tikitik abandoned the grove. I'd seen the "glows" the Om'ray relied upon; they were intended to fail and need replacing. Forced dependency. Obligatory interaction. We were finding more and more examples of it, which made the Ouds' rejection of the Agreement between the races even more troubling.

Or terrifying.

"I'll inform Pirisi and Agem. They arranged our families and supplies." Barac looked over to where his Chosen sat with a friend. "Ruti suggests we send M'hiray to the village in the morning to 'port the Sona's belongings here."

"Have her look after it, please. I'm sure they'd appreciate it." The pair were becoming leaders, to my relief.

I'd no interest in it.

Morgan sat up, his chin on my shoulder. *What made them so eager to move in with us? We're still on e-rations, last I heard.*

Our greater number calls to them, Aryl answered. *Waking, sleeping.*

They'll feel joy as well as relief to stop resisting the urge to be together, as Om'ray should.

As M'hiray would. "We'll be one Clan," I decided. "One people." We had a language in common, common problems, a shared future. Surely that would be enough to ease the remaining differences. Even together, we were still so few.

So few, and living in an ancient starship.

Ancient starship in a swamp.

Starving—I stopped there. We had beds. We were clean. As beginnings went, it could be worse.

Morgan had followed my thoughts. His breath warmed my ear. "It's time, Witchling."

Use this moment, when the M'hiray were happy and feeling safe, to tell them the rest.

About to agree, I changed my mind. "Maybe not."

There being a delegation heading our way, with Tle di Parth in tow.

Interlude

HE'D STAY AT SIRA'S SIDE through peril and joy. Not this, Morgan assured himself with an inner smile. What brought an infuriated Chooser with an escort of two much older Clanswomen and yes, there were more behind, hurrying to their Clan's leader had nothing to do with her Chosen. Maybe the M'hiray weren't as concerned about his being Human anymore, but he knew when to make himself scarce.

Especially with Tle involved. If she tried to 'port him away? Just say there'd be an entirely different problem.

Problems weren't on his mind at the moment. A growing, dreadful surmise was, cobbled together from half-formed notions and a scattering of facts. Thought Traveler said he already knew the Makers' purpose. Better to say, the Human told himself, he hoped he was wrong. If he was right?

Well, there was a reason he hadn't told Sira yet. She was determined to be open and honest with her people. Before she faced them with this, he had to be sure, either way.

Morgan walked through the Dream Chamber, responding to greetings with a smile, a dignified nod to acknowledge those who fell silent to watch him pass. More greetings than before, especially from the younger M'hiray. Well enough.

The remaining M'hir Denouncers kept together, as he'd

expected, claiming eight beds in a row, then rigging tables at their ends. Tables, he was interested to see, covered with what hadn't come from Stonerim III. They'd been busy.

The brothers, Arla and Asdny, grinned to see him, their parents, Holl and Leesems waving distractedly, heads bent over one table. Andi was off playing with her new friends, but her parents, Josa and Nik, were sitting cross-legged on one of the beds, a dismantled instrument between them. Morgan hoped it wasn't broken. They'd no spare parts.

The Oud did. His refurbished comlink among the reasons Morgan sought the scientists, he pulled out the device as he approached.

First to spot it, Arla made an odd gesture, passing his hand back and forth over his eyes.

Asdny noticed. "Can you tell what happened to it?"

"Different," Arla told his brother, squinting through fingers.

"That it is." Morgan handed the device to Leesems. Josa and Nik stood and came over to watch. "An Oud took it apart and rebuilt it." Without leaving a trace of that reconstruction on the exterior. "How did you know?"

"Arla's a Looker," Asdny explained, the words coming faster and faster. "He sees what's changed. The First Scout was impressed—"

"Asdny!"

"He was. He gives us special duties."

"Because Asdny's a great climber," Arla clarified.

The Human carefully didn't smile, though at a guess, those duties would be anything to keep the pair safe. "We're fortunate to have your help," he told them. To their father. "I want to rig it for sleepteach tonight. What do you think?"

In other words, would he be scrambling something important if he connected an Oud-touched object to his subconscious?

Leesems nodded. "Nik and I should be able to check that."

"That's not why you're here, is it?" Holl's eyes searched his face. "You've learned something." She lowered her voice. "So have we. Come, sit with us."

They sat on the centermost beds, facing one another across

the gap. The brothers kept busy at the table. Lookouts, Morgan judged, not that anyone would bother them. The rest of the M'hiray had become accustomed to the scientists' tendency to cluster in conversation that most couldn't understand.

Or chose not to understand. He'd been aware since first meeting Barac and Kurr that the Clan as a whole regarded technical expertise as unimportant, almost demeaning. After all, they'd Humans for what little their Power couldn't accomplish. Art and music? Hobbies. Mere interests. As was any scholarship.

Seeing the earnest faces around him, sensing their *commitment,* Morgan wondered if Mirim had realized what she'd done, gathering those with such unClan-like passion for knowledge, such open minds. On second thought, knowing her daughter? He'd no doubt at all.

Holl spoke first. "I've analyzed the samples we have so far. I'm confident we can put together a decent diet. For you, too," she added.

At last, some good news. "Thank you," the Human said sincerely. "That was quick work."

"We'll need to be quicker." Her thick brown hair curled at the ends, a sign of tension. "The Sona must stop eating dresel—at once. Sira has to convince them."

That, he hadn't expected. "Why? What's wrong with it?"

"Nothing. Everything. Dresel contains the key nutrients, as we predicted, but that's not all it has. It's full of engineered compounds." Holl leaned forward, her sober gaze fixed on Morgan. "In my opinion, those compounds have one function: to speed Om'ray metabolism dangerously beyond normal." Her eyes narrowed. "You knew."

"Not about the food," Morgan replied. "Sira's age surprised the Tikitik. He said, 'Our Om'ray burn faster.' That's what this means, isn't it?"

" 'Faster'?" She sat back. "Burn out is more like it."

"Why?" Josa asked. "If the populations suffer from food shortages, an accelerated metabolic rate would only make it worse."

"Would it shorten generations?" Morgan shared what Aryl had told them.

"Definitely, but if this is deliberate, what's the reason?"

Nik gasped. They all looked at her. "Surely you see it," she said. "The Tikitik and Oud—they've been breeding Om'ray. Breeding us!"

The M'hiray fell silent. "Go on," the Human urged. They shouldn't be shocked. Hadn't the Clan Council been doing the same?

They began a hushed murmuring, each finishing the other's thoughts. "Shorter generations—"

"Birthrate's still low. Could compensate—"

"Changing between Oud and Tikitik drastically alters each Clan's environment—"

"Creating selection pressure—favoring adaptations related to survival, reproduction—"

"A monster killed Deni!" Holl covered her mouth.

Silence again, this time grim.

Then Nik spoke. "Accelerated, targeted evolution. Everything points to it, even the way Om'ray unChosen needed permission—tokens—to cross to another Clan."

A puzzle, Morgan thought, putting itself together. Tokens and Speaker pendants . . . the Tikitik had a sense to locate them. A "favorite" food for every Clan? No doubt who'd engineered it. The way the Tikitik's cilia had *tasted* Sira, learning what she carried, its parentage?

"The Tikitik look after the biotech," the Human concluded. "The Oud reshape the physical landscape. Cersi isn't a world—"

"It's an experiment," Josa, his eyes round. "But whose?"

Transmitters in the pendants. A starship marking the location of each "Clan." Moons that housed the Tikitik's "Makers." The Old Ones of the Oud, leaving relics that responded to the M'hir. The Stratification of Om'ray and M'hiray.

Everything snicked into place when Morgan added that one final piece: the Hoveny Concentrix.

"Yours."

Chapter 54

"MATTERS OF CHOICE are decided by Council," Tera di Parth insisted. "Sona has a Council. Therefore the matter should be up to—"

"The Chooser," Tle responded grimly. "I'm not letting strangers dictate my Choice." She looked at me.

I looked at Enora, who was doing her utmost not to smile. Making that difficult was the glowing figure of Ermu sud Friesnen beside her, Chooser no longer. *Joy* came off her in waves. I shook my head. "In the shower."

Nothing innocent in those sparkling eyes. She'd waylaid Oseden sud Parth, that was the truth of it, though he'd been more than happy to take her hand and I couldn't, quite, bring myself to object.

It wasn't as if a Joining could be undone.

No need. This is a good one.

I blinked. Before I could chase that disturbing notion, Aryl went on, *The problem is Tle. Her Power-of-Choice has begun to call.*

Hence the escort and anger.

On one hand it was ridiculous. Our remaining unChosen were now in the Council Chamber, restrained for their own safety. Sona's unChosen had tried to leave his village—in truenight—and was similarly trussed until, according to Destin, his brains returned.

On the other, it was tragic. Whatever happened next, someone would pay the price for the Clan's mistakes.

"The Sona will be here, with us, tomorrow," I said, focusing on the angry Chooser. "With their unChosen."

"Noil di Rihma'at is the son of their Speaker and by all accounts a fine young Om'ray," Enora volunteered. "He's—" a delicate pause "—eager to be offered for your Choice, Tle."

"He lives in a tree."

Peace, Tle. It wasn't polite to send during such a meeting, but I'd other matters to attend to, more important ones than a stubborn Chooser and antsy unChosen. "Has anyone checked on Jacqui?"

"She's as yet unaffected."

MINE THE CHOICE!

There was the real answer, I thought, wincing with the others at Tle's shout. The weaker Chooser wouldn't contest Tle, not while this close to losing control. Just the same, we'd best make sure Ruti's Birth Watcher stayed out of the shower.

"The Sona have somgelt." Tera folded her hands in her lap. "And a Council. All we need do is observe the proprieties."

Somgelt being the drug used to "ease" the mind during Choice, smothering fear and doubt. As for the "proprieties?" I understood, all too well. I didn't blame Tera for clinging to what we'd known, in the Trade Pact, how we'd been.

But it hadn't worked then. It wouldn't now. "I'd prefer," I said in as reasonable a tone as possible, "we don't introduce ourselves to Sona's families by killing their unChosen."

"He wouldn't fail," Tle claimed, her head high. "I can *hear* him. He's strong."

I glanced at Ermu. She'd Commence within days; be whole as she'd never been. Tle deserved the same. Maybe, I thought hopefully, this would end well.

"But I don't want him." Sullen as a child. "I won't Choose him." Or not.

Tera threw up her hands. "See what we've been dealing with?"

Enora, however, nodded. "Ah. I see."

"Sud!" Tle glared at her. "You see nothing."

I resisted the urge to *SNAP* at the irate Chooser. Sud or not,

Enora's Talent was undeniable. No shield, no Power, could keep her from reading the emotions of others if she chose. Something was going on here. "Enora?"

She inclined her lovely head at Tle. "Please. Tell Sira. Trust her."

Tera shook her head. "It's unnatural—!"

"It's how we were. How we're supposed to be. Mirim—" Thinking of my mother, Tle's outrage subsided. "Mirim told me of the right way. The better way." Her scowl reformed. "If you'd just give us time—"

"'Us'?" I repeated with a sinking feeling. "Don't tell me you think you can wait for Asdny di Prendolat."

"He'd never survive your Choice, you fool," Tera scolded.

"He would—he will!" Tle focused on me. "Sira, your mother told me Choosers and unChosen should live together, learn about one another. Fall in love if we can. She brought me to Asdny, urged me to stay as close to him as I could. I do—I do care for him."

She does, Enora sent. *I know you understand, heart-kin.*

Who better? I thought sadly. My mother's dream of what we should be was just that, a dream. Tle's affection for Asdny wouldn't protect him.

They'd brought me unChosen to meet, children really, ever hopeful. I'd felt affection for them all.

And killed the first offered for my Choice.

My Joining with Morgan almost killed him. That it hadn't was due to the depth of our love, yes, but also his great strength and courage.

I couldn't allow this.

I rose to my feet, the others doing the same. "Tle di Parth. You cannot remain a threat to our unChosen." As I'd been. "Tomorrow you will offer Choice to Noil di Rihma'at or leave us and live apart."

As I had.

Her face was a study in anguish.

You may not have Asdny, I told her. *If you decide to leave, to protect him and the others, I promise to find you another Choice, a good one. There are more unChosen on this world, Tle. You're strong enough to wait. I did. I know you can.*

Something eased the pain in her face. "I accept exile," Tle announced. *Let Jacqui have the Sona. She's waited longer.*

While that wasn't her decision to make, I gestured gratitude.

The others bowed, gesturing respect. I hoped the rest of the M'hiray were going to approve of what I had to tell them. Even more, I hoped I could live up to my promise to one.

Enora let the others leave. "Well done," she said.

"I never thought I'd act like my father," I admitted ruefully. "When did that happen?"

"You are nothing like Jarad." *I've watched you search for answers, heart-kin, until you fell asleep over your machines. I've seen you find hope for all of us, fight for all of us, time and again. That's why we believe in you, even Tle. It's not about Power. You care—for all of us.* "Rest, Sira," she finished aloud, smiling. "Tomorrow's a new day."

I smiled back. "And full of hope?"

Her dark eyes twinkled. "I don't need to tell you that."

Having discovered actually useful Keeper-memories, I showed the M'hiray how to set the lighting above their beds. By the time Morgan and I sought ours, most of the Dream Chamber had dimmed. There was a distant brightness marking where Holl and the others continued to work; others where people stayed awake, talking over what I'd told them, in whispers or in outward silence.

As did we. The beds to either side were vacant, a courtesy. Morgan and I nestled together on one, it being wider than our cot on the *Silver Fox,* neither of us interested in sleep.

Forget I'm here, Aryl had told us smugly the instant we'd pulled up a blanket. *I need sleep too—and I've no interest in being a spectator.*

I'd blushed at Morgan's chuckle, but we both knew why her presence faded away the closer we came to one another. Enris. She now spoke of her lost Chosen—Enris this, Enris that—with ease, sharing light-hearted moments. On recognizing the embossed metal bracelet Enris had made for her, so long ago and on this world, she'd consoled Barac with her memories of its gifting, and urged from him memories of his brother.

I wore the bracelet now, my cousin insisting, though I couldn't help but think it only added to the unimaginable pain filling Aryl di Sarc, a pain she disguised, one she used for strength.

As I drew upon joy. I snuggled closer, my hair cloaking Morgan's shoulders and chest, loving how his arm curved warm and strong around me. "I think that went well," I said after a moment. "I didn't *pry*, of course." I paused, feeling him breathe. "Did it go well?"

Low and in my ear. "We've food and beds. The Healers put Tle and Jacqui to sleep for the night. You could have told the M'hiray the world was ending and they'd have smiled."

"Is it? Ending." When he didn't answer right away, I twisted to face him. "Morgan."

"Sorry. Poor choice of words."

Jason.

He traced my jaw with a finger, then sighed. "Maybe."

" 'Maybe' the world's ending?" I went to sit up.

He wouldn't let me. "You heard Thought Traveler. 'The world will end in fire.' Some Tikitik believe the Makers will destroy Cersi if the Balance ends."

I had a bad feeling Morgan no longer considered the Tikitik beliefs superstition. "You think there's an installation on the moon. Moons," I corrected, feeling numb.

"Nothing we can do about it if there is," he said pragmatically. "But something stopped the Oud in midair. My best guess? An automated system, like this ship. Or from this ship and others like it. A perimeter field, cued to specific life-forms, would do it."

"This starship." I'd told the M'hiray. Other than the scientists among them, they'd been more impressed by, as Morgan noted, food and beds. "We came here in starships. First." I removed any distance between our bodies, pressed my face against his chest. We'd had a starship.

"Or at the same time." His voice rumbled through my cheek. "About that—"

I sighed, guessing I wasn't going to want to sleep after what Morgan had to tell me. "What about 'that'?"

"Do me a favor. Change the word 'Balance' to 'Parameters.' "

"All right."

"Now 'Clan' to 'Test Group.'"

That sinking feeling was becoming familiar. I tensed, waiting for it.

"Last, but not least, 'Cersi' to 'Experiment.'"

Not going to sleep, at all. Ever. "If Cersi is some grand experiment," I mumbled into Morgan's chest. "Was Thought Traveler right? Do you know its purpose?"

"I believe it was to produce you, Om'ray with the ability to manipulate the M'hir."

"Us?" It made a terrible kind of sense.

I wasn't a mistake? Aryl, more hesitant than I'd ever heard her. *What I did, what we did, wasn't wrong?*

That, I thought to myself, depended on the consequences. As for her *listening*, I'd have roused too, hearing the world was ending.

"Experiments come to a conclusion." I closed my eyes, pretending Morgan's arms made the universe safe and comprehensible. "The M'hiray are here now. Is that it? Is it—over?"

A shrug. "The neighbors seemed to think so."

Okay, not safe and comprehensible after all. I pushed away, trying to see his face. "You don't. You think there's something else."

"Thought Traveler said the Makers would restart the world if they saw failure. Does that mean a time limit? Unlikely. From what we've seen here, I'd say this experiment's gone on longer than ever intended. Those who started it are dust.

"Another measure of success then," Morgan went on. "If it was the splitting off of the M'hiray, you'd think something would have changed here. Other than the Oud grabbing Human tech and getting ambitious, that doesn't appear to be the case."

A trial awaits. A test.

I nodded. "I agree. But what sort of test?"

I didn't expect an answer; Morgan had one. "The Hoveny Concentrix."

"Pardon?"

"This planet is full of Hoveny ruins and technology. The object the Oud wanted you to activate responded to the M'hir. What if Hoveny technology did as well? What if Om'ray—the original Om'ray, the Oud's Old Ones, the Tikitik's Makers—knew that and set up this experiment to try and take advantage of it? To produce individuals capable of awakening the past."

It was the Clan Council dictates about Choice taken to—I'd no words for where this had gone, nor did I care about the past. "Did they steal children?"

"Sira—"

"These 'original' Om'ray had to start their breeding program somewhere. Criminals. Political prisoners." The too-small rooms, all in a row.

Generation after generation. How many had been born on this world? How many had died?

And for what? Machines, buried in the ground.

I pushed aside my questions, stretched my awareness into the M'hir, *sensing* who slept, who stirred. Food they'd done on their own, and more. Tomorrow I'd thought to offer them hope, to celebrate the beginnings of a new Clan and future.

Which we'd do. After they heard the truth about the old.

Tomorrow.

Sira? With *concern.*

I tightened our link, shared my *resolve.* Then hugged my Chosen as tightly as I could. *You sleep. Learn the language.*

I'd watch over him, just in case.

I'd watch over them all.

>Keeper<

I'd been asleep. I hadn't meant to—

>Keeper<

—and was asleep, something in me realized. I opened what weren't eyes.

Pinpricks ot black light. Each the end of a thread. So many I couldn't see a gap or end to them, so close they stirred with what wasn't breath—

>*Keeper, welcome*<

—no, this wasn't happening. I'd known to disable the Dream Chamber, had put it to sleep. It took Identity—

>*Keeper, welcome*<

—and the Will of an Adept, my will—

>*What is your will, Keeper?*<

—to wake up!

>*You are awake; the body sleeps. I am Sona. What is your will, Keeper?*<

—if I was dreaming and awake, I wanted answers. I want answers!—

>*Ask.*<

Interlude

CHANGE! Choking on the *taste,* Morgan fought to wake up. Change!

Had something gone wrong with the sleepteach? Processing that much input could muddle the head, but usually no worse than a night at a bar.

CHANGE!

His eyes shot open. Morgan found himself staring up at a seething mass of tendrils!

He flailed at them with the hand that wasn't pinned under Sira, relieved when they curled up and away as if hairs caught by flame.

"Sira!" They were still on the bed, a bed now descending. It had been—it had been near the ceiling. The Dream Chamber! Not again.

I warned her—Aryl sounded furious—*nothing good happens here!*

Descending? The bed fell. Morgan threw himself over Sira, held on and waited for the impact.

Instead, politely, the bed slowed and stopped, exactly where it had been.

Morgan jumped up to find the rest of the chamber improbably normal, filled with sleepers. If he'd disturbed any, they were pointedly ignoring a Chosen who'd shouted his partner's name.

Turning, he put his hand flat on her forehead. *SIRA. WAKE UP!*

Chapter 55

STARS CRUSTED THE SKY. I felt as though I hadn't seen them in years, like old friends I hadn't known how much I missed until seeing them again.

"Unfamiliar. No surprise there."

I dropped my gaze to Morgan. Or rather, to where he sat. I'd 'ported us here the instant my eyes had opened. He'd waited, a shadow fairly bursting with *impatience,* for me to explain what had just happened.

"I didn't do it on purpose," I said finally, it being important to get that out of the way. This wasn't a case of my trying the wrong switch or button.

"I wasn't actually worried about that." As if I should have known.

And did. I relaxed. "It turns out the Keeper is more like a comtech." Odd, how what I'd learned from Morgan and the *Fox* mattered more here than all my years as Clan. "Falling asleep where I did, with my mind full of questions, activated Sona. The—" I waved my hands. Being dark, that didn't help. "—the ship."

"That's—" I felt the effort Morgan expended to curb his excitement. "Tell me what happened. Everything."

"I heard it, like a voice. Like Aryl's from the crystal. I was a little—startled." I heard him shift; our experience with uninvited voices hadn't been good. "But it wasn't an attack or threat. It was like—you know, talking to the ship."

"People don't talk to ships." Patiently.

"You do. Did." Move on, I told myself. "The point is, Sona answered questions. The couple I had a chance to ask it."

Before someone yanked me out of a perfectly comfortable sleep, demanding answers of his own. I'd 'ported us here more to protect those still asleep, if any, than for privacy.

Though privacy was pleasant.

"I'll apologize later," he said grimly, making that in no way a promise. "Go on."

"The Maker Oud was right." I looked up at the stars. "The Om'ray started all this. They sent volunteers, the best and most able; invited the Oud and Tikitik for their skills. They were to work together, Morgan, but something happened. The trial was never to last this long. They were supposed to go home." To a world out there, one where we'd evolved—

Where we'd belonged, once.

"I asked it why." I raised my arms, reached as if to touch that world. A tear slid down my cheek, as cold as the space between, tribute for those who'd risked so much only to fail.

Arms went around me, held tight. My hair slipped around his neck, binding us together. His kiss found my tear and he asked, "Why, Sira?"

"Because everything was taken from us," I told him. "Cersi was our last chance to reclaim what we'd lost.

"We were the Hoveny."

Interlude

BARAC SETTLED BACK against the wall with a yawn. Hadn't sounded like passion, that shout, but when he'd gone to check Sira and Morgan's bed was empty. He'd like to know where they'd 'ported. A little privacy would be nice, sooner than later.

He grimaced, working his tongue around his mouth. Emergency rations. He suspected Humans made them tasteless so they wouldn't be eaten on a whim. Just as well Holl had—

He straightened. Not food, that *taste*. Change. Should be getting used to it by now, he thought grimly. Barac started down the aisle between the beds—

A figure, swathed in white, *appeared*. Another! Two more over—

"Intruders!" Shouting that warning, *sending* at the same time, Barac pulled free his blade as he ran at the nearest.

Others were in motion too, some *disappearing*—'porting from the chamber to escape. Lights came up.

The figures were beside the children's beds! Barac wasn't the only one running now.

Enora got there first, tried to protect Andi. Barac saw her fall—saw Andi's terrified face as a stranger snatched her up and they *disappeared*.

"GO!" He slashed through legs, on the backstroke removed a head, stumbled over his mother's body, and kept running.

They're outside! They're outside!

Figures came and went. Barac split another in half. The M'hiray had no weapons, but he saw Pirisi wrap his arms around an invader.

Disappearing together, where he couldn't follow.

Screams, inside and out. *SIRA!* He'd never imagined an attack like this—never dreamt he'd be fighting for survival against his own kind.

Here! Sira *appeared* with Morgan.

Too late.

It was over.

Barac sank to his knees in the sudden quiet, sobbing with the rest.

Chapter 56

"VYNA." Destin used her boot to roll over the limp body of a Clansman. Other than his hairless head and white clothing, he might have been of Sona. "And those who serve them." Her eyes were hard as stone. "I told you. They steal children. The unChosen."

Barac's warning had reached them. I'd sent my own summons, but they'd been coming already, risking the swarm with what glows they could carry.

"We'll get them back," Morgan promised. "Them" including Sona's one unChosen as well as ours, and our children.

Andi.

We'd lost six forever, a new and terrible grief. Pirisi di Mendolar—dropped in the M'hir, his Chosen, Ru, dying soon after. Kele and Celyn sud Lorimar, cut down in the hall as they'd fled, for some of the intruders had been armed.

Dear and gentle Enora. Agem, ever puzzled by the world.

They call us "lesser Om'ray," Aryl sent, her mind voice as *dark* as I'd ever felt. *They won't sully their breeders with our blood. They'll use those they stole, then toss them aside.*

We'd another body to examine. A Vyna. Tall for a Clanswoman and obscenely thin. Her shoulders and knees protruded under her clear garment like great knuckles, her skin everywhere colorless, tracked with the blue of blood vessels. Her hands had four fingers and two thumbs, like Sona's Speaker, but her digits were half again as long; the nails were missing. A tight beaded cap covered her hairless scalp, and her eyebrows were beads of gold.

A disturbing face, even empty of life.

She'd been pregnant, the swell of her abdomen the only roundness to her body. Jacqui had checked, disgusted anyone would so risk their child, but the life within the Vyna had died with her.

The Vyna's frail appearance was a lie, I thought. There'd been but two of them, with their "servants," but they'd 'ported here with others and sent them away again with their captives, along with what supplies they'd been able to grab. Formidable, that said of them.

Greedy as well as callous, that too.

Unfortunately, they'd hidden those they'd taken well enough I couldn't *grab* them back. We'd an answer for that.

Morgan stood by Barac, busy allotting weapons the Sona provided among those willing to use them, which were all of the M'hiray. The Sona, led by Destin, were determined to come as well, a chance to strike back at their tormentors worth the risk of the M'hir. The chamber boiled with anger.

None of it mine. What I felt I kept to myself; every so often, Morgan would give me a searching look.

Knowing me as he did.

Peace, I told the mothers waiting nearby. *Wait.* They were desperate to go, the severed links to their children like bleeding wounds. So far, they'd listened, but I was ready to block their 'ports if need be. We couldn't lose them too.

Slipping into the M'hir, I'd found the *burn* of Vyna passages, followed to the blinding nexus where they converged and overlapped: their home. They must have been raiding the other Clans for generations.

Since we taught them how, Aryl sent.

You say they respect Power.

That was then. Sira, are you certain?

Certain that if we were to live on this world, among its Om'ray, the Vyna couldn't continue to be a threat? Yes.

Certain more death wasn't the answer? Yes.

That I alone could stop it?

We'll see, Great-grandmother. The nexus wasn't enough for a locate, of course, but I had what was: Aryl di Sarc's vivid memories of the Vyna Council Chamber.

It was time. *Morgan.*

Even across the chamber, I could see the blue of his eyes when he turned in answer.

Coming?

Interlude

MORGAN FOUND HIMSELF inside another Council Chamber.

With Sira.

And only Sira.

He winced, thinking of those they'd left behind, let alone facing them again—especially Barac. But this was her call and he'd trust it.

Especially with—he stepped forward, staring out the tall arched windows, so like those of Sona's Council Chamber, seeing a clear night sky, filled with stars—

—if stars wheeled in formation, creating the outline of something very large and disturbingly curious. Morgan squinted. Somethings, he decided, tapping a finger on the pane. "What are they?"

The rumn, Aryl informed him. *It's unfortunate they've been attracted. With them close, we may not be able to 'port.*

Given that was how they'd arrived—and would leave—Morgan looked at Sira. "They part of the plan?"

She gazed at what swam past the windows with a thoughtful frown. "I don't know. What are Rugherans doing on Cersi?"

Rugherans? He found his mouth open and closed it. This complicated matters. The species existed, partially, within the M'hir.

They'd encountered them on a couple of occasions, the last he'd thought with success.

There'd been sex. Of a sort. Some type of happy conjunction had taken place, though on a planetary scale. The details were a bit hazy. It was often the case when Drapsk were involved.

Morgan watched the nearest moving constellation, trying to make out tentacles or a head—not that Rugherans had heads. "Sure it's them?"

"Yes. No, but they feel—alike." Her gray eyes clouded. "I hadn't noticed the M'hir was unsettled here, at least no more than usual. That's where we've found them before." She chewed her lip. "They aren't talking, not to me."

The rumn can talk?

They aren't always here, *or aware of us,* Sira explained. *Let's hope that continues.*

Unaware and not here would suit him too. Putting aside the chill such otherworldly beings gave him, Morgan looked around the chamber. The Vyna Cloisters was underwater—completely, from the memories Aryl shared—and accessed by an enclosed staircase. The Clan's living space was carved into a spire of black rock rising from the lake.

A lake of something other than water, the whole was ringed by tall cliffs of more black rock. Morgan guessed they stood within a volcanic crater, itself surrounded by a sere landscape of once-molten stone. A fortress, without Oud or Tikitik.

Or reason. "Why?" he asked suddenly. "What's here worth protecting?"

We are.

As quickly as that, five of the six tall backed chairs on the dais were filled with Chosen, so alike to the corpse in Sona they might have been clones.

All pregnant. *Councilors,* Aryl supplied.

One problem resolved. If the Vyna could 'port near the rumn, so could they. Maybe they'd come to an agreement.

He was, the Human thought, doing rather well not to be terrified at the thought.

The door had swung open at the same time. In floated four

quite different chairs, these each filled with the oldest Clan Morgan had ever seen. They were wrapped in blankets and two unChosen accompanied each.

Adepts. This with utter *loathing.*

Compared to these Vyna, Sira was life incarnate, the red-gold of her hair burnishing the walls and floor, the healthy glow of her face like the sun, the lush curves of her body making those in the chairs look skeletal.

I love you too, she sent, with a warm sidelong glance, then became all business. *I've found our people, the children. They've been put into a false sleep. It won't take much to wake them. First things first.*

She stepped forward, hands by her sides, waiting for the Adepts to settle into place.

Be watchful, Aryl warned him. *They can't be trusted.*

Oh, he was sure of that. Morgan surreptitiously checked various pockets, items he'd promised to use on only one condition.

If Sira failed.

Chapter 57

I LOOKED UPON THE VYNA and grieved. Choosers Commenced without Choice, bearing empty offspring to host the dead. Adepts, prolonging their lives at the cost of others', until they died and were reborn. It was as if what was new mustn't be tolerated. As if Vyna must never change.

The disturbing thought kept me silent when I might have spoken, busy rethinking so many things. Why were they different? Was it because they lived with such strange neighbors?

Could this one Clan have soured the Hoveny's hope, trapping Om'ray, Oud, and Tikitik in an endless experiment? Why hadn't the Makers restarted the world, if that were possible?

Or had they? Molten rock surrounded Vyna, lay at the heart of what had been Tikitna. How—

The leftmost Adept lifted a gnarled finger at Morgan. *NOT-REAL!*

Yet you *hear me.* His sending, in their language, was strong enough to echo in the M'hir.

Sleepteach. Vastly clever, my Human.

He caused a stir among the ancients. Thin lips worked, some drooling. One summoned her unChosen, taking his strength with the touch of a feeble hand. Another chittered, then covered her mouth in haste to mute the sound.

Vyna's Councilors remained still, observing. They were the key, I decided. Jealous of their Talents, unwilling—perhaps unable—to share Power. These would be the Vyna who 'ported from Clan to Clan, taking what they felt they deserved. The ones to stop.

Are you sure? Aryl asked.

I've known their kind all my life, I assured her. Their selfishness was their vulnerability.

I made the gesture of greeting between peers who were not equals. *I am Sira Morgan.* I let them test their Power against mine, for once glad to *dominate.*

It seemed I'd made the right decision. Heads nodded. Thin lips smiled. *We glory in your Power.* From the one at the far right.

We do not acquiesce to it! From the middle.

From the rest: WE *are superior.*

I smiled my father's smile. *You are welcome to think so. I truly don't care. What I do care about are those you stole from me. Return them, and we'll leave.*

You are not Vyna, to give orders here. The middle one rose, holding out a languid hand. *Yet you bear within you a Glorious Dead, who may be.* Paired green rings glinted between the first and second knuckle of fingers and thumbs as they closed and opened. Beckoning me closer, I thought with a chill. *Let me greet Her properly.*

I didn't turn at the menacing *snick* from behind me, well aware of Morgan's growing distrust.

I need no proper greeting from you, Aryl sent, her mind voice like the sounding of horns. *The last time we met, Tarerea Vyna, I promised to drop you in the M'hir.*

Yet left us a magnificent gift, Aryl di Sarc. Sona's Adepts. The hand lowered. *How else could we save so many?* As if we should be grateful for their theft.

Save them? Aryl began, her *rage* beating through me.

Though I shared it, I sent, *Wait.*

Something tried for my /attention/. Something regrettably familiar. /here/attention!/

I looked past the Vyna to the window. More rumn/Rugherans had arrived—or a larger one—pressing themselves/itself against the transparent barrier. Unlike before, it didn't move, the stars patterning what I assumed was a body as still as if I gazed at a night's sky.

Now it wanted to communicate? I wasn't about to dip into the M'hir with it. *Excuse me, but I'll have to talk out loud,* I informed the Vyna, then walked to the window. "What do you want?"

/attention/~urgent~/

Gasps, good and loud, from behind me. I assumed the Vyna hadn't heard from their neighbors before.

"Not the best time," I replied. Morgan's reflection appeared beside mine. How he'd hidden a blaster that size in his coat was a question for another time. I did find it a comfort, though unlikely of use. "Do you know who I am?"

/attention/ trouble~anomaly~trouble/leave/

That'd be yes. "We'll be leaving."

/leave/determination/leave/determination/ It retreated and I breathed a sigh of relief. Leave we planned to do, just as soon as—

BANG!

Apparently it had retreated in order to have room to ram the window. A Vyna shrieked, likely for the first time in her life.

/leave/~!~leave/ BANG!

Morgan shouldered his blaster. "I'd say we've outstayed our welcome, chit."

I agreed. I sent a call outward, knowing the minds I had to *reach. WAKE!* Waited until groggy minds turned to frightened, then determined ones.

We're here, Sira, from Asdny. From others. Sparks of warmth in the dark. *Where's here?*

It doesn't matter, I assured them. *Go home—take Noil with you. Your families are waiting.*

Some with weapons they'd hoped to use, all no doubt furious I'd left them behind—especially Sona's First Scout—but this had never been about fighting a battle.

It was about finding peace.

BANG! /leave~anomaly~leave/determination/

Don't forget the part about getting clear ourselves, if we can't resolve this, my Chosen reminded me.

Together we turned to face the Vyna.

The Adepts were in full flight, chairs speeding toward the door, servants running to catch up. The Vyna Council were on their feet, but stayed, either of sterner stuff or too afraid to move. No, I decided cheerfully, it was fear.

How is this possible? Tarerea Vyna demanded. *The rumn—how have you made them speak?*

Questions I couldn't answer, so I didn't try. What I could do was seize the opportunity like a true trader. *We are the M'hiray. As you can* sense, *you can't steal from us. We will no longer tolerate—*

They're gone! Fury shredded my shields, burst into my mind. *What have you done!?*

I recovered, pushed back. *I saved them from you—*

From us? Vyna is the final sanctuary, you fool. We were saving what little's left. Tarerea Vyna covered her face with her hands.

Can you not hear the screams of the world?

Interlude

*S*AVE THOSE YOU CAN.

The order came with a locate and an *urgency* that numbed Barac even as he obeyed, gathering those he wanted with a quick *summons.*

What's going on? Ruti hadn't wanted to stay behind. Now she crowded close, Jacqui hovering behind. There were other groups forming. Other questions.

A figure formed in their midst, spun with a curse, then stopped, hands at his sides. Morgan.

Alone.

"The Oud have attacked the remaining Clans," he told them, his voice unrecognizable, eyes blazing. "We'll save those we can."

Sira's words, Barac thought, even as he nodded with the rest. "Go."

Barac formed the locate and *pushed* . . .

. . . finding himself in a long wooden building. The floor was tilted, tables and benches having slid to one end, and he braced himself against the nearest wall, seeing the other M'hiray do the same. Lamps—glows—illuminated shocked faces, haunted eyes. Om'ray.

And the glint of metal. An ax. A pot. "You can't have our children!"

"We're not Vyna," the First Scout said quickly. "We're here to save everyone." The building moaned, a sound Barac sincerely hoped he never heard again. Dirt began pouring in, through the windows, through what had been doors. "Trust us or die here."

"We can get you to Sona," Destin urged.

They came forward, coughing, choking. Three held children. Another an armful of—coats? Barac didn't care what they carried, he wanted to be out of here. "Take them."

Tle nodded, put her hand on the nearest and *disappeared*. She was back for the next before Degal left with his, this time taking two.

Power she had.

Barac turned. "Where are the rest?"

Destin held out an empty hand. "Amna's gone."

The floor cracked beneath their feet. Barac lunged for the Sona Scout, concentrating with desperate speed even as the floor opened . . .

. . . and Oud burst through.

Chapter 58

*T*HIS WAY.

Holding a child's hand, I walked through a nightmare. This—this had been a grove, like Sona's.

Until the Oud had sucked it dry, then plowed it under. What had been rastis lay shattered, so many sticks caught and tossed. The air was thick with dust and acrid, burning my lungs, and everywhere, hands or feet or the faint shine of hair—

Don't be sad, Andi told me, her mind voice *peaceful. They aren't gone. I still hear them.*

Try not to listen, little one, Aryl advised.

Advice I did my best to take. The M'hir was a cacophony of horror, the Watchers howling names, ghosts trying to reclaim them, the fading echoes of lives. How Andi could bear the *sound* was beyond my understanding.

How she remained untouched? I could only be grateful. I needed her Talent. Those left—

There are, she assured me. *This way.*

Had the ground been soft, we couldn't have moved. As it was, we were forced to walk between mounds twice my height and horrifying in their regularity. How anyone could have survived—

Here.

She'd stopped, so I did, though I saw nothing. *Where?*

Here. Andi pulled free, dropping to her knees, and began to dig. She paused and looked up at me, her eyes somber. *You'll have to help. They're a long way down.*

Because, I realized with a lurch under my heart, the Oud had buried the Cloisters.

I'll help. Picking up the child, I opened my awareness—

Then *reached.*

Hoping to find more than the dead.

Interlude

THE STENCH OF DEATH masked all other scents, but it was the silence Morgan noticed most. Not a whisper of air stirred the leaves or cooled his face. Whatever could fly had already left. What lived in the trees was hiding or gone. He gripped the railing with both hands, knuckles white, and wondered how long a forest took to die.

The water had gone first, stolen before dawn. The black muck left behind had squirmed with the desperate and dying for hours. Nothing moved now.

He supposed he should be comforted that the Tikitiks' Makers hadn't rained fire upon the planet. Yet.

Other, smaller, hands appeared, gripping the rail beside his, and the Human closed his eyes in relief. "You're back."

"Twenty from Tuana, thanks to Andi." Sira's voice had a ragged edge. Rage, that was, not exhaustion. He didn't know if the Vyna had given her the locates for the remaining Clans or if she'd ripped them from their minds.

She'd sent him back first. Ripped, then.

"Barac brought nine from Amna," he told her. "And some coats."

Coats?!

His sense of Aryl faded after that outburst. "Is she all right?"

Sira sighed and leaned into him. "As right as anyone. The Vyna didn't exaggerate. The Oud have devastated every Clan but theirs."

"And Sona's next." The rastis had folded their fronds to preserve moisture; so doing only served to let the sun through to evaporate what water remained and bake the mud-coated corpses. He nudged her gently. "Look."

A solitary esans stood at a distance, striped in sun and shadow, its rider sitting astride. Morgan couldn't see who it was.

He didn't need to. On impulse, he raised his hand.

As if in answer, the beast gave its shuddering shriek, then turned and walked away.

"Thought Traveler has the right idea," he said after a moment. "This is no place to be, Sira." They'd saved all they could of those willing to be saved, the Vyna confident in their sanctuary. A sanctuary too small and rumn-infested to offer hope to anyone who didn't want to be a "servant." "So, chit. Here we go again. Where do we 'port?"

Her pause had a little too much *thinking* in it for his comfort. Morgan turned, taking Sira's hands in his. "You did hear me. We might as well leave sooner than later."

She looked up, an unexpected gleam in her eyes. "It's a starship."

"You can't be—" serious, but he didn't finish. Of course she was, so he made himself think out loud. "A starship half buried in muck and dead swarm bits. A starship with no power source. A starship older than the Trade Pact. Need I go on?"

"You *pushed* the *Fox* through the M'hir."

To save her life, at the cost of—taking that determined chin in his fingers, he tilted her face to look up. "This is bigger. And yes, in this case, that matters."

She kept looking up, her nose wrinkled. "Came here, so it's flown before."

"Not necessarily. Could have been dropped from orbit like lifepods." Morgan shook his head. "Sira, I'm the first to believe you can do the impossible, but we don't even have a manual for the thing."

She lowered her gaze to meet his. "Say that again."

"We don't know how it works—"

"That's not what you said." The gleam in her eyes had become a glow. "You said a manual. I know who—what to ask. The ship!"

He shouldn't encourage her. Any delay—still. Morgan looked up. The petalled walls, the shaping. A beautiful design.

Once. "Lifepods aren't intended to go back into space on their own."

"The ship told me the Om'ray were supposed to go home. What if that's the conclusion to the experiment—the finale to all of this? We just go home."

"In this."

"Why not this? It's tech." She glanced up again, making a face. "Okay, it's big, but it's still a machine. What we've seen of it so far works. Maybe all it needs is—us!" Her hair lifted in a cloud.

"Promise me—" what? To consult, to waste time, to—"I'm coming with you."

That smile he loved, then the dying jungle disappeared . . .

Replaced by the Dream Chamber.

Chapter 59

BARAC REACHED ME FIRST, hands on my shoulders. "That was—" he shook his head, my cousin for once without words.

Destin nodded. "Agreed." She looked around the room. "We're here," with a certain wonder.

Which was what mattered. I sent *reassurance.*

Easy to give, when you'd no idea what you were doing.

Is that so? Aryl felt as though she was making herself comfortable. *I for one am in favor of seeing this thing fly. A much more civilized way to travel.*

As if she had reason to fear another long 'port. *I won't risk you, Great-grandmother.*

Unlike the others in your care, Sira, I've lived my life. Whatever happens, remember that.

Whatever happened was going to be now and in front of everyone, the Om'ray and M'hiray having gathered—as I should have realized—together in the chamber. All talking at once.

I stepped up on the nearest bed, getting my balance. No one noticed. I readied myself to *reach* to all of them. "We—"

The word filled the immense room, turning heads and silencing conversation.

Well now. Being Keeper had some advantages. "We don't have much time before the Oud finish reshaping Sona," I said bluntly.

"We can't stay here. I see two choices: Vyna's one. They believe they'll survive. Maybe they will, but I don't trust them."

Angry nods. *Agreement.*

"The other is to leave Cersi. Those of you who've just arrived— I ask you to accept that we can travel the same way, much farther. Where, is the question. It's one we thought we'd resolved by coming here."

"There's no going back," Tle said, her voice loud enough to be heard. She looked around at the others. "The Trade Pact's too far for most of us. The passage we used to reach here leads to a trap—or solid rock."

"It's all been for nothing." Degal sank on the nearest bed, head in his hands. I felt *despondence* spread; knew their *anguish.*

"It's been for this." I *reached* out, dropping my shields, letting them feel my *love* and *determination.* "We are the answer our ancestors wanted so desperately to find." I *pulled* them into the M'hir with me, floating in that darkness . . .

. . . becoming light. Morgan's, nearest and warmest. Flickers steadied as those new here found their courage. Glows marked those sure of their place. We saw one another and were glad . . .

. . . we couldn't stay long. I felt the *interest* of Watchers, but they were not what sought. *SONA!*

>*Keeper. What is your will?*<

To go home.

Interlude

THE EARTH BECAME AN OCEAN and the great rastis and nekis, able to bend to the M'hir Wind, fell like twigs to float away and drown. Buttress roots snapped and clawed at air, spinning helplessly before being dragged under. What lived above ground tried to flee, only to be sucked down and smothered.

Worker Oud continued to dig, appendages smoothing rough walls. Others swept aside the unpleasant leavings of the surface, conveying those deeper, to where iglies waited to scavenge this bounty. These Oud were incapable of imagination; those who could dream rejoiced in a clean new Cersi. Best.

The reshaping Oud reached Sona's Cloisters, moved along the metal-taste, opening space, conveying dirt. They weren't to stop until they'd brought this splinter to the greater depths.

The ground vibrated.

Every Worker went still.

The vibration deepened.

Every Worker crouched, tucking its appendages safely inside flesh. It was necessary to pause and wait for the rumble to end before digging resumed. Until secured with beam or body, tunnels collapsed. The Oud were wise in the ways of the earth.

But the rumble grew stronger and louder. Tunnels did collapse, then the ground above them, then the surface fell away.

Safely crouched, thoroughly buried, the Worker Oud didn't see the proud tapered starship shake free. Didn't see it rise into the sky above Cersi and disappear.

A Tikitik did, with all four eyes.

It barked its laugh, before heading out to sea.

The Om'rays' great experiment had concluded. The Makers received the notification signal, so long overdue, and sent out the required response.

Not "restart."

"End."

Those Cloisters still asleep answered. Those buried in the earth ignited, ending the lives of innumerable safe and oblivious Worker Oud along with the dreams of their brethren.

That of the Vyna summoned its Om'ray and prepared to take them home. Tarerea Vyna stood with her sisters, their shock turning to triumph. Their virtue was rewarded. The Pure had been Chosen!

Until arms made of darkness and stars took hold, and a voice like the M'hir itself said—

/ours/

Epilogue

"HOW FAST ARE WE GOING?"

Morgan cracked open an eyelid. "Fast."

I poked him under the ribs. "Can't you tell?"

"No more than you can tell me where we're going."

He had a point there.

The streaks of color that should be stars weren't necessary to know we were moving. We could *feel* the great starship leap through space. Not through the M'hir, which had surprised us all.

But using the M'hir. The small rooms I'd thought prison cells were filled now with that darkness. We'd *pulled* it into place, the ship guiding us, then stood back in wonder as the panels along the corridor had come to life, color streaming the walls between. Color that *beat* like a giant heart.

Hoveny tech. Our heritage. How strange and wonderful to have one. Our scientists could hardly sleep.

I was ready to sleep the entire way. That and eat. Holl was still exploring the storerooms below. The ship had been ready.

I propped my elbows on Morgan's chest and peered into his face. "We're going somewhere," I assured him, kissing his nose. "That's what matters."

Morgan buried his fingers in my hair, cupping my head. "No."

He looked up at me, the blue of his remarkable eyes the most beautiful color of all. "It's going there together."

Our lips met, our hearts joined, and I gave my full agreement to what happened next.

My Human being right, as usual.

M'hiray and Their Associates, on Cersi

M'HIRAY

Andi sud Prendolat, child, Birth Watcher, M'hir Denouncer
Arla di Licor, brother of Asdny, M'hir Denouncer
Asdny di Licor, brother of Arla, M'hir Denouncer
Barac di Bowart, Chosen of Ruti, former First Scout, cousin of
  Sira
Celyn sud Lorimar, Chosen of Kele
Cha sud Kessa'at, Chosen of Deni, M'hir Denouncer
Deni sud Kessa'at, Chosen of Cha, M'hir Denouncer
Ermu sud Friesnen, Chooser
Holl di Licor, Chosen of Leesems, mother of Arla and Asdny,
  M'hir Denouncer
Inva di Lorimar, Chosen of Bryk, Council Member
Jacqui di Mendolar, Chooser, Birth Watcher
Josa sud Prendolat, Chosen of Nik, father of Andi, M'hir
  Denouncer
Kele sud Lorimar, Chosen of Celyn
Leesems di Licor, Chosen of Holl, father of Arla and Asdny,
  M'hir Denouncer
Nik sud Prendolat, Chosen of Josa, mother of Andi, M'hir
  Denouncer

Oseden sud Parth, unChosen
Pirisi di Mendolar, Chosen of Ru
Rasa di Annk, friend of Andi
Ru di Mendolar, Chosen of Pirisi
Ruti di Bowart, Chosen of Barac, formerly of Acranam
Sira di Sarc (Sira Morgan), Chosen of Jason Morgan, former
    Council Member, Speaker
Tle di Parth, Chooser, former Council Member, M'hir Denouncer
    (on occasion)

OM'RAY

Destin di Anel, Chosen, First Scout, Sona
Eand di Yode, Chosen of Moyla, Council Member, Sona
Gurutz di Ulse, Chosen, Scout, Sona
Moyla di Yode, Chosen of Eand, Council Member, Sona
Noil di Rihma'at, unChosen, son of Odon, Sona
Nyala di Edut, Chosen, Council Member, Sona
Odon di Rihma'at, Chosen, Council Member, Speaker, Sona
Tarerea Vyna
Tekla di Yode, Chosen, Scout, Sona
Teris di Uruus, Chosen, Council Member, Sona

OTHER SPECIES

Jason Morgan, Human, Chosen of Sira
Maker, Oud
Speaker, Tikitik
Thought Traveler, Tikitik
Worker, Oud (also called the Mindless)